# DARK BRIDE

# DARK BRIDE

3 Gates of the Dead: Book II

Jonathan Ryan

OPEN ROAD
INTEGRATED MEDIA
NEW YORK

978-1-4976-6308-4

Published in 2015 by Open Road Integrated Media, Inc.
345 Hudson Street
New York, NY 10014
www.openroadmedia.com

Dedicated to the abolitionists
who are fighting modern-day human trafficking

# DARK BRIDE

†

# CHAPTER ONE

**"THE CHURCH IS A WHORE. THE CHURCH IS YOUR MOTHER."**

I broke the silence as I read aloud to Father Neal, Reg McClelland, and Darrin Francis. All of them looked up from their books and pints of various imported beers. Our weekly Sunday-night pub discussion had turned into a quiet study session. Books and papers lay scattered across the table where everyone sat reading. The pseudo-Irish pub that hosted us was almost empty, with only a few hipsters nursing their beers on the long wooden bar across from our table.

Father John Neal, dressed in priest black and a white collar, held a battered copy of *Pride and Prejudice* in his liver-spotted hands. Since Monday was his day off, he could afford not to work on a Sunday night. The white of his hair glowed in the dim light of the pub, and his wrinkled face stretched into a smile. "Ahh, the blessed Augustine. If you use that in your sermon, you are bound to get some attention, my lad."

I smiled as I looked at my commentaries, books, and Bible in front of me. "At least that quote will. I can't seem to get my thoughts together tonight."

Darrin laid down his huge tome on Shakespeare. The computer tech guy for our little Scooby-Doo paranormal investigation group, he spent his days preparing his doctoral thesis on religious symbolism in the works of the Bard. He stretched and ran his hands through his tight brown curls. "Maybe the two pints of Guinness has something to do with that."

Reg took a drink and wiped beer from his walrus mustache. "Aidan is Irish; two pints of Guinness sharpens his mind."

"I would suspect that bottle of Irish whiskey," Father Neal said, pointing his wooden cane toward the top of the bar, "would have to be emptied before Aidan could have his sermon instincts dulled to the point of incomprehension."

"I guess that must explain why my congregation is in a stupor on Sunday morning; they can't handle their whiskey."

We laughed and the hipsters at the bar turned their eyes from the Reds baseball game on the TV. Usually, we sat outside, but the oppressive heat wave gripping Columbus had driven us inside for the night.

I smiled as I looked at the guys I hadn't even known a year ago. We had bonded over our paranormal investigations, demon fighting, and thwarting the plans of the evil magicians who wanted to unleash hell on central Ohio.

Reg, our resident skeptic, Ohio State physics professor and terrible poker player, provided a good balance to the group's founder, Zoe. She often drifted into crazyland and needed Reg to bring her back to reality. He had saved me from being torn apart by a demon at a house investigation just a few weeks ago.

The professor fingered his gray-flecked mustache. "It's an interesting quote. Did Augustine really say it?" His position as the group skeptic, a product of his job as a physics professor, helped keep all of us in check from crazy flights of fancy.

Father Neal leaned back in his chair. "The quote is attributed to him, but no one is exactly sure."

I sipped my beer. "The tone always sounded like Luther to me."

"Luther would tell the devil to kiss his ass. My kinda guy, but

I'm guessing neither of those quotes will make it into your sermon, Preacha." Darrin chuckled, hands on his diminishing beer belly. His girlfriend, Kate Collins, made him run with her every evening. They made an odd couple. Darrin looked like Seth Rogen's younger brother while she bore a strong resemblance to Emma Stone—though scars from a mysterious attack marred her flawless white skin. Kate possessed a razor-sharp mind and had just received her PhD in English. She served as our group's historical researcher.

"Why not?" asked Father Neal.

"A bit coarse for the ol' church crowd."

"The Bible is full of coarse language, crude bodily illustrations, and blunt language. God doesn't share our scruples about language when he is trying to get our attention. This is especially true when the Bible talks about God's people playing the whore," Father Neal said, hands on his cane.

"I don't think the fine people at Knox will appreciate being referred to as whores, do you?" Darrin said with a smirk.

Father Neal smiled, marked his book, and closed it. "Most likely not, but they need to hear it. Being good Presbyterians, they'll just have to listen, I'm afraid. The subject of God's people as a whore, and a bride, is a common theme in scripture."

I leaned forward. "You should see the passage in Ezekiel. God's people are described as spreading their legs like a prostitute. The whole passage is beyond anything Tarantino could come up with on his best day. And then there is Hosea, which I just started preaching from this morning."

Reg spun his glass on the table. "Who is Hosea?"

"A prophet of God from the Hebrew Bible. God commands him to marry not just an unfaithful woman, but a downright slut."

Darrin stopped smiling. "Why does God do that? It sounds vaguely sexist."

Father Neal chuckled. "Not in the least, my boy. God is presenting Himself as a jilted lover who will do anything for His people. His wrath in the Old Testament largely comes from the distress of His people walking away from their one true love."

Reg looked over at Father Neal. "Really? I didn't know that. I thought the God of the Old Testament was all fire and brimstone."

Father Neal leaned back. "He most certainly is, but it's the fire of a lover, not the fire of a dictatorial judge."

"Still, why I haven't heard this whore/bride stuff in Sunday school?" Reg asked.

I snorted. "Some of those passages wouldn't make for good flannel graph material."

"Too true, my lad, too true," Father Neal chuckled.

Darrin shook his head and muttered, "Church humor."

Father Neal continued. "The church today could use a good dose of that sort of language. We have been whoring after our own gods way too long. For instance, in America, the church has a warped desire to be credible to everyone. The problem is, what is credible to one group of people isn't to another. In the end, both are chasing lovers who are hung like stallions."

Darrin looked shocked at Father Neal's language, and I laughed. "He's quoting from Ezekiel, bud. Father Neal won't be contributing to the curse jar anytime soon."

"What's our jar up to now?" Darrin said with a laugh, raising his beer glass.

"Jen counted it last night. It's up to fifty dollars. Your artful display of the *F*-word during the last Reds–Pirates game filled it very nicely."

"Damn Pirates," Darrin mumbled, handing another fifty cents to me.

Father Neal smiled. "I'm sure the kids at Saint Stephen's mission will enjoy their new Wi-Fi when you reach your goal."

I nodded and remained quiet for a moment before saying, "This has been my sticking point for a long time. Things are a little better at Knox since Mike, uh, left, but not much. I still have to deal with the same amount of petty crap and political showdowns."

Father Neal nodded. "Well, the church is a family, isn't it? Since when is a family well behaved behind closed doors?"

Darrin smirked. "If it's anything like my family, there's a lot of broken furniture in the house that's been used as flying projectiles."

I took a sip of beer. "Furniture hasn't been thrown, yet."

"What's your future at Knox look like? Are they going to hire you as the head pastor?" Reg asked.

I shrugged. "They talked about it, but presbytery most likely won't allow it. The normal rule of thumb is an assistant pastor can't take over for a head pastor, but exceptions can be made, especially given the circumstances. I told them I wouldn't accept even if they offered. I didn't say I'm considering leaving the Presbyterian Church. . . ."

Reg broke in. "Presbytery?"

I smiled. "Sorry, church terminology again. It's the regional governing body for local churches. In our case, the presbytery that presides over the state of Ohio."

"They basically act like bishops, yes?" Reg asked.

I burst out laughing. "Essentially, but I would never use that terminology to any good Presbyterian. Having one asshole in control and telling them what to do? Horrifying thought."

I placed fifty cents on the table, the price for saying the word *asshole.*

Darrin smiled. "So, instead, they have several assholes telling them what to do?"

"Nailed it," I said.

Father Neal rapped my arm with the end of his cane. "That's a very cynical view, boys."

"Yes, Father," Darrin and I said together.

I continued. "I'm still working out the church stuff and my future. There are a lot of questions in my head. What does the church do? What should it look like? How do we go about it? Should I stay a Presbyterian? What is the nature of the church? I'm not sure what I should do next."

Father Neal poked me with his cane. "Just try to be a good minister and churchman."

"Will you stop with that cane, old man? I'm starting to get bruises. After the past year, I can't go back to where I was, I mean, especially after I saw—"

Father Neal's eyes narrowed and he held up his hand. "Enough, Aidan. I told you not to speak of it."

I didn't say anything more as I furrowed my eyebrows. Ever since I saw a glowing cup in Father Neal's hands at Serpent Mound, he'd refused to talk about it.

Whatever it was, the very sight of it unsettled me in ways I couldn't explain.

"Well, at least Mike got what was coming to him yesterday," Darrin said as he motioned to the *Columbus Dispatch* in front of me. The headline read, "Cult Cemetery Killers Sentenced to Death."

Along with visions of Father Neal holding a glowing cup, I couldn't shake the evil memories of that horrible night at Serpent Mound. Testifying at the trial brought a fresh round of nightmares filled with the leering, broken faces of the damned. Mike Johns and Daniel Mueller stared at me the entire time with blank eyes. Even though Father Neal told me he had injected them with another dose of "magick away," as I called it, before the trial, I kept expecting them to summon back the spirits of the dead. I celebrated my testimony by getting so drunk that Darrin worried about me choking on my own vomit. Not my finest hour. Still, it's not every day your former boss goes on trial for the murder of your ex-fiancée.

This entity, the Grinning Man, whatever he was, had been freed from the Newark Earthworks around the same time, but refused to show himself in any way. I preferred a face-to-face confrontation instead of the unknown. Father Neal pointed out more than once this is how agents of pure evil usually work—in the shadow of our own doubt and misery.

I decided I didn't need any more nightmares tonight, so I changed the subject.

"I just can't go back to being the good assistant pastor at Knox. I mean, I think I'm still going to be a pastor, but I don't think it's at Knox. In fact, I'm pretty convinced of it."

Father Neal nodded. "Have you told your elders?"

"Not yet. I want to see how Cole, the intern, works out."

Reg scratched a few red marks on a student's paper. "How is he doing?"

I shrugged. "He is a guy who just graduated from seminary, which means he thinks he has the solutions to all of the church's problems. I think he stands in constant amazement of how 'the church, as a whole, just doesn't get it,' " I said, making quotation marks in the air. "The guy is like the greatest hits collection of fix the churchisms. He's charmed the little old ladies and impressed the session with his drive. Meanwhile, I put up with epistle-length emails that would shame Saint Paul."

Father Neal chuckled. "Lad, you are only four years out of seminary yourself. You shouldn't sound so cynical and jaded. That attitude is for ministers my age."

I sat back and took a drink of my Guinness. "I suppose. I mean, I think I'm much better than I used to be."

"As long as you have a few ghosts to feed you a dose of reality." Father Neal laughed again.

Darrin lifted his glass. "Score one for the old English priest."

We went back to our studying, and I noticed Darrin kept looking at me through his stack of books.

"What? What's wrong?" I asked.

Darrin cleared his throat. "What does Ms. Jennifer Brown think about all of this?"

I tried not to wince. Jen and I hadn't exactly won any communication awards in the past few weeks. "She's supportive, of course, but she is so wrapped up in some mysterious new task force that we haven't had time to talk about our, I mean, my future. I know it sounds bad, but I almost wish Weaver had passed her over for this investigation. But I know what she's doing is important, so I try to keep my mouth shut."

Darrin rubbed his beard. "What's the task force?"

I shook my head and stared into my beer. "She can't say. Apparently, the FBI is involved, and she's been sworn to secrecy."

Darrin frowned. "But she hasn't told you? What's up with that?"

"She takes being a cop very seriously and is playing by the rules on this. Part of me admires that, and part of me just wants to scream every time I hear, 'I can't talk about that, Aidan.' " I mimicked her voice and then regretted it. I know I'm an asshole sometimes.

Father Neal turned in his seat. "Did you get into a fight about her secrecy last night?"

I stared at him. "How did you know? Did you read my mind?"

He sighed. "What you feel is all over your face, all the time. Anyone can read you. It doesn't take magick to do it."

"Yeah, we fought, and I said some pretty stupid things."

Darrin crossed his arms and nodded. "Yeah, Kate and I have had a few of those. I think I'm learning to control my mouth."

"Is that even possible?" Reg asked with a chuckle.

Darrin smiled. "More than you know."

The table began to vibrate. Reg, Darrin, and I looked down at our phones. I saw Jen's picture come up on my phone and smiled in spite of the raw feelings over our fight.

I quickly answered, "Hey, babe."

"Where are you?"

I grimaced. "Well, hello to you, too."

Father Neal furrowed his eyebrows at me.

"Aidan, I don't have time for a fight. Just tell me where you are."

"I'm at The Drunken Priest with the guys."

I heard her breathe a sigh of relief.

"Fantastic, I need all of you. Can you please come to the old quarry near Shrum Mound?"

Curiosity got the best of me. "Of course, what's wrong?"

"I need your advice on something. You'll see the police cars near the entrance. They have instructions to let you through. When can you be here?"

"All we need to do is pay our bill. The quarry isn't far from here, so I'm thinking twenty minutes?"

"Great. I'll see you then. And, Aidan?"

"Yes?"

"I do love you, you know."

I felt myself melt on the spot. "I know, I love . . ."

Darrin made kissy faces at me. I gave him the finger and lowered my voice.

"I love you, too. See you in a few minutes." I hung up the phone and glanced at my companions who gave me questioning looks. "Who is up for tromping around the old quarry tonight? Jen needs our help."

Father Neal examined me as the lines in his face tightened. "Did she say why?"

I shrugged. "No, but it must be some sort of crime scene. She didn't say it was a murder, and I think she would have told me."

"Let's not keep the lovely lady waiting, let us go forthwith," Darrin said as he gathered up his books.

I shook my head. "Someone has been reading too much Shakespeare."

Darrin grinned. "Verily, fucking good, sir."

"More money for the jar," I said.

After paying our bills, everyone piled into my car. I turned the air-conditioning on full blast as the night hadn't brought any relief from the humidity. The heat combined with alcohol made sweat roll down my back.

We traveled a few miles down Fifth Street before turning. I saw Shrum Mound rise above the quarry and smiled as I thought about all the time I'd spent with Jen there. No one comes to the mound, so it was a private place to be together.

Darrin leaned over the seat. "Why does everything happen to us around mounds?"

Father Neal glanced up. "Because, mounds are places of

power, didn't you learn your lesson from Serpent Mound and the Newark Earthenworks?"

"I thought it was just those particular mounds."

"No, all mounds are places of magick; some more than others. There are some . . ." He broke off and stared at the mound.

"Some are what?" Reg asked.

"Some might be paths to other worlds."

Reg looked at Father Neal. "You can't be serious."

"I am, and you of all people would know that's possible."

At first, I couldn't figure out what Father Neal meant, but then I remembered Reg's study of alternate worlds in theoretical physics. I reminded myself to ask Father Neal about this later and wondered if the glowing cup had anything to do with it.

Police cars came into view, and I pulled up alongside. Rolling down my window, I motioned to a beefy uniformed cop with dark hair. "Hey, Joe, I'm here to see Jen."

"Hey, Preacher, good to see you. You doin' okay?"

"Can't complain, other than the heat."

"Yeah." He shook his head. "I moved to Columbus from Florida to get away from this kind of soup."

I smiled. "Where is Jen waiting for us?"

Joe motioned down the road. "Go around the workstation. You'll come to an old mine pit. Park the car outside of the tape."

"Uh, what exactly are we going to see?"

Joe paused and looked behind him. "I think you should find out for yourself."

I nodded slowly and rolled up the window. "What in the world was that about? He actually looked scared."

Father Neal's hands gripped his cane. "Magick, Aidan."

Walls of gray Ohio limestone rose above us as we drove into the open-air mine. Yellow POLICE LINE—DO NOT CROSS tape stretched across a tunnel. Two uniformed police officers stood guard. We got out of the car and a rancid odor assaulted my nose. The two pints of Guinness in my stomach began to churn.

Darrin put his shirt over his nose. "What the hell is that smell?"

Father Neal stared grimly ahead. "It's rotting flesh of some type. I'm hoping it's not human."

I only nodded, afraid I would throw up.

We walked up to the police officers, who raised the tape without asking any questions. They directed us toward the tunnel. Approaching the entrance, a hint of coconut drifted through the stench. Jen stepped out of the tunnel to greet us.

"Hey, love, what's going on?"

"I'm not entirely sure. I was hoping you could tell me," she said, and then turned to Father Neal. "I'm glad you're here. This one is, uh, a bit unusual."

Darrin looked past Jennifer into the dark tunnel where large police lights illuminated the canyon inside. "Murder?"

Jen chewed on her lip. "No, but, well . . . Just come this way. Don't worry, I've cleared it with Weaver. You guys are good."

We walked through a small tunnel to another opening and stepped into a rounded open-air mine, about twenty yards deep. The walls of limestone contained thousands of ancient sea creatures.

Staring at the stone walls full of fossils, I wished I'd brought my fossil hammer with me. My next thought as we stepped out onto the canyon floor turned into a prayer.

*Christ have mercy.*

# CHAPTER TWO

**BEHEADED CHICKENS LAY STREWN ACROSS THE ROCK FLOOR OF THE** quarry, each body carefully arranged to form a full circle, leaving an empty space in the middle. In the center of the circle, chicken skulls were stacked in a neat pyramid, staring at the opposite wall.

Two paths split the circle on each side. One path led from the opening where we stood to the center. The other led to the far wall where a symbol, written in blood, covered the lower rock face. I squinted but couldn't make out the symbol or its meaning. A message of some sort, but of what, I couldn't imagine. My mind wandered to the square of empty earth we found at the Newark Earthenworks, the open tomb of the Grinning Man.

We began to walk toward the center. What I assumed to be chicken blood oozed into puddles of water left over from a recent rain. The water looked as if Moses had placed the curse of the Nile on it, as the thin red blood swirled in the inch-deep puddles.

"So much for my secret desire to be a chicken farmer," Darrin said.

We reached the middle of the circle and looked around. Father Neal bent down slowly to examine the chicken heads. As he did, I noticed bloody red *X*s all around us, covering the bottom third of the quarry walls.

"What happened here?" Reg asked.

"The *what* is easy to guess. As for the whom and why . . ." Father Neal trailed off as he stepped through the chicken corpses to the canyon wall.

I followed him to one of the trio of *X*s. The police lights illumined his face as Father Neal traced them with his fingers, mumbling something in Latin. I tried to translate with my sketchy Latin grammar, but nothing made sense. Walking alongside the rock wall, I heard him mutter a few times, "The message, what is the message?"

I decided to leave him to his investigation and went back to Jen in the middle of the circle. "Who reported this?"

She gave me a smile. "Apparently, some kids making out on Shrum Mound."

"Yeah, I heard it's a good place for that. Wanna try it some time?" I winked.

"If you're lucky." She arched an eyebrow and took out her notebook. "They called the station around eight o'clock and said they saw a bright flash explode over the canyon. They also heard a female screaming something at the top of her lungs."

Female. I stopped walking. Again, my mind flashed back to the magick used at the Newark Earthenworks. Female magick, Father Neal told us as we stared at the opening in the ground six months ago.

"What did the voice say?"

Jen stopped and frowned. "They couldn't make it out. The 911 operator asked them that. They said . . ."

"What? What did they say?"

"Well, remember they're two scared teenagers."

"Okay."

Jen shook her head in disbelief. "They said it sounded like her voice was commanding, as if giving orders. One of them even said, 'It sounded like she was casting a spell.' "

I looked around, almost expecting the woman to jump out at us. "You didn't find the body of a woman, no drag marks or anything? Footprints? Clothes?"

She smiled. "Someone has been studying the books I gave him."

I begged Jen to teach me forensics, and she gave me a crash course in the basics through her old textbooks. "I have, want to see me apply my knowledge further?"

"By all means."

We walked over to the canyon wall and looked closer at the *X*s drawn there.

"Have you looked at these?"

Jen nodded. "Yes, but forensics hasn't been here yet. Since this isn't a murder, it's not a high priority at this point. They're working a couple of murder cases as we speak. So, don't touch anything."

"I won't. It looks like the *X*s were done by someone shorter than me."

"Why do you say that?"

"Because, they are about to my chest. I'm assuming they wrote at their eye level, so I'm thinking they're around five three or five four." I lifted up my hand to show the measurement.

She smiled. "Go on."

"The *X*s are in groupings of three, which means they're part of the message."

She looked surprised. "How do you know that?"

"Father Neal has grudgingly been teaching me how to recognize magick signs."

Her face clouded, and she frowned at me. Jen didn't like the subject of magick, considering she was almost murdered at the hand of dark magicians.

Never a good sign, I thought, and took a step back.

"You never told me that."

I shrugged. "You don't tell me everything, either, so what's the difference?"

She crossed her arms, and I knew I should have kept my mouth shut. Why couldn't I stop jabbing her for something she couldn't help?

"That's different, Aidan. It's my job and there are . . ." She stopped.

"There are what?"

"There are lives on the line."

I looked at the ground feeling stupid, but I wasn't about to admit defeat. "Don't you trust me?"

She sighed. "It's not about trust, Aidan. I gave my word."

"I know. I'm sorry. I'm trying, it's just hard. Because of—"

Jen touched my lips. "I realize having secrets in a relationship can ruin it. Just know, I'm not trying to keep anything from you on purpose." She motioned toward the wall. "What else do you see in the *X*s?"

"The blood looks fresh, but it's starting to congeal. And from the smell, I would say this happened four hours ago at the most."

She listened intently, and I continued. "They seem to have been drawn with a finger, not a brush. The rock has been scraped by a fingernail. I wonder if you can get any DNA from that."

She shrugged. "Maybe, maybe not. Probably won't matter much anyway."

"Why not?"

"DNA labs are busy. A chicken massacre isn't exactly on the priority list. We might get fingerprints, but I'm not sure what sort of crime we would charge the person with."

"What do you mean?"

"We might get them for animal cruelty, or some kind of health code violation or maybe vandalism. The problem with vandalism is that the blood will wash off in the rain, so any decent defense attorney could get a 'no contest' plea. This person would probably be sentenced to picking up trash on the side of the road. PETA would hate them, but no one else would care. Maybe we could get them on a cruelty to animals charge. Or, it could just be a stupid high school prank." She wrinkled her nose.

I could tell she was not convinced. "You don't believe that."

"No, I don't. I feel like something nasty is going on here, and given everything we've been dealing with down at the station since the Grinning Man's release, this is just another item on the weird shit list."

We both glanced at Father Neal, who made his way back to the center of the circle slowly. "If that's true, he'll be able to tell us."

Father Neal stopped and stood still in front of the pile of chicken skulls. His body tensed and his head shook slightly.

Touching him gently on the shoulder, I said, "Father?"

He didn't respond and began walking along the other path, staring at the symbol as he went. I watched as he shuffled toward the wall, almost as if dragged against his will. A grimace crossed his face. His lips moved wordlessly as he leaned toward the scrawl on the limestone.

Father Neal stood rigid as he examined what looked like an elaborate cross with blue whorls at each end and small, wafer-size circles in each quadrant. They were colored dark red by the congealing chicken blood.

I walked over to him. "What is it?"

Father Neal didn't answer, and I touched him again.

"Don't touch me. No matter what happens."

"I don't understand."

He pointed to the symbol with his cane. "It is a veve."

"A what?"

Father Neal touched the center of the symbol. His arm and body went rigid, and he started to shake as if he'd touched a live wire.

I reached for him and his head turned toward me. His eyes clouded white, and he spoke in a deep voice not his own.

*I . . . said . . . don't . . . touch . . . me . . .*

Everyone rushed over as they saw Father Neal shake with an unseen force. Jen reached out to him, but I grabbed her arm.

"No. Don't."

I watched in horror as Father Neal continued to vibrate, his lips moving in a quick rhythm. I couldn't make out his words at first, but as I leaned closer, I heard one phrase.

*Elle est dangereuse*, he growled out in a deep guttural voice.

I looked at Jen, and she whispered, "She is dangerous."

"How do you know?"

"Semester in Paris."

With a final shake, Father Neal yanked his cane out and dropped to the ground. I bent over and saw his eyes turn back to normal color. After a few moments, he looked at me with a crooked smile. "That was somewhat unexpected. Did I say anything?"

Reg, Darrin, and Jen stared at him, their faces a mask of utter shock.

I slowly nodded. "Yeah, you spoke in French. You said, 'She is dangerous.' "

He looked perplexed. "Did I? How long have I been here?"

I frowned. "Are you okay? Maybe you had a stroke."

He looked at me, puzzled, and then said, "No, I haven't had a stroke. Just receiving the message."

Jen kneeled down. "What message?"

He pointed up to the symbol. "That, my dear, is a veve. It is used in Voodoo to open the gates to the spirit world for messages. It appears one was left for . . . someone."

Darrin looked at it. "For whom?"

Father Neal attempted to stand, and Jen and I helped him up. He took out a handkerchief to wipe the sweat from his face. "That is the question. I don't know. The danger to everyone else has passed."

Jen looked at the symbol again. "You said Voodoo? Who does Voodoo in central Ohio? I thought that was a Gulf Coast thing."

Father Neal gave a soft laugh. "You and me both, my dear. But it all fits." He turned to the chicken skulls. "Voodoo practitioners often use chickens in their rituals. And *X*s, especially when in threes, have a special power in Voodoo." Father Neal looked back at Jennifer. "I don't know if I have much to offer you for your investigation other than research Voodoo in central Ohio. I'm guessing you won't find much. As for why, who, where, and how come, I can't tell you. Not yet, anyway."

Jen nodded. "What happened to you when you touched that wall? Why wouldn't you allow anyone to touch you?"

Father Neal began to walk toward the tunnel. "Because you would have been in serious danger from the spirit in that sign. I alone could handle it, and I did, but barely."

I ran to catch up with him. "Surely, I wouldn't have been in danger, after everything you've taught me. And does this have anything to do with the woman who raised the Grinning Man?"

He stopped and gave me a glare.

"You already have an interest in magickal things, Aidan. I try to limit your temptation as much I can. Not to mention you've seen the cup and you're now marked to be . . ."

"Be what? What are you talking about? Marked with what? And, I'm already involved with magickal stuff. That started six months ago when Mike and Daniel murdered Amanda. And now we have some woman on the loose who is murdering chickens. Probably the same one who raised the Grinning Man."

He knocked his cane on the ground. "No, you don't get it, Aidan. You are in danger of becoming what I am and always in danger of being tempted. The doors in your mind and heart are open. Any more exposure and you may fall. And now, now that you're walking both worlds, I can't protect you anymore."

The others stayed several yards away from us as we argued.

"You're going to have to start explaining things, priest. If you can't protect me, then I want to know what that cup is and why you get so distressed every time I mention seeing it."

Father Neal stopped. "What you saw, I wish you'd never laid eyes on. You don't understand. You don't know how beautiful and terrible it is to be—"

"To be what? I don't understand."

He looked at me, eyes filling with tears. "You will, my son.

God help me, you will. It appears the choice has been made. The Five Sorrows have chosen you."

Afraid any more questions would strain him further, I shut my mouth. Still, I knew that every time I laid down to sleep, I could hear the otherworldly music, see the glowing cup and the bright white light that saved us at Serpent Mound. Often, I'd see glowing beings out of the corner of my eyes when I'd walk in the woods alone. Wild animals would walk up to me and nuzzle my hand. I wanted to know what the hell, or heaven, was happening to me.

We walked in silence through the tunnel, and when we reached the other side, he said, "I'm sorry, Aidan. It seems God is speaking. I'd hoped to spare you this cross."

I gripped his arm. "It's okay, Father. I would do anything you asked."

He gave me a thin smile. "I'm not the one asking." He hesitated, staring at me for a long moment as though debating something that weighed heavily. Finally, after a stretch of silence, he sighed. "I will tell you a few things, but not all. I don't even know what I just saw. And I won't talk about the cup yet, agreed?"

I nodded.

He took a deep breath and started walking. "I have told you, and I don't think you quite believe me, but magick is a branch of science. When you do a chemistry experiment, it always leaves residue. Or, in a more extreme case, such as splitting an atom, it leaves a very nasty residue. Do you follow me so far?"

"Yes."

"Very good. A magician can read these signs. In some cases, you can plug yourself into the experiment, as if plugging into a telephone line."

"So, you plugged yourself in back there?"

He limped toward the car. "That's correct. The thing is, I wasn't prepared for . . . well, for that powerful of a spirit message in the residue."

We paused as we waited for the others to catch up. The oppressive heat made it impossible to do anything quickly.

I whispered, "What's the message?"

He shrugged his shoulders. "I have no idea, at least not yet. It might take some time . . . to figure out the images I saw."

The others appeared out of the tunnel, looking nervous. We both smiled as they drew closer. Jen walked up to us. "I guess I'll have to tell Weaver that Voodoo has come to central Ohio."

Darrin replied, "I'm guessing that'll make you the butt of jokes at the station."

Jen rolled her eyes. "They call me 'spooky girl' now because Weaver gives me these kinds of cases when I'm not working on the task force. I guess he thinks I'm some sort of expert. And given the weird crap we've seen lately, I think he likes my connection to Father Neal."

The priest smiled. "Scott is an excellent man. He also has very fine bourbon." Before we all got into the car, Father Neal looked back toward the tunnel. "My sons and daughters, we have a job to do. The Grinning Man is here, and his followers are increasing."

"To what end?" Reg asked. "To take over the world?"

Father Neal stared at the police lights shining into the canyon. "That is what we must figure out."

Looking back at the mine, my skin crawled. Even though the night heat baked my skin, I shivered.

# CHAPTER THREE

**WE DIDN'T TALK MUCH ON THE WAY BACK TO THE BAR.**

Father Neal stared out the window and kept mumbling, "'She is dangerous.' "

Darrin and Reg exchanged worried looks before giving me a questioning glance. I shook my head. I knew very well that Father Neal wouldn't share more information with us until he thought we could handle it.

I dropped Darrin and Reg at their cars and then drove toward Saint Patrick's. I kept glancing at Father Neal. His skin looked paper-thin in the soft green dashboard light. He appeared to have aged five years in the past hour.

"Why do you keep staring at me?"

"I . . . uh, well, you just don't look well, Father. It's like the veve took something out of you tonight." I ran my hands through my sweaty hair.

Father Neal smiled. "It did. It always does. Magick comes at a price that must always be paid. You have to sacrifice, but there is no resurrection. It takes away from you and only offers an illusion back."

"And that illusion would be?"

He gripped his cane. "The illusion of the serpent. The dream that every human being chases, but always in the wrong ways."

I gripped the steering wheel. "'Ye shall be gods.'"

Father Neal nodded. "The desires of all magician/scientists—knowledge, control, and mastery—in and of themselves are not bad things. But when used for selfish ends . . ." His voice trailed off as he gripped his cane. "But what they don't understand is that magick uses you up. It's not meant for us sinners, Aidan. I knew I would pay a price for putting my cane in the middle of that symbol. But I needed to know. Someone was trying to get our attention. She did her job well."

"You're sure it's a she?"

Father Neal nodded. "The type of magick we saw tonight is female folk magick. It's earthy, elemental, unlike the cold reason of European magick. Usually, folk magick is used by women in locations where being a female magician is considered a high honor. Not a witch, not in the way you are thinking. Many cultures have had the 'wise woman' of the village, who dispensed herbs, practiced some sort of fortune-telling, and was generally considered a good thing. Even among your Scottish Presbyterians, this was true; many of the early Calvinists practiced astrology."

I laughed. "You have to be kidding me. I think you must have hit your head. Presbyterians aren't exactly the magick types, Father. Can you imagine John, one of my elders, reading his horoscope?"

He smiled. "It's true."

I couldn't wrap my mind around my puritanical theological forefathers gazing at the stars for their destiny, but I let it go.

"I thought you said the magick down there was Voodoo."

Father Neal nodded. "It was, well, a mixture of Voodoo and some other folk magick. Voodoo often mixes things from other magickal traditions. It's very fluid."

As we pulled into the parking lot at Saint Patrick's, I asked, "Why do you think so?"

Father Neal paused for a moment. "The whole atmosphere,

whether you could feel it or not, was charged like an electric conductor. Then there was the veve. That alone confirms someone who practices Voodoo, or some kind of blend magick."

I turned off the car and rolled down the windows so we could breathe.

"What happened to you when you touched that thing? You said it was like plugging into a telephone. USB port seems like a better analogy. Did you see something?"

Father Neal gave me a thin smile. "Yes, it was like a rush of images in my head. Things . . . images that I'm not sure I understand."

"Why don't you tell me what you saw? Maybe I can help?"

"Yes, I think you can. There is a reason Mike was interested in you."

Mike, my former head pastor and supposed friend, murdered my ex-fiancée Amanda and his secret girlfriend. The mere mention of his name made me want to run my fist through a wall.

I looked at him. "I don't get that part. Why did he want me? I have been thinking about that for six months. I mean, he killed two women just to . . ."

"Just to get to you? Yes, I know. But, Aidan, you don't see yourself as you are. Women are drawn to you like magnets. You command a room and people follow. You have a scientific mind that is quick to sort through information. In short, you have all the qualities of a magician."

Father Neal's knuckles went white.

"And the Grinning Man wanted me."

He gave me a thin smile. "Not just him, something . . . someone . . . else."

I ran my hand through my hair. "Okay, Father, I'm trying to understand here. I thought the Grinning Man was the biggest, baddest bully around."

Father shook his head. "First, he's terrible, very terrible, but not the biggest bully around, you should know that. The masters he was buried with, the Nephilim, well, I shudder to think if they ever walked the earth again. Second, the person I'm talking about is not evil, but he is dangerous."

"I'm not sure I understand."

Father Neal sighed. "Let's at least do this in the coolness of my office with some fine Irish whiskey. I think it's time you know about some things."

"Okay."

As we got out of the car, I looked up at Saint Patrick's. The light gray stone shone in the moonlight and my whole body relaxed. Vines crawled up the side of the building and the flowers in the memorial garden were a riot of color. I smiled. No matter what was going on around me, this building made me feel at peace.

We walked into the office and a blast of icy air hit me. Father Neal couldn't stand the heat, so he kept his personal space close to Arctic temperature. As I sat down, I took in his office. Books lined the walls on stained oak bookshelves. Icons of Christ, Mary, and Saint Peter covered the rest of the open spaces. On the wall, to his right, hung the painting of the Fisher King. Father Neal took out glasses, poured in two fingers of scotch, and gave me a glass.

I raised it to him. "To the answers."

"That I can drink to," he said, taking a sip.

He sat down, sipped some more whiskey, and then said, "We must start with the Grinning Man. It is a name given to, well, a man, I think. Even though the name dates from the twentieth century, his origins are far older. He has appeared in numerous places associated with various paranormal phenomena. Most famously, he appeared during the events at Point Pleasant."

"Wait, the whole Mothman stuff? The winged creature a bunch of drunk teenagers supposedly saw in the 1960s?"

"Much more happened in that town than just the Mothman. What concerns you now is the Grinning Man. He was sighted numerous times in the year before the Silver Bridge collapsed into the Ohio River. That happened because I failed," Father Neal said, staring at me with clear blue eyes.

"What do you mean, you failed?"

"Story for another time, lad. I need you to focus right now."

I took another sip of whiskey. "So, what else about his history?"

"The early European settlers found him waiting for them. The Puritans of New England had many names for him. Hawthorne called him the 'Black Man.' I believe he might have ruled this land in a variety of different forms. I think his unusual affinity for the Newark Eathenworks is telling."

"Because the Nephilim are supposedly buried there?"

"Yes, or at least I guess so. He is not Nephilim, or we would be in darker waters. Many Native American tribes had legends of a dark destroyer who sought them out for destruction. When the Europeans first came over, he started to influence them to destroy the First Nations people."

"How do you know?"

"Think about it. First contacts with Native Americans and European people are filled with peaceful promises. Something corrupted their relationship and played on people's natural fear of one another. The whole early history of this country is written in blood. The strife, the anger, the greed, all of it didn't just come from ordinary sinful hearts. Plus, there were the hideous Salem witch trials. He is mentioned as the main culprit that tempted men and women to witchcraft. At the trials, he is referred to as the 'Black Man.' "

"Yeah, but, weren't the Salem witch trials just an example of mass hysteria?"

He nodded. "Partially, but I have no doubt the Grinning Man was behind it. He pops up in various guises in American history and always in relationship to some paranormal event. You might say he is America's own personal demon, and a powerful one at that."

"We have our own personal demon here?"

"Haven't you noticed that America, no matter how beautiful of an idea it is, has this dark, bloody undercurrent throughout history?"

I thought about our massacre of the Native Americans, slavery, the sterilizations of the unfit through the eugenics movement in the early twentieth century, and our willingness to destroy anyone who gets in our way. "Yeah, I have."

"He didn't do it alone. Back when the Europeans first started coming to this continent, the dark magicians joined them. The Grinning Man, whoever he is, found them and made contact. Their unholy alliance has influenced this country since its very early days."

"Who were they?"

"Are they," Father Neal corrected. "The club still exists."

"Club?" I frowned.

"Yes, a club of dark magicians who called themselves the Hellfire Club in England; a center of dark depravity that supposedly even Benjamin Franklin checked out from time to time."

"So, why are they interested in the Grinning Man?"

Father Neal paused and raised a shaking hand to his forehead. "They are interested in the secrets of the Nephilim, which the Grinning Man supposedly holds."

I didn't know how to process all this so I changed the subject. "Okay, what does he look like?"

He gave me a thin smile. "He appears as he wants, or so it seems. Sometimes, I think he alters his appearance to be comical. In many cases, he appears in green overalls."

I laughed in spite of the sick feeling in my stomach. "What?"

"But, then, it's the face that causes fear."

"What do you mean?"

He drew his finger across his mouth. "He is often described with a wide sinister grin and deep, beady black eyes."

"So, what is he? A demon? What? How would he know the secrets of the Nephilim's magick? How could he have lived so long? I thought you said magick used you up."

"Oh, it does, Aidan, never doubt that. But, there are ways, many ways, to keep existing. I wouldn't call it living, either."

"So, I'm missing something. How does he play into tonight? I didn't see any grinning faces around the chickens."

"No, you didn't. I told you, it's a different sort of magick. However, when I touched the center of the veve, one of the images I saw was the Grinning Man."

"What else did you see?" I asked, draining my glass.

He wrinkled his brow. "Several things I don't understand. Flashes of a snake, an old black woman's face, a white woman's face, a mansion of some type, dark woods, and then . . ." He paused. "Well, I can't tell you the rest just yet."

I shook my head. "I can't make any sense of that. Seems pretty random to me."

"Oh, it's not random. There is a pattern. We just have to figure out what that pattern might be," Father Neal said, staring at the ceiling.

I leaned forward. "When we figure out the pattern, we'll get the message, right? What is it? That Michigan sucks? Step back or I'll kill you?"

He smiled. "It is a message, but I'm almost positive it is a threat. In fact . . ." He trailed off as he looked back at me, then said, "Aidan. It is like a large caution sign in a foreign language. We just have to figure out the language."

"How do we do that?"

"Well, given that this is obviously Voodoo combined with some Appalachian folk magick, we must begin there. I will look in my books for some clues. You check out the Internet," Father Neal said as he stared up at his painting of the Fisher King.

I didn't say anything as I looked at the painting, too. The large, warriorlike king held a glowing cup in his hand.

The Fisher King. The revelation hit me like an Ohio State linebacker. Everything clicked into place. I dropped my whiskey glass to the floor and stood.

"My son, what's wrong?" Father Neal asked as he struggled to get up.

Everything came together in a rush of images. I thought about Father Neal holding a glowing cup that defeated the dark magick of Mike and Daniel. I remembered the detail: wooden, simple, and as Indiana Jones said in *The Last Crusade*, the cup of a carpenter's son.

"You. I can't believe I didn't understand before . . ."

"Understand what?" he asked as he limped over to me.

"It all fits. The slow aging, the wound in your leg . . . You're the guy in the painting, the Fisher King, the one who's guarded the—"

No, it just seemed too crazy, too fantastic.

"Speak the truth, my son," Father Neal said, a small smile on his face.

I flashed back to Serpent Mound and saw the glowing cup in the priest's hand. I remembered the detail, how it looked like golden wood, bronzed by a deep inner heat.

I lowered my eyes. "The Grail. You're the guardian of the Holy Grail."

A deep chuckle came from Father Neal. "No, Aidan, not just of the Grail. I'm a member of an order, the Order of the Five Sorrows."

"I don't understand."

Father Neal stood and leaned against his cane. He stared at me for a moment, examining me with his clear blue eyes. "Yes, I'm sorry to say, it is time."

I furrowed my brow. "Time for what?"

He closed his eyes, muttered something I couldn't hear, and then said in Hebrew, "Behold."

The air shimmered around me, and I felt a searing pain in my eyes, as if someone had peeled off a scab. Everything glowed with a white light, just like the holy dead at Serpent Mound. Five beings appeared inside the light, and I fell to the ground in front of them.

"Stand, my son," I heard Father Neal say, "and look at your fellow servants."

I grabbed the arm of my chair and tried to pull myself up. My knees felt as though they would give way at any moment, and I could feel heat radiating from the five beings.

"Look at them, Aidan. It can't be helped now, and you must know," Father Neal commanded.

"Father, I don't know if I can."

"You must. You have no choice."

I raised my eyes and saw them standing in front of me. They wore white robes streaked with blood that flowed with the cloth as the beings moved. Their faces bore the resemblance of created creatures: a large angelic man, a lion, an ox, an eagle, and one with a face that rotated between all four.

Each held a different object. The being with the face of a man held a wooden cup, the lion carried a Roman-style spear, the ox bore a wooden cross beam, the eagle carried a hideous crown of large thorns, and the being with many faces held a linen cloth covered with dark red splotches.

"What . . . Who . . . Don't . . ."

Father Neal chuckled and it sounded as if the whole earth laughed. I looked up and staggered backward. No longer was he an old man. Instead, he looked like a Greek god, bronzed by the sun with long black hair hanging to his shoulders. His beard contained flecks of gray. I looked down to see his heel bleeding. "What, who are you?"

Father Neal walked over to me, and I took a step back. He looked at me with a frown and uttered something I didn't understand.

My eyes glazed over, and I blinked. Everything returned to normal. I fell into the chair, and my hands shook.

"Son?" Father Neal said, his normal voice back.

"I'm gonna need a minute."

He poured another glass of whiskey and handed it to me. I swigged it with a huge gulp and didn't feel the familiar burn.

"Do you mind telling me what I just saw?"

Father Neal bent his head. "It is the next stage for you, my son, for you and the Order."

"What Order?" I pressed.

"Did you notice the five objects the seraphims held?"

"Hard to miss," I said, pouring more whiskey.

"They are the objects of the Five Sorrows of Christ: the spear that pierced His side, the cup He drank from at the Last Supper, the cross beam, the crown of thorns, and the cloth that wrapped Him in the tomb."

As he spoke, I felt faint and leaned forward. I could barely process any of it. "So, these things actually exist?"

He smiled. "You just saw them. Each object is guarded by a Seraphim and a human being, the Order. We each bear one of the wounds of Christ as our mark."

"What, like stigmata?"

"Of a type, but not all five. As you saw, I bear the wound of Christ's heel. The other four of my Order—two men, two women—bear the other wounds."

"Are you the leader?"

Father Neal chuckled. "Not a bit. I'm not even the oldest member."

Thoughts raced through my brain too fast to harness. "So, I'm supposed to replace one of you, is that right?"

He bowed his head. "So it would seem. The moment I discovered you had seen the cup, I knew you'd been marked."

"By whom?"

"The Elder."

"Who is he?"

Father Neal shook his head. "You can't know that, not yet. In order to know that, you must meet him yourself and become a novice. When it is time to take the place of one of us, you'll become a full member."

"Why? Why is the Order of the Five Sorrows even needed in this world?"

"You know the answer."

"I do?"

"We hold evil at bay, Aidan. That is our job; all of us chosen by the Elder."

"This is making my head hurt," I said, rubbing my temples.

"Your vision is complete now."

"Father, I—"

"No more tonight, my son. It's late, and I'm sure Bishop needs to go out."

I stood up and felt weak.

"Can you drive home?" Father Neal asked.

"Yeah, yeah, I think so."

In truth, I didn't think I'd have the ability to walk. I felt shaky. The world spun on its axis. And none of this had to do with the alcohol.

Father Neal gripped my arm. "Go home and try to sleep. We must figure out what is going on, and what the next steps might be in regards to you."

I walked out into the night. The vision I'd seen filled my mind, and I couldn't shake it. Everything around me seemed changed. If I didn't know any better, I'd think I had developed night vision. Trees, bushes, and animals were illumined by a light source I couldn't see. The dark didn't seem that . . . dark. "What's wrong with me?" I muttered aloud.

As if to answer, I saw someone walking just out of the corner of my eye. "Hello? Anyone there?"

I kept seeing people on the edge of my vision, but every time I turned, no one was there. The visions reminded me of the righteous dead I saw at Serpent Mound.

I got in my car, drove home, walked Bishop, and finally fell asleep.

# CHAPTER FOUR

THE NEXT MORNING, I SAT IN MY OFFICE, NURSING MY STEAMING COFfee. As my head pounded, I reminded myself to drink more water the next time I shared whiskey with Father Neal.

*You are to be a member, chosen by the Elder.*

Father Neal's words kept echoing in my mind, and I tried to forget them. My head hurt too badly to think about much, so I decided to troll the Internet for information on Voodoo. Most of the sites turned out to be worthless, written by obviously white, modern, New Age people who knew no more about Voodoo than Scooby and the gang. Every site emphasized the folk nature and private instruction of Voodoo practitioners. It didn't seem likely they would just throw up a site and invite people into their circle.

Stumped, I leaned back into my chair and rubbed my temples. The pounding in my head started to diminish, and I let out a sigh of relief.

"Late night, Boss?"

I turned to my intern, who stood in the doorway of my office. "Hey, Cole, yeah, you could say that. I had a late-night sermon discussion with Father Neal and the guys."

He sat down and I forced myself not to smile. If Plato invented an ideal form for young Presbyterian ministers, Cole MacArthur would have been the model. He wore a blue golf shirt with light khaki pants. His dark brown hair lay neatly with the close, stylish trim of a frat boy. Cole spoke with a slight Southern accent that the ladies in the church found irresistible. If anyone ever decided to do a Men of Ministry swimsuit calendar, my intern would be on the cover.

"How was the early round of golf with John this morning?"

He smiled. "Well, I was hard pressed to try to lose. He isn't very good. The ol' golf champion instincts had to be held back so I didn't totally crush him."

I laughed. "Well, that's why I'll never play golf with you. Did Abby catch her flight okay this morning?"

He nodded, face tight with concern. "Not sure if it's entirely safe for a woman six months pregnant to fly, but she insisted. I guess I'm being the overprotective first-time dad."

Cole did and said everything right. I couldn't help but be a little suspicious.

"So, what's the sermon about?" he asked.

"Oh, a fairly safe topic: God's people as a bride and a whore."

Cole stretched out his lean frame and laughed. "Well, that should wake up the Blue Hairs."

I realized that I had my laptop open to the Voodoo sites. I turned and closed out the search window.

"So, what's up?" I asked.

"I dunno, I thought maybe you wanted to grab some lunch. I have some questions about Knox."

I raised my eyebrow. "Is that so? What kind of questions?"

He smiled. "Oh, just some things John talked to me about this morning. I would rather not discuss them here."

"Probably wise. Where do you want to go?"

"Actually, there is a new Cajun restaurant that opened up in Franklinton. I read about it in the paper this past Sunday. Would be nice to get a taste of Gulf Coast food again."

The look of eagerness and his Southern-tinged voice betrayed his Mississippi roots.

"Hmmm, I didn't know about that place. Sounds good. Although, it's an odd place for a restaurant."

He stood up. "Why is that?"

"Well, Franklinton is not exactly a hip, up-and-coming area like the Short North or German Village. It's a mostly blue-collar, white Appalachian area mixed with some African American folks. Not exactly the place I would pick for a Cajun restaurant."

"This should be an interesting lunch, then."

We walked out to the reception area of the church, and I turned to tell Sherry we were leaving for an early lunch. She stared straight ahead, the color drained from her face, as she played nervously with her necklace.

"Sherry, we're getting ready to . . ."

She didn't turn to me or show she had heard me.

"Are you okay?"

She responded by pointing a shaky finger to the door. I looked in that direction and saw Sheila, Mike's wife, coming in the door. My heart did a quick double beat.

"Who is—" Cole started.

I held up my hand.

Sheila walked toward us. She wore a simple blue dress shirt and a gray skirt. Her long red hair flowed to her shoulders. I took a quick glance at my phone to see if anyone had made an appointment with her. Nothing.

"Sheila, hi, can I help you?" My words sounded wooden and strained as I walked to meet her.

She gave me a small smile. "Aidan, yes. I'm here to clear out Mike's office."

Mike's office. I realized that for the past six months we had all avoided the subject. None of us had even gone in there. It's as if we had an unspoken agreement to avoid it at all costs. A murderer had occupied that office, and no one wanted to be tainted with the stain.

"Of course. Cole, give me a few minutes."

"I'll be in my office, Boss. Let me know when you're ready."

I led Sheila to Mike's office. I hesitated as I touched the door handle. I felt Sheila's cool touch on my hand.

"It's okay. Mike's not hiding behind the door, you know."

I looked at her, and she smiled.

"It looks like both of us need to do this. Open the door."

I opened it, and a slightly musty scent wafted into the hall. Even though the room had all of Mike's church possessions, it felt empty, empty like the soul that used to occupy the space. I flipped on the light, and Sheila walked straight to the pictures behind Mike's desk. She took the family picture I had often admired and threw it in the trash.

Stunned, I didn't know what to say. She stared at the trash can for a moment. "You think I'm cold, don't you?"

I found my voice. "No, why would you think that?"

She looked up and gave me a tight smile.

"Most women would have kept that picture no matter what had happened."

"No, I don't think you're cold, not under your circumstances."

She nodded. "Not a usual set of circumstances, is it?"

"To say the least."

She looked around the office. "I really don't want anything in here, Aidan. I don't want the taint in my life."

I didn't say anything as I waited for her to continue. I got the sense she really wanted to unload.

"I have put this off for a while."

I mumbled, "Understandable."

"But it's time now. The trial is over. We are moving back home with my parents. We need a new life, Aidan, a life where I don't have to protect the girls from hearing their daddy is a . . ." Tears began to pour down her cheeks. "How, Aidan, how could I have been so stupid?"

I grabbed some tissues from Mike's bookshelf and handed them to her. She took them and whispered, "Thank you."

I touched her arm. "He had us all fooled, Sheila. That's what he did. He was a consummate liar."

She blew her nose. "I could have forgiven the affair. But everything else . . ."

"I know."

She looked at me. "Aidan, how . . . how do I tell the girls their father is going to die? Even worse, how do I tell them he deserves it?"

She fell into my arms, gripping me tight. I held her as she flooded my shirt with her tears.

"I pulled them out of school right after he was arrested. I have been homeschooling them and not letting them watch the news."

I held her as every hidden emotion of the past six months came out in wracking sobs. After several moments, she calmed down and pulled away from me, collecting herself. A new person emerged, and I knew she would no longer mourn Mike. In her eyes, he was already dead, before the State of Ohio stuck him with a needle.

Sheila touched the wet spot on my shirt. "Thank you, Aidan. I'm sorry about your shirt."

I looked down and smiled. "That's okay; I think I had egg yolk on it from breakfast this morning. You helped me clean it."

She gave me a watery laugh. "That's why I've always liked you, Aidan. Funny at just the right times."

She looked around the office again. "You can give all this stuff away or throw it out, for all I care. Maybe take the books to a used bookstore. Keep the cash or donate it. Would you?"

I couldn't deny her. "I will."

She nodded and then looked over to the framed, blood-spotted Bible page from the Salem witch trials. She crossed the room, grabbed the frame off the wall, and walked back to me. "I want you to have this, Aidan."

"I can't. That belongs to your family." I didn't touch it. Something about that artifact had always creeped me out.

She pressed the edge of the frame into my stomach.

"Please, I don't want it in my family, not anymore. Someone else needs to keep it. There are too many bad memories for me."

Her desperate pleading broke down my reluctance. I took the frame from her, and the feel of the wood sent chills up my arms. The page shimmered, and I thought I heard faint screams coming from the frame. I gritted my teeth and resolved to get rid of it as soon as possible.

Sheila relaxed and walked to the door with a handful of picture frames.

I stopped her with a light touch. "Are you sure you don't want anything else in here?"

She didn't turn around. "No, Aidan. I don't even want to touch those things."

As if I did, I thought.

"Burn it all, it might be the best thing." She turned to me and said, "Thank you, Aidan, for everything. God be with you."

She left without another word.

I took a deep breath and walked out. At least the spell of not going into Mike's office had been broken. Sheila cleansed it somehow.

I put the frame in my office and then went to the waiting area. "Sherry, I want you to get quotes from a janitor service to clean Mike's office. Ask them what they would charge to take everything away."

"But . . ."

"No buts, Sherry. Get me the quotes by the time I get back from lunch. Sheila won't be coming back here, and I don't blame her. All that stuff in his office just needs to go. Understand?"

"Yes, Pastor Aidan."

Cole stuck his head out. "Are you ready to eat, Boss?"

"I'm ready."

We walked out to my 2009 Honda Civic, which Jen had made me buy a few months ago. Giving up the Geo that I'd had since high school was a deeply emotional experience. To be fair to Jen, the bottom of the car had rusted through so that I could see the road as I drove.

"So, spill some water?" Cole pointed at the dark pool on my shirt.

"If you are going to be a pastor, Cole, you should get used to this sort of stain."

"What happened?"

I started the car and pulled out of the parking lot. "Long and short of it, I doubt we will be seeing Mrs. Johns ever again."

"I'm surprised she came back at all."

I looked at him. "She needed to put him to rest."

He nodded without saying anything.

We drove in silence for a while. Cole kept stealing glances at me until I said, "Well, what do you want to ask?"

"I'm just curious about Mike. I mean, no one ever talks about him. I get why, but I can't help being curious as to what he was like."

I dreaded this question, but I couldn't blame him for asking. "Do you want an honest answer?"

"Of course."

I got on the highway before responding. "He was like an older version of you."

Cole furrowed his brow. "What do you mean?"

"Well he is—was—very put together in a Presbyterian sort of way. I mean, look at you, Cole: every hair in place, every stitch of clothing perfect, cute pregnant wife. Everything looks perfect on the outside, but I can't help wondering what's going on here." I pointed to his heart. "You say all the right things, you do all the right things, and the elders love you. I still love you even if I am suspicious of you. Forgive me if I'm a little skeptical of the whole package."

He looked at me, stunned. I felt bad as I stared straight ahead while I drove. It's not his fault, stupid, I thought. You can't blame him because he lived a perfect life. You've gotta stop taking out your anger on everyone. It's getting old.

He gave me a low laugh. "Well, I'm not Mike. I haven't killed anyone recently."

I gripped the steering wheel. "I should hope not."

Cole's face turned fire-engine red as he realized what he had said. "Aidan, I'm sorry. I . . ."

I waved my hand. "It's okay. You just got here, after all. You are only now beginning to understand the devastation Mike caused. In fact, maybe it was good for you to see Sheila this morning."

"I think you are right. I'm sorry, Aidan. I just needed to understand."

We talked about sports the rest of the way to the restaurant. It's times like these that I'm thankful for sports. Nothing covers up awkwardness between men like a conversation about how much Dusty Baker is a punk and how Yadier Molina, the Saint Louis Cardinals catcher, is the game's greatest player.

The affluence of Upper Arlington gave way to the city as we drove down State Route 315. I reached the exit for Franklinton. We drove through the streets and the rundown brick Midwestern houses.

"So, this is Franklinton? I see what you mean."

"Yeah, it's a tough neighborhood, also known as The Bottoms. A strange mix of people and the oldest part of the city."

"How do you know all of this stuff?"

I smiled. "Jen. She is a nut when it comes to local history. She's been teaching me."

He laughed. "Such a trial for you, I'm sure . . ."

"Well," I smiled. "They're the best history lessons I've ever had."

I pulled into the parking lot next to an old brick building. We walked down the street, and I looked at the GPS. "Well, according to this, the restaurant should be—"

"Right here," Cole said.

I looked up and laughed. Green and purple skeletons decorated the windows as they danced around the sign MADAME CELESTINE'S NOLA HOME.

"I think this is the place."

We opened the door, and Louis Armstrong hit our ears with a trumpet blast like Gabriel at the end of days. Foreign spices filled my nose, and I became dizzy from the sensory overload. Posters of jazz greats, Louisiana bayous, and scenes from the French Quarter along with more colored skulls dominated the walls. We'd left the Midwest and entered a different world.

"Ever been to New Orleans, Boss?"

"Can't say that I have. You?"

"A few times, once right after Katrina and once on my honeymoon."

I smiled. "Talk about contrasts."

"That's New Orleans, really, contrasts and contradictions mixed into one truth of the city."

I stared at Cole. "That's the most un-Presbyterian thing I've ever heard you say."

He laughed. "Should I take that as a compliment?"

"Yes, yes you should." I looked around the restaurant. "Seems we got here early, I don't see anyone else."

"Well, it's only eleven fifteen."

"Yeah, I wonder if they're even—"

"Open, honey? Of course we are open. We rarely close, like my beloved city, no?"

We turned to see a young woman, probably mid-twenties, with flawless café-au-lait skin. Her full red lips curved into a mysterious smile as her deep brown eyes examined us. To keep with the spirit of the place, she possessed curves like the Mississippi River kept in bounds by a short, trim figure. She wore a curious head wrap dotted with strange whorls and animals. She looked like the gatekeeper to another world. When she spoke, she had a liquid Southern accent tinged with something else I couldn't place.

"So, does the cat have your tongue?"

I shook myself and said, "I'm sorry, uh . . ."

"Celestine. And who might you be?"

"Oh, I'm Aidan and this is Cole."

She put her hand on her hip. "And, Aidan and Cole, what is it exactly that you are looking for?"

The question took me aback. I looked at Cole, and he gave me a goofy grin. He seemed about as out of sorts as I was. "I guess you could say we are hungry."

The smile left her face as her eyes bore into mine, searching. She frowned. "And what are you hungry for, Aidan?"

I didn't know what to say other than, "Food."

She smiled again. "Why didn't you say so, my loves? Celestine will take care of you. Come and sit."

Cole and I moved like drunken men to the nearest table.

"Take your ease, lovelies. Here are the menus. I'll be back in a moment to take your wishes."

She swayed rather than walked out of the room.

"Well, too bad God made her so ugly," Cole said.

I realized that I'd been watching her the whole time as she left. "Uh, yeah, right. Sorry, Cole, I—"

He laughed. "No need, Aidan. She is what we down South call a 'force of nature.' Hard to ignore those."

"Yes, indeed."

I knew there was something else to Celestine that I couldn't place; something other than her just being beautiful. I felt as if this restaurant inhabited one of those "thin places" that Father Neal talks about, places where the seen and unseen world grated up against each other in a tangible way. I couldn't tell Cole. He and the church had no clue about the world I inhabited on the weekends.

We looked at the menu and I had just decided to order a muffaletta when Celestine returned.

"Well, sweeties, have we found anything to our liking?"

I didn't even hear her walk up. It's almost as if she appeared out of thin air. "Uh, yeah, Celestine, thanks. I'll take a muffaletta and a water."

She nodded and turned to Cole. "And you, honey?"

"The gumbo please, with a soda."

She smiled, took our menus, and walked back to the kitchen.

I recovered myself enough to ask Cole, "So, the questions about Knox you want answered, I'm guessing they asked you to consider applying for the church."

He looked stunned and I laughed.

"You are a talented preacher, energetic, with a picture-perfect family, like I said before, with the knowledge to match. All you need is some real ministry seasoning, and you'll be ready for the table so they can devour you."

"I figured they would want you."

I shook my head. "First, it would be a huge undertaking with the presbytery to make that happen. I'm an assistant pastor, and they don't take kindly to assistants taking over a church. Doable, but I doubt they'll want to go through the trouble. Second, I told them I had no wish to take the position. Third, I'm not going to stay."

He raised his eyebrows. "John didn't say anything about that. That's why I was worried."

"No need to be. John, for all of his faults, doesn't spill personal secrets. I think many people in the congregation expect me to take over. The elders are the only ones who know I won't and that I'm thinking about leaving."

He crossed his arms and looked at me.

"Why won't you?"

At that moment, Celestine walked up to us with our drinks.

"To quench your thirst, *mes amours*."

"Thanks, Celestine. Can you answer me something?"

"Of course."

"Are you from New Orleans?"

She smiled as she gave me a saucy look. "Now, why do you want to know that?"

I motioned at the decor. "Well, obvious, yeah?"

She looked around and whispered, "Yes, I'm from New Orleans. My sisters and I moved up to Columbus after the storm."

"Katrina?"

She looked at me with her brown eyes blazing. "Yes, *mon amour*, what other storm has there been in NOLA in the past six years?"

I nodded. "But you just opened this restaurant?"

She gave me a look of withering pity. "It took us some time to get back on our feet."

I blushed. "Right, sorry."

"It's not your fault." She smiled. "Most people don't realize how bad things were for us refugees. The worst thing is being away from our lovely city. Maybe, one day, we'll return."

She sighed and then said, "I'll be back with your food."

I looked back at Cole. "Now, to answer your question. I'm not sure what my future is at this point. I'm still trying to figure that out."

He nodded. "When will you?"

"When the next pastor is hired. So far, we aren't even close. You know how these search processes go. They take forever."

He looked at the people who came into the restaurant. "You aren't bothered that John talked to me about taking the job?"

I shook my head. "No, not at all. I think it shows they have their head in the right place, instead of up their butts, for once."

He laughed. "Is that so?"

"Yes, that is so. They need to be shaken up a little, and that's a good thing." I paused to sip my water. "Remember one thing, though: people are never that simple, and certainly not in the church, Cole."

He didn't say anything until Celestine brought our food.

"There you go, gentlemen. Your fine food made by Celestine herself."

I breathed in deep and smelled the combination of warm olives and spicy Italian meat.

"It looks amazing, Celestine, thanks."

We ate without talking, and I got the sense that Cole didn't want to continue the church conversation. I didn't press it, as I'm certain I had given him more than enough to think about.

Celestine returned. "Well, *mes amours*, will there be anything else this fine day?"

I looked up to tell her that we just needed the check when I caught a symbol in Celestine's head wrap. I nearly choked on my words as I saw the veve from the canyon wall on her head wrap.

"Yeah, actually Celestine, tell me about your head wrap. We don't see those much around Columbus."

She put her hand on her hip and said, "Well, now, that's easy enough. It's called a 'madras.' My ancestors would wear it because it's one of the few things we were allowed as slaves to wear that contained any sort of self-expression. Normally, we would have to wear plain outfits to mark our slavery. However, we were allowed to wear whatever we wanted on Sundays, and we would wear the most colorful things we could find."

I nodded, still staring at the symbol. "And does that include interweaving Voodoo symbols in the design?"

The effect of my question on her demeanor startled me. Before, she had put off a vibe of soft sensuality that had enchanted us. Now she stood up straight, and her eyes crackled with fire. The whole room seemed to dim as if she commanded the light in the room with her soul, the force of nature become a gathering storm. Cole didn't seem fazed by the sudden change in her appearance or the darkening of the room.

"And why, Aidan, do you ask about Voodoo?"

I decided to tell her the truth, at least, as much as I needed to get answers.

"Let's just say I have a professional interest. I'm a pastor of a church in Upper Arlington, and I date a detective who got called to the site of a Voodoo ritual last night. At least, we think it was Voodoo."

She slowly relaxed and covered her reaction with playfulness. Light returned to the room. "And why would you think I would know about such things? Because I'm from the land of Madame

Laveau? Because I may or may not have a Voodoo symbol on my madras?"

"Who?"

She laughed, and the room seemed to shake. "The boy asks about Voodoo and doesn't know about Madame Laveau. My sweet pastor, Madame Marie Laveau was the Voodoo queen of New Orleans in the nineteenth century. She was a powerful woman, at least, powerful for a free woman of color."

"I thought you said you knew nothing about Voodoo."

She gave me a slow smile. "I am a Creole woman, Pastor Aidan. Stories of Madame Laveau are our bedtime legends, yes?"

"Sure," I said, a bit confused.

"Now, as you are my first customers of the day and such lovely men, your meal is on me this afternoon, as long as you come back."

The abrupt dismissal took me by surprise, but I took the hint.

Cole looked back in the restaurant as Celestine waited on other customers.

"What was that all about? Voodoo? Why did you ask about that?"

"It's just as I said. Jen investigated a crime last night and asked my advice. The crime scene contained elements of a Voodoo ritual."

"How do they know that?"

"Can't tell you that, I'm afraid. Part of the investigation."

He shrugged and began walking to the car.

I watched Celestine a little longer, convinced she knew more than she was telling. Maybe she had performed the ritual. If so, why?

I resolved to tell Father Neal when we met.

# CHAPTER FIVE

"THERE'S SO MUCH SUGAR IN APPLE JUICE. I CAN'T BELIEVE YOU WOULD advocate giving it to our children. It's bad enough we are killing their brain cells with VeggieTales videos, but now we are trying to make them fat? We should be teaching them how to take care of their God-given bodies." The argument was coming from Nicole Barrens, a short, thirty-something soccer mom.

"They are kids; it's not going to hurt them. And VeggieTales are funny, and they teach good lessons. Sugar isn't a sin, you know," shot back Katie Burr, a brunette former beauty queen.

I looked back and forth between the grizzly-bear moms. There's nothing more uncomfortable than watching two women take out their frustrations with life on someone else. Nicole, ignored by her career-focused husband, controlled every aspect of her kids' lives. She fought nearly everything we tried to do if it didn't line up with the plan she had for her kids.

Katie fought her insecurity about being a career-oriented mom by letting her kids have everything their little hearts desired. This sort of family plan resulted in her kids being the terrors of Sunday school teachers everywhere.

They glared at each other, and I wondered if I would have

to break up a fight. I realized that I'd have to be Solomon in this situation and figure out how to split the baby.

"Katie, Nicole, please . . ."

They turned their glares at me, and I had to think fast. I didn't want to be grizzly fodder.

"Listen, I think you are both right."

Their looks of anger turned to mystified confusion.

Good, I stopped their momentum.

"Nicole, you have an excellent point. Sugar can be bad for our children in excessive amounts. We need to be sensitive to that concern. Plus, there might be kids who aren't allowed to have it for various reasons, like your own, correct?"

Nicole nodded. "In addition to my kids, Dakota has diabetes and the Sanderson kid has ADD. Any sugar will send him through the stratosphere."

"And, Katie, would you agree with that?"

"That kid could become a human molecule if we let him. His parents got mad about the juice, too."

I smiled. "So, is there something out there that is juice with no sugar or at least, very little?"

They nodded, the last of the anger fading from their faces.

"Good. So, get me a list of good, sugar-free alternatives. Then we can decide which is the best. Does that sound okay?"

They looked at each other, smiled a little, and said, "That sounds doable."

Silence fell, and both women seemed embarrassed. Both of them began to sniffle, and their eyes watered as they looked at each other. I grabbed the tissue box and held it out. They each grabbed a few.

Katie said, "I'm sorry, Nicole. I got a little too bossy."

Nicole wiped her nose with a tissue. "It's okay, Katie. I guess I got a little out of control myself."

They both hugged each other in a watery embrace.

Katie said, "Should we get together for coffee tomorrow morning? I can take the morning off so we can chat."

"Yes, I'd like that. The older kids will be in school, and Jodie will be in day care. I'll have a free moment to myself, thank God."

They broke apart and continued to clean up their faces with tissues. Katie looked at me and then smiled. "How is Jen, Aidan? You two have any wedding plans yet?"

Ugh, the dreaded wedding plan question. I knew it was a natural question. Still, I didn't know what my own future would be, much less how Jen related to it.

"Um, well, not yet. But, you never know what God is going to bring in the future."

They both looked at each other and smiled. A few minutes ago, they stood ready to tear each other apart, and now they seemed to be keepers of some secret they wouldn't be sharing with me.

I'm pretty sure I don't understand women at all. Truth be told, that is one of the main truths of my life. The mystery of women keeps growing as my own understanding recedes.

"Well, keep us posted. We'll get the juice stuff after we meet for coffee!"

They both walked out of my office chatting and making plans. I took a deep breath and reached into my drawer for the bottle of Irish whiskey. It had been a present from Father Neal. He called it "full-moon tonic" in reference to a conversation we had about how the full moon seems to bring out the craziness in church people. I poured a little in my coffee and spent the rest of my day preparing my Wednesday-night lesson that I would give tomorrow.

I wasn't in a hurry to get home, as I figured Jen would be working late again and wouldn't be coming over for dinner. Still, I needed to walk Bishop. So, with a sigh, I headed out the door and drove home. I walked to my condo door with my head down and found my door unlocked. I opened up the door, and Bishop greeted with me a soft woof.

"Hey, bud, did you unlock the door for me or something?"

Bishop looked toward the kitchen, and I heard the clank of pots and pans.

Was it possible?

"Hey, sweetie, come into the kitchen and give me hand, will you?"

I smiled and went into the kitchen. All of the stress drained from me at the sound of Jen's voice. My tension drained away as I breathed in the scent of coconut and Italian spices. As I rounded the corner to the kitchen, I caught sight of Jen in her running shorts and her toned, tanned legs. She wore a pink apron as she cooked up a storm.

I leaned against the doorframe. "Now, that is a sight I could get used to, a hot woman in my kitchen making me food."

She gave me a saucy look. "Does a man really need anything else besides a warm woman and a full belly?"

I laughed. "Not really, truth be told. If all women understood that about men, we might have fewer problems in relationships. Well, sports on TV might be a close third, too."

"Can you help me reach the glass bowl on the top shelf? I can't reach it."

I reached up and got the bowl. As I did, I turned around and almost ran into Jen. She took the bowl from me and placed it on the counter. Then she put her arms around me and I took her into mine. We hugged for a moment as I felt the warmness of her body against mine. I kissed her head and breathed in deep, savoring the smell of her fruity shampoo. She responded by kissing me deeper, and I held her tight. I could taste her tongue and Italian spices.

"I love you," she said.

"And I you, Jen. I'm sorry I have been such a jerk lately."

She smiled. "That you have, my love. But then, I've been a secretive little witch lately, too."

I moved my head to gaze into her eyes. Our lips touched in a gentle kiss and then our passion took over. I held her tight as the tension between us dissolved into warm kisses. My hands ran through her hair, and we only broke apart as Bishop nudged himself between us.

"What's the matter, buddy, jealous that I got the girl?"

Bishop gave me a soft woof.

"I know, I know, no contest; you win, right?"

Jen smiled as the scar stretched across her beautiful face, "No fighting, boys, we have work to do. Set the table, Aidan."

I grabbed her. "Why? I think I like it right here."

She smiled and swatted my butt. "Do it, boy. Your dinner is getting cold."

I set the table, lit some candles, and Jen brought in the food, a delicious pasta dish of rigatoni and homemade red sauce with spices thrown into the mix. She'd also made bread, and the smell made my stomach growl.

"Mouthwatering."

She gave me a flirty grin. "What is, me or the bread?"

"Both."

We prayed, and then ate for a moment as we enjoyed the silence. Jen looked at me and smiled. "So, surprised to see me?"

I swallowed my food. "Yeah, to be honest, that's why I got home a little late. I put it off until I thought Bishop wouldn't be able to stand it anymore."

She smiled. "I took the evening off. I told Weaver I wasn't feeling well. I guess I bent the truth a little, but only a little. Considering I never take any time off, he can deal with it, I'm sure. Besides, the Cardinals are playing the Reds tonight. I figured we could fight about baseball instead of our lack of time together."

We laughed and then I said, "I love you, you know."

"Even if I'm a Reds fan?"

"Well, no one is perfect."

We finished eating and we cleaned up together. I took every opportunity to steal kisses from her, and we made our way to the couch. Turning on the baseball game, we sat on the couch and Jen snuggled up close. We both started to fall asleep as the baseball game made its way into the middle innings.

The phone rang and jolted me out of my drowsing. I had to hold on to Jen as she nearly fell out of my lap.

"Sorry, love, phone."

I reached over and looked at the caller ID. It was Brian Little, my best friend.

"Who is it?" Jen whispered.

"It's Brian. Should I take it?"

"Of course, I have to go the bathroom anyway."

I answered, "Yo, buddy, does this nasty heat and humidity make you feel more at home?"

"Hey, man, how are you?"

Brian's tone made me sit up.

"What's wrong, are you okay?"

"Not really. Something is going on here at the farm and I don't know what to do."

"What, the corn not growing fast enough?"

"I'm serious."

He sounded dejected. I realized he'd sounded like that since he'd moved with his family to Columbus two months ago after buying Olan and Edna's farm. I'd just ignored it. Grimacing, I said, "Okay, talk to me, buddy. What's up?"

"I think it would be better if you just came out here to see."

"What, right now?"

"Yes."

I gripped the phone and sighed.

"Brian, I mean, I don't know. Jen's here, she took a night off just to be with me. We are watching baseball and—"

"Aidan, please, I need you. Bring Jen with you."

The desperation in his voice set alarm bells off in my head. We hadn't been able to talk much in the past three weeks, so I wondered what I'd been missing.

"Okay, let me ask her."

Jen had just come out of the bathroom and said, "Ask me what?"

I covered up the phone so Brian couldn't hear. "He wants me—us—to come out to the farm."

She wrinkled her nose. "Tonight? Why?"

"He said something is going on at the farm that he wants me to see. He sounds a bit desperate, actually."

Jen sighed. "Well, at least we'll be together."

"Are you sure?"

She smiled. "Of course. Besides, I'm a bit curious, aren't you?"

"I am, actually. Something is going on there."

"Okay, let's go."

I uncovered the phone. "Hey, Bri, we will be there in about thirty minutes or so, sound good?"

"Yes, I doubt it'll have stopped by the time you get here. See you then."

He hung up before I could ask him what "it" was. I must have had a weird look because Jen asked, "What? What is it?"

"I don't know. Something isn't right. . . ."

"What?"

"He just . . . He said something wouldn't have stopped by the time we got there."

"Should I put Bishop in the crate or bring him along?"

"Leave him here. But . . ."

I paused as Jen looked up at me. "What?"

"Bring your gun."

She smiled. "Never leave home without it, my love."

She put Bishop in his crate and we got in the car to drive to the farm.

# CHAPTER SIX

"I MISS OLAN AND EDNA," JEN SAID AS WE PULLED INTO THE GRAVEL driveway. "Are they loving Arizona?"

"They love being around the grandkids. I think Olan is enjoying golfing all the time. 'I needed to rest, love my kids, and enjoy God's creation on a golf cart,' " I said, imitating Olan's booming Midwestern farmer's voice. "Never thought he would leave the farm, but seems he doesn't mind it one bit."

Jen smiled. "It's a good thing Brian was able to buy the house then."

"I still don't understand the whole situation and why they moved up here. They are Southerners. They are going to hate the winters."

"Well, Ashley's uncle got him a good job, didn't he?"

"Yes, but he already had a great job with one of the best firms in Nashville. If you were a Southerner, would you move to the frozen North?"

Jen didn't say anything else until we pulled up to the house. "Have you asked him about it?"

I shrugged. "I tried but he just gave me some lame excuse that it was time for a change. He said that since I lived here and some of Ashley's extended family lived here, Columbus would be a good fit. I figured he'd tell me when he is ready."

We got out of the car as Brian walked out of the house. His face wore a look that I had only seen a few times in our friendship. One of those times included when he took a swing at me during a pickup basketball game.

"Hey, bud, what's wrong?"

He shrugged. "I just want to show you both something."

Jen made to walk toward the house and Brian stopped her.

"I wouldn't do that, Jen. Ashley and I just had a pisser of a fight. Give her a few moments."

Jen and I looked at each other. I gave her a slight shake of my head as I said, "No problem, what did you want to show us?"

"This way."

He led us along a path toward an all-too-familiar field, and I shuddered as we drew closer. This had been the same field where Olan showed me the footprints of his dead son, and I had avoided it at all costs. It seemed as if every aspect of my life would be haunted by the events of a few months ago.

When we got to the fence, Brian said, "They aren't doing anything right now. I guess that gives me time to give you the whole story."

Jen grasped my hand, and I squeezed back as we gazed into the dark field.

"A few weeks ago, I strolled through this field for an evening walk. As I reached the middle of the field, I nearly tripped over a piece of stone. After I made sure my toe wasn't broken, I looked at the stone. It formed a perfect rectangle about eight inches long and about six inches wide. Someone had taken care to polish it smooth and slick. On the face of the stone, characters, trees, and whorl lines were carved in a style I had seen on Native American stones at the Ohio Historical Society."

I nodded. "Olan found ancient Indian stuff here all the time. He had a box full of ax heads and arrowheads. He even had an archaeologist come out to look at the field. The guy told him it had probably been some sort of battleground."

"Really?" Jen asked. "I didn't know that."

"Olan was very proud of it. I can't believe he didn't tell you."

Brian said, "Well, that would explain it. Anyway, this is what I found."

He pulled out the stone and handed it to me. I took out my phone and turned on the flashlight app. The light illuminated the artwork. Whorls dominated the corners as the lines swirled around a figure with deep hollowed out eyes and a huge grotesque grin. One hand held a small human-shaped figurine with a look of pain, and in the other was a grotesque wolf-shaped statue.

"That's a bit disturbing," Jen said as she traced the carved lines on the figure.

Brian said, "Well, if it was the only disturbing thing I had to tell you or show you, I would be happy."

I looked at him. "What do you mean?"

He looked off into the field. "A few days after I found this stone and removed it, stuff started happening."

I felt a chill that had nothing to do with the weather. "Like what?"

Brian paused for a moment. "You know I'm a rational guy, right? I mean, even all the ghost stuff you told me a few months ago, I believed it, but I couldn't help feel a little skeptical. I mean, I believe in all this stuff, but, well, I guess it's another thing when it happens to you."

"No doubt," Jen agreed.

He took a deep breath. "It started with a kangaroo."

I tried not to laugh. "A kangaroo?"

"I know it sounds crazy, so just listen. We had decided to eat dinner on the picnic bench, and just as we sat down, we saw something hopping across the fields. We couldn't believe our eyes as this kangaroo-looking like thing hopped up right to the fence."

I looked at Jen and she shrugged.

"Go on."

Brian thrust his hands in his shorts. "I know it sounds unreal."

"Jen and I have seen crazier things."

"Well, maybe I'll be able to top it. We were so stunned by a kangaroo thing in our field that we didn't notice its face." He shuddered. "I still wish I hadn't. It haunts me, and I can see it staring at me as I try to close my eyes at night."

"What do you mean?"

Brian stood there for a moment. "It was horrible, like a cross between a man, a demon, a feral animal, and something else I really can't describe. And the eyes. Dear God, black and full of evil."

He rubbed his face and put his hand on the fencepost. "Peyton ran up to it and started barking. The thing looked at him and lifted up its head in a long, ear-splitting howl. Poor Peyton was scared out of his mind as he ran into the house. He still won't come outside unless one of us is with him."

"Did the thing hop away?"

Brian shook his head. "It just disappeared."

Jen said, "You mean, hid?"

"No, it's like the thing dissolved into thin air. We stared at the spot for about five minutes. I think we were in shock."

"I bet that's the understatement of the year," I said.

"We tried to put it out of our minds, but things kept happening around the house. Things would disappear and would reappear. Strange phone calls came in the middle of the night—"

"What kind of phone calls?"

He shook his head. "I don't really know. All I could hear when I answered was some sort of electronically garbled voice."

Jen pecked at her phone as she wrote down what Brian told us. "Did you catch any words?"

He stared out into the field.

"Brian?"

He answered, "Most of the time, the voice said, 'We are watching you.' But, it changed yesterday to 'We are here.' And then last night, that's when those started showing up." He pointed toward the field. A bright red light in the shape of a ball had begun to move in the distance.

Jen gripped my hand again, and I winced. "What is that, Aidan?"

"I . . . I don't know."

The red light began to gather speed as it crossed the field, then shot straight up into the air and disappeared into the night sky.

"Brian, what—" I couldn't finish my sentence.

"It's not over."

The red light reappeared in the field and joined three others. Each light began to move in its own pattern, dancing across the fields. I needed to give them a closer look.

"Where do you think you are going, Aidan?" Jen grabbed on to my shoulder as I began to climb over the fence.

"Are you kidding? I have to see these up close."

Brian shook his head. "I don't think so. I tried last night, and they won't let me get close."

Almost as if in response to his words, one red orb broke away from the pack and sped toward us. It moved so fast we had no time to react as it drew within twenty feet of the fence. A low hum emitted from the sphere, and I could feel a low-grade heat building up on my skin.

Brian fell to his knees and held his head. "I know. I know. I shouldn't have. I shouldn't have."

He collapsed to the ground writhing in pain.

"Jen!" I yelled as I dropped to the ground, and she joined me.

She felt his pulse. "It's still strong, but his heartbeat is erratic. We have to get him back to the house."

The red sphere continued its low hum, but I realized I could make out words being whispered: *He is ours. His family is ours. She will be our slave. The lover of the Grinning Man is here.*

I stood up and climbed over the fence before Jen could grab me. I walked closer to the sphere as it began to back up. The heat radiated from its core as it began to burn my face.

Something tugged at my mind, and I pushed back with

force. Whatever this orb thing was, it was trying to invade my thoughts.

"Get out! Out! Leave him and his family alone, whatever you are. You have no place here. In the name of Christ, go."

White light shot out of my fingers and penetrated the sphere. Voices screamed as it backed up across the field. The other lights joined with it, and they disappeared in a flash.

Jen yelled, "Aidan Schaeffer, get your ass back here, now!"

She didn't see anything, I thought. I looked down at my hands. What the hell? How did that happen?

I stumbled back toward her and bent to the ground to throw up. My whole body felt weak, unable to move. I made it to the fence. "Jen, I don't think I can make it over the fence. Can you help me?"

Jen took my arms and supported me as I climbed over the fence.

When I did, I collapsed near Brian, who'd stopped holding his head.

# CHAPTER SEVEN

JEN STARED DAGGERS AT ME AS WE HELPED BRIAN BACK TO THE HOUSE. It took everything in me not to throw up again as the world seemed to be turning upside down.

"Why, in God's name, did you go into that field? What the hell were you thinking?"

"I guess I wasn't thinking," I rasped. "Can we not talk about this now?"

She looked at me as she bit back a real crusher, but she didn't say anything. Heat radiated from my face as if I had drank a gallon of Tabasco sauce. We reached the back porch, and I knocked as hard as I could.

"Ash . . . something has happened . . . let us in."

The porch light flicked on and Ashley Little opened the door. Even now, my breath caught in my throat at Ashley's beauty. Light red hair had been straightened from her normal curls, but otherwise she looked almost exactly like she did in college.

"Aidan. What happened?"

She drew near, and I nearly dropped Brian. Her eyes were almost swollen shut from crying.

"The lights in the field . . . they did something to him . . . to us," I said between gasps. "Can we come in?"

She paused as if she wondered if it would be a good idea to let us in, and Jen's firm voice broke in. "Now. He's hurt."

Ashley nodded and stepped aside. We carried Brian to the couch.

"Get me a cloth soaked in cold water. Quick."

I went into the kitchen, ran cold water on a towel, and came back into the living room. "Here." I handed her the towel.

Jen looked up and turned white. "Aidan, your face."

I touched my cheek and yelped in pain. Jen turned to Ashley. "Aloe?"

Ashley stared at Brian like a zombie. Jen stood up and grabbed Ashley's arm. "Aloe, Ashley. Please."

Ashley pointed to the bathroom. I walked to the bathroom and shut the door. I opened the medicine cabinet and found the bottle of aloe. As I closed the cabinet door, I caught my reflection in the mirror. I gasped as I saw my face glowing like a scarlet Buckeye jersey. Red welts had begun to form on my cheeks, and it looked as if an intense Florida sun had burned me. I winced as I applied the aloe. The blue-green goo did its magic, and the heat began to fade. I still felt sick, but at least I wouldn't be a walking radiator.

I made my way back into the living room. Ashley sat in a chair and watched Jen attend to Brian. She looked at him with dead eyes.

Jen dabbed the cloth on Brian's face and checked his pulse.

I knelt down next to her. "How is he doing?"

She looked around at Ashley. "He is doing fine. His heartbeat is regulating. I don't think we will need to take him to the hospital, but"—she looked sideways at Ashley and leaned into my ear—"she hasn't said one word since you went in the bathroom. You would think she would be concerned, but she just keeps staring at us. It gives me the creeps."

I nodded. "Well, glad we won't have to take him to the hospital. Isn't that great, Ash?"

Jen and I looked back, expecting a reply. For a moment, she just stared at us.

"Ash? Are you okay? Do you need some water or something?"

"Water? No. No, I'm okay. Just worried about . . . him."

I had to bite my tongue. If she cared about Brian, you could slick back my hair and call me a Baptist.

Jen glanced at me. "He is going to be fine. He just needs some rest."

"Should I leave him on the couch?" Ashley asked.

Brian stirred and mumbled, "It's where I have been sleeping anyway, so what does it matter?"

Ashley rolled her eyes. "And whose fault is that?" She left the room leaving a tense silence behind.

"I'm sorry you had to see that," Brian said.

I gripped his shoulder. "It's okay, man. We're like brothers. But, what's going on with you two?"

Brian shook his head. "Not yet, Aidan. I feel too sick right now to even get into it."

"But . . ."

"Aidan." Jen gripped my hand. "Leave it."

I looked at Brian, who seemed a shell of his former self. I wanted to help. I wanted him to talk to me. I hated seeing him in pain. Something had attached itself to his mind, his soul, his whole family.

"I'm sorry, Brian. I'm just—"

"Worried, I know. One day soon, we will talk, I promise. I need to sit up."

Jen and I helped him, and he gave me a weak smile. Noticing my face, Brian frowned. "Aidan, what happened? Did the lights do that?"

I looked at Jen, who had just taken Brian's pulse again. She nodded.

"Yeah, they burned me. The heat from those things is incredible."

"I'm so sorry."

I waved my hand. "Don't worry about it."

Jen began taking notes. "Have these lights ever gotten that close before?"

Brian shook his head. "No, never. I have always watched them from a distance, and they seemed to be unaware of me. That is, until tonight."

"What happened to you?" I asked. "Why did you drop to the ground and say, 'I shouldn't have . . . I shouldn't have?' "

Brian didn't respond as he stared out of the window.

"Brian?"

"I . . . I can't tell you everything. But I'll tell you that those things, whatever they are, were talking inside my head. It's as if someone had turned on a radio full blast in my skull. Voices laughing and telling me . . ." He shuddered and then looked at me. "They kept saying over and over again, *She comes, the Dark Bride comes. And you have summoned her.*"

The lights seemed to dim and I glanced at Jen. Looking back at Brian, I asked, "Do you . . . do you know what that means?"

He shook his head. "No, I don't know. I was hoping you would."

He looked so white that I moved so he could lie back down.

"What can I do, Aidan? I need help."

"That you do, in more ways than one, it seems. I think we need to get the Scooby gang out here. What do you think, Jen?"

"Yes, I think so, if you are willing, that is." She touched Brian on the arm.

Brian nodded. "I don't know if Ashley will be, but I'm worried about Lily. I need to protect them both, even if Ashley doesn't want it. Please, Aidan, will you ask them to come out here, especially Father Neal?"

"Of course. As long as you keep your stupidity about SEC sports to yourself. I don't want to soil my friends."

He smiled thinly. "Yes, dear."

"Brian, we should go. Can I get you anything before we leave?"

He motioned to the table at the end of the couch. "Just the remote, if you don't mind."

Jen handed him the remote and smiled. "Get well. Let us know if you need anything else."

"Thank you."

Jen and I walked outside. I looked toward the field, but I didn't see any red lights. "I guess frying someone's brain and burning my face was enough for one evening."

Jen gave me a look, and I knew I would get it once we got in the car. She waited until we got on the road before she started in.

"Do you mind telling me what you thought you were doing?"

I shook my head. "I don't know . . . I just, I guess I was trying to help Brian."

"By putting your own life in danger?"

"Isn't that what you do on a daily basis?"

She glared at me. "Don't change the subject, Aidan."

"I wasn't trying to . . . just making a point."

Jen folded her arms. "And that would be?"

"If you can risk your life for total strangers, why can't I risk mine for my best friend?"

"I don't do it right in front of you."

I laughed and then checked myself. "So, um, that makes a big difference, does it?"

She sighed. "I guess I see your point. I just care about your sorry ass."

"And I care about yours. So, now that we've established we care about each other's butts . . ."

She laughed. "Why is it I can't be angry at you for a long time?"

"Because I'm so charming and witty?" I offered.

She shook her head. "You wish. You are infuriating sometimes, you know."

"And yet you stay with me, what does that say about you?"

"I'm a glutton for punishment, that's what." She grabbed my hand, and we rode in silence for a while.

"So, are you going to call Father Neal in the morning?"

I sighed. "Yeah, he has a lot on his plate, but I don't think we can ignore this."

"Has he figured out that whole quarry thing?"

"No, he hasn't. I'm reluctant to throw more cares on top of everything, but I don't see where we have any choice. Brian and his family are in serious danger."

Jen gripped my hand. "In more ways than one, it would seem."

I cleared my throat. "Yeah, I know."

"I have never seen anyone be that cold, that distant, when the person they supposedly love is suffering from some kind of physical harm. Has Ashley always been like that?"

"Not to me, and I've never seen her like that with Brian."

We pulled into the parking lot, and I stopped the car. Leaning over, I kissed Jen as long as I could with a burned face. She kissed me back, melting into me, and then I hugged her tight. "Do you want to come in for a while?"

Jen's whispered response tickled my ear and I squirmed. "If I did that, I wouldn't leave, and that wouldn't be good for the respectable pastor's reputation."

"You would be surprised. Most of the church probably thinks we're sleeping together anyway."

"Aidan, don't tempt me. I'm weak tonight. When you went into that field . . ." She gripped me tighter.

"I'm sorry, my love. I didn't mean to scare you."

Jen broke our embrace as we stared into each other's eyes, and she whispered, "Please, please just be careful."

"Says the woman who carries a gun everywhere."

She arched her eyebrow. "Give me a good ol'-fashioned criminal over that stuff we just saw in the field. I can shoot a bad guy. What do you do with burning red lights?"

"That, my love, is what we must figure out."

I didn't know why I couldn't tell her what happened in the field. Maybe I didn't want to admit, even to myself, I'd been changed and couldn't go back. I just wanted to hold on to being normal as long as possible.

If I could . . .

# CHAPTER EIGHT

"LOOKS LIKE THE ALOE IS STARTING TO DO ITS WORK," FATHER NEAL said as he bent down to look at my face.

"Yeah, finally. I had to sleep on my back last night. Every time I turned over, I nearly screamed in pain."

Father Neal's fingers hovered over the burns without touching my face. "And the lights disappeared after you confronted them?"

"They did. I don't think they came back that night."

"The light that came out of your fingers, did it shoot or ooze out?"

"Why does that matter?"

"It tells me how far along you are in your transformation into the Order."

Father Neal made it sound like I'd been inducted into the Justice League with my newfound powers. Transformation? What happened to me when I saw the Five Sorrows? Did they do something to me?

"It shot."

Father Neal nodded. "Forgive me, my dear boy."

Before I could ask what for, he jabbed me in the face with his finger.

"Oww! What the hell?" I backed away from him holding my face.

"I'm sorry. I needed to see if there is any . . . evil residue . . . on you."

"Isn't there a less painful way to do it?"

He shook his head. "No. I'm sorry, there isn't."

"You obviously know what did this. Can you tell me?"

He leaned on his cane. "Very often spirits, mainly elemental spirits, manifest with glowing lights, heat, just like you mentioned. Many people mistake them for UFOs. Indeed, I'm pretty sure they're the source of all the alien abduction stories and the modern UFO movement. Given the history of that field, it's not surprising. Elementals are often found in places of death."

"Why are they manifesting now?"

He shrugged his shoulders. "There could be any number of explanations. Most likely, Brian disturbed something by taking up that stone. How is he, by the way?"

I frowned. "He is back at work today. We are supposed to spar at the gym, and he texted me to see if we were still on."

"Spar?"

"We are both taking bataireacht. You know, Irish stick fighting. Separate classes, but we decided to practice together. We've not been able to get together at all since he got here."

Father Neal nodded as he finished scanning my face. He limped back to his desk and sat down with a sigh. I watched him for a moment, then said, "Are you okay?"

He smiled. "Okay? Yes, I'm okay."

I didn't let it go. "How about better than okay?"

Father Neal was staring at the pictures of his wife and his daughters. "Aidan, ever since I saw them at Serpent Mound, I'm pretty sure I'll never do better than okay until the day I join them."

"Can't you, you know, see them?"

He looked at me as tears brimmed. "No. The second sight never works like that. I have no wish to summon them at will.

That's too much like the people we are fighting against. I have to constantly resist the urge."

We sat silently for a moment, and then I said, "I'm sorry, I know you didn't join them because of me."

He smiled. "Well, as Saint Paul said, it's better for me to remain in the body for a little while, for more people than just you. My work is not finished. Not just yet. You must be trained, and I'm not entirely sure you will be replacing me in the Order."

"Let me guess: vacancy only comes through death."

"No, sadly, there is also the loss of faith or betrayal. Both have happened in the long history of the Order. Now, back to Brian. What do you think is going on between him and Ashley?"

"I have no idea. I'm planning on asking him today."

"Do, because that is going to be important."

"Why?"

"Somehow, I think the activity is related to the stress going on in the house."

"Why would that be?"

He shrugged. "I'm not sure of the why; I just know that such activity can be activated by stressful situations. It's a well-known fact among paranormal investigators and priests, for that matter. Think about it, Aidan. How often have you seen strange things happen around people undergoing severe emotional stress?"

I rubbed my chin. "You know, now that you mention it, I have spoken to a few doctors who talked about strange things happening around dying people."

"Yes, that's because in times of stress, the veil becomes thinner."

"I guess my job is to find out the thin place in their lives, is that right?"

Father Neal nodded. "Correct. If we are going to bring the team in on this investigation, I want to know everything we might be dealing with, seen and unseen."

"Fine, but no one else can know."

Father Neal made a face. "Trust me, Aidan. No one else needs to know what is going on with Brian and Ashley. But you and I must know everything that is at play. Do you understand?"

"Not entirely, but I trust you, so that's good enough for me right now."

He smiled. "Thank you, my dear boy. I'll call a meeting of the team for this evening. You can tell Brian that we'll help them."

"Sure. Anything new on our little message from the land of Voodoo?"

He shook his head. "I'm in the process of drawing out all the images in my head."

"I didn't know you could draw."

Father Neal pointed up to a sketch of Westminster on the wall. "That's my work right there. The archbishop loved it so much, he commissioned it be sold in the abbey bookstore. It's on everything from tea cups to towels."

"One day, I'll get a tea cup and remember you when I'm at the abbey," I said. "Anything coherent in the images?"

"I'm still in the process of searching my brain for what I saw. I drew the ones I told you about, because they are the ones I can remember. The rest, I have to think harder on. It used to be easier when I was younger. There is certainly a message there, and it's about the Grinning Man."

My shoulders slumped. "We already knew that, didn't we? I was hoping you would know more."

"Courage, my dear boy. All will be revealed when it is time. Whoever did this must be found. They are very dangerous to have walking around. "

I remembered the restaurant and Celestine.

"We may not have to wait for your drawings, Padre."

Father Neal leaned over his desk. "What do you mean?"

I told him everything that happened at the restaurant, and he looked thoughtful. "It could be just a coincidence," I said.

He shook his head. "There is no such thing, Aidan. Everything is connected. The real question is: Does this connect with our little situation? Or something else entirely?"

"Well, we could check things out, couldn't we? I could take you out for lunch. The food is pretty amazing."

He stared out of the window. "Yes, yes, I think we should do that, but not yet."

"Why not?"

"Not enough evidence. At least, not enough for a direct conversation. I want to know more about this . . . magician—if that's what she is."

I looked down and sighed. Celestine seemed to be a powerful Voodoo queen, no doubt. But did that mean she was evil as well? "I guess if there is no immediate danger, we don't need to worry about it."

"There is always immediate danger. I'm just not sure if the danger is ready to present itself."

I looked at my phone. "I have to get to sparring with Brian. I'll let you know what happens. Call me when you know more about the group."

My stomach clenched into a knot as I pulled up to the gym. I didn't know if I wanted to hear what Brian would tell me in our conversation. Ashley's look from the night before told me everything I didn't want to know. Things weren't just bumpy in Brian's house. His happy home seemed to be sinking into a hellhole.

I made my way into the locker room, changed into my workout clothes, and grabbed my shillelagh. Brian was already there, twirling and feinting on the mat. His face fixed in intense concentration as he assaulted an invisible opponent.

"So, are you winning?"

He stopped and smiled. "Of course. Easy to beat an enemy you can't see."

I stepped on the mat. "I can promise you, that's not the case."

He walked over and stood in front of me. "Are you ready?"

I lifted my shillelagh in a defensive stance. "Born."

He raised his stick in a salute, and I did the same.

"Begin."

We sparred for ten minutes straight, sticks cracking, as we

tried to find weaknesses in each other's defense. Breathing hard, I held up my hand. "Need a break."

We sat on the mat and I said, "Quite a night, eh?"

Brian looked at me with bloodshot eyes. "Yeah, I guess you could say that. I'm sorry about your face."

"I'll live. Aloe does wonders."

He looked away and stared out the window. "So, will you be able to help us? Will Father Neal?"

"That's the good news, Brian. Father Neal is getting the team together tonight. Usually, we just do people's houses. This sort of investigation is going to be a bit more complex. It might take a few days to set up."

He let this pass without comment as I continued, "But, Brian, there is something else that I need to ask."

He looked at me and said, "What?"

I leaned in. "I think you know what, so don't be a dick. Your fight with Ashley last night . . . Coldness came off her like an open refrigerator. Something is going on that you haven't told me about. I'm your best friend, damn it."

He smirked. "The righteous preacher and his potty mouth."

"Shut up. This is serious."

He twirled his shillelagh in quick half circles. "Yeah, thanks, I think I know how serious this is, asshole. It's my family."

"Then you better start talking, jackass. Because, as much as I love you, I'm not going to put other people at risk."

He sneered at me. "So, I get to air my dirty laundry to a bunch of people I don't know?"

I rolled my eyes. "Come on, you know better than that. The only people who'll ever know what is going on between you two are Father Neal and me."

He didn't say anything and for a moment, I thought he would hit me with his stick. Brian gained control of his temper, and his shoulders slumped.

"I guess I just don't see the connection."

"Father Neal said there might be a link to what's going on.

He feels like something may have been set off by your troubles. Apparently, that happens with this paranormal crap. That's why we need to know."

He covered his eyes. "It's all my fault. I'm sorry I haven't told you. I just feel so ashamed."

"Dude, really, ashamed? I'm guessing there isn't anything you have done that—"

He looked up. "No, Aidan. Stop. Don't say any more."

I grew quiet and motioned for him to continue.

"It starts with why we moved up here in the first place. Haven't you wondered?"

"I did. I think at the beginning I was thrilled you were moving up here. I figured you would tell me the reason soon enough."

He gave me sad smile. "I'm glad you thought that, but if it wasn't for this—burning lights stuff—I never would have told you."

Brian took a drink of his water. "The truth, Aidan, is that I got fired from my job in Nashville."

I couldn't believe it and began to search for answers. "So, what, the bad economy got to the Christian music industry? Couldn't afford to pay their lawyers?"

He shook his head. "No, I mean, you know my boss, stand-up Christian guy."

Yeah, not many of those around, I couldn't help thinking.

Tears began to form in his eyes as he said, "I got caught . . ."

I wanted to cover my ears for what would come next.

". . . with porn on my computer."

My stomach unclenched a little as I said, "What? I didn't know you had a porn problem. I thought we had a long conversation about how that stuff didn't do it for us. You could have told me about the temptation, you know."

He shook his head. "No, it wasn't that sort of porn."

"Okay, then I'm not getting it."

"I started talking on some erotic chat sites."

It finally clicked. I'd dealt with this issue quite a few times over the past few years with weeping men in my office. Lonely, tired, and stressed, they reached out to find someone, anyone to understand them.

"So, you talked sexy with these women on the Internet? And what, the firm's filtering software picked it up?"

He nodded. "My boss brought me in and said they had all the transcripts for the chats. He gave me the option of quitting or public exposure through firing. I quit, and I had no intention of telling Ashley. However, the gossip hounds did their work, and she found out shortly after we moved here, thanks to the lovely Christian community."

It all made sense. The cold look. The fight. Everything. Brian pounded the mat with his fist, and I wanted to feel sorry for him. On the other hand, hitting him seemed like a great idea, too. I'd begun to realize how complicated life is, especially with the people we think we know. Do we ever really know anyone? People are a mystery almost as much as God is.

"How could you, Brian? I mean, Ashley is the total package, isn't she? What could possibly make you get on the Internet and chat with strange women? I don't get it. You have everything with her."

He grimaced as he looked up. "You know what your problem is, Aidan? You always idealize women. That's why Amanda broke up with you—couldn't bear the burden of your idolatry—and if you aren't careful, Jen will walk out the door as well."

I felt as if he'd punched me. I wish he would have. "Shut the hell up." I stood and so did he. We faced off as he turned red.

"It's true, Aidan. You make women into these perfect goddesses who aren't real. You always blame the guy and whatever his problem might be in the marriage. Let me tell you, bub, that's only half the story. You always had this crush on Ashley, and until I married her, I thought for good reason. She seemed like the total package. However, the day after our wedding, she showed her true colors. Our honeymoon was a disaster. She screamed at me over one stupid thing after another. I wondered if she didn't really want me, she just wanted the security I provided. I felt alone, isolated, and I finally cracked after years of stress."

I waved my hand. "Be that as it may, you still sinned."

He clenched his stick shillelagh as tears began to roll down his cheeks. "I know, Aidan. I know, okay? What was I supposed to do?"

"Well, how about not cybersexting women? That might have been a good start."

He swung the shillelagh at my legs. I tried to block it, but I missed. The sound of wood on skin echoed through the gym. I went down in pain on one knee and struck out at him in anger. Brian went down like a shot and groaned. We both lay on the mats nursing our bruises and gasping in pain.

"Feel better, Aidan? Punished me enough? You damn Pharisee. You have no idea what it's like to be married to a woman who doesn't love you. No clue."

Pharisee. The word went in deep and cut me more than if he told me to go fuck myself.

Every part of me hurt as I croaked out, "No, man, I feel horrible."

"You and me both, bub."

Brian pushed on his shillelagh to help himself up and got to his feet.

"Brian, wait. I'm sorry. Please . . . sit down."

He hovered between sitting and standing as he tried to decide. "The only reason I'm not walking out of here is because I don't know where else to go for help, I hope you know that."

"I'm sorry, bro. Please sit."

He sat down with a gasp and said, "So, Elder Brother, what should I do next?"

I winced. "I'm sorry, Brian, I didn't mean to come across like that. I just, it's hard for me to believe . . ."

"Hard to believe that your best friend is a human being?"

"No, I just didn't realize things were that bad with you two, that's all."

He nodded with a grimace. "I guess I should have reached out to you before I got to this point. But, to be perfectly honest, I did a good job justifying my actions to myself."

"Amazing how we justify drinking our own poison, eh?"

Brian put his hands over his eyes as he whispered, "Yes, and I drank deep. Now, I don't know what to do if all this scary shit is my fault. I love Ashley and Lily. I don't want anything . . ."

Brian broke down, and his whole body heaved with the sobs of a broken man. I stared at the mat and waited for him to pull himself together. It's the closest thing guys have to holding each other, giving a fellow guy space while he cries his eyes out. I looked around to see if anyone was watching. Everyone seemed occupied with knocking the shit out of each other.

After a few moments, he looked up and said, "What am I going to do, Aidan? My whole life has been flushed down the toilet, and now it seems I'm being tortured by some invisible force I don't understand."

"Yeah, about that, what happened when the sphere spoke to you? Why did you grip your head?"

He rubbed his head. "It seemed like the voices planted themselves in my head and took over all of my senses. I couldn't see anything, and it sounded like . . ."

"Like what?"

"Like a full stadium at the Horseshoe after Ohio State scores a touchdown. Thousands and thousands of voices speaking all at once and at full volume."

"What did they say?"

"Probably what you heard, I'm guessing. Stuff about the Dark Bride coming, that my family belonged to her, and that I was the one to blame."

I looked up and gripped his arm. "Brian, I promise you, I'll do anything, anything, to help you. You believe that, right?"

"Even after what I did?"

"You act like I think everyone is perfect. I don't. We're sinners. We have to fix this, the unseen stuff and the seen stuff, everything with Ashley."

He shook his head. "I don't think the last one is possible. Ashley doesn't forgive, Aidan. Ever. She may not divorce me, but she'll use this for the rest of our lives. You saw how she was last night."

What I had seen disturbed me to the core. I couldn't recall ever seeing a look of loathing and pure disgust like the one I saw on Ashley's face.

"We can do something about this. Nothing is irredeemable, you know."

He looked up at me. "Do you really believe that, Aidan?"

I nodded and said, "Yeah, man, I do. I have seen it work. Redemption is always possible, but—"

"But what?"

"The cross always has to come first, you know. There is going to have to be a lot of death between now and that point. You know that, right? You can't have what you had before with Ashley. That is dead. Hopefully, what gets raised up in its place will be better."

He turned to me and smiled. "Man, you've really grown, you know."

"What do you mean?"

"What you just said. The Aidan of last year never would have said something that painful and true. Plus, if I can be honest, selfish Aidan would have turned all of this around to be about you in some way."

"Yeah, well, I have seen some shit, you know?"

"I guess that is the understatement of the year."

Brian stopped chuckling as he turned to look at my burned face. "Although, something tells me you are going to see a lot more before it's all over."

I touched my face without thinking. "Yeah, well, being around Father Neal guarantees that."

"Just Father Neal? I don't think so; I think it's not just him. I think it's you, Aidan. Something is changing in you, and it's not just being more mature."

I let that pass without comment. "I'll give you a call in the morning after we meet tonight. Don't worry, we're gonna help."

He nodded. "I know you will. I never doubted it, bud."

As I climbed off the mat, leg still smarting, I gave Brian my hand and helped him up. "You can call me anytime, man—you know that, right? No more secrets."

He nodded. "No more secrets. Promise."

# CHAPTER NINE

I RODE BACK TO THE CHURCH WITH BRIAN'S TURMOIL ROLLING around in my head. His look of utter helplessness had shaken me. He had always stood strong for me in my trials and tribulations. Now his life was in utter shambles, and he'd broken apart right in front of my eyes. I'd learned to handle people's pain and darkness being dumped on me. With Brian, though, his troubles might as well have been my own.

I walked into the church, and Sherry looked up. "Pastor Aidan, Elder John is here to see you. He went into the sanctuary to check on some things for Sunday's worship."

What did he want? I really wasn't in the mood to deal with John's crap. Although things had gotten a lot better between us in the past few months, he still got on my nerves, mostly because he couldn't learn to communicate in twenty-first-century English.

I walked into the sanctuary and saw John as he adjusted the pulpit so it would be dead center on the stage.

"Hey, John, sorry, I was getting lunch with Father Neal." I didn't want John to know what was going on with the good priest.

He smiled. "Well, I hope you got nourishment for the body and soul."

"Uh, yes, I did. Thanks. Sherry said you wanted to talk to me?"

"Yes, I did. Let's sit down."

He motioned toward the pew, and I sat.

"Aidan, what do you think the Lord has in store for you in the future?"

I shrugged. "Not sure, to be truthful, John."

"Do you ever see yourself leading the Lord's flock in a head pastor role?"

"I have thought about it, but I'm not entirely sure that is what he has called me to do."

John nodded. "Well, the Lord moves in mysterious ways, I'm sure he will make his calling clear in amazing and beautiful ways."

"I'm sure." I couldn't figure out where this conversation would be leading.

He leaned back in the pew. "Do you feel any urgings from the Holy Spirit to pursue being the head shepherd here at Knox?"

I shook my head. "No, John. I think I made that pretty clear to you a month ago. I'm either called to be an assistant here or move on to another church. I appreciate your patience in this."

"Well, I feel like God has everything in hand. He is good"—he paused, as if waiting for me to say something—"all the time." As John completed his own phrase, he beamed.

I felt no urge to participate in this absurd evangelical liturgy. Of course God was good all the time, good grief. "Right, so why are you asking all of this?"

He looked around and then leaned forward. "Well, to be honest, many of us are interested in interviewing Cole. We wanted to talk to you about it first."

As much as John annoyed me, you had to leave it to him to do things in the good ol'-fashioned Presbyterian way, decently and in order.

I smiled. "I think you are making a wise choice. He is everything that Knox needs in a pastor: young, enthusiastic, and biblically sound, and has a lovely family."

John nodded, pleased with my response. "He is most certainly.

All the elders are struck by his godliness and his drive. His wife is lovely, a Proverbs 31 woman. So, you wouldn't be affronted by us pursuing him as God's candidate?"

I hid my smile. "No, in fact, I would encourage you to do so."

He concurred, pleased. "Aidan, you are one of the godliest men I have ever met. Your humility is truly a credit to a man of God."

I didn't know what to say. For John, this was pretty much akin to him slapping my back and telling me he loved me.

"Thanks, John. That means a lot."

He looked up at the pulpit and frowned. "The pulpit was out of place this morning. The youth must have been messing with it last night. I wish they had more respect for the things of God."

"It's just a wooden pulpit, after all. It's not like they spit on it."

He looked at me and then smiled. "You know, you are right. We mustn't be in love with things, only the one who makes such things possible, amen?"

"Amen."

"Well, I need to get back to my bride. She is waiting for me so we can make some spirits."

I decided not to wonder if he meant wine or a little lunchtime quickie.

I sat for a moment allowing the peace of the empty church to wash over me. Very rarely did I get to sit still and think. The way my life seemed to be going, I wouldn't be able to do that until I bent with age.

Brian. Jen. Voodoo. Father Neal. The Order of the Five Sorrows. The church. What would I do about all of them? Each had its own set of complications that I wasn't sure how to handle. I wanted to marry Jen. There was no doubt about that. I didn't give a damn about her previous marriage. The guy beat her and cheated on her. I would marry her with a full heart, but I knew I brought my own baggage to the party. Her long and strange work hours on that unnamed task force stretched my thin trust factor to a dangerous point. I hated myself for thinking that, but it was there.

I knew in my head she would never do anything to hurt me. The heart, however, constantly gave me pictures of her cheating on me with Lieutenant Weaver or anyone in her life who spent time with her. Not rational, but whoever said the heart was rational? She didn't deserve that distrust, and I needed to work through it before I could propose to her.

And the church, and therefore my career—all those questions had their own complications. My faith had been on the mend for the past six months, but I still couldn't figure out what the church should be to me or my role in it. I no longer felt comfortable in the evangelical Presbyterian circles, but I couldn't say why. My cynicism still remained about the culture surrounding the church, but I clung to its teachings. Still, I couldn't shake the feeling that the church I saw in the evangelical world seemed incomplete at best, laughably ridiculous at worst with its strange and bizarre subcultures. No matter how they clung to the idea of "scripture alone," they'd splintered it into so many divided voices. And none of them made sense.

A thought struck me. It's never just scripture alone, is it? There is always a framework people interpret the Bible through, whether it's Reformed Presbyterianism, Weslyanism, or good ol'-fashioned Americanism. Despite assurances I received, no one agreed on very much and the fact is, everyone became their own little Bible gods. I realized the Bible itself never asked for us to read the Bible on our own. It's always done in community, in church, not just the invisible church, but also a visible one.

I looked up to the cross and said out loud, "What do you want me to do? I love your church, but I'm not comfortable with it right now. What should I do? Where do you want me?"

The empty cross stared back at me with no answers. Not that I expected God to speak in an audible voice. It just felt good to get it all out to him. Somehow, I knew the answers would present themselves in one way or another.

Sighing, I stood up and walked back to my office. My phone buzzed, and I looked at it to see a text from Darrin.

"Preacha, meeting at Saint Patrick's tonight. Padre Neal said get all the info you can on Voodoo and bring it along. He also said to put something together on Brian's farm, if you can."

I sighed. At least I had something to do this afternoon other than sit in my office trolling Cardinal baseball news. I spent the whole afternoon in my office doing research on Voodoo and preparing a presentation for the team. Jen called me around five saying she'd taken Bishop for a walk but had to run back out for an investigation. I took the opportunity to have a nice quiet dinner by myself at North Star Café.

I made my way to Saint Patrick's around eight thirty and walked to Father Neal's office. I knocked lightly on the half-closed door and heard rustling inside.

"Come in, Aidan."

I went in and saw Father Neal writing at his desk on an old typewriter.

"Seriously? A typewriter? Why don't you let me pick out a good laptop for you?"

The keys kept clacking like a train as he typed away with surprising speed. "Because I would be lost with a computer, Aidan. I'm old and I'm going to be dead soon, so I'm not really concerned with catching up with new technology."

Father Neal flipped a switch into kick-ass priest and I doubted it would go away soon. I would've killed for his sense of command and air of authority.

I smiled and sat down. "Can't teach an almost-dead dog new tricks, eh?"

He looked up over the rim of his glasses. "Yes, that would be correct, my lad. Did you bring the presentation on Voodoo and Brian's farm?"

I nodded. "I feel more comfortable with the stuff on Brian's farm."

"Why?"

"Well, I don't exactly have my bachelor's in Voodoo arts. The Internet is a crazy mess on this subject. Plus, it seems to me that the real Voodoo is done away from prying eyes. All the stuff we know about is probably tourist-oriented to get people down to the French Quarter. Everything on Appalachian granny-magick is even worse."

Father Neal took off his glasses and leaned back. "Yes, I figured as much. I just wanted to see what you would find. I'll give the presentation on Voodoo, and you can fill in with what you found on the Internet."

"You really think there is a connection between Brian's farm and this Voodoo ritual?"

"Yes, isn't it obvious?"

I leaned back in the chair. "Yeah, the Grinning Man is the obvious connection, with the stone Brian found in his field and what you saw in the veve. But that begs the question: Why? Do you know if the Voodoo person who did this ritual was trying to call up the Grinning Man? If so, why? And why at Brian's farm?"

He held up his hand. "I think after tonight we might be closer to that answer. I'm a little tired, so I don't wish to repeat myself. I would rather give all the information at once."

A little disappointed, I said, "Jen isn't going to be joining us. Weaver called her into a special task force meeting tonight. Not sure what that's all about."

Father Neal looked at me and asked one of his uncomfortably close to the truth questions. "Does that bother you?"

I rubbed my forehead. "I wish it didn't. I just wish she could tell me."

"Secrets aren't a bad thing, you know. Sometimes, secrets are kept for a very good reason. I think in Jen's case, we can be sure that's the truth."

I nodded as we heard the door open. Zoe Othmeyer, an ex-drug addict in her forties with long, wispy gray hair, struggled inside with her computer projector. She'd founded our little Scooby group a few years ago after she joined Father Neal's parish. I grinned, thinking about the first time she had come to my office. She announced that my dead fiancée had visited her and had a message for me. Not sure why I didn't call the cops at that moment.

"Hey, let me help you."

"Oh, thanks, Aidan. You're such a sweetie."

We walked into Saint Patrick's boardroom. As we arranged the projector, she asked, "Do you know what this is all about?"

"Partially, and I'm thinking this is going to be the biggest investigation we have ever had, other than Amanda's murder. Some very weird stuff is going on."

She peered at me through her thick glasses. "There's always something weird going on."

I smiled. "Yeah, I guess so, but I'm guessing this might qualify for ultra-strangeness, even for you."

Everyone piled in to the conference room, Reg, Darrin and Kate holding hands, and finally Father Neal, hobbling into the room. I set up the projector with my computer and nodded to Father Neal as a picture of the old quarry came up on the large white screen behind him. The ghostly glow illumined his face, making him look like the Fisher King painting in his office. Or maybe like Merlin, the prophet of the Holy Grail. I wondered how the two stories related.

"Thank you to everyone for coming on short notice. I know you all have busy lives, but there are some pretty serious events that have happened in the past few days. Some of you know parts, but not all. So, I thought it would be good for all of us to get on the same page."

Everyone nodded as they waited for him to continue. "All of this began with a phone call from Jen on Sunday night."

He explained everything that had happened at the quarry in remarkable detail. Anyone who ever thought that Father Neal might be losing a few marbles would have had that illusion busted in the chops. He remembered small things that even I couldn't recall.

Darrin raised a hand. "Are you going to tell us what you saw in the vision?"

Father Neal paused. "I will, because I'm hoping you can help me make sense of the images." He motioned to me. "Could you grab the large sketchbook in my office along with the easel? I'm not as high-tech as you."

I nodded and walked to his office. As I bent down to look at the sketchbook, I saw a drawing peeking through the folded cover. I fought the urge to take a glance at the sketches and brought everything back to Father Neal as he continued, "The first page is actually the last image I saw. It is the most important. It is the Grinning Man."

Everyone looked around with uneasy expressions on their faces. I knew what they felt. I had no desire to see him either; this phantom haunted my own nightmares.

"Aidan, if you please . . ."

I took a deep breath, put the sketchbook on the easel, and flipped open the page. I stood back, a sickening feeling growing in my stomach as I stared at the face of evil.

Father Neal had drawn a figure with a wide, sinister grin on its face. The grin drew me in and made me ignore every other feature. The lips stretched wide as if the mouth wanted to eat the whole world and found the world's destruction a joke. Being a geek, I couldn't help but think of the Joker from Batman. Except that this face scared me more than any comic book character.

I looked away from the mouth and saw the dark, beady black eyes. Visions filled my head as I imagined I could almost see figures dancing in the coal-colored eyes.

"This"—Father Neal's voice broke the silence—"is the face I saw in my vision. He is the figure mentioned at Serpent Mound. He is dreadfully interested in us, most especially Aidan."

Everyone turned to me, and I didn't meet their eyes. I didn't want them to see my fear.

Reg broke the silence. "Is this the same Grinning Man associated with the Mothman sightings and Woodrow Derenberger?"

Father Neal nodded and Kate spoke up, "I'm sorry, who? I know about the Mothman stuff and the men in black, but not Derenberger."

"Woodrow was a lovely man who didn't understand any of the things happening to him," Zoe said. "The Grinning Man appeared to him at the side of the road down in Parkersburg, West Virginia, in 1966, around the same time as the Point Pleasant sightings of Mothman. The Grinning Man eventually drove Woodrow half insane and destroyed his life with mysterious appearances and horrid phone calls."

I looked up at her. "Phone calls?"

"Yes, why?"

I looked at Father Neal. "Brian has started to get strange phone calls. I'll talk more about it in a bit, go on."

"Woodrow never could understand why the Grinning Man chose him and why he told him his name: Indrid Cold," Zoe said.

I couldn't figure out why that name always made me tremble with fear every time I heard it.

Reg broke in. "So, with the Mothman sightings, it wasn't just the sighting of some winged creature?"

Father Neal shook his head. "No, Reg. If that was all that happened, it might be dismissed as a mass hallucination or some large bird. The sightings of the actual Mothman were only a small part of the problem in that area. Strange lights in the sky, voices, the men in black, and the horrible tragedy of the Silver Bridge collapse combined for a horrific year for the people along the Ohio River."

Reg sat back in his chair. "I didn't know all of that."

"So, ol' Indrid decided to show up in Ohio? Are he and the Grinning Man the same person?" Darrin leaned back, twiddling his ever-present unlit cigarette.

"I don't know the answer to that, Darrin. If he is not here now, he is about to be, as we will relate in a moment." Father Neal motioned to me. "Aidan, the next picture, please."

"Wait, I want to know something."

Father Neal said, "Go ahead."

"The Grinning Man, we know he has shown up in various forms in American history—Salem, the Bell Witch, Point Pleasant, maybe others—but what is he?" I said. "Where does he come from? You never really answered that question."

Father Neal stood, leaning on his cane. "As I told you before, Aidan, he is not a what. I'm pretty sure he is a *who*. He is one of the servents of the Nephilim. From what I can tell, they are magicians who, well, for lack of a better way to put it, walk between worlds. I have every reason to believe he is seeking to wake his fellow dark servants."

I noticed that Father Neal left out any mention of the Hellfire Club.

Reg leaned forward. "So, interdimensional beings of a type?"

Father Neal nodded. "Yes, this is why they act strange all of the time. For example, one of the men in black at Point Pleasant played with a pen as if he'd never seen it before. Their constant jumping back and forth has, well, scrambled their brains, not to put too fine a point on it. And, from what I can tell, the Grinning Man is one of those types. Aidan, next drawing, please."

I flipped the page, and the veve from the canyon wall stood out in vivid blue.

Father Neal pointed with his cane. "This is the veve, a Voodoo drawing filled with the power of the spirit world. It's an invitation for the spirits to enter our world and speak to us. Dangerous, as we all know. However, this particular one had been designed to give a message to someone through the spirits."

He paused. "Any questions?"

Darrin spoke up, "Yeah, what the heck is it doing in the middle of Ohio?"

"That is what we must find out. Aidan has an idea."

I stood up. "As all of you know, after Katrina, people from New Orleans scattered to the four winds. They are starting to form little communities wherever they are located. One of them, I think, has found a home here in Columbus. There is a new Creole food place that has opened up in Franklinton."

I told them about my experience with Celestine.

Zoe spoke up, "Just because Celestine is mysterious

doesn't mean she is practicing dark Voodoo or anything like that, does it?"

Father Neal shook his head. "No, it doesn't. However, the coincidence is too strong to ignore. She'll be one of the pieces of the puzzle we have to explore. The next image is more disturbing. It was one of the first images I saw after I touched the veve."

I flipped the page, and the whole room gasped. At first, I thought Father Neal had drawn a grotesque-looking spider, but it turned out to be a human being with limbs bent back into impossible angles. If this person had been real, they would walk like a Lovecraftian crab.

I pointed to the picture, toward the figure's neck. "Is that . . . Is that what I think it is?"

Father Neal nodded. "It's a steel collar like the ones used in the South to punish slaves. This figure, from what I can tell, is some horribly tortured man. From the position of the limbs, it looks as if someone broke the bones and reset them at horrible angles."

Kate looked as if she would be sick. "It's . . . He's not real, is he?"

Father Neal closed his eyes. "From what I can tell in the message, this really happened."

The whole room went silent. After a few moments, I whispered, "Dear God, why?"

"I don't know, Aidan. Maybe the next picture will help us."

I turned the page and said, "That's Celestine . . . or, no—"

I looked closely at the picture. Certainly, it looked like her, a beautiful young black woman with lovely red lips and her hair bound. But the eyes seemed different from Celestine's.

"No, it's not her. Someone very much like her, though."

Zoe said, "She's very beautiful. I wonder who she is. Anyone have an idea?"

Father Neal broke in. "No, but don't overlook the snake; that might be a key."

Sure enough, a large snake was wrapped around the woman's neck, and her hand rested on its head.

"Voodoo practitioners identify with snakes," I said. "They think snakes are images of Legba, the main spirit that can put you into contact with other spirits."

"So, the devil then," Darrin said.

Father Neal answered, "Well, maybe, maybe not. It's hard to say. Voodoo practitioners would certainly deny they worship the devil. But I really don't know. It's complicated. At best, they are messing with things they shouldn't mess with, at worst . . ." He let the sentence hang in the air as he motioned for the next drawing: a beautiful white woman with lips curved in a smile.

"This is the drawing that doesn't fit into anything Voodoo-wise or the Grinning Man legend."

"Could she be the one who sent the message? You did say Appalachian folk magick had been used in the ritual," Kate asked, chewing on her lip.

Father Neal considered the face for a moment. "It is possible, but I'm not entirely convinced. I'm not sure why the magick is mixed."

"You mean these pictures form one message?" Kate said, leaning forward. She had just finished her PhD in linguistics.

"Yes, Kate. It could be read this way. 'The black woman, whoever she is, sends this message: the white woman tortures slaves for the Grinning Man.' Or, it could be 'The white woman,' — whoever she is—'sends this message: the black woman tortures slaves for the Grinning Man.' "

Reg rubbed his head. "But there are no slaves in Ohio, are there?"

Father Neal leaned on the podium. "None that I know of, Reg. The slave in the previous picture seems to have been tortured at some point in the past. How far in the past, I can't say. I just know it happened."

"How could you tell?" Zoe leaned forward.

Father Neal closed his eyes. "I heard his screams as his limbs were broken."

Silence took over the room.

"Aidan, that is all I have. It is your turn to talk about Brian's farm."

I related the events of last night and showed them my burned face as proof.

Darrin whistled. "I thought you just had a really bad sunburn. Good grief, Preacha, you have a pair on you."

Kate hit Darrin as he protested. "What, he does! Running out in the middle of that field . . ."

I shrugged. "My friend was in pain. I had to do something."

Reg butted in. "Aidan's courage aside, what do we do about all of this?"

"We will do what we do best, we will investigate," Father Neal said. "Brian has cleared it so that we can come out to the farm on Friday night. Can everyone do that?"

Darrin leaned back. "Yeah, not excited about that field, but I'm there."

"Reg, how many cameras do we have?" Zoe asked.

"Four, but I have been meaning to buy two more."

I chimed in, "I'll buy two as well, and that way we'll have enough to cover the property."

Father Neal smiled. "Good. But I must warn you all, we are now encountering powers we have never dealt with before, even at Serpent Mound. Look at Aidan's face, and you will understand the danger. These spirits are not bound by any rules, and they are commanded by one who has lived longer than you can imagine."

He let his words sink in as he looked around. "Now, all of you go home, it's been a long night. It's time for sleep."

Father Neal raised his hands. "May Michael Militant guard you as God's own and enfold you with his wings in the strength of the Father, the Son, and the Holy Spirit."

# CHAPTER TEN

**I WAITED UNTIL EVERYONE LEFT, AND FATHER NEAL MOTIONED ME TO** his office. After he poured us whiskey, he sat down and asked, "So, what do you think?"

"I think everyone is nervous."

He pointed to my burned face. "They ought to be. I'll be honest; I don't think I have seen this level of magick in a long time."

We sat in silence for a moment. "What do you think we can expect?"

Father Neal shrugged. "I'm not sure. This Grinning Man doesn't seem to play by any sort of game plan we would recognize."

"Why didn't you bring up the Hellfire Club?"

"No one is to know about the Order. You must protect them, even Jen. They are not to know. None of them. It would put them at serious risk, do you understand?"

Nodding, I finished my drink and stood up. "Well, that's me gone. I better get home to Bishop. Will you be okay?"

Father Neal nodded. "Of course, lad. I'm glad you are with me on this. In truth, you are starting to become like the son I never had. I'm glad the Elder chose you, even as it saddens me."

I didn't know what to say. My throat began to tighten and I looked away. I realized that I loved this withered old man in front of me. But how could I tell him that?

"I . . . Father, you have become the only person I can trust, other than Jen."

He smiled. "I'll take that as a compliment. Although, one day, you'll have to start learning to trust more people." He paused. "Speaking of which, how are things with Knox?"

"They're fine. John told me they're going to interview Cole. Most of the church is pretty hot on him, from what I can tell."

Father Neal leaned back in his chair. "And how do you feel about that, lad?"

I leaned against the doorframe. "I don't know. I like Cole very much. The guy is the real deal, as far as I can tell. He has the drive, he is a good preacher, and he can most certainly lead. You would think he is the second coming of Tim Keller."

He nodded. "But what do *you* feel about him?"

I sighed. "I feel fine about him. As I said, he will make a good Presbyterian minister. The only thing that worries me is his whole 'choose who you lose' attitude."

Father Neal frowned. "What do you mean?"

"Cole has this whole plan to change Knox into a 'lean, mean, missional machine.' He wants to do away with the organ, get rid of Wednesday nights, and go to all small group meetings during the week. I told him that the older church people wouldn't like it. He just shrugged."

"So Cole's response to Knox's deadness is to beat the corpse?" Father Neal asked.

I laughed. "That's about the size of it."

He pointed his cane at me. "But could you work for him? Could you support everything he is doing?"

His questions rocked me a little. I felt stupid for not seeing the implications. "I'll be honest, I hadn't really thought about it."

Father Neal nodded. "I think God is drawing you to a decision point."

"Yeah, I know. I still don't know what to do about my future. I'm really torn between two ways of thinking that I don't like."

"Then maybe it's time to consider a third way."

"What do you mean?"

"Become an Anglican priest. We can marry, you know. Study under me and become a novice of the Order. I'll work on getting money for a position here at the church. It'll take an intense year to get you ready, but I think you can handle it. Normally, I wouldn't encourage someone to leave their denomination, but these aren't normal circumstances. I've much to teach you and very little time to do it. Besides, you've reached a crisis point."

I shrugged. "I wouldn't call it a crisis point, more of a 'fed up with the shit' point."

We both laughed. Father Neal said, "Indeed. But I want you to consider my offer. It's an option, anyway. Do some study on your own. Figure out what you want and I'll help you, lad." He looked up at the painting. "I must train you to be a member of the Order because my time is growing short."

I didn't know what to say to this last statement. My throat tightened again at the thought of this man leaving my life just as he came into it.

"I will think it over, and talk to Jen."

He smiled. "And she is in your future, too, you know."

"Did you stare into the future, O Conjurer?"

"I have seldom seen two people so in love with each other. Enjoy it. It is a rare thing. Now, off with you. This old body needs rest."

"Thanks, Father. You've given me a lot to think about."

I walked out to my car and drove home. As I walked up to my condo door, my phone rang. I looked at the screen and saw the name *Indrid Cold*.

Indrid Cole. The name the Grinning Man used at Point Pleasant when he would call random people.

I stared at the phone as it rang with the tones of the doxology, a melody I didn't remember putting on my cell. The doxology smacked of old-school Presbyterianism. Everyone played it after the offering and before the sermon during a worship service. Normally, I avoided cliché pastor ring tones and went for the voice talents of Eric Cartman from *South Park*.

The Grinning Man was using the old-school church hymn to mock me and get my attention. He had it, and I tried to turn off the ringer. It didn't work. Finally, I couldn't take it.

My skin crawled as I answered, "Hello?"

A warbled electronic voice spoke in a language I couldn't make out.

"Who is this? Indrid? Are you there?"

Slow, manic laughter answered me.

"Indrid, sorry, my minutes don't include calls from the other-world."

I hung up the phone and went inside. Chills ran and up down my spine. How in the hell could the Grinning Man change my phone like that? The thought unnerved me as I took Bishop out for a walk.

As he did his business, the phone rang again.

My hands trembled and I steeled myself with my usual sarcasm.

"You're worse than a bill collector, and you're getting on my nerves."

The garbled electronic voice spoke in English. *Oh, I'm about to get on more than your nerves, tehehehe, tehehehe.*

I gripped the phone. "And what does that mean?"

The voice laughed. *My bride has come and will show you my ways. My interest is in collecting women. I love women. They serve me and those who love me.*

"I don't really care." My hand trembled.

Garbled laughter. *Oh, you will. You will have much interest, very soon. I shall see you on the farm.*

With that, Indrid hung up. My hair stood on end, and I ran back to my condo. The phone calls went on for an hour, and finally I turned off my phone. I couldn't figure out how to block them, as Indrid didn't exactly have an ordinary number.

My email notification dinged and I opened an email from Jen that read, "Where are you? Been trying to call you for the last half hour. Worried."

I picked up the phone, turned it on and saw that Indrid had called a hundred times. I dialed Jen.

She answered, "Where have you been? Are you okay?"

"I'm okay, I promise."

I told her about Indrid's phone calls. She listened and then said, "Aidan, those phone calls are happening all over the city. Plus, it seems someone cranked up the Weird Shit O'Meter for Columbus tonight. Weird things are happening all over the place."

I sat back on my couch. "What do you mean?"

"The 911 center nearly crashed a few hours ago. Phone calls are coming in from all over the city reporting strange things in the sky, in their yard, and in their house."

"Like what?"

"Like UFOs, for one thing. They sound like the ones we saw on the farm. About a hundred people at a midnight basketball tournament called about five lights chasing each other in the sky. The tower at the airport picked them up on radar and had to shut down the airport for half an hour. I think they even scrambled jets from Wright-Patterson Air Force Base."

"What else?"

"Strange bigfootlike creatures seem to be peeking into windows, and lions are roaming around Dublin."

"I'm sorry, did you say lions? In Dublin, Ohio?"

"Yeah, lions as in plural. This isn't the first time, you know. Lions have been reported in Columbus and its suburbs a few times."

"What? Seriously?"

"Yes, back in 2004. At first, the force thought it was just a pet lion that had escaped from an illegal zoo. But despite numerous credible witnesses, no one could find any evidence. Now it's started back up again."

"Are you still at work?"

"Yeah, some really ugly things have happened that are in the task force jurisdiction."

"Like what?"

"You know I can't tell you that."

I rubbed my head. "I know. I'm sorry. Nosy Pastor Reflex."

She sighed. "Aidan, I love you. I know it's hard on you not to know everything."

I shook my head. "No, it's fine, love. I need to trust you more. You aren't Amanda."

I could almost hear her smile over the phone. "No, I'm not, baby. Trust me when I say this task force is one of the most important things going on right now. Soon, I promise, I'll be able to tell you about it."

"I'm sure you will."

"Aidan, what is going on in this town? It's like someone hit the WEIRD SHIT button. I didn't think Columbus had that sort of thing. I mean, we aren't Roswell."

"Neither did I, Jen, but maybe we will have some answers soon. The team met tonight, and we are going to investigate the farm on Friday night. I'm thinking that's ground zero."

She sighed. "Okay. Just be careful, okay? No more running into fields?"

"It's not like I tried to get burned by mysterious balls of light," I joked.

"I'm serious."

"Sorry. Hey, I talked to Father Neal and he offered to give me a job at Saint Patrick's. What do you think?" I said.

"I love it."

"Really? Why?"

She paused. "Truth be told, I feel much more comfortable at Saint Patrick's. Maybe because I still have a Catholic heart, or maybe it just feels more like home. I can't tell. Knox just doesn't feel right to me. I'm there because you are, that's about it. The people are nice, but I can't ever get settled."

I sighed. "Yeah, I know. I'm just not sure if I'm ready to make that leap yet, but I think I need to make the decision soon. I want us to make this decision together."

"Really? Do you see me in your future, Aidan?"

I paused, swallowed hard and said, "Yeah, I do."

She didn't say anything for a moment, and I thought maybe I overplayed my hand.

"Jen, are you there? Are you okay?"

"Yes, I'm more than okay." She sounded as if she would cry at any moment.

"I didn't mean . . . I hope I didn't upset you."

"No, no. You didn't upset me. Just the opposite."

I wasn't sure what to make of that. "We can talk about it more later. I'm tired and I'm sure you are as well. Hopefully, Indrid Cold has gotten tired of the frat prank calls for the night."

Silence on the other end of the line.

"Are you okay?"

"I don't think Indrid Cold is a laughing matter."

"I wasn't trying to—"

She cut me off. "I don't want to hear it. I want you to be careful, do you understand?"

"Yes, dear."

"Don't 'yes, dear' me. I agree with Father Neal. This thing or person, or whatever it is, seems dreadfully interested in you. More than I'm comfortable with, that's for sure."

"Okay, I'll be careful. Happy?"

"No. I'll be happy when we can figure all this crap out. It seems like it started with the Voodoo ritual. Whoever performed it set all this stuff in motion; it's like they lit a match to kindling that was already here, you know?"

"What do you mean?"

She paused. "I dunno. It's as if Columbus had some kind of unseen paranormal jack-in-the-box. It seems as if the ritual wound the crank."

"Father Neal thinks that's possible. We just aren't sure of the intent."

"Well, I'll see what I can dig up on everything that's happening around the station. Now, bedtime."

"I love you, Jen."

"And I love you, Aidan. Good night."

# CHAPTER ELEVEN

I WOKE UP ON THURSDAY MORNING WITH A GROWING SENSE OF DREAD and the urge to pee. The latter I took care of with a trip to the bathroom, but the other wouldn't go away with the flush of a toilet.

As I made my way downstairs to fix coffee, I began to think about our investigation at the farm. It would be a long and tiring night of research, not to mention the possible emotional explosion I might get from Brian and Ashley. The last thing I wanted to do was sit in the church office all day. I checked my phone for my daily schedule and realized I didn't have any appointments. I dialed the church and found my way to Sherry's voicemail.

"Sherry, this is Pastor Aidan. I'm going to do some work at the coffee shop this morning, so I won't be coming to the church. Please hold off telling anyone where I am, as I'll be busy with sermon writing. If it's an emergency, take a message, call me, and I'll deal with it. Thanks very much. Oh, and feel free to close the office around two. Take the afternoon off; take your grandkids to the pool or something. Tell Cole unless he has appointments today, he can go home at noon."

I hung up the phone, satisfied I had taken care of my staff.

Given that most of our congregation were on summer vacation or headed to the lake for the weekend, I figured no one would really need us today.

I put on a pot of coffee and took Bishop out for a walk in the warm, soupy atmosphere that gripped Columbus. As he sniffed around, I tried to gather my scattered thoughts. I could feel the pressure building in the atmosphere and I wondered if severe thunderstorms would strike later this afternoon. It didn't bode well for tonight.

Come to think of it, nothing boded well for tonight. The whole world seemed about to erupt into something violent, scary, and terrible. I wasn't sure what scared me more: the Grinning Man, or Ashley and Brian. My friends had given the perception of my idealized version of a relationship for a long time. Brian had it wrong, at least partially. They really had loved each other. You couldn't fake what they had had between them.

Now their marriage lay in pieces. Everything on the farm tonight promised to be a perfect storm of ugliness.

Being lazy sounded better than doing actual work. I decided to take Bishop back to the condo, pour myself some coffee, and sit on the couch to watch the last three episodes of *MythBusters*. Just as I started episode two, the phone rang. Without looking, I answered.

"Hello?"

"So, playing hooky, are we?" Jen's voice greeted me.

I smiled. "Hey, love. Not exactly. I'm planning to go to the coffee house to work."

Jen laughed. "And when would that be? When *MythBusters* is over?"

"You caught me. I have to confess, I'm not in a hurry to get this day started."

"Because of tonight?"

"Yeah. I mean not just the whole ghost stuff, but Ashley and Brian. It has me wondering, can anyone really be happy?"

She sighed. "I know, I have been wondering the same thing. I mean, I'm happy with you, but then, I thought I was happy with Chris."

"I know. He nearly killed you. And Amanda had an affair with a married man and was killed by magickal wackos. We make quite a pair, you and I. Neither of us has *stable* stamped on our forehead."

Jen laughed. "I guess so. But I'll take the risk. You are worth it. None of us know the future."

I swallowed hard. "So, you see a future with us?"

"Yes, isn't that obvious?"

"I just didn't want to . . ."

She laughed. "Assume? I think you can assume it, boy."

I changed the subject. "Are you going to be there tonight?"

"I am, actually. I just got off a long night, and Weaver gave me the next two nights off. We made a ton of progress last night. We are so close to nailing these— Sorry."

"It's okay. I figured you were working on nailing someone's ass to the wall. Someone who probably deserves it."

Jen lowered her voice. "You have no idea. We are chasing the scum of the earth right now. There are some days I want to get into the shower and never get out."

"One day, you can unload everything on me."

She sighed. "I wish I could do that now. So, do you want to meet at your place and we will have dinner together?"

"That would be great. See you at five."

"Love you."

"Love you. Get some rest."

I hung up the phone. Jen wanted a future with me. She really did. As I sat on the couch to digest that fact, I wondered what I should do next. I hated waiting around for stuff to happen. I needed to do something. No, not do something, talk to someone about Jen. I picked up my phone, dialed her father, and waited for the phone to ring.

"Hello?"

"Mr. Brown, this is Aidan Schaeffer."

"Aidan! How are you? How are those Cardinals doing? Wanna go to the game when they come into Cincy?"

"That would be great."

"So what can I do for you?"

I had made this call without much of a plan, so I didn't know where to go from here.

"Well, I, um, I wondered if you were busy for lunch today?"

"Let me check."

As he did, I wondered if I'd lost my mind. Why did I want to pile one more stressful thing on top of this day?

"As a matter of fact, I am free for lunch. Come to think of it, I have the whole afternoon free. Want to grab lunch at the club and a round of golf with me?"

I hated golf, at least golf where I couldn't swear every time I sliced the ball into the rough. I liked Mr. Brown a lot, but I didn't want to show him the darker side of my personality. At least, not today, but I realized I didn't have much of a choice.

"Yeah, that sounds great. I'll finish up some work this morning and meet you at the club around noon?"

"That sounds great. Thanks for getting me out of a boring afternoon. We can talk about investing, so I can say I worked for the afternoon."

"Now that sounds fair. See you in a bit." I hung up the phone and stared at it, amazed at my own audacity.

I finished watching *MythBusters*, took a shower, and walked Bishop one more time. I put him in his crate, then drove to the club. After giving my keys to the valet, I waited in the lavish lobby of the country club and took deep, slow breaths to prevent a panic attack.

Mr. Brown arrived right at twelve. He looked like the perfect, stylish businessman with a close-shaved head, a gray goatee, and a scarlet golf shirt.

"Aidan, thanks so much for calling me. I needed to get out of the office."

I smiled and shook his hand. "Rough day?"

He waved his hand. "Oh, this whole Libya mess has the stock market in a shambles. And as you might expect, investors are as nervous as Jim Tressel in a high-scoring football game. I have spent my whole morning trying to get people not to panic."

I laughed. "Now that is nervous. I thought I had it bad with church people."

"Let's eat. I'm starving and I need to talk baseball. My girls won't let me talk any sports, so it's nice to have a male in my immediate life."

Jen's younger sisters still lived at home with Mr. Brown and his wife. I wondered if the poor guy ever had a chance to use the bathroom.

We ate a great lunch of steak and salad while we chatted about baseball. Mr. Brown had loved the Reds since he was a kid. He knew every batting average for every Red that ever played.

We started our round of golf, and I couldn't believe how well I played. As we reached the ninth hole, he said, "So, Aidan, did you call me to just get out of the office yourself, or did you have another reason?"

I leaned on my golf club. "When I woke up this morning, I had no plans to call you at all. I had planned just to work from home. Maybe it's better this way."

If he knew what I would ask, he didn't show it as he put his tee in the ground.

"Go on, son."

"Mr. Brown, Jen and I have been dating for several months. We both have things we have had to work through, and we have. We talk a lot about our previous relationships, our trust issues. There is really no subject off-limits."

Mr. Brown stared toward the green. "I'm listening."

"We want a future together, I think. We are working on that. I'm just trying to understand Jen better, and I'm hoping you can help."

He didn't answer as he put the ball on the tee. With a mighty swing, he drove the ball about 275 yards straight down the fairway. He watched the ball bounce and come to a stop, then turned to me. I couldn't read the expression on his face, but I didn't back down as he asked, "How can I help?"

"Is there anything you can tell me about her that I don't know? The situation with her ex-husband? And do you think I'm good for her? I know you don't know me very well, but I'm hoping you can give me some answers."

He chuckled. "Aidan, first, knowing your children is a difficult thing, especially with Jen. My other daughters tend to stay around the house. Jen was never like that. She is independent, strong-willed, and has always done her own thing. Just like her father."

We got in the cart and started to drive. Mr. Brown looked thoughtful as he said, "But being strong-willed, she married someone I told her not to marry."

"Oh?"

He nodded. "I could tell Chris was bad news the moment she brought him home."

"How?"

"He was too nice, if you want to know the truth. In my experience, people who are too nice tend to put a knife in your back."

"I can relate."

"I told this to Jen, and she laughed at me. Then when things went down, it traumatized her. There were times when she would call me up and cry on the phone for an hour."

He looked at me as we got out of the cart. "Did she tell you this?"

"No, she didn't. I know what happened with him, of course. Nothing more disgusting than trying to have sex with underage girls."

Mr. Brown grimaced. "Yeah, I know. I'm a very forgiving man, Aidan, but I hope that peckerwood gets what he deserves in prison."

"You and me both."

We got back in the cart and he said, "I don't know if you knew this or not, but when Jen first brought you home, it was a big test."

I smiled. "I didn't know that exactly, but I had a feeling."

Mr. Brown laughed. "When you started giving me shit about Reds the first time you shook my hand, I knew you weren't like Chris. Jen called me up after you both had left, and I gave her my hundred-percent approval."

We got to the green, and he leaned on his golf club. "I love my daughter, Aidan. I want her happy. I have never seen her as happy as she is with you. And I care for you more than I ever did Chris. The only thing is that I wish you were Catholic, but I'm not worried about that. I just want to know what your future plans are at this point. Will you keep being a minister?"

I prepared my putt and sunk it with one swing before I answered. "I'll keep being a minister. I can't just lay aside that call. But I'm going to change addresses. I'm going to become an Anglican priest."

The words came out before I realized what I said. I examined the truth of the statement and found I meant every word. This seemed to be a day for deciding things.

I turned to him and said, "So, yeah, it's not Rome, but it's Canterbury, which is a lot closer to you than Scottish Presbyterianism."

He looked at me for a moment and laughed. "That's what I love about you, Aidan. Straightforward and honest. Have you always been this way?"

I shook my head. "To be honest, no. This is a recent development."

"Indeed. Could never tell," he said, then paused. "So, do you promise to take care of my daughter to the best of your ability?"

"Yes, sir."

"Do you promise not to harm her in any way?"

"I would rather die, sir."

He nodded. "Then you have my blessing, as if you needed it anyway. This is a bit old-fashioned, you know."

"I tend to be an old-fashioned guy, Mr. Brown."

"So do I, truth be told. But there is one thing that I must insist on."

I swallowed hard, wondering how far my resolution would stretch.

"You have to call me Jerry for now, and then Dad when you two decide to get married."

I smiled as we climbed into the cart. "Gladly, Jerry."

He took out two cigars. "These aren't really permitted on the course, but everyone smokes them. This is another test. Chris hated smoking."

I took the cigar, smelled its brandy-dipped flavor, and cut off the tip. Jerry gave me his silver Zippo lighter, and I lit my cigar. We puffed our sacrament as we sat in silence gazing out on the course. He smiled. "Word of advice, though."

"Give it to me."

"Get your own bathroom."

We finished our round of golf, and I sped home. I wanted to beat Jen so I could take a shower. She didn't like it when I smoked, even if it was with her dad. I saw her black Mustang in my parking space, and I knew I would have to think up a story.

When I walked inside, she greeted me at the door with a kiss. Her nose wrinkled as she gave me a pouty frown. "Have you been smoking today? Are you that nervous?"

I smiled. "No, I didn't break our rules, if that's what you meant."

She raised an eyebrow. "You were with my dad today?"

"Yep. I called to ask him a question, and he wanted to see I if I would help him play hooky from work. We ate lunch at the club and played a round of golf."

I tried to avoid her questioning glance. One of the perils of dating a police detective is that it's hard to lie to them.

"You played a round of golf with my dad?"

"Yep. He had some cigars. I didn't think it would be wise to refuse. Sorry, I know how you feel about them."

I hoped the discussion about cigars would sidetrack her questions.

She sighed. "I'm sure Mom doesn't know about those. I should probably tell her."

"Why would you do that? Let a man have his smoke."

Jen raised her eyebrows and frowned. "Is that so?"

I looked her in the eyes. "Yes, that is so. A man needs his space sometimes."

She crossed her arms and tossed back her hair. "Is that what you are saying, you need some space?"

I grabbed her and pulled her to me. "Not at all. But sometimes it's good to just be a guy, you know?"

The sides of her mouth twitched. "I would kiss you if you didn't stink so bad. Go take a shower or the odor of tobacco will scare away the ghosts."

I grinned. "Want to join me?"

She spanked my butt. "Go and stop tempting me. I ordered a pizza, so it should be here by the time you are done."

I grinned to myself as I walked up the stairs. Even detectives could be misled, it seemed. I took my shower and put on shorts. I figured if I would have a night of confronting pure evil, I would at least be comfortable.

After we ate pizza, we walked Bishop. Jen touched my hand. "You aren't going to tell me the real reason you played golf with my dad this afternoon?"

Crap. I should have known better. "Listen, Detective, can't two guys hang out just because?"

"Not when it's the two most important men in my life, who have had limited contact up until now. A girl gets suspicious when such things happen."

I laughed. "Especially when said girl is the star detective in Lieutenant Scott Weaver's detective service."

She hit me on the arm. "I'm serious, Aidan."

I rubbed my arm. "So am I. Seriously, I got a ticket to the Cardinals/Reds game. I thought it would be good to get to know him better."

"Is that so? And why is that?"

I smiled. "So I could get to know all of the bad stories about you."

"Aidan Schaeffer, you are so frustrating."

I kissed her on the cheek. "And yet you still love me."

She sniffed. "Don't play that card too much, mister."

"It's the only one I've got, so I have to use it often."

We walked back to the condo holding hands.

# CHAPTER TWELVE

**I COULDN'T REMEMBER A TIME I HAD PULLED UP THE GRAVEL DRIVEWAY** leading to the farm with such a feeling of impending doom. This place had been such a source of comfort and warmth that had radiated from Olan and Edna. Now it pulsed with a sinister menace, from Brian and Ashley's imploding marriage and whatever occupied that field. The black and green clouds swirling above me suggested an impending tornado, but when I looked up the weather report, I saw no storms.

Guess we are in for it tonight, I thought.

I pulled up next to the house and took a deep breath.

Jen put her warm hand on my arm. "Are you okay?"

I put the car in park and didn't answer for a moment.

"Aidan?"

"I don't want to do this," I said.

She nodded. "I'm not exactly thrilled about it, either."

I gripped her hand. "I have no idea what to expect tonight. Nothing could happen, but somehow, I doubt that."

"Yeah, the air is too thick for that to be true."

I chuckled. "You can say that again. It's as if an epic thunderstorm is about to break. I thought we would get nailed with storms this afternoon. But, so far, nothing."

Jen glanced up at the rolling, turbulent gray sky. "Yeah, I thought so, too." She looked at her phone. "Oddly enough, there is nothing on the radar."

We sat for a moment staring at the farmhouse and then I said, "All right, let's get out there."

We got out of the car as Peyton greeted us with his head down and a slight wag of his tail.

"Even Peyton feels it," I said. I bent down to pet him, and he gave my hand a few halfhearted licks. "I'm betting we won't see him at all when this gets started."

Jen nodded and bent down. "Peyton, find a nice dark hole. I wish I could join you."

No one else had arrived, so we knocked on the farmhouse door. We didn't hear any movement in the house, so I knocked again. The door swung open, and Ashley greeted us. She no longer looked like the pale, withdrawn waif of a few nights ago. A white summer dress clung to her elfin body and her curly red hair hung to her shoulders.

"Ash, you look beautiful this evening."

Jen gave me a sideways glance.

Ashley giggled. "Thank you, Aidan. Come in!"

Jen frowned at her as she turned to go in the house.

I leaned in to her. "What?"

She shook her head. "Later."

We walked into a house that had been scrubbed clean. A scent of cinnamon hung in the air, and everything had been put exactly into place. A smell of something baking wafted in from the kitchen. The atmosphere of the house had a thin layer of southern hospitality painted over its dark secrets, as if we stepped into a Flannery O'Connor novel.

Ashley beamed at us. "Please sit. Would you two lovebirds like some iced tea? Lemonade? You will have to wait on the cookies baking, I'm afraid."

Jen and I looked at each other. She had put on her detective face that gave away nothing. The message to me seemed pretty clear. *Say nothing.*

"Uh, sure, Ashley, we'll have some tea, thanks."

We heard tiny footsteps run into the living room as mass of red hair and giggles jumped into my lap.

"Uncle Aidan! I missed you!"

I hugged Lily tight. "Hey, Lil' Red, how are you?"

She giggled. "I'm fine. Do you like my new dress?" Lily danced around the floor, displaying her butterfly-printed dress for us to see.

Jen smiled. "Lily, that dress is so beautiful. Did you just get it?"

She ducked her head and blushed. "Yes."

"It's so pretty. Do you love butterflies?"

Lily smiled and danced a little more. "Yes."

Jen leaned in. "I wish I had a dress just like it!"

"Thank you. Morgan thinks it's pretty, too."

Jen smiled. "Is Morgan your dolly's name?"

Lily shook her head. "No, she is my friend. She talks to me at night. She said she speaks Celtic, but I can understand her because I'm special. She says so."

Ashley walked in with a tray of iced teas and laughed. "Oh, my dear flower, you and your imaginary friend."

Lily gave her a beautiful pout. "She isn't 'maginary. She's beautiful."

I smiled. "I'm sure she is, Lily, but not as beautiful as you."

Lily giggled as she twirled out of the room. Ashley put her hands on her hips. "Oh that child of mine, such an imagination!"

With a sigh, she sat down in a blue wingback chair and crossed her legs. "Well, tonight should be exciting, shouldn't it? We really want to know about those lights and whether we have a little ghostly presence around here! How interesting. My grandparent's plantation has a lot of ghosts, you know."

Ashley spoke in full Scarlett O'Hara mode, every word dripping with Southern honey. Jen stared at her in mild disbelief, and

I remembered she'd never been down South. She'd never experienced Southerners trying to put sugar on a rotting corpse through sweet talk and rambling on about nothing in particular. I almost smiled in spite of the circumstance as I said, "Yeah, should be interesting, to say the least."

Ashley wagged her foot like a sorority girl. "Goodness, I felt so terrified the other night with you and Brian. I think we will all sleep much better once you have this figured out. However"—she leaned forward, then whispered—"I'm a bit uncomfortable with this Catholic priest being here, Aidan. What would my daddy say? Can't you just handle all of this by yourself?"

I shook my head. "Father Neal isn't Catholic, Ashley. He's Anglican. He was actually married for fifty years."

She leaned back. "Oh, that's good. I'm so relieved. I couldn't handle the whole Catholic thing in my house. Such strange people."

Jen's body went tense, and I could almost feel the anger radiating off her body. I grasped her hand, and she recovered her detective calm. Ashley, however, wouldn't shut up.

"Not that Catholics aren't lovely people, bless their hearts. They just don't understand Jesus at all. And that praying to Mary and the saints business! And goodness, they treat the pope as if he is Jesus himself! Those robes, incense, and eating Jesus! So strange." Ashley shook her head and laughed. "Ah well, Jesus loves them, too, I suppose; but I don't understand them."

Jen got up. "Ashley, where is your bathroom?"

Ashley pointed to the hall. "Last door on your left. Use the spray if you need to!"

Jen walked out of the room and Ashley whispered, "Is she okay? She seems a little tense tonight."

"She has a rough job, Ashley, and tonight isn't exactly going to be a normal ghost hunt."

She leaned forward, touching her fingertips together. "Hmm . . . Hmmm. Yes, probably not. But you two are probably worried for nothing. I'm sure it's nothing. Jesus has it all in hand, doesn't he?"

I wanted to stand up and shake her. I wanted to grill her with twenty questions about her and Brian. I wanted to ask her why she had gone from the hateful ghost I saw the other night to the fresh Southern angel before me. There is no question which one creeped me out more.

I nodded. "He does indeed. Of that, I'm very sure."

Jen walked back into the room. "Thanks, Ashley. Had a little too much water today."

"Oh, no worries, Jennifer. I remember when I was pregnant with Lily and we were on a road trip with Brian. I had to have him pull over every forty miles! That little girl could kick the bladder!"

The little kicker walked into the room and said, "Mommy, Morgan and I want cookies. Are they ready?"

"Almost, sugar love. Let's check on them."

She got up and led Lily into the kitchen. Jen leaned over to me. "What the hell is going on?"

"I'll explain later."

Jen stared toward the kitchen. "Such a passive-aggressive bitch."

"What are you talking about?"

"She doesn't like me, and she has been expressing that from the moment we got here."

I shook my head. "You are imagining things, Jen. It's just the way Southern people deal with stress."

She shook her head. "You have a lot to learn."

"I never denied that, dear."

Jen smiled and kissed me on the cheek. "Just stay close to me tonight, got it, boy?"

I put on a fake Southern accent. "Yes, ma'am, as long as you do likewise."

Ashley walked back in with a plate of cookies and I asked, "Hey, where is Brian?"

"Oh, I sent him to the store for some ice. He'll be back in a bit."

Lily came in munching a cookie and carrying one in her hand. "I'm taking one to Morgan, Mommy."

"That's very nice, darling."

Brian came in the door to spare us the Southern onslaught.

"Hey, Aidan, Jen. Glad you are here! I think the team just pulled up behind me. Aidan, can you help me with the ice?"

I looked at Jen and then went out with Brian. Zoe's van had begun to make the journey down the long gravel driveway.

"Ashley is in rare form tonight."

He nodded. "She started acting like that the morning after the attack. I think she is in serious denial about everything. At least the hostility is gone for a while. I honestly thought about getting a motel for a few days."

"Don't blame you. Are you feeling okay?"

He paused as he handed me a bag of ice. "I guess I'm surviving. I'm trying to be strong for Lily. She needs one parent who isn't about to lose it."

I put my hand on his shoulder. "We are going to do what we can."

He smiled. "I know, thanks. You have no idea how much it means."

The van pulled in with Reg's SUV not too far behind. Zoe waved at us from the driver's seat, and Kate got out. "Aidan, where should we park?"

"Right beside me."

Kate walked up to us. "I really didn't want to ride with her. She is scarier than ghosts."

I laughed. "And why is that?"

She rolled her eyes. "She can't talk and drive at the same time. She has to look at you when she talks. It's terrifying. I think we almost died twice on our way here."

Brian and I laughed. Father Neal climbed out of Reg's SUV and limped toward us.

"Brian, my lad, how are you? How are things?"

"Father, great to see you. I'm doing okay, as best as I can anyway."

Father Neal put his hand on Brian's shoulder. "Rest easy. We will get this all figured out, I promise."

Brian nodded as he looked out into the field. "I'm counting on it, Father, I really am."

# CHAPTER THIRTEEN

WE WORKED HARD TO UNLOAD THE VAN. ALL OF OUR EQUIPMENT LAY out on Brian's front porch, which would become our command center. Darrin, Reg, and I set up the table as Brian took everyone else for a tour of the farm.

"So, Preacha, ready for this evening?"

"As ready as I'm going to be. To quote everyone on *Star Wars*, 'I have a bad feeling about this.' "

Reg grunted. "Don't know if we can ever be ready for something like this."

I plugged in a few wires to the back of the monitors. "Are you two nervous?"

"Nervous doesn't cover it. Downright scared out the ass." Darrin pulled out a quarter. "For the swear jar."

I chuckled. "I think we are going to be filling that tonight. Besides, I don't think 'ass' counts."

Reg fiddled with the wires under the table. "Why not?"

"Well, 'ass' is not really a curse word. Same thing with 'shit.' I have been tempted to switch to *skubulos* in front of church people."

Darrin started switching on the computer and video screen. " '*Skubulos*'?"

I laughed. "It's Saint Paul's word for 'shit.' That is the literal translation. That is, 'my righteousness is shit in comparison to the righteousness of Christ.' "

Darrin laughed. "Saint Paul had a bad mouth? Now I don't feel so bad."

"And then there is the time he encouraged false teachers to cut off their junk," I said with a grin.

Darrin and Reg laughed. "What?"

"It's true. Some people were misleading the Galatian church, teaching them they had to be circumcised to be true Christians. Paul said they might as well cut off the whole damn thing if they are so in love with cutting their penises for the hell of it." I smiled.

Reg shook his head. "I'm learning more and more about the Bible every day. Moaning whores, Paul's swear words, and now the chopping off of a man's twig and berries."

Darrin practically fell on the ground. "Twig and berries, Reg?"

Reg smiled. "It's what we called it growing up in Ohio, usually with a few whispers and glances toward the house to see if Mom was around."

After the tour, Father Neal, Kate, Jen, and Zoe walked up to us. I jumped down to meet them. "So, did you find good places to put the cameras?"

Jen nodded. "Yep. I'm going to take Darrin, and Kate is going to take you."

I frowned. "Why can't you take me?"

Father Neal said, "Because you need to concentrate and so does Darrin."

"What about the girls? Why aren't you worried about their concentration?" Darrin asked as he joined us.

"Women are better at multitasking. All you would do is think about kissing your lovely ladies. I need your minds in the game."

Darrin and I shrugged as we went for the cameras. Jen grabbed me and whispered in my ear, "I think Father Neal overrates my concentration ability with you around."

I smiled. "On the other hand, his assessment of my ability would be right. You distract me."

Jen pinched my butt and then walked down the stairs.

I went with Kate to the field. As we walked, she kept glancing at the sky as the clouds rolled and swirled.

"The sky is pretty scary-looking, isn't it?"

"Yeah, but I wasn't looking at that."

I stopped. "What were you looking for?"

"Owls."

I looked at her. "What?"

She smiled and said, "I have a thing about birds, especially right now."

"Can I ask why?"

She kept walking as she touched the scars on her face. It made me think of Jen, who had a thin scar marking the corner of her mouth, courtesy of her ex-husband.

"Let's just say that animal manifestations make me nervous."

"Animal manifestations?"

Kate waved out to the field as we approached the fence post. "Brian talked about the kangaroo, right?"

I nodded. "Bizarre, right?"

She shook her head. "No. Animal manifestations are very common with land hauntings, for lack of a better term. Most of them are evil, but not always."

Kate touched her scars again. I figured this would be a great time to ask how she got those scars, but then I thought better of it. She could tell that story when she was ready, not because I asked.

"Where should we put the cameras?" I unrolled the cable I had been carrying.

Kate pointed to a post at the center of the fence. "Right there. Zoe thought that would give the best overall view of the field."

I set up the camera on top of the fence post. As I tied it down with wire, Zoe called over the walkie-talkie.

"Hello. Aidan, can you adjust the camera a few degrees to the right?"

I moved the camera for her.

"That's perfect, darling. We can see most of the field right now. Come on back!"

Kate and I walked back to the porch in silence. She kept looking to the sky, and I pretended to ignore her. Jen knew her story, but she told me that Kate had made her swear not to tell me.

Zoe clapped her hands as we climbed the stairs. "Good, that's Kate and Aidan. We're all here. Brian and Ashley, do you want to see this?" she called in through the screen.

Brian came out. "Ashley is putting Lily to bed. She is being a bit of a pill, saying how much she wants to watch the lights."

Father Neal smiled. "Lovely girl you have, Brian. She reminds me of my own."

"Do they get less troublesome the older they get?"

I winced. Brian had no idea that Father Neal's daughters had died in the same crash as his wife.

Father Neal answered it with good grace. "No, but when they reach thirty they realize how much their daddy loves them."

Zoe said, "Let's look at the camera angles. Reg?"

Reg turned his head a little. "Right. Camera one is on the picnic table facing toward the house. We are hoping to see if any of the lights go near the house." He clicked on the mouse as camera two popped up on the screen. "This is in the barn in response to the strange noises that Brian heard last night."

I looked up at Brian, and he nodded. "I heard some weird noises, like people wailing in pain."

"Do we have cameras in the house?"

"Camera three is pointing up the stairs, and camera four is in Lily's room," Reg said.

Jen leaned forward. "Why Lily's room?"

"Father told us to put one there."

I looked at Father Neal and asked, "Why?"

"It seems Lily has an imaginary friend, Aidan."

Brian looked disturbed. "Is that a problem?"

Father Neal shrugged. "Under normal circumstances, no. Right now, I'm not taking any chances. I hope you understand. Ashley gave us permission."

Brian relaxed. "Oh, okay, then it should be fine."

"Camera five is pointing into the middle of the field. We have nailed a great view of the field."

I noticed an unused camera. "Why aren't we using that one?"

Reg shrugged. "Wasn't sure where we would put it."

"I have an idea." Everyone looked at me and I continued, "I think we should put it on the end of the fence, facing toward the line between the field and the woods."

Father Neal smiled. "An in-between place, then."

"Yeah, and it's where I saw the footprints this past winter."

Reg handed me a cable as I walked down the porch. I handed him the male connection side for the camera board and started walking.

The sun began to slip toward the western horizon, flooding the swirling gray clouds with light. Sunset colors of green, orange, and blue blazed over the field as I unspooled the camera cable to the end of the fence. The woods, bathed in the orange sun, looked like the unconsuming fire of Moses's burning bush. Light always broke the darkness.

Then I heard it: a soft, low female whisper. *Aidan.*

I looked around to see whether Jen had walked up behind me. My skin prickled and the hair on the back of my neck rose. "Amanda? Is that you?"

A soft female laugh mixed with a low animal growl. *No, Aidan, it is us, for we are many.*

Noises began to pour from the woods. I couldn't make them out at first because they spoke in an incoherent babble. They reminded me of the voices around Serpent Mound.

*He talked to us. Talked to us and called us. He invited us.*

I shouted, "Who did?"

They all laughed and began to babble in an unknown language.

*He called her here, so many prisoners to be had.*

"God damn you all. Shut your mouths in the name of Christ."

Shrieks of pain that brought me to my knees erupted from the woods. I put my hands over my ears as I thought my eardrums would burst. The voices stopped. I removed my hands from my ears and listened. My hands started pulsating with light, and I took a deep breath as I tried to calm down. No sound except the wind moving through the trees. As I pulled myself up on the fence, my phone rang.

"Hello?" I gasped.

"Aidan? Are you okay? What's wrong?"

I leaned against the post as Jen's voice soothed me. "I'll tell you when I get back. I'm going to set up the camera; give me a sec."

I put the camera on the post and tied it in place with wire. After I plugged in the camera cable, I got back on the phone. "Okay, how does that look?"

"Just a few inches to the left, Reg says."

I moved it and Jen said, "Looks great. Get your ass back here, and tell us what's going on."

"Will do."

I hung up the phone and looked to the woods. I could hear the whispering beginning again, mixed in with animal sounds as if someone dumped the whole Columbus Zoo into the woods. A lion roared, a donkey brayed, and monkeys chattered. I just hoped they wouldn't start flinging their ghostly monkey shit everywhere.

As I turned to run back to the house, I heard a singsong female voice. *I hope you are ready, Pastor Schaeffer. Tonight is going to be* un cirque.

The French brought me up short. "A what?"

*A circus,* mon amour, *as your lover said to you. Tonight is for lovers.* The voice gave a soft chuckle.

"Something tells me you don't know the meaning of the word."

The voice seemed to move around me as it said, *Consume, love, it's all the same thing,* non? *Each using the other for their own pleasure?*

"True love is sacrifice, as Christ does for the church." I recited Father Neal's words.

A low laugh. *Oh yes, I listen to Father Neal's sermons. Entertaining. Tonight, we shall consume, for my lover comes.*

With a shudder, I started to move. I tried not to imagine feminine fingers reaching for my neck.

I found myself running back to the house.

# CHAPTER FOURTEEN

AFTER I GOT BACK TO THE PORCH, I TOLD EVERYONE WHAT HAD HAPpened by the woods.

Father Neal leaned on his cane and ordered, "No one goes to the woods tonight. No one. Is that understood?"

We all nodded, but I found myself gazing back toward the fence. I felt a hard smack on my leg. "Oww, what the hell?"

Father Neal whacked me again with his cane. "I'm serious, Aidan, this goes especially for you. Do you understand?"

I rubbed my shin. "Yes, Old Priest. I hear you loud and clear."

"Then stop gazing at the forest. Concentrate on what we need to do. Now, everyone join hands; we are going to pray for our protection."

I tried to concentrate on Father Neal's words, but the feminine voice kept rattling around in my head. I wanted to go back to the woods. I wanted to figure out what I had heard and the source of the voice. Jen kept shooting me glances and frowning. She knew something was eating me, but I didn't want to tell her just yet.

That thin place begged me to step through it.

"Amen!" Everyone let go of one another's hands, and I woke out of my reverie.

"Okay, everyone," Zoe instructed, "here are the assignments for the first two hours. Jen and Kate, you have the barn. Aidan and I will take the field watch. Father Neal and Reg, you get the first watch at the command center."

Father Neal said, "No."

Zoe looked at him. "I'm sorry?"

"I'll take the field with you. I want Aidan at the command center."

"What? No! I'm going to the field."

Father Neal shook his head. "No, I don't want you out there right now. You need time to get your head clear."

"I am clear, priest. I'm fine, really."

"I'm not giving you an option or a choice, boy."

We stared at each other in a showdown I knew he would win. I wouldn't question his authority in front of everyone, and he counted on my obedience. I relaxed and shrugged my shoulders. "Whatever you say. I have walked through those fields too many times anyway."

The sun had set, and darkness pervaded the farm. Brian shut off the security lights, and the only illumination came from the computers on the porch. Everyone grabbed their digital recorders and cameras as they headed into the dark. Reg and I sat before the glow of the monitors. Sweat began to drip out of every pore of my body. The heat had not relented with the setting of the sun.

"So, why do you think Father Neal wanted you to stay behind?"

I shrugged. "I have no idea. Guess he didn't want me to get my face burned again."

Reg looked at me and didn't say anything.

"What? Why are you staring at me?" I asked.

"Sorry, I didn't mean to stare, just wondering something."

"What?"

Reg turned his eyes back to the monitor. "Did you have any

experiences in all of this before everything that happened with Amanda?"

"A few things happened to me in college. Brian used to call it 'Ghost World.' Nothing like what we have seen in the past six months."

Then I remembered the visitors of my childhood. My skin crawled as the memories came flooding back.

"Are you okay?"

"Yeah. I just had some childhood memories."

His eyes flickered to me and then back to the monitors. "Care to share?"

"I'm not sure if this is a real memory. It might just be a dream I remember."

"Do tell."

"We lived in an old farm house, and weird stuff would happen all the time. My dad would dismiss it, because he was an old-school Presbyterian with a full dose of Scottish rationalism."

Reg laughed. "My dad was the same. If you couldn't see, touch, taste, smell, or hear it, it didn't exist."

"That's about right. Anyway, my brother and I had separate rooms. I hated it. I hated being alone, still do, as a matter of fact. It's why I got Bishop. Plus, the visitors would always come to me in the dark."

"What did they look like?"

I shook my head. "I can't remember much. Their bodies were tall, thin, and hollow-eyed."

"Like the grays?"

"No, not like the grays at all. When I say hollow-eyed, I don't mean black. It's as if someone took a drill to their faces. Their mouths were the same way. I can't remember any other feature because those stood out the most. They would float near my bed and just stare at me, watching me."

Reg shivered. "That's horrible. Why didn't you tell your dad?"

"I did, and you can probably imagine his answer. Dad was a

great guy, but he had no tolerance for supernatural weirdness. He told me it was just a dream, and finally I learned to stop talking about it."

Reg nodded as he stared at the screen. "Did they go away?"

"Not until I went off to college."

"Did they ever communicate?"

I shook my head. "Not that I can remember, but they kept opening and closing their mouths. My parents always thought I left my light on because I fell asleep reading."

Reg rubbed his walrus mustache. "I think that's the wrong story to tell right now."

I chuckled. "Sorry, Reg, it all just came pouring out. I blocked it, apparently."

Reg held up his hand as we watched something dart across the woods camera. "Did you see that?"

"I couldn't make it out. It went by too fast."

Reg looked stunned, and I put my hand on his shoulder. "What did you see?"

"I'm, I'm not sure. I'm not sure if . . ."

At that moment, another shadow appeared at the edge of the woods. I stared at the tall, thin figure floating about three inches off the ground: a figure with hollowed-out eyes. Its mouth opened and closed in a wordless message to me.

I stood up and grabbed a camera. Reg grabbed my arm. "No, Aidan, you can't go out there. Can't you see that's what it wants?"

We gripped each other as a dark black hole began to form on the TV screen. The hole began to grow until it filled the entire screen and obscured my nightmarish friend. A figure emerged from behind the receding circle and raised its thin arm. Five more figures emerged from the blackness, and the dark circle disappeared. The figures formed into a circle around the original entity and began to move.

Reg gripped my arm. "What the hell is that?"

I leaned in close. "The question might just be: What the hell are they?"

The figures stopped circling, and the leader pointed toward the farm. They broke apart and disappeared in bright flashes.

"Reg, get everyone back here now!"

Reg lifted his walkie-talkie and said, "Everyone, get back to base, ASAP. Move your asses!"

We got nothing but crackling static in response.

"Father Neal, Jen, Darrin, respond!"

A soft female voice began to sing in French, and then in an unknown language. Somehow it seemed familiar to me, but I couldn't place it.

"What is she singing? Is that one of the girls?"

I shook my head. "No, it's not. It's her."

"Her? The voice you heard earlier?"

"Yes."

A soft laughter drifted over the speaker. *Correct,* mes amours. *It's time to play.*

I heard a loud scream come from upstairs, and I bolted inside. Brian, who had agreed to pray for us, had nodded off. He sat bolt upright as I ran into the living room.

"Aidan? What—"

Another piercing scream from Lily upstairs echoed through the house. I ran full tilt up the stairs and almost tripped over the top of them. When I reached Lily's room, she flung herself at me.

"Aidan. Aidan. Aidan."

She whimpered into my neck as I held her tight.

"What is it, Lil' Red? Tell me."

She sobbed. "Sk-sk-skinny man . . . no eyes . . . open mouth."

Her little arms gripped my neck with surprising strength and I loosened them so I could speak. "It's okay, girl. I've got you."

Ashley and Brian came running into the room. Lily reached for Ashley. Ashley held her. "What's up, baby?"

"Skinny man. Dark mouth."

Ashley said, "Shhhh, it's okay, darlin'. Probably just too much excitement."

"No, Mommy, no. He was here. Right in that corner."

All three of us looked up. Nothing.

Brian put his hand on his daughter's shoulder. "You need to go back to bed, darlin'."

"No, Daddy. Please, no, don't leave me."

She nearly climbed up Ashley's body. Ashley and Brian looked at each other. Brian nodded. "I'll stay with her a bit and then you can take a turn."

To my surprise, Ashley agreed. "That's probably best."

Brian took Lily and said, "It's okay, Lilybug. Daddy's going to be with you. I'll keep you safe."

Lily answered with a whimper. Brian looked at me. "Is that okay? I know I promised to pray, but . . ."

"Take care of her, Bri. We'll be fine."

I made my way downstairs, thinking about the figures of my childhood dreams. How had they just appeared in the woods and in Lily's bedroom on the very night I remembered them? The Sherlock Holmes in my head told me there was no way it could be a coincidence. Could whatever this thing was be reading my mind?

As I reached the porch, I heard soft, hysterical crying.

Kate.

Darrin held her tightly as she said over and over, "Just like last time. Owls. Owls at my face, my hands . . . everywhere."

Father Neal limped up the porch with a speed I didn't think possible for him.

"What is going on? What happened? Jennifer?"

Jen held Kate's hand. "I'm not sure, Father. We decided to separate in the barn. I took the loft, and Kate took one of the abandoned stalls. I think I must have fallen asleep because the next thing I knew, Kate screamed. I scrambled down the ladder and found her in the corner of the stall. She held her hands to her face and kept screaming, 'No! No! Not again! Please, leave me alone!' "

Father Neal leaned down to Kate. "Love, can you speak?"

She shook her head as she continued to sob into Darrin's shirt.

"That's not the only thing that's happened, Father," I told him.

He stood up. "What do you mean?"

Reg and I took turns running down the events of the past ten minutes.

Father Neal looked at me. "Are you sure the figures are the same ones you remember as a kid?"

"Positive. I don't know how I blocked the memory of those things all those years, but there's no question about it."

Father Neal nodded. "Things are starting to happen, then."

"Damned British understatement."

Father Neal gave me a thin smile. "The show is about to begin, my friends. Let's hope we survive it."

He looked down at Darrin. "Take Kate inside and lay her on the couch. Stay with her until I come inside, do you understand?"

Darrin nodded and lifted Kate up. She clung to him in the same way Lily clung to Brian. He gave me a little smile as he passed me. Darrin loved being Kate's white knight.

Father Neal motioned for all of us to circle up. "All of this takes things to another level. I think we can assume something is listening in on our conver—"

A singsong Welsh accent crackled over the walkie-talkie. *OOOOO, I love a man with a British accent, reminds me of home, you damned Saxon. . . . Especially a sexy priest like you, one who knows the magick, the sex magick. You know it, don't you . . . Faaatherrrrr?*

The voice laughed and sang in the unknown language I heard earlier. "What language is that?"

I could see Father Neal's face tighten in anger. "A form of Celtic, Aidan, an ancient form."

*Yessss, Father. I know your sins. For they are . . . LEGION.*

The voice laughed and sang as we watched Father Neal. He stared at the radio and ordered, "Name yourself, spirit."

The voice laughed. *Oh no,* mon amour. Je ne donnerai pas mon nom si facilement.

Everyone looked at Jen. "She said, basically, 'I will not give my name to you so easily.' "

The voice laughed. *Lovely. Jen knows how to play. You are delicious. I shall have a taste of you, soon, I think.*

I shuddered and grabbed Jen's hand.

*Come to the woods, Aidan. Come to the woods and I'll leave everyone alone for the night.*

I stepped forward. "Gladly. I'll be there in a few minutes."

Father Neal put out his cane. "I said no."

Jen grabbed my arm. "He's right; we can't give in to its demands."

The voice on the radio crackled. *Bitch, bitch, I know you. You have your hubby's love bite on your face, don't you?*

Jen took out her gun, shot the radio into pieces, and then gave us a wicked smile. "Boring conversation anyway," she said, quoting Han Solo.

Dear Lord, how I loved this woman.

We all laughed and the tension drained out of me.

"What do we do now, Father?" Reg asked as he continued to look at the monitor.

Father Neal sat down in my abandoned chair. "We keep up the investigation, Reg. We aren't going to back down from this thing."

Brian ran out the door with a bang. "Father Neal, Aidan, upstairs."

I helped Father Neal to his feet, and we went upstairs. Jen followed us as Brian led us into his bedroom.

"I came in here to get my iPad to read and she—"

He pointed to the bed where Ashley lay stiff as a board. Her eyes stared at the ceiling, and her mouth moved at a rapid pace.

"What is wrong with her?" I went to touch her, but Father Neal grabbed my hand.

"Don't touch her. Something has a hold of her."

"Can you do something about it?"

He said, "Go downstairs and . . ."

Ashley let out a low, sensuous moan as she began to move around on the bed.

She moaned out, "Oh, lovers, lovers in my bedroom. My real lover is coming soon."

Father Neal grabbed my arm. "Go. Get my prayer book and candle. Now."

I ran downstairs and grabbed everything, including a book of matches from Brian's kitchen drawer. When I got back to the room, Father Neal knelt at the bed and had begun to pray: "In the name of the Father, and of the Son, and of the Holy Spirit. Wash me, O Lord, make me pure in your eyes. Let no darkness be found in me through the mercy of Your Son, Jesus."

I laid the book on the bed and lit the candle. The light chased away some of the darkness. Father Neal stood up. "Brian, you are going to have to stay with Lily. Keep watch with her and pray. Jen, I'm going to ask you to attend me here, can you do this?"

Jen nodded. "No problem. I don't know what help I can be, but I'll do whatever you ask."

Father Neal said, "That is all I need, a willing heart."

He turned to me. "You are going to have to lead the investigation now, Aidan. This thing, whatever it is, is taking us out one by one. But it wants you. Do not, under any circumstances, go into those woods. Do you understand?"

"I got it, Father. No problem."

He gave me a skeptical stare. "I mean it, Aidan. Don't be a hero tonight. This is not the time. Too many things are at stake."

"Okay, O Annoying Priest, I got it. Run the investigation, but don't go into the woods. Anything else?"

He gripped my hand. "Pray, lad, like you have never prayed before."

I went downstairs and saw Darrin stroking Kate's hair.

"How is she?"

"She is asleep, thank God. I think she'll be okay for now."

I nodded. "Ready to get back to investigating?"

He stood up and handed me a dollar. "What the hell is going on here, Aidan?"

I shrugged. "You have been at this longer than I have. I thought you could tell me."

He shook his head. "No way, man. I mean, we have both seen some weird shit, but this . . ."

"I know."

"What is this thing? It's not a normal ghost or anything."

"I wish I knew. I mean, we've only been at this what, an hour? What's next, Bigfoot going to start walking across the barnyard?"

I motioned for Darrin to join me outside. He kissed Kate on the head, whispered something I couldn't hear, and joined me on the porch. Reg and Zoe held cups of coffee in their hands. Both took obligatory sips as they watched the monitors.

"What do we do? Should we go?" Reg asked.

"No, I need you here. We can't quit. Now, I think we should go in a group of three with one person back here at the—"

Before I could finish my sentence, all the screens flashed white and then went dark. We stared at them a moment, and then we looked at one another.

"Well, I guess that solves that problem. Darrin, you are with me, Reg, with Zoe. We will take the field, and you all take the barn."

Reg rubbed his mustache. "Okay, Aidan, but just remember—"

"Yeah, no woods, I got it. I'll be fine. Let's get to work."

# CHAPTER FIFTEEN

**I COULD TELL THAT DARRIN DIDN'T REALLY WANT TO GO TO THE FENCE.** Truth be told, neither did I. My old reluctance to confront the supernatural slipped away, replaced by a desire to know exactly what was happening.

We got to the fence and watched the dark field in silence.

Darrin looked at me. "You want to go to the woods, don't you?"

I gripped the rails of the fence. "I don't know what you are talking about."

He chuckled. "I thought preachers weren't supposed to lie."

"We aren't, but sadly, we do it as much as anyone else."

Darrin turned to me. "So tell me the truth."

The truth. I couldn't tell him about the Five Sorrows, nor what they had done to me. I could feel myself changing, growing, and full of power. Father Neal had forbidden me to tell anyone. I understood the need for secrecy, but it also made me feel isolated.

"I'm standing here thinking of a way to get to those woods without you or anyone else knowing. Something there is calling me, and if it will help us stop this, I'm going, no matter what anyone says."

He raised an eyebrow. "Even Jen?"

"You won't break the bro code, will you?"

"Damn it, you are putting me in a bad spot. Jen specifically told me before we went out not to let you near those woods."

I shrugged. "Just tell her that I started walking along the fence and the next thing you knew, I leaped over it."

I started walking as fast as I could to where the woods met the fence. I leaped over the fence before Darrin could come after me. Looking back at the now-illuminated house, I sighed and then began walking along the edge of the field with the dark woods on my left.

As I walked, I felt as if silent eyes watched every step I took. Every stereotypical scared-body reaction gripped me, from a cold sweat to a rapid heartbeat. I took out my flashlight and shined it into the darkness of the forest. The beam penetrated only a few feet into the trees, which told me the darkness in the woods wasn't natural. Whatever roamed the woods now hated light of any type.

I didn't know what I expected. More lights? Ghosts? Voices? I wished something would happen, because the silent darkness filled my imagination. Sweat rolled down my back and face, driven from my body by the humid, still heat.

"Hey, is anyone here? I heard you earlier."

No answer.

"Why are you here? Why are you picking on my friends? Leave them alone."

A faint whisper of wind blew around me and a barely audible voice whispered in my ear. *I'm here because your friend called me.*

I whipped around, looking for someone behind me. Nothing. "My friend called you? My friend isn't into magick or ghosts. Try again."

Another whisper of wind. *Oh, but he did. He stepped into my domain, and now his family is mine.*

My hand balled into a fist. "Yeah, we will see about that, ass-hole."

A whisper of wind. *I have been watching you a long time, Aidan.*

"Should I get a divine restraining order?"

No answer.

"Did that shut you up? Was it that easy?"

I heard a loud, hair-raising cackle coming from the woods.

*Come deeper into the woods to know my secrets.*

"No thanks. I don't have any desire to stumble through the woods in the dark. I have this thing about broken bones. I hope you understand."

The cackle started low and then reached an earsplitting pitch. It sounded as if a male and female had mixed their voices together in an amplified sexless human voice. I kneeled in pain and covered my ears.

*I'll show you the path, Aidan, if you'll follow.*

Every instinct in me screamed not to go into those woods, to run back to the house, to tell Father Neal. Then another instinct, one that had grown since the day I found out about Amanda, kicked in, and my spine stiffened. I didn't need Father Neal or anyone else to confront this thing.

"Fine, Spirit o' the Woods. Tell me your secrets, if you are stupid enough to show me. Just remember, my heart belongs to the Slain Lamb . . . and . . . I belong to the Order."

The last words sprang out of mouth before I realized what happened. A faint song of chanting monks filled the air, and I clenched my fist. I would confront whatever had set up shop in those woods and chase it out.

I felt a stream of heat race past me, and an orb of reddish light took shape. It began to move up the path along the field, and I followed it. I could hear Darrin shouting at me, but I ignored him.

*Please, God, don't let me him follow me, for his own safety.*

The orb veered to the right and hung among the trees. I caught up and saw a faint path through the thick brush. I stepped on the path and nearly fell over as the world turned upside down.

Air shimmered around me just as it had in Father Neal's office, and I felt the scab-ripping sensation. I looked around to see trees blazing in light as colors ran together in a riot of bright lights. My hands pulsated and I looked down. White light engulfed them, and I could see the inner workings of my body as if under an X-ray. I couldn't find the source of the light and energy.

A constant low-frequency pulse assaulted my body until my inner ear burst, and I threw up in the bushes. The pain drove me to my knees, and I could only crawl along the path. Something told me this was exactly what the spirit wanted.

As I looked back, I couldn't see the path behind me. The only way to figure out this mess was to press forward.

I crawled for what seemed like days until I reached a little clearing in the woods. The pulsing slowed, and I felt the pressure ease. I lifted up my head.

The clearing blazed with light. I looked up and, much to my surprise, the sun blazed in the sky above me. As I looked behind me, I saw the darkness of the woods. Confused, I turned back around to see a roughhewn log cabin with a stack of chopped wood by the door. The wood looked fresh, as if it had been cut just yesterday. I stood up and made my way to the door. Before I could knock, someone opened it and grinned in my direction. A large, well-built African American man waved at me as he came outside. He wore what looked like a nineteenth-century cotton shirt and pants held up with a rope.

I raised my hand in greeting as I said, "Hey, I think I'm lost."

The man didn't react to my words, just stared behind me. A smile lit up his face as he bent down, and a child ran past me into his arms.

"She's cute, what's her name?"

No answer from the man or his daughter. They moved their lips and laughed. No sound. I couldn't figure out why I couldn't hear them or why they didn't react to me. Then I realized that a vision of something from the past had started to play like a movie, a residual haunting. I seated myself on the stack of wood and watched them with a smile on my face.

The father and daughter laughed while they played in the yard. An African American woman with a head wrap like Celestine's stepped out of the door and said something to the wrestling pair. They laughed and began to walk to the house. Then the man stopped and looked over his shoulder. His eyes went wide with horror, and he turned to his ladies. The man shouted and pointed to some place beyond the house. They began to run, but something made them pull up short. Their mouths opened in a silent scream.

I stood up and felt something brush past me. A man in a long, dark cloak walked in front of me and pointed to the father. I saw veiled figures pour out of the woods as they grabbed the mother and daughter. The figures threw back their hoods to reveal some of the most beautiful women I'd ever seen. Each one had long, blonde, almost white, hair. They grabbed the fugitives and dragged them to the ground.

"No, no, stop!" I shouted, but none of the specters paid any attention to me. They grabbed the mother and daughter to pull them apart. Both of them kicked and screamed until the figures beat them into submission. The father started to run after the figures until the man in the long black coat held up his hand. The man fell flat on his face, unable to move.

A black-veiled figure moved out from the others and approached the man on the ground. She knelt and lifted her veil to show her face to the man on the ground. A look of utter loathing contorted his features. I tried to turn away, but I found I couldn't move my head. The figure in the veil took out a long knife and began to cut into the man's head. He screamed and thrashed on the ground as he bled.

I couldn't turn away. I couldn't help. I could only watch.

The veiled figure motioned to the blonde women, and they came to grab the man on the ground. They carried him screaming into the woods with his wife and daughter. The woman approached the man in the long black cloak, and they embraced.

Then the scene dissolved until only the man remained. He turned to me, mouth spread in a fixed grin, teeth shining in the light, and black almond-shaped eyes fixed on me. The air vibrated with power as reality distorted, moved, and flowed all around me. I felt like I'd stepped into a time warp.

*So, Aidan, we meet at last.*

# CHAPTER SIXTEEN

**I REGAINED CONTROL OF MY BODY AND BOWED MY HEAD. I DIDN'T** want to look into that face.

*So, you decided to face me without the old man, hmmm? Very brave of you. And foolish. You're not a member of the Order yet, and you're now in an interesting phase in your . . . development*, the Grinning Man said. There was a slight British tinge to his accent.

His voice echoed in my head and in the woods. My stomach clenched and my knees felt as though they'd give out at any moment. Still, I could feel the presence of the Five Sorrows, and I drew from their strength.

"Well, I have been known to do foolish things."

The man laughed. *Indeed, you have. You are quite entertaining to watch, Aidan. Mike thought much of you, you know.*

"Mike is a murdering asshole."

The Grinning Man sighed. *Yes, and a foolish one. He allowed his—ah, shall we say—desires to get in his way of my waking. He tried to do his own experiment with the ladies. Thankfully, my Bride fixed his error.*

"Goody for her."

*You never let anything get in your way, do you?*

I paused for a moment. "What do you mean?"

He chuckled. *Your whole life, you never paid the slightest attention to what anyone else had to say. Your parents, your brother, your teachers, professors, lovers, and now Father Neal—all of that has led you to me.*

I shrugged. "Don't flatter yourself, jackass. If I'm not going to listen to them, what makes you think I'm going to listen to you?"

*You haven't been broken enough yet to answer that question. But don't worry, I'll break you.*

"I don't break so easily."

*Oh no? Amanda? The hypocrites in the church? Jennifer's secrets?*

"What secrets?"

*Oh, dear, I have said too much. Oh well, you'll figure it out soon enough.*

"Not Jen. No. She has no secrets other than her job. You are a liar." Right? An utter liar.

*Oh, I never lie. The truth is much more effective for destroying someone.*

"I don't believe you, Grinning Man."

He laughed. *Of all my names, I find that one the most interesting. Something terrifying about a grin, isn't there? People are so much more afraid of a grin than a frown, don't you think? People really can't stand humor and laughter as much as they say.*

I heard the rustle of his cloak as he bent down. I kept my head lowered.

*Do you like the work of my Bride? She always had a thing about hunting down darkies. Ohio became her own personal playground after they kicked her out of the Granny Circle in North Carolina and your government passed that wonderful law. Ohio became her happy hunting ground. She gathered some sisters and, I must say, she was, and is, really, very effective.*

Despite myself I asked, "What law?"

*Tut, tut, you should listen to your ravishing woman when she talks about history. The Fugitive Slave Law.*

"So, your Bride and her mean girls hunted escaped slaves in Ohio, is that it?"

The Grinning Man chuckled. *Oh yes. Her love of keeping humans in slavery is beautiful to see. But that is only part of the picture, Aidan. Only part . . .*

"Is? Slavery ended a hundred and fifty years ago, jackass. I don't know what that has to do with now."

*Do you not? And do you really think slavery ended with the Civil War?* He sounded puzzled. I kept trying to place his accent as he spoke. His pronunciation combined Shakespearean English, Southern drawl, and modern Midwestern businessman. My sense of the dislocation of time and space increased.

"No."

*You are a bright lad, I'm sure you'll figure it out. Do you know why I brought you here?*

"No, I don't."

I could hear the creak of leather as he turned from one side to another.

*People have been worshipping me here for hundreds of years. Natives fought a battle on this land, as you seem to know.*

I nodded.

*But more has happened here on this ground. Your old man friend . . . he knew.*

"What are you talking about?"

*The vision you saw really happened.*

"I figured that."

*Not just once, Aidan, many times. Different people, different families, but all of them met my Bride and her sisters in the end.*

I lay down in the dust, too tired to kneel anymore. "I don't understand."

He patted me on the shoulder, and I felt electricity give me a small jolt.

*Maybe you should come back here in the daytime after you have a talk with that*—he grimaced and clenched his hands—*man and his horrible wife who used to live here.*

I raised my head, looking at his knees. "What's the matter, afraid of little ol' Olan and Edna?"

A hand grabbed me by the shirt and lifted me a few inches off the ground. He hissed as drool oozed out of his mouth onto my head. *I'm afraid of no human, boy. I served the Nephilim when they walked this land, back when they built the mounds. We raised them with the power of the watchers. My destruction is not in your hands but in the hands of the watchers, and only through their dark magick.*

"So, a group of voyeuristic pervs are in charge of your destiny?"

I flew across the clearing and landed hard. I coughed and struggled for breath.

*Do not mock the watchers or their servants the Nephilim. They listen. They hear.*

The temptation rose within me to call on the Five Sorrows for rescue, but I resisted. I wanted more information.

"And what about the Hellfire Club. Who are they?"

The Grinning Man didn't say anything for a while. Then he responded, *They are powerful magicians, but they do not know the secrets of the Nephilim . . . not yet.*

"More powerful than you?"

He grabbed me by the throat and hissed, *Look at my face.*

I closed my eyes tight and fought him every inch of the way, but I didn't want my neck to snap. His fingers pressed on my eyes and slowly pulled up my eyelids. I fought hard not to cry out and keep my eyes closed. I failed in both respects.

I saw him, the Grinning Man, whose face haunted me. Whose name caused me to shiver the first time I heard it from Mike. His eyes dominated the upper half of his face, while a wide, sinister grin dominated the lower half. His eyes and his grin hypnotized me.

Staring into his eyes, I felt a rushing wind as he sucked me into his mind. I saw flashing images: a man in a robe and hat staring into a crystal stone; a woman walking to the gallows as she screamed her innocence; the faces of terrified slaves as someone bent their limbs into unnatural positions; and girls, thousands of girls, screaming in pain. Their cries pierced my heart, and I curled into the fetal position in pain.

I cried out in a loud voice in Hebrew, "Behold!"

A flash of light erupted in the forest, and the Grinning Man roared in pain. The last thing I heard was, *How? Only the old priest was supposed to be . . .*

Everything went dark.

# CHAPTER SEVENTEEN

I WOKE UP TO DARRIN SHAKING ME. STARS TWINKLED IN THE NIGHT SKY above me. The storm clouds had vanished.

"Man, what the hell do you think you're doing?"

I pushed myself up off the ground. "Looking for lightning bugs."

"Damn it, Aidan, if you'd of gotten yourself killed, Jen would have skinned my hairy ass. I just happened to hear shouting, saw a flash of light, and ran toward it."

I laughed and then winced. My ribs felt as if someone had put me on the rack. I gasped for breath and coughed.

He shined his light around in the forest, and then he looked back at me. "What happened to your eyes?"

I reached up to touch my eyes and felt some sort of fluid oozing out of them. "I don't really know."

Darrin bent down and helped me stand. He shined the light on the side of my face just enough to see clearly. "Dude, you're bleeding out of your eyes, and the area around them looks like somebody smeared you with red crayon."

I touched the side of my eyes and cried out. "Holy hell, that kinda hurt."

Darrin put his arm around me. "Yeah, well, not as much as we are going to hurt when Jen sees your sorry ass. I don't like to cross chicks who can shoot me."

"Probably a smart rule."

We didn't say another word as Darrin supported me all the way to the house. As as we made our way from the field, everyone except Father Neal stood watching us. I could make out Jen's figure, tense as a coming thunderstorm, her arms crossed in disgust.

"Let me . . .. let me try to walk on my own."

Darrin let go, and I nearly fell to the ground. He caught me and pulled me back up. "I think you are just going to have to live with me holding you up, Preacha."

As we got to the porch, I tried to deflect Jen's anger. "A funny thing happened to me near the fence."

She brushed that aside. "What the hell do you think you were doing out there, Aidan? Darrin, you obviously didn't stop him. I could shoot you both."

Darrin whispered, "See, I told you."

"Honey, I'm okay. Really."

She marched up, grabbed Darrin's flashlight, and shone the light into my face. I winced and everyone gasped.

"Aidan . . ." Zoe broke off.

They all stood in silence as my face radiated heat and pain. Jen's expression went from intense anger to worried concern. Her soft hands reached up to my cheek.

"What happened to you, baby?"

Father Neal came outside, took one look at me, and said, "Let me see. Now."

Darrin half carried me to the nearest chair and sat me down. Father Neal and Jen bent over me. Father Neal studied my face and eyes.

"Can you possibly tell me what got into your damned thick skull going into those woods when I told you not to?"

"Quarter for the Wii, Father," I said, giving him a weak smile.

He didn't respond as he searched my face.

Jen frowned. "I would like to know that myself."

I started to explain when Brian walked outside on the porch.

"Father, is Ashley going to be okay? Lily just got to sleep."

Father Neal looked at me for a moment; I nodded and he said, "Come inside, Brian. We will talk. There are some things we are going to need to do."

Jen knelt down next to me as she looked at my eyes and cheeks. "You need to go to the hospital."

I shook my head. "I feel fine, love. It just stings a little. Besides, how are we going to explain this? Doctor, you see, there is this old servant of the Nephilim running around and . . ." I broke off as they all stared at me.

"Sorry, I should tell that to Father Neal first."

Zoe knelt by Jen. "I think I can fill that in for you, Aidan. It was the Grinning Man."

"I . . . How did you know?"

"Your injuries, dear. They have happened before."

"Where? Who?"

She patted my arm. "You never read those paranormal books I gave you, did you?"

"Well, no. I've been reading Jen's forensic books."

Zoe clucked her tongue. "Those are good, Aidan, but if you want to stay with us, you need to read the books I gave you."

"Uh, Zoe, my injuries . . ."

"Yes, they happened down in Point Pleasant during the Mothman saga."

Everything clicked. "Indrid Cold."

She nodded. "Some people who saw the creature called the 'Mothman' often came away with red eyes and bleeding, as if they had been burned."

Darrin knelt down. "Then why is he here? At this farm?"

I had an idea, but I didn't feel like explaining it to them. It would mean dragging Brian's private life in front of everyone.

Jen touched my arm. "The bleeding has stopped. You should really go to the hospital."

I shook my head. "No, Jen. I have to preach on Sunday."

Zoe gripped my arm. "No, Aidan. You need to rest."

I sighed. Truth be told, I couldn't figure out how I would get into the pulpit. I could barely stand, and my ribs ached. Thankfully, Jen didn't know about the ribs. She would have drawn her gun on me and forced me to go to the emergency room. Still, I couldn't help the warm feeling that spread over me. She really did love me.

I sighed, took out my phone and dialed Cole's number.

"Hey, Boss, what's up?"

I turned on my sick voice, which wasn't hard. "Hey, bud, I have some sort of virus and I can barely stand."

"Oh man, are you okay? Do you need anything?"

I winced as I shifted in my seat, and Jen raised an eyebrow at me. "I, uh, no, Cole, that's okay. But I do need for you to take over worship and preach for me on Sunday. Can you do that?"

"No problem. I actually have a few sermons laying around."

"Awesome, thanks, bud. I owe you one. I hate doing this to you."

"Nah, it's good practice. Sorry you are sick. Get better."

I hung up the phone and winced again.

"Is there something wrong with your ribs?" Jen asked.

"Uh, yeah, they are just a bit sore, that's all."

She lifted up my shirt and gasped. "Sore, my ass." Her fingers reached down to explore, and I shied away.

"No, it's really . . ."

She got a finger on a rib, and I nearly passed out. "That's it, bud, you are going to the hospital. Right now."

I held up my hand. "No, not until Father Neal is done with Brian. Okay?"

She stared at me with a look that made me afraid and made me want her at the same time.

"Fine. But if you are permanently crippled, I'm not going to feel the least bit sorry for you."

I grinned. "I'll keep that in mind."

She huffed as she stood and started giving orders. "All right, everyone, we need to start breaking down for the night. I think whatever was out there, Aidan restrained it somehow. Let's get to it."

No one questioned her as they dispersed to gather the equipment.

Father Neal walked out with Brian, who looked as if he would come apart at any moment. They sat down next to me and were quiet for a while.

Brian bumped my shoulder with his. "I'm sorry about this."

"Not your fault, man." I gasped.

"No, it is my fault. I invited all of this."

I glanced over at Father Neal, who shook his head.

"No, man, whatever this is, whoever this is, it's something beyond what you could have invited, no matter what you did."

"That's what Father Neal said, and I wish I could believe you both." Brian put his head in his hands, and his body began to shake. "And now you. Look at you."

"Well, I'm certainly not posing for a magazine any time soon, unless it's *Weird Shit Weekly*."

We all chuckled a little.

Father Neal said, "Jen is making you go to the hospital, isn't she?"

"Yeah, I don't know what I'm going to tell them."

"Just tell them you fell off Shrum Mound in the dark with Jen."

I looked at him. "How did . . ." My mind flashed back to a certain night two weeks ago.

Father Neal laughed. "I may be old, boy, but I'm not blind."

Everyone finished gathering the equipment and loading the van. They all came back on the porch, and Brian shook everyone's hand.

"What do I do? What if everything starts happening again?"

Father Neal shook his head. "It won't. Not tonight, Brian. The entity got what it came for tonight in talking to Aidan. I think you'll be fine until morning."

We heard a little cough and whimper coming from the living room. Lily came out on the porch, clutching her teddy bear and blanket.

Brian leaned down to pick her up. "Hey, honey, what's up?"

She buried her face in Brian's chest. "A woman in a black dress is in my room. She keeps smiling at me. I don't like it. She scares me. She says she is Morgan, but I don't believe her."

Brian looked at us in agony.

"It's okay, darlin'. It's just a bad dream. Daddy will stay with you for a while."

He opened the door and then turned to us. "Let me know when you know anything. Please. This can't go on."

We all nodded as he went inside. Jen put her hand on my arm. "Hospital. Now."

# CHAPTER EIGHTEEN

**I WOKE UP WITH A GROAN AS BISHOP PAWED AT ME.**

"Oh, buddy, you gotta be careful with that."

The painkillers the doctor gave me for two bruised ribs had worn off. I reached up to touch my eyes, and I winced. The doctor hadn't asked too many questions, but I wondered what he thought. Given Jen's unruffled appearance, he probably thought she'd beaten me to a bloody pulp.

I sat up and leaned my head against the headboard. As I did, my hand hit a piece of paper. I picked it up and read:

*My Love,*

*I had to run to the station. I didn't want you to think I left you like this. I hope to be back later this afternoon. Darrin is bringing you lunch around two. Take it easy and DON'T get out of bed. Darrin will take Bishop out when he gets there.*

*Love,*
*Jen*

*P.S. I love you, but take your damn medication.*

I chuckled and rubbed Bishop's head. "Your mommy sure knows me, doesn't she? Well, I can't take it just yet. Got a phone call to make."

Bishop gave me a sleepy dog look and closed his eyes.

I reached for my phone and looked for Olan's number. "All right, Olan. You are about to get a big apology."

I used to tease Olan and Edna about their farm. They always told me weird stuff happened all the time, and I never believed them. That is, until Edna's dream about their dead son and everything that happened with Amanda. I never apologized for the teasing, and now I would eat a whole bunch of crow.

"Aidan, my boy! How are you?"

"Oh, I think I'll live, Olan. How is Edna?"

"Doing great! We are actually in Santa Fe for an art festival. She is selling her paintings and making a killing."

I grinned. "Sounds like retirement is treating you very well."

"Oh boy, you don't know the half of it. I thought I would get bored, not running the farm and all. Turns out, playing golf every day and traveling with Edna suits me just fine."

"So, basically, you are puttering around."

He chuckled. "That's right. And I love it. So what can I do for you?"

I paused, not wanting to break the mood.

"Aidan, what is it, son? Is it Jen? Father Neal?"

"No, no, they are both fine. Better than me, in fact."

"I don't understand."

"Well, it's about Brian and the farm." I told him everything, including my encounter with the Grinning Man in the woods. When I finished, I couldn't tell if he had hung up.

"Olan?"

"I'm here, Aidan. Just thinking about everything you just said."

"Does it surprise you?"

"No, not a bit. I always told you my farm is—"

"I know. I'm sorry about that. I shouldn't have made fun of you."

"It's okay. Really. It's all hard to believe until you experience it."

"Why do you think the Grinning Man wanted me to talk to you?"

I could almost hear his brain whirring. "Well, I know for a fact that the farm used to be a stop along the Underground Railroad during the years before the Civil War."

"Yeah, but the house isn't that old, is it?"

"No, it's not. The house was built at the turn of the last century, 1901, I think. In your vision, you saw a cabin. The foundation is still out in the woods."

My heart began to race. "I didn't know that."

"I didn't tell you. I never went near the place much myself. Too many bad feelings. I'm guessing the ol' Grinning Man wants you to find something. I wouldn't recommend going back there at night."

I laughed and winced. "Even if I wanted to, Olan, do you think Jen would allow that? Or Father Neal, for that matter?"

He chuckled. "No, I guess they wouldn't. There is one thing that troubles me, Aidan."

"What's that?"

"Well, rumors surround that cabin. I've got papers, somewhere, that say a circle of Appalachian witches lived near there."

"Yeah, but we're not in the Appalachians."

"If you look at a map, boy, you'll see we are actually very close. Besides, you don't need to be in the mountains to practice magick, I'm guessing."

"So why did they come to your land?"

"Huh. Well, according to the legends, they were a group of evil witches, terrible, and they hunted runaway slaves."

My skin crawled as I remembered my vision.

"Yeah, sort of a hit squad of some type, so they say," Olan continued.

I wrote everything down and realized the shadowy figures must have been the witches. "A hit squad for whom? Do you think it was for the Grinning Man?"

"Hmmm, I dunno. Maybe? That question would be for Father Neal."

I worked hard not to sigh with impatience. "Did you find any papers that have the rumors written on them?"

"Sorry, son, no, I don't. I just heard the stories from the guy I bought the farm from. He warned me weird stuff happened. Well, you know the rest."

He paused as he muttered to someone off the phone. "Edna told me to tell you she believes our farm is a nexus point."

"A what?" I said, sitting up and then wincing.

"We talked about this before, son. Place where the veil is thin, weird things leak through all the time. They didn't directly attack us for some reason."

I smiled, thinking of the Grinning Man's fear of them. He couldn't stand the untainted holiness of their power.

"Wonder what set everything off?"

"I can't tell you that, Olan. But your instincts are right. Something did happen."

"I thought as much, son. You'd better be careful."

I put a hand on my wrapped ribs. "Thanks, Olan. I'll keep that in mind."

"The missus and I will be praying hard for all of you. Tell me what you find at the cabin."

"I will. Give Edna a hug for me."

"Will do. You and Jen come out and see us. We have two spare bedrooms."

I smiled. "I'll talk to her. We might both need to get away after this one."

"Keep me updated, Aidan. Good-bye."

"Bye, Olan."

I hung up the phone and looked at the bottle of pain pills on the table. If I took them, I would probably be out of it the rest of the day. The evidence review would be tonight at Saint Patrick's, and I couldn't miss it. Something told me the cameras and voice recorders had caught more information. Plus, the investigation would be incomplete without visiting the cabin. I looked over at the clock. 1:50 p.m. Darrin would be here any moment. If I could get him over the fear of being shot, he would take me to the farm. Jen didn't sound like she would be back until dinner, so that gave me plenty of time to get there. She wouldn't let me go to the evidence review if she knew I'd been tromping around the woods.

I dialed Brian's number and he answered, "Hey, Aidan."

"Hey, Bri. Is everything okay?"

"Well, Ashley is still in bed, and I'm watching Lily play with Peyton. So, probably as good as it gets right now."

"Of course."

"How are you? What did the doctor say?"

"Oh, a few bruised ribs, nothing serious."

"What about the eyes?"

"They stopped bleeding long before I got to the hospital. They just looked really inflamed. The doctor just thought it might be bruising, nothing to worry about." I paused, then continued. "Listen, I need to come back out to the farm."

"Will Jen allow that?"

"She isn't here. She went to the station. Darrin is bringing me lunch at two and I'm going to convince him to bring me out there."

"Okay. We aren't going anywhere. See you in a bit. I don't think you should get out of bed, but I know you, stubborn."

I hung up the phone and shook my head. I'd never heard Brian sound that dejected and defeated.

A shower seemed too painful at the moment, so I slowly put on some clothes. The dull ache of my ribs made every movement a trial. I went down the stairs, taking each step one at a time. As I reached the bottom, the doorbell rang.

I opened the door and Darrin lifted up a Tommy's pizza.

"Hey, Preacha, I brought food. Hungry?"

My stomach growled. "If you weren't so ugly, I would kiss you right now."

Darrin grinned. "I'll pass on that."

He came in and while he got plates, I tore into the pizza, enjoying the greasy goodness.

"It's bad manners not to wait for your guest."

"Yeah, well, my guest doesn't have cracked ribs, and he had breakfast this morning."

We ate in silence for a bit, and then I said, "Darrin, I need to go back to the farm."

No response as he turned on the TV and began watching a rerun of *Pawn Stars*.

"Not happening, Preacha. I got orders to sit with you until Jen gets back."

"I have to go. It's important."

"So is my ass. Jen said to tell you if you want to go to the evidence review tonight, you had to take your pain medication, sleep, and then she would take you herself."

"I have no doubt she said those exact words. But she didn't know about the cabin."

He stopped chewing. "The what?"

I told him everything Olan had said.

Darrin sighed. "Now you have *me* wanting to go."

I grinned. "I hoped so."

He looked me over. "Do you really think you're up to walking?"

"Of course. I'll take ibuprofen. I'm sure I don't need the Percocet or whatever they gave me last night."

He looked doubtful. "Man, I've had bruised ribs before. I don't believe that for a second."

"Maybe you were just a wimp."

"Not funny. I was out of commission for two weeks. I don't believe you're going to be able to even get to the car."

"Preachers have superpowers, don't you know that?"

He sighed. "Well, Jen already wants to shoot me, so I might as well go the whole way."

We finished our lunch, and I popped four ibuprofen. The pizza made me feel better, and the medicine began to do its work. I walked out to Darrin's car with a fast old man's shuffle.

"You realize that Jen is going to be überpissed, don't you?"

"Not if she doesn't find out about it."

He arched his eyebrows. "Yeah, good luck with that one."

We drove out to the farm, and Brian greeted us as we pulled into the driveway.

"Why are you here? Seriously, man, you need to be in bed. I only let you come out because you never listen to anyone."

I shook my head. "Do you really need me to answer that after all you've done for me?"

He looked at me for a moment, then said to Darrin, "How did he dupe you into coming here?"

"I got tired of his whining and nothing good on TV . . . blah, blah, blah."

Brian gave us a smile. "All right. Let's do this and get you home."

We walked by the house, and I saw Ashley in a rocking chair. The slow creak of the wood matched the rhythm of her foot as she pushed. She stared off into space and didn't acknowledge us as we passed.

"How long has she been there?"

"About ten minutes. I just put Lily down for a nap and came out to find Ashley on the porch. She hasn't said one word." He paused, then asked, "Has Father Neal said anything to you yet?"

I shook my head. "We haven't had time to talk. Hopefully, tonight."

"I'll let him tell you everything then."

They both helped me over the fence as we made our way to the woods. While my skin started to prickle, I pressed on. The desire to discover the cabin and confirm everything I saw last night drove me forward. We reached the small clearing in the woods.

"Is this the place you went to last night?" Darrin asked.

"Yeah, this is it. Look for some sort of outline in the grass, stone, anything."

The hot humidity and my ribs made breathing a chore. I fought to take in air as I looked around in the grass. We searched for about twenty minutes until Brian called out, "Here, I think I found something."

Darrin and I walked over to kneel down by Brian. We saw a gray stone slab full of fossils.

"Ohio limestone," I said. "Out of place in the middle of the woods."

"It's not a foundation stone," Brian said, running his fingers along a fossilized trilobite.

Darrin shook his head. "No, but I bet it's a hearthstone."

"What?"

"Everyone put in a hearthstone back then. They built their fireplaces on it."

I nodded. "So, is that it?"

Darrin shrugged his shoulders. "I didn't see anything else around here that stuck out, did you?"

Brian and I shook our heads. Darrin smacked the stone. "I'm an idiot. I bet something is under here."

"Why?"

"Sometimes families would put a token or valuable under the hearthstone so that it would bring good luck or whatever."

We all looked at each other, and I said, "I can't turn it over. Can you two do it?"

They both nodded.

"All right, well, go for it."

Brian and Darrin grunted, groaned, and sweated as they tried to pick up the stone. They pushed it over with a final *oomph*. I looked at the worm-ridden ground underneath, and I saw another stone tablet. It bore the likeness of the Grinning Man.

The carved lines were faded with age and wear. How long, I wondered, had the Grinning Man walked on this continent? Father Neal seemed to think he'd been here even before the Native Americans. The carvings looked older than anything I'd seen at the Ohio Historical Society. Still, the rock looked clean, as if someone just placed it there for us to find.

I picked it up and saw a glimmer of white sticking out through the dirt.

"What is that?" Darrin asked as he leaned down.

"I don't know. Let's find out."

We brushed away the dirt and found a white stone box with an old-fashioned metal lock holding it into place.

"How are we going to get it open?"

"The metal is so rusted, we could probably just pick it open," Brian said, touching the hole in the lock.

Darrin took out his Swiss Army knife. "Old reliable should help us." He fiddled with the various knives and devices until he found a long, thin metal pick.

Brian grabbed his hand. "Let me."

In a few seconds, Brian picked the lock and the box came open. We stared at the contents of the box in disbelief. An ornate knife, like the one I had seen in my confrontation with the Grinning Man, gleamed in the sunlight. It looked as if someone had just forged it and placed it here in the woods. I picked up a doll made out of rough cloth and yarn. A white wedding veil covered two slashes for eyes, and I shuddered as I felt the energy humming up my arm.

"What the hell is this?" Darrin asked.

"The knife looks like the one I saw in my vision, but that's not possible. This looks as if it has just been made."

"I don't get it."

I shrugged my shoulders. "Neither do I, but maybe Father Neal will know." I grabbed the box, and we walked back to the house. By the time we reached it, my ribs felt like they were on fire. "I gotta sit down for a bit, guys."

"But Jen . . ."

"I know, Darrin. I just need a minute."

We sat down near the rocking Ashley and didn't say a word. She broke in with a small, weak voice. "What did you find in the woods?"

We all looked at each other and then I said, "Nothing much. Just a box, a knife, and a weird-looking doll."

"Let me see the doll."

I looked at Brian and he nodded. I pulled out the doll and held it up.

Ashley screamed, her face contorted in horror. She tried to climb up the back of the chair. Brian reached out his hand to steady the chair so it wouldn't fall. She kept screaming, tears rolling down her face.

"The Bride. The Bride. She's after me. She's after me."

# CHAPTER NINETEEN

WE PULLED INTO SAINT PATRICK'S JUST AS MY PHONE RANG.

Darrin looked over. "Who is it?"

I looked and grimaced. "Guess who?"

"We're fucked." He took out a dollar.

I answered, "Hey, love."

"Where the hell are you?"

"Um, just pulling into the parking lot at Saint Patrick's."

"Why aren't you home resting?"

"I wanted to talk to Father Neal before the review."

"You could have used the phone, you know," Jen said in her cop voice. "Please tell me you didn't drive."

"Uh, no."

"Tell Darrin I really am going to shoot him someday."

Darrin whispered, "What did she say?"

I pointed a finger gun at him and pulled the trigger. He grinned as I said, "When are you coming?"

She sighed. "I'll be a little late. Things are really starting to go to hell around here."

"Oh, why?"

"I'm going to tell you later—it's time, I think. Just please take it easy."

I blurted out before I could catch myself, "I'm a grown man, Jen. Things are serious here. My best friend's family is coming apart."

Dead silence.

"Jen?"

"Tonight, we're going to discuss what it means to take care of yourself for once." She hung up.

I looked at the phone, stunned. "What the hell?"

Darrin made a face. "Guess that didn't go the way you wanted."

"I'm not sure I even understand what she meant."

"Living in the mystery that is woman?"

"Evidently."

We got out of the car and Darrin helped me to the rectory. I knocked on the door and Father Neal answered, "Come in, you two."

He led us to his living room decorated in quaint English cottage–style, circa 1940s. Father Neal sat down and motioned us toward the couch.

"I had a feeling you two would show up before the review."

I wrinkled my brow. "And how is that?"

Father Neal chuckled. "You needed answers, and Jen probably took your keys." He motioned to the kitchen. "Darrin, get us three beers out of the fridge."

Father Neal looked at me. "Now, tell me about the Grinning Man. I want to know everything he said or did. Leave out no detail."

I told him everything I could remember. Father Neal sat with his eyes closed, and at one point I thought he fell asleep. "Are you awake?"

"Yes, Aidan. Please keep going."

Darrin came in with bottles of beer, placed one in Father Neal's hand, and gave one to me.

I finished my account of last night, and Father Neal said, "And you called Olan?"

"Yeah. That's when I decided to go back to the woods."

"So what did you find on the farm?"

Darrin laid the box on the table. Father Neal leaned forward and opened the box. He pulled the dagger out first.

"Such beauty wasted on an instrument of destruction."

"Knives don't always have to be used to kill."

Father Neal shook his head. "No, my boy, this is more than a knife."

Darrin and I looked at each other in confusion.

"I'm not sure I follow, Father," I said.

"Magick always uses everyday objects to focus its power. This knife helps, or helped, concentrate the mind and focus for the practitioner."

"What, like a wand?"

Father Neal took a drink of his beer. "Crudely, yes. No one who practices magick uses a wand. They use an object that means a lot to them to focus their power, their essence, and their will. Do you understand?"

We both nodded.

He held up the doll and the knife together. "When these two are combined, the magick becomes more powerful."

"I know the doll is serious from Ashley's reaction. But when we found it, I actually laughed at it. It looks like a three-year-old made it," Darrin said.

Father Neal smiled. "That's because culture has trained you to think so. Have you two never seen anything like this before?"

Darrin pulled out a cigarette and began to twirl it in his fingers. "I saw these toy Voodoo dolls in New Orleans that kind of look like the same thing."

"Exactly. The Voodoo doll in pop culture is silly: a throwaway thing, not even real Voodoo. Still, it reflects something real."

"So, I can still give Darrin stomach cramps by poking a doll of him in the stomach," I said with a smirk.

Father Neal shook his head. "Not exactly, no."

He held up both again and then moved the knife toward the doll. The knife began to penetrate the threads causing a small ripping sound.

"When you take your will and focus on the object of your will, you can make things happen. My guess is that this doll is being used to influence the house and cause all the havoc with Ashley."

I leaned forward. "What?"

"Ashley is very obviously under the influence of magick. Something has a hold of her," Father Neal said as he took another sip of beer.

Darrin twirled his cigarette. "The question is: Why didn't Aidan see that person in the woods last night? I mean, if this supposed magician had been wandering around the woods, wouldn't Aidan have seen him or her?"

Father Neal shook his head. "No. *He* wasn't exactly in our world."

"Then what world was I in?" I asked, raising my eyebrow.

Father Neal leaned back. "I don't know. One of the mysteries of the Grinning Man, I'm afraid, and the magick of the Nephilim he guards."

"The other mystery is why he would lead us to the cabin and to a magickal object belonging to one of his servants," I said.

Father Neal nodded. "Yes, that is something I don't understand at all. I don't know why he showed you this. Some sort of trap, maybe."

He looked at the knife. "This knife, I can't place it. I thought it might be recent, but it keeps changing, did you notice?"

Darrin and I looked at the knife. To my surprise, it no longer looked like something made in the twenty-first century. The object seemed to have grown in length and elongated figures had appeared on the blade.

"What the—" I started to pick it up.

Father Neal grabbed my wrist. "The less you handle it, the

better. Something about this knife disturbs me more than anything we've seen so far."

Darrin crushed the cigarette in his hand. "Uh, that's kinda saying a lot, Padre."

"Yes. Whoever the Dark Bride is, she was given this knife, I think. She didn't make it. For some reason, the Grinning Man wanted us to have it and took it from her. That is the mystery here."

"That and why did those bastards attack Brian and his family? What would be the point? They couldn't be any real threat, right?" I asked.

"I doubt they are the real targets, but just a side benefit. You've seen enough to know what we are dealing with, Aidan. Evil loves to destroy, no matter how big or small a person might be." Father Neal stared at the portrait of the Fisher King.

"Yeah, and it doesn't help that Brian invited her there."

Darrin stared at me. "What? How?"

I sighed. "The Internet, Darrin. Brian chatted with women he didn't know. Maybe one of them was the Dark Bride."

Darrin sat back and made a silent *O* with his mouth.

"That would explain everything: the insistence of invitation to the home, the torment, Ashley's oppression, all of it," Father Neal said, "but there is more." He looked at me and I understood. Brian invited the darkness in, but it came because of me. I rubbed my forehead, trying not to fall apart.

"So now what?" I asked.

Father Neal drank the last of his beer and got up. He limped to the desk to pour himself a large glass of whiskey and took a huge gulp before he answered.

"We must figure out the identity of the Dark Bride. She is very obviously not a ghost or whatever the Grinning Man might be. She is flesh and blood."

I picked up the knife and doll. "Because of these things, right?"

Father Neal nodded. "Yes. A magician needs concrete reality, unlike the Grinning Man, who is . . . something we don't understand just yet."

"Where do we even begin? Go through Brian's chat records? That's not something I want to do."

Father Neal shook his head. "I don't know. I should hope not. At this point, I don't see the need. We might have more clues after the review."

As if on cue, we heard car doors slamming.

"Let's go to the conference room."

# CHAPTER TWENTY

I MET JEN BEFORE SHE WENT INTO THE CONFERENCE ROOM AND PULLED her into the sanctuary.

"Listen, I'm sorry . . ."

She held up her hand. "I get it, Aidan. Brian is your best friend. You would die for him."

I stopped, taken aback because I expected her to rant and rave. She just stared at me with a grin on her beautiful face.

"It's one of the reasons I love you, you know. You'll do anything for those you love, even at the expense of your own damn health."

I smiled back. "You are in a sanctuary, you know."

She looked around. "God knows how impossible you are. He led me to you to straighten you out."

I held her and then moaned. She looked up at me. "But, after tonight, you will go home and rest, right?"

"Scout's honor."

She led me out of the sanctuary with her arm around my waist. "Were you even a Boy Scout?" she asked.

"For a few years."

We walked into the conference room. Darrin set up the projector as Kate held the cords for him. Zoe talked to Reg as they sipped coffee, and Father Neal fiddled with something I couldn't see.

"Hey, everyone, sorry, I needed a word with my beautiful girlfriend."

Zoe looked up and smiled. "Aidan! How are you feeling, dear?"

I grimaced. "I could do without the pain every time I move."

Reg came over and put his hand on my shoulder. "What did the doc say?"

"Bruised ribs. Guess the Grinning Man didn't want me dead yet."

Father Neal looked up. "Of course he doesn't want you dead. He wants you."

"He has a funny way of showing his affection. A card, flowers, and a long walk on the beach are probably the best way to get my attention."

Jen guided me to a chair. "Shut up and sit down."

I looked over at Kate, who looked like she would come apart at any second. "Kate, how are you?"

She gave me a thin smile. "I'm here, Aidan."

I nodded as Father Neal raised his hands. "Okay, everyone, pay attention. It's time to offer up our prayer."

He made the sign of the cross in the air. "In the name of the Father, the Son, and the Holy Spirit."

We all responded, "Amen."

He continued. "Father of Light, guide us, and protect us with Your sure hand. May our minds think Your thoughts. May our mouths speak Your words, and may our hands do Your work. Send Michael Militant to protect us and guard us from the ancient enemy. In the name of the Father, and of the Son, and of the Holy Spirit. Amen."

We agreed with an *amen* and looked up at Father Neal. He leaned on his cane for support, and his face was pale from some inner stress. He didn't look good, and I decided to stay after the review to check on him.

"Well, we had quite the interesting night."

I mumbled, "Understatement of the year."

"You all know what happened, except for what went on in the bedroom with Ashley. Jen and I will give a full account of that in a moment. But, before we do, Darrin and Reg, do we have any evidence?"

Darrin looked over at Reg, who stood up and walked to the screen.

"The interesting thing about this investigation is the seeming failure of the equipment later on in the night. I didn't think we would have much to review."

He paused. "Turns out, that's not the case."

Darrin clicked on the keyboard, and a video popped up on the screen. The camera view showed us the dark field as lights began whizzing over the ground. They filled the screen, giving us a psychedelic light show as they zoomed around.

"As you can see, these lights are forming patterns, breaking apart and forming again."

The video ran on for three minutes as we watched in silence. Reg motioned for Darrin to stop.

"Believe it or not, these lights went on for most of the night. We have hours and hours of footage, odd considering we thought the equipment had broken."

"What are they?" Jen asked.

Reg shrugged his shoulders. "I have no idea. I can tell you what they are not."

He took out a laser pointer. "They aren't car lights from any road. The nearest road that would provide this sort of activity is about four miles away. No amount of atmospheric conditions could give this sort of light reflection. It's just not physically possible. Even if it was, there would have to be a traffic jam of epic proportions on that road. Clear, so far?"

We nodded.

He pointed to the woods. "I'm pretty sure they aren't any sort of gaseous light. The field is very high and dry. No chance for swamp gas." He smiled, and everyone chuckled.

I raised my hand. "Am I missing something?"

Darrin laughed. "It's a common 'go-to' skeptical explanation for mysterious lights. Sometimes it works, but most of the time . . . not."

Reg continued. "Atmospheric discharge or some sort of unknown form of lightning is possible; I can't rule it out. However, two major things argue against it. Does anyone see the arguments?"

Jen spoke up. "I'm seeing the constant forming and reforming into patterns."

Reg smiled. "Good, and?"

"The clouds looked nasty, dark, and horrible. Yet we didn't have any storms all night."

"I checked the radar on my phone all through the night. No storms ever showed up on the radar."

"We have ruled out all the natural explanations. What else do we have?" I asked.

Reg shrugged his shoulders. "I have no idea. None of us really do. We have never seen anything like this."

I looked at Father Neal. "Surely, you have some idea."

He shrugged. "Some idea, yes. In England, we call these faery lights. They are present whenever the lines between worlds are thin."

Jen leaned forward. "What do you mean?"

"In folklore, when the faery folk enter our world from theirs, they are recognized by lights that are dangerous for mortals to follow."

"Uh, so, Tinker Bell and her cronies were dancing in the field last night?" Darrin chimed in.

Father Neal shook his head. "Faery, not fairy."

"What's the difference?" I asked.

"Sweet little impish fairies are a purely modern invention. The fae are, well, residents of another world. From the old tales, they are dangerous at best for humans to approach and sometimes, outright deadly."

"Okay, so what does that have to do with our lights?" I was getting impatient.

Father Neal motioned to Reg. "Well, I have a theory about that. I think the lights appear when something 'bursts through the veil,' maybe in this case the blonde women Aidan saw in his vision."

Jen furrowed her brow. "Reg, you are a scientist, and you are talking about the faery world?"

Reg shrugged. "I don't know anything about the faery world. All I know is quantum physics and some of the new theories concerning other worlds."

Jen raised an eyebrow. "Other worlds?"

"Yes, many physicists are beginning to theorize and find evidence for other worlds; worlds that may scrape up against our own."

"Seriously?"

Reg smiled. "Seriously."

"So, what, every time the veil between worlds is breached, there is a release of those lights? Then why do they go into formation?" I mused.

Reg paused. "I wish I had that answer."

"Has this happened in other places?"

"At a place nicknamed 'Skinwalker Ranch,' " Reg said.

"Where?"

"It's a place in Utah. A friend of mine did an investigation there a few years ago. Many of the things observed are very similar to what we are seeing here."

I nodded. "And let me guess, he had no explanation for them, either?"

Reg shook his head. "No, but we both have a theory that a great deal of energy makes all of this stuff happen, a burst of power, if you will."

"What else did we see?"

Darrin punched up the next video. Jen gripped my hand as we watched ghostly figures move in front of the camera placed in the barn. The body of a man with the head of a wolf walked through the field, looking left and right. The next figure looked like a huge hulking figure that reminded me of the blurred Bigfoot pictures on the Internet. Shadow images began to fill the camera field, and I couldn't make out any other distinct forms.

Reg pointed with his laser pointer. "Another similarity to Skinwalker, unexplained humanoid figures."

Darrin pulled up the next video as Reg said, "And this last video I find the most distressing and sad."

Before I could ask why, the audio came up. Loud, human screaming echoed through the conference room. On the screen, writhing ghostlike figures moved.

"What camera is this?" I asked.

Darrin found his voice. "The camera we placed in the house."

*Help us . . . free us*, said the voices. *She holds us . . . tortured . . . pain. Limbs broke . . . cut . . .*

All of us stared in silence at the pleading figures on the screen. Reg broke the silence. "I have no scientific explanation for any of it. There are only two times we've heard a direct appeal for help. Now"—he nodded toward me—"and when Amanda reached out to us during that whole mess."

"Thank you, Reg." Father Neal stood up and limped to the front of the room. A brown leather drawstring bag dangled from his hands. He set this down on the table as the light from the projector illuminated his heavily lined face.

"Now we have seen the evidence. It's time for me to fill in the gaps." He opened up the leather bag to pull out the knife and the doll. "Aidan and Darrin found these in the woods near the farm this morning. Aidan, explain your vision and what you found."

After I did, Zoe said. "So, whoever used the knife and doll spoke through Ashley the night before?"

Father Neal nodded. "So it would appear."

We all sat in silence until Kate broke in. "The Dark Bride. She was in the woods last night."

"I do believe you are right, my dear."

"I guess now we have to figure out who the Dark Bride is and where she came from," I said.

Father Neal motioned to Darrin, who switched off the projector and turned on the lights. "I think we can figure out where she might have come from." He picked up a marker and wrote one word on the board.

*Voodoo.*

"That is the key, everyone," Father Neal began. "The brand of magick the Dark Bride uses is some form of Voodoo. We have dead chickens, the veve, and the doll as evidence to that, along with some traces of Appalachian folk magick she probably learned from West Virginia or North Carolina. The voices in French are another clue. What locations in the United States have all those things in common? I think we can rule out Africa and the Caribbean islands."

Darrin typed on his computer and turned on the projector. Google maps came on the screen with the words *New Orleans*.

Father Neal nodded. "Yes, New Orleans."

"So, the Dark Bride is a Voodoo queen who has made her way to Ohio?"

Father Neal raised his hand. "She is a practitioner of a *form* of Voodoo, a twisted form. The woman is powerful; there is no doubt about that. In fact, there is only one female magician that would fit the bill."

"Who is that, Father?" Jen asked.

He paused for a moment. "That would be Marie Laveau."

Kate finally spoke up. "What, seriously? But she has been dead for a hundred years."

Father Neal nodded. "Yes, supposedly. I'm just telling you the facts. Marie Laveau was the most powerful Voodoo queen ever to practice and, indeed, one of the most powerful magicians ever known. She had the whole city of New Orleans in her grip for fifty years."

Images of New Orleans, Marie Laveau, Voodoo, and food ran through my head, then it hit me.

"Celestine."

Father Neal looked at me. "I think, my boy, we are going to have lunch Monday."

Kate broke in, "I just can't believe it could be Marie Laveau."

"Why not?" Jen asked.

"Her daughter insisted all the rumors about her weren't true."

"How do you know that?" Darrin asked.

"I read a biography of her. After Marie's death, her youngest daughter insisted that Marie died a Catholic in good standing, that she never practiced evil in her life," Kate said.

"Yeah, but what about those rumors that she sold her own people into slavery, owned a house of prostitutes, and encouraged women to sleep with married men?" Zoe asked.

Kate shrugged. "I don't know. Maybe she did all those things, and the daughter lied. I have no idea. If she is behind all of this, then maybe she did."

Reg turned to me. "What color was the woman in your vision, Aidan?"

I shrugged. "I couldn't tell. She wore a veil, remember?"

Father Neal said, "Well, we have enough to go on right now. Darrin and Kate, I want you to investigate Marie Laveau, Voodoo, and how they relate to the slave trade. We might be missing some link here. Jen, keep your ear to the ground at the station for anything unusual. Aidan, we go to Celestine's, sound good?"

We all agreed, and then he asked, "Is there any other evidence we should see tonight?"

Darrin jumped in, "Well, there is one picture that I wanted you all to see—a few, actually. I have been taking them all around town while doing a photo essay for *Columbus* magazine. At first, I just took them because I thought they were funny. Now, with this whole Grinning Man thing, I have been wondering."

He showed us pictures of smiley faces drawn on walls, park benches, and schools around Columbus. Each face painted in blood red. "Any ideas?"

Father Neal shook his head. "Anyone?"

No one responded, but Jen dug her fingernails into my hand. I looked at her, and she worked her lip like chewing gum.

"All right, we will keep those in mind. It might just be a vandal trying to make everyone smile by defacing public property."

Everyone laughed except for Jen, who almost drew blood as she gripped me harder.

"Go in peace, everyone. Let's meet back here as soon as we get the information we need."

I looked at Jen for an explanation, and a tear ran down her cheek.

# CHAPTER TWENTY-ONE

I LEANED OVER TO JEN AND WHISPERED, "WHAT'S WRONG?"

She didn't say anything as she stood and led me into the sanctuary. Her eyes shined in the light of the candles as she wiped away the tears.

"Those smiley faces, Aidan."

Her body trembled, and she wrapped me in a fierce hug. I held her for a few moments as I fought my guy impulse to fix everything. "What's wrong, love? They're just silly smiley faces."

She drew away from me and faced the altar. "No, Aidan, they aren't just smiley faces. They're something terrible, more terrible than you would guess."

I didn't know what to say, so I waited as I watched her struggle.

"You can tell me anything, you know."

She shook her head. "No, Aidan, that's just the point. Those faces . . . they relate directly to what I'm doing on the task force."

I walked up to her and gripped her shoulders. "Are you sure?"

She wiped away the tears. "I am."

"Is there anything you can tell me about them?"

She paused for a moment and said, "The smiley faces are a symbol for a group, or at least we think it's a group."

I had never seen her so messed up about something. Her whole body tensed as she fought for control of her emotions. "A group, based here in Columbus?"

She nodded and said, "Yeah, and most of Ohio."

"What does this group do? I'm assuming something really serious."

Jen covered her face with her hands. "You have no idea, Aidan. I never thought this crap happened on American soil. The videos and pictures I have seen. The conversations . . ."

She broke down and began to cry, her whole body shaking with grief.

"I have . . . I have been wanting to talk to you about it. Dying to talk about it. I want to clean my head of everything. But I can't, not yet."

Everything in me wanted to pressure her, to badger her to tell me. I wanted to know what she had experienced that had been so horrible. I wanted to fix it, but I needed to make a choice and think of what Jen valued most. She valued keeping her word. Even more, she valued bringing some sort of justice to the victims of whatever horror she'd been fighting.

I held her tight and kissed her head. "You don't have to tell me, love. I'm here whenever you need to talk about it."

She buried her head in my chest and cried. Then she looked up at me. "I love you, Aidan. I promise, the moment I can tell you, I will."

The smiley faces flashed in my head again, and I thought about the stone in Brian's field.

"Jen, do you think those smiley faces have anything to do with what's going on at Brian's farm? I mean, it's obvious when you think about it: smiley faces, Grinning Man."

She looked up at me, tears gone and the muscles of her face hardened. "I hadn't thought about that, but I don't know now."

I shrugged. "I just can't help feeling there is a connection somewhere."

Jen sat in a pew, and I joined her. Her brow furrowed in concentration. "I may bring you in on the task force work after all. I have to talk to Weaver. The problem is, it's not just him who has to approve. The FBI needs to give an okay, and I'm not sure how to do that just yet. The agent in charge, she is a bit, uh, hardcore about secrecy."

I nodded. "If there is anything I can do to help, I will."

She chewed her lip and held up fingers in a pinch mode. "We are this close to nailing these bastards. We just need one break, and the whole damn thing will come apart."

She stopped. "Sorry, I shouldn't do this to you. It's a horrible tease."

I smiled and hugged her to me. "I understand, babe. I'm done being the jerky, jealous boyfriend."

She leaned into me, and we enjoyed the silence of the sanctuary. "You know, I can see you here. This is your sort of place, I think."

I hadn't had much time to think about my impending decision whether to stay with Knox or join Father Neal. Jen's comment brought it rushing back with a vengeance. "You think so?"

"I do. You don't fit being a Presbyterian. I think you know that."

I nodded. "Yeah, I think I have always known it. I just tried too hard to fit in and worked to be the ideal Presbyterian."

"Because of your parents?"

"That's probably part of it. It's just the culture I grew up in and all that I knew. I fought hard to fit in, but it just never worked. I always felt on the outside because I saw things in a different way."

I paused as Jen sat up and listened to me ramble. "I mean, it's not that I think that Presbyterians are bad or terrible. I did think that for a while, you know."

She nodded.

"But not anymore. Father Neal was right in making me stay for a while. I couldn't make the decision to leave, at least not the way I felt. It would have been wrong."

She touched my arm. "And now?"

I looked up at the cross, the glowing candle under the monstrance that held the Body of Christ, and breathed in the slight incense smell.

"This is where I belong. I need the symbols, the visual reminders of Christ's Incarnation. I can't live in my head anymore."

"You know, that's the biggest problem I had at Knox. Everything seemed so stripped bare and brutal. There was no sense of holiness, of God's presence, or even any real joy."

I chuckled. "Well, not all Presbyterian churches are like that."

Jen smiled. "I know, I have been to Scotland. I guess my point is, it's nice to have the beauty to remind you of God's presence. Ever since I met you, my faith has returned, and I've been trying to figure out what to believe. I can't say I have changed my basic Catholicism all that much. I mean, I really need Jesus here rather than just in my head."

I pointed up to the monstrance. "Yeah, and the real presence of Christ with his people."

"You know, I think I have always believed. But meeting you, all of this, has made my faith in him so much stronger."

I looked at her and smiled. "Really? Even though I'm a cynical ass sometimes?"

She smiled. "You aren't cynical; you just haven't found your home yet." Jen motioned around the sanctuary. "I think this is your home and mine. We'll find out more about him here, I think."

I nodded as I looked up at the glowing candle, signifying the presence of God as it hovered over the tabernacle that held the communion hosts.

Her hand intertwined with mine. "So, will you take priestly orders?"

"What do you think?"

"I think yes. You were born to be a priest. God made you for it. And I can't think of a better teacher than Father Neal."

I gripped her hand. "Neither can I."

"When are you going to tell everyone?"

I sighed. "Not right now. Knox needs to figure out who their next pastor is going to be. I can't just leave them. Plus, I want all of this with Brian to be over. For some reason, I think it's going to get worse."

We sat for a moment until we heard the creak of the sanctuary door. A familiar clunk sounded in the aisle as Father Neal made his way toward us.

"Are you two okay?"

Jen got up and hugged him. "We are, Father, thank you. I just got a bit emotional about some things."

Father Neal crossed himself in front of the altar. "Yes, this investigation is troubling, my dear. In so many ways . . ." He paused and looked at her. "Or is it something else?"

"We both think . . . well, possibly, anyway, that Darrin's smiling faces are more than just a juvenile prank."

His face fell. "Of course. How could I not see it? The Grinning Man . . . stupid of me, really. I'm afraid I really am getting old."

Jen said, "Plus, those faces are related to a case I'm investigating. It's possible they are all tied together, but I can't say how just yet."

Father Neal nodded as he gazed at the cross. "Yes, they are related. I can feel it. Figuring out how will be our main goal."

He turned to Jen. "When can you tell us?"

"I have to check with Weaver and some others. I have to figure out how to make a case to bring you both on as consultants. Not exactly sure how to do that just yet."

Father Neal wiped his face with his hand. "I'm sure you'll think of something."

Jen and I looked at each other. I said, "Are you okay, Father?"

He smiled. "Late night and old age just don't mix well. I have been feeling it more and more, Aidan. My strength doesn't return after a good night's sleep, either." He paused before saying, "And that worries me for all of you."

"Why?"

"The Grinning Man. I'm afraid of him. I'm afraid for you. All of you. I don't know if I have the strength to fight him."

I stood up and gripped his shoulder. I noticed he didn't mention the Five Sorrows, but I couldn't figure out why.

"I'm here, Father."

His eyes searched my face. "So you have decided then?"

"I have. I'm ready to become a priest. I'll join you, if you'll have me."

"My boy, I have been praying for nothing else for the past six months."

I furrowed my brow. "And why didn't you tell me that?"

"Because, my dear boy, you had to make your own decision. I thought that would be obvious. I had no desire to influence you in this."

"I suppose you're right."

"Plus, the people at Knox needed you during this transition. No one else could have guided them through the turmoil with Mike."

Jen smiled at us both. "The two of you together. That's going to be interesting."

Father Neal chuckled. "As long as this stiffnecked boy bows his head in obedience, we shall get along fine, my dear."

I snorted. "Please, priest, I'll listen to everything you have to say."

Jen and Father Neal laughed.

"What?"

Father Neal rapped me with his cane. "You don't listen to anyone, boy. You are too headstrong."

I frowned. "Well, I try."

Jen kissed me on the cheek. "Sure you do."

We all left the sanctuary side by side. Father Neal walked us out into the night and I said, "What should I tell Brian?"

Father Neal sighed. "Tell him what we found. There is no need to tell him his family is in danger. That is something he already knows."

"And the Dark Bride?"

"I wouldn't tell him about that until we know more."

"Why not?"

Father turned to me. "Because the less he knows, the better. He is a man about to come apart at the seams. We need him to stay strong. If he knows all of this is happening because of what he did, it will probably break him."

"Good point. I'm just trying to get him to be on his guard."

Father Neal scoffed. "Don't you think he already is?"

"Yeah, but if there is a real person out skulking around the woods, I guess he does have guns."

Father Neal gripped his cane. "I don't think guns will kill the Dark Bride. Do you?"

"You tell me."

"I can't, not yet. I need more information."

I frowned. "I know you have some idea, Father. I can see the ancient gears whirring in your head from here."

He rapped my legs with his cane. "Show respect, boy, especially to the man who is about to become your spiritual head."

"Fine, tell me, oh fountain of knowledge, your esteemed guesses."

"I think the Dark Bride has undergone some sort of transformation."

"What sort of transformation?"

"That is something I don't know. But she is going to be older than you think."

"I don't understand," Jen said.

"Let me just say she might not have been born in this century or the last."

He let that statement sink in before he continued, "The knife, which I'm assuming belongs to her, is old."

"It looked brand-new to me," I interrupted.

"Yes, it looks that way, but it bears magickal marks that could have only been put there through long use of magick."

"What, the scrollworks on the knife? They looked new, too."

He shook his head. "No, my dear boy, invisible signs. Feelings and emotions. Too many for five or even fifty years to explain them."

"I don't know what to say to that," I said.

"Neither do I. So, let's be off to bed and rest. I need it," he said.

He gave Jen a kiss on the cheek and hobbled to the manse.

"As much as that man aggravates me with his mysteries, I love him."

Jen laughed. "And I think you are the son he never had."

I nodded as I kissed her. "Be safe going home."

She hugged me tight and whispered, "Thanks for understanding, Aidan."

I whispered back, "Anytime, love."

She kissed me, got in her car, and drove away.

I looked up at the church steeple and smiled as I remembered the first time I saw Saint Patrick's. I'd imagined the church as a dark, sinister place, out to get me, to bring me into the fold. The old church succeeded. It devoured me and I couldn't be happier.

I thought about the Order and Jen. She would need to know someday. At the same time, I couldn't tell her what I didn't understand.

As if to answer my thoughts, Father Neal came back out.

"Thinking of the Order, Aidan?"

"Yeah, and not to mention the Five Sorrows. Are they real? Just visions? Can you summon them at will?"

"No, you cannot. They don't respond to human commands, but they are bound to the Elder and the Order."

"Who is the Elder?"

Father Neal smiled. "All in good time. You're not a member yet."

"So, did they, the Five Sorrows come to me in the woods when I said 'behold'?"

"As to that, I'd say probably. They are responding to your voice now and recognize you. Someone's days in this world are coming to a close."

Father Neal embraced me. "I wish I could have spared you this life, Aidan."

"You keep saying that, but I'm not sure what you mean."

"It is a life of constant danger, not just of the body, but of the soul," Father Neal said, gazing up at the stars.

"Why are they here? I mean, yes, you said to fight evil, but that's kind of vague."

He looked at the floor for a moment. "That is not for me to say. You must hear it from the Elder, when it is time."

I sighed. "Fair enough. I have to keep my promises to Jen. You gonna be okay?"

"Always, my son."

# CHAPTER TWENTY-TWO

MY MONDAY MORNING BEGAN AS I SIPPED AT MY COFFEE AS BISHOP sniffed around in the grass. "Should I get you a magazine? Will that help?"

Bishop just kept sniffing, ignoring his owner's stupidity.

"What do you think, Bishop, ready to live up to your name and be an Anglican dog?"

He woofed and found his spot.

"About time, dude."

We walked back to the condo. I let Bishop wander more than normal because I wasn't in a hurry to get my day started. I wasn't looking forward to the round of interviews with Cole and the search committee. Unless Cole laid a big egg in the interviews, the conclusion wasn't in doubt. I couldn't even ask that many questions as moderator of the meeting, so my boredom would be guaranteed. Thank God I could play Angry Birds on my laptop or I would go crazy. Combined with taking Father Neal to Celestine's, I had a very strange day ahead of me.

I showered and got to the church around nine. After wading through some emails, I leaned back in my chair, sipping my second cup of coffee for the morning. I thought about my conversation with Jen from the previous night. Her eyes, her tight hug as she cried, and my conversation with Jen's father came rushing back to me. Protect her, he had said. I wanted to do just that.

It's time, I thought. I wanted to marry her. No more doubt.

The realization made me sit up. With everything going on, I hadn't thought I'd be searching for an engagement just yet. But now the desire overwhelmed me. There would be no getting rid of it, nor, I realized, did I want to anyway. I didn't feel giddy. I didn't feel a huge rush of emotion. I just knew it. I just wanted her there with me, never going home, never sleeping in another bed except ours.

"Hey, Boss, you okay?"

Cole had leaned against the doorframe, and I didn't even notice him. I shook myself out of my avalanche of thoughts. "Hey, yeah, just a lot on my mind."

"Such as?"

I smiled. "Oh, just thinking about Jen and our future."

He raised an eyebrow. "Our?"

"Yeah, just had the realization that I can't live without her."

Cole laughed. "It's amazing how long it takes for us guys to reach that sort of conclusion."

"Yeah, and we both have pasts, so maybe we made it more complicated than it needed to be."

I didn't want to reveal any more so I changed the subject. "Are you ready for today?"

He looked up and down the hall. "I'm scared out of my mind."

I couldn't quite believe it. Cole almost never admitted weakness or fear. Sweat beaded on his forehead, and he looked a little green.

"Are you going to make it there, bud?"

He swallowed hard. "I hope so. I'm trying very hard not to throw up right now."

I pointed to the chair. "Sit. Relax. Talk to me about it."

Cole sat and put his head down for a few moments.

I put my hand on his shoulder. "What's up, man? Tell me, are you afraid of the committee?"

He shook his head. "No, not at all. I just . . ." He gulped. "I just don't feel worthy to do this."

"What do you mean?"

"Being a minister. I mean, I feel like such a sinner."

I tried not to laugh. "I see, so you think that disqualifies you as a minister?"

He nodded. "I'm not pure, man. I struggle with sin all the time. I can't help it. There must be something wrong with me. How can I lead anyone in Christian morality?"

I sat back in my chair and realized what he needed.

"Cole, do you remember the passage where Jesus says that to look at a woman and want to have sex with her is committing adultery?"

He put his head in his hands. "Yeah, and it tortures me. It's so convicting."

"Yes, it is. However, there is something there you might not be seeing."

Cole raised his head. "What do you mean?"

"Think about it. Everyone who heard Jesus was pretty smug in their keeping of the law. They thought if they didn't actually have sex with someone other than their wife, they were pretty much free and clear to do whatever they wanted. And therefore sin-free, right?"

He nodded.

"And Jesus brings the hammer down and says, sorry, guys, if you even think about another woman in a sexy way, you are committing adultery. What is he telling them?"

I could see the lightbulbs turning on his brain. "That they are basically in a constant state of sin and that the heart matters as well as the actions."

"Yes. And why does he tell them that?"

"To make them let go of their pride and show them their need."

I smiled. "Exactly. In Saint Paul's words, their righteousness is shit."

He laughed. "Right."

"So, what does that mean for being a minister?"

Cole frowned. "That's my sticking point. I feel it disqualifies me."

I leaned forward and gripped his shoulder. "Cole, if you are disqualified, then I am, and every other person who ever stepped into the pulpit is disqualified." I pointed toward the sanctuary. "No one is qualified to stand there and lead the people of God. Yet He asks us to. For some unknown, mysterious reason, he chooses us to lead His people. If that thought doesn't buckle your knees in humility, there is something seriously wrong with you."

He didn't say anything for a while, but his muscles relaxed. He looked up and smiled. "Thanks. I take it you have been thinking about this for a while."

I nodded. "I wish someone had told me the same thing before I started. I hope it helps." I raised my hand. "I should warn you, though, you are taking up a heavy burden. Not just you, but your family as well. Are you ready for it?"

"I . . . I'm not, at all. But I am willing."

I smiled. "Now you have it."

Cole leaned back in his chair. "How do you think the interview will go?"

I laughed. "Cole, unless you go into that conference room, unbuckle your pants, and take a crap on the table, you'll pass with flying colors. They want to love you and you are good. Don't get cocky, just lean on Christ and you'll be fine."

He smiled. "Will you pray for me?"

"I will."

We bowed our heads in prayer until it was time for us to go to the conference room. The morning interview went very well. Cole answered questions like, "Tell us about your walk with Christ, and your personal prayer times." Once he settled in, he knocked each question out of the park. After the interview, I worked on administrative work until it was time to pick up Father Neal to go to Celestine's. I didn't have to park the car and get him from the manse. He was waiting on the sidewalk, dressed in full priest black and a white collar. I noticed the same brown leather bag he'd had with him at the evidence meeting.

He climbed in the car and said, "Well, my lad, are you hungry?"

"Yeah, I'm in the mood for some Cajun. Have you ever had it?"

Father Neal nodded. "Yes. I went to New Orleans for a priest conference a few years ago. Lovely people, but very strange."

"Yes, it's like its own world, barely a part of the States at all." I glanced at the bag. "So, I'm guessing that's the knife and the doll?"

"Don't ask questions, boy."

I sighed. "Old man, one of these days, you are going to have to tell me all your secrets."

He smiled. "One day. But that's not today."

"Frustrating old goat," I mumbled.

He chuckled. "Name-calling won't help you."

I changed the subject. "So, are you ready to take me on as your pupil?"

"More than ready, actually; the vestry is very excited about the idea. I think they are getting tired of the bleating of this old goat."

I shook my head. "I'm not coming to replace you."

He smiled. "So you think. God may have other ideas."

I frowned as I got on the ramp to the highway. "You aren't going anywhere."

"I'm old. I may not look it, but the effects of being in the Order wear on you after a while. I've earned my rest. And to be honest, I'm looking forward to it. I needed someone to take my place. And God sent you."

I shrugged. "I'm sure the bishop would have found someone."

He shook his head. "Not what I'm talking about, Aidan. There are other things, other roles you must fill."

"Let me guess, you aren't going to tell me those, either."

He didn't say anything for a moment as he stared out the window.

"Aidan, the past year, you have stepped into a larger world, wouldn't you say?"

"To say the least."

"Do you think you have explored the limits of that world?"

"No, something tells me I'm just a babe in the woods."

He shook his head. "No, you are a new fetus, just conceived."

"Okay, so what does this mean? Are you finally going to teach me magick?"

He gripped his cane. "No, absolutely not. But, you will be shown secrets . . . secrets you'd never believe. When you see the Five Sorrows again, you'll understand."

"Yeah, well, I think I'm past the nonbelief point after all that's happened."

Father Neal shrugged. "We shall see, my son."

We drove to Celestine's, and I parked the car. I looked over at him. "So, do you have a basic strategy for all of this? Questions you are going to ask? What we are looking for?"

Father Neal opened the door and looked over his shoulder. "Our strategy will be for the Holy Spirit to guide us. As to what we are looking for, hopefully we will find the Dark Bride herself."

I got out of the car and looked over the roof. "Do you really think Celestine is the Dark Bride?"

"Celestine will either lead us to the Dark Bride, or she is the Dark Bride. One or the other."

I frowned as we walked to the restaurant. "Maybe, but Celestine looks to have African American ancestry, Father. I have a hard time believing she would force her own people into slavery."

"It happened all the time in New Orleans. If she is Creole, like you said, thcy often owned their own slaves."

"Yeah, but, the hunting down of other slaves? That's another level of sadism, don't you think?"

He nodded. "That is the one possible flaw in my theory. I'll be honest, dear boy, I have no idea which road we will go down once we step into this restaurant."

We reached the restaurant and I put my hand on the door. "Well, we are about to find out, aren't we?"

# CHAPTER TWENTY-THREE

WE WALKED INTO THE RESTAURANT, AND FATHER NEAL STAGGERED A bit. I steadied him and whispered, "Are you all right?"

He gripped his cane. "Yes, magick."

I looked around for Celestine and didn't see her. A teenage girl chewing gum asked us, "Two?"

"Please."

She led us to a table under the huge portrait of Marie Laveau I had seen in my earlier trip with Cole.

"Will here work?"

I looked at Father Neal, who smiled. "That will be fine, my dear, thank you."

Her face broke into a huge grin. "Oooo, you're from England! I'm saving my tips for a trip next year. I love your accent."

"My dear, you'll love England, I'm sure. Thank you."

We ordered drinks, and she hurried away into the kitchen.

Father Neal gazed up at the picture, and I didn't interrupt his thoughts. He stared at her face for a while and said, "Well, there is no doubt about it."

"No doubt about what?"

"That Marie practiced magick."

I raised my eyebrows. "You doubted that?"

He shrugged. "No, but one has to be sure."

"How do you know?"

Father Neal pointed up to the picture. "She has the mark in her face."

I frowned. "I don't see a mark on her face."

"No, son, it's not visible to the naked eye. It's in her facial expression, a little wild, a little out of control."

I looked at him and said, "I don't see it in your face."

He smiled. "And you wouldn't. I don't practice anymore since I started serving Christ and became a member of the Order." He pointed with his cane. "Marie, at least when this portrait was painted, practiced magick on a daily basis."

I tried to see the markers he pointed out, but I couldn't.

"Well, whatever she did, she certainly was a beautiful woman."

"That she was, she stole the breath of many New Orleans admirers and made them full of jealousy, too," a feminine voice said from the direction of the kitchen.

I turned around and saw Celestine staring at both of us. Father Neal smiled. "I'm sure, and you look just like her, my dear, in so many ways."

She stared at him. "Is that so, Father?"

"Yes, that is so. The marks are all there."

Celestine gripped her pencil, and her knuckles went white.

"Why are you here?"

"To eat, of course. My good friend Pastor Schaeffer told me about this place and I, having been to New Orleans, had him bring me here."

Celestine forced a smile. "Well, we have the best Cajun food not in New Orleans, Father. What would you like?"

"I'll have the gumbo, please."

She turned to me, a look of cold fury on her face. "And you, Pastor?"

"Shrimp po' boy, please."

She stalked off to the kitchen and the lights seemed to dim. I glanced up and said, "I don't think she is happy we are here."

He shook his head. "Doesn't seem to be, does she?"

The other four diners looked up, and almost as if obeying a summons, walked out the door without finishing their food or paying their checks.

"Did you see that?"

He nodded. "I think we might have walked into a trap."

As if to confirm this, tables slid across the floor and blocked the door. The blinds went down on the windows, and the objects on the wall began to rattle. Lights darkened, and a wind blew from an unknown source. A deep female voice echoed all around us, *Who are you, Magician? Why are you here?*

Father Neal stood up, his hair whipping in the wind, and bowed. "I'm here because of what you are doing in this city. It's wrong and you must stop."

*I don't know what you are talking about, Priest.*

"I think you do, Madame Celestine. There are signs of Voodoo all over this city, and this restaurant is full of magickal marks. You aren't exactly hiding, are you?"

The voice cackled with laughter. *I have no wish to hide. I'm looking for a great magician, John Neal.*

"You have found him, my dear, but I'm no longer a magician. And why are you looking for me? How did you know I lived in Columbus, Ohio?"

The voice paused. *I was told.*

"Told?"

*By Madame Laveau.*

Father Neal looked puzzled for the first time. "You aren't Madame Laveau?"

The voice laughed. *No, Father, I am not.*

The lights went back on, the wind died, and Celestine came out of the kitchen with her hair sticking straight up. She looked about ready to tear apart her own restaurant. I tensed, but Father laid his hand on me.

Father Neal turned to Celestine. "But you look so much like her."

She smiled. "I'll take that as a compliment. My great-*grand-mère* was a beautiful woman."

Father Neal leaned on his cane. "Why are you here?"

"I am hunting, Father. But allow me to bring your food. I'll explain as much as I can."

She went over and turned the open sign to CLOSED. She locked the door and went back to the kitchen.

I said, "Well, that's different. Why do you look puzzled?"

"I thought . . ."

"You were about to have a magickal throwdown?"

He nodded. "That's about the measure of it, yes."

"If it's any consolation, I thought the same."

He looked confused. "I don't understand. Is this a game of hers? I'm almost positive she is the Dark Bride. There are too many signs for her not to be."

"Maybe she is."

She came out bringing three plates of food: Father Neal's steaming gumbo, a huge shrimp po' boy sandwich, and a muffaletta for herself.

"I'm going to be joining you, gentlemen, if you don't mind."

Father Neal looked at her. "By all means, my dear. We would like nothing better."

We all sat down at the table and looked at each other. Celestine smiled. "Father, will you pray for us?"

He nodded, obviously mystified. "Father of all that is good, bless our food and our conversation. Restrain the hand of the evil one who wants to destroy our bodies and our souls as we eat. In the name of the Father, the Son, and the Holy Spirit, Amen."

To our amazement, Celestine crossed herself at the end of the prayer. Father Neal's face relaxed, and his grip loosened on his cane.

"Now, eat, my lovelies. The food will get cold."

Father Neal smiled. "But I have questions, Celestine."

She lifted her sandwich and smiled. "I'm sure, Father. And I'll have answers, after we eat."

We finished our dinner, and Celestine daintily wiped her face with her napkin. She smiled and said, "Now, Father, you may ask your questions."

"Who are you, and where do you come from?"

"My name is Celestine Glapion, and I'm from New Orleans."

Father Neal prodded. "How long have you been practicing Voodoo?"

"Since my mother trained me, seventy years ago. She has since gone to sleep with her ancestors."

"I'm sorry."

She bowed her head. "Yes, she was a wonderful woman. Brave, loving, and hated evil. She died fighting during Katrina."

"Fighting?" I asked.

"Yes, it was a dark time for our city, Pastor Schaeffer."

"Call me Aidan."

She smiled and touched my arm. "Aidan, then."

Father Neal interrupted, "And why were you looking for me?"

"After the death of my mother, I visited Madame Laveau's tomb for guidance. My ancestors often have, when they needed guidance for the fight."

"And Marie spoke to you from the dead?"

She nodded. "She doesn't with just anyone, you know, only women sworn into her service."

Father Neal wrinkled his brow. "Her service?"

"Yes, Father, there are many women in her service in New Orleans, continuing the good works she did." She paused and shuddered. "And fighting the sisters who practice dark magick, slaves to the Hellfire Club. Madame Laveau discovered their presence, their local chapter, and how it corrupted the city. They now hold the city in an iron grip, as all of us have been chased out. Only the church stands against the darkness there."

Father Neal nodded. "Then why are you here? Is it because of the Dark Bride?"

She set her jaw. "That is one of her names, yes."

"Why do they call her the 'Dark Bride'?"

"She has given herself willingly to the Hellfire Club, who gave her to the Grinning Man a long time ago. The Bride used to be called Morgan Wedig. She came over as an indentured servant with the first colony at Roanoke."

"Wait, the Virginia colony that disappeared?"

Celestine grimaced. "We've got every reason to believe Morgan destroyed it when she met the servant of the Nephilim, or the Grinning Man, as you call him."

"Then what happened?"

"We know bits and pieces. She would move with him to different towns, start chapters, and move on. The one in New Orleans became darker than most, and at one time, Madame Laveau, in her youth, participated in their rituals."

I held up my hand. "Listen, you two, I think I'm missing huge chunks of a story here."

Celestine nodded. "Yes, *mon amour*. From the beginning, I think."

"Please."

She took a drink and frowned. "I think we all are going to need something stronger."

Celestine walked into the kitchen, and Father Neal looked at me with a smile. "It appears, my boy, you are witnessing a rare event."

"And that would be?"

"Me being wrong."

I scoffed. "Please, Priest, I have witnessed that event too many times in the past six months, especially with your obscene love for soccer."

Celestine retuned with a bottle of red wine and three glasses. "Yes, Celestine takes care of her men. Drink, *mes amours*."

We drank as she scooted next to me. Her warm skin touched mine in the closeness of the booth, and I reminded myself that I loved Jen.

"Now, allow me to tell you a story that will bring understanding." She pointed up at Marie Laveau. "My *grand-mère* practiced Voodoo, Father. This you know."

He nodded.

"While she was drawn to the Hellfire Club, she discovered their horrific intent early on. Madame Laveau never practiced the dark elements of Voodoo, contrary to popular opinion. She always sought to help, heal, or soothe, never to curse, unless someone practiced evil. Then she could be . . . formidable."

Father Neal took a sip of wine. "Of that, I have no doubt."

"Many people in New Orleans came to her for help, guidance, and instruction. Wealthy people, influential people and even, much to the shock of everyone in that century, white people."

"White people came to her?" I asked.

"Yes, *mon amour.* While my *grand-mère* always worked for the good, she was a shrewd woman. Many think she worked magick to accomplish everything, but she rarely did. All she did was keep an open eye and open ear. She learned many secrets that enabled her to serve the good."

"How so?"

She smiled. "White politicians and businessmen would often try to enact measures that would rape the poor. But she knew their secrets and would often use them to her advantage."

I chuckled. "Clever woman."

"Yes, no need to use magick when information will serve."

Celestine twirled her glass. "So many lies have been told about Grand-mère. She was a good Catholic all her life and laid down her Voodoo practices after . . ."

She grimaced and Father Neal grabbed her hand. "After what, my dear?"

"After the Dark Bride betrayed her and seduced Marie's daughter, my aunt."

"Go on."

Celestine took a deep breath. "A powerful and wealthy French woman came to her one day, asking to be taught the ways of Voodoo. Her name was Dalphine LaLaurie."

He looked at Celestine. "What happened when Madame LaLaurie approached Madame Laveau?"

Celestine frowned. "Many bad things, Père, but none of them my *grand-mère*'s fault. Madame LaLaurie was beautiful and persuasive. She convinced Marie that her intentions were honorable, so the training began. Soon after, slaves began disappearing all over the city, politicians no longer consulted my *grand-mère*, and the whole thing began to unravel. Marie began to suspect that Morgan, the witch who had hidden herself in our city, was behind it all. Sure enough, she had begun to delve into the dark side of Voodoo, using it and making it look like Marie's work. Both of them wanted to frame my *grand-mère*."

She took a sip of wine. "So she visited the LaLaurie mansion one night and found . . ."

She shuddered, and Father Neal said, "Found her experiments?"

"*Oui*, she and her husband, a dark and mysterious figure, had been experimenting on slaves, horrible experiments like breaking limbs into unnatural angles, crude sex-change operations, and removing the skin from a woman's body in slow, agonizing strips."

She took a deep breath again. "Marie knew Morgan had finished Madame LaLaurie's training after Grand-mère had stopped. She had used the pain and blood of her slaves to open the dark regions to increase her power."

Father Neal nodded, and I understood what I had seen last winter. The pain and suffering of others was used to empower dark magicians.

"So she helped a slave woman start a fire in the kitchen of the house, so that firemen would look through the whole house, exposing Madame LaLaurie to chase her out of the city. In the dark of the swamps, Marie killed LaLaurie by drowning her."

Celestine looked up at Marie's picture. "Morgan went underground in New Orleans and continued her dark work, pinning on it on my *grand-mère*, who went to Père Antoine to renounce Voodoo. She became even more committed to the Catholic Church and spent her life battling Morgan, the Dark Bride. She formed a group of women who swore to fight the Dark Bride's works. But unknown to Marie, her daughter, Marie the Second, had been seduced to the dark arts. It broke her heart when she had to kill her eldest daughter near Bayou Saint John one fateful evening."

She sighed. "My great-*grand-mère* realized that the Dark One, whom you call the 'Dark Bride,' wasn't aging at all. She figured out that the Dark One had discovered a way to live, if not forever, longer than my great-*grand-mère* could. So she passed on leadership of her group to her youngest daughter, my grandma, with the charge to watch, fight, and hunt down Morgan, wherever she may go."

Celestine drew herself up. "I am now the leader of our circle. It is for this reason that I am here in Ohio. She has come back to her old hunting grounds with her husband."

Father Neal leaned in. "Do you know the identity of her husband?"

She shook her head. "No, other than that she must be keeping him alive in the same way."

Father Neal and I looked at each other as I said, "I think it might be the opposite, Celestine." I told her everything about the Grinning Man and the events of the past few days.

She sat back in her chair. "Who is the Grinning Man?"

We both shrugged as I said, "We have no idea, other than that he is someone who has haunted the history of our country in one way or another."

She crossed herself. "An unholy union."

Father Neal nodded. "To say the least."

"I still don't get why she and the Grinning Man are here torturing my friend," I said.

Celestine took a drink of her wine. "Yes, that is the question, isn't it, *mon amour*."

"You mean you've been tracking her all this time, and you don't know how she chooses her victims?"

She frowned. "I might practice Voodoo, but that doesn't give me knowledge of her secret plans."

Father Neal smiled. "So, was it you with the chicken heads, trying to get my attention?"

She nodded. "I figured I needed a big blast, as I had no idea where you might live. I found the most magickal place I could, at the foot of that mound, and performed the ritual. Did you feel it?"

"No, but thank the Lord, Aidan's girlfriend is a Columbus police detective."

She looked at me. "You have *un amour*, Aidan?"

"Yes, I do."

"And she is the *amour* of your life?"

I nodded. "Yes."

Her face fell. "Of course."

I tried to change the subject. "So, the ghost of Marie Laveau told you to find John Neal in Columbus, Ohio?"

"Yes. I had no idea he was a priest. Sometimes Marie doesn't give complete information. But I found him. That is all that matters."

Father Neal finished his wine. "I'm sorry that I suspected you, my dear."

She waved her hand. "Perfectly reasonable, Père. I can understand why."

We sat in silence for a moment, and then I looked at my watch. "Great. I have to run. Father?"

He looked at Celestine. "My dear, do you mind talking to an old man for a few more hours? There is much that I wish to know."

"As my mission was to find you, Père, I think I have all the time in the world."

He brought out his bag. "Then maybe we can discuss these." He took out the knife and the doll.

Celestine gasped. "Where . . . where did you get these?"

I told her about the woods. "Do you know what they are?"

"The doll, yes, is an influence object. The knife is . . . it is hers, Père. It is her object of concentration and how she uses her power. I cannot believe you have this."

"Nor can I, my dear. It is a mystery to me that I can't figure out."

"And the Grinning Man led you to this?"

I nodded.

"It must be a trap of some kind."

"Yeah," I agreed. "We kind of figured that. But, would Morgan willingly give this up?"

She shrugged. "She may not have had a choice, if this Grinning Man is as powerful as you say. Without it, her power is wild, uncontrolled and unfocused. There's no telling what might happen next. She'll do anything to get it back, if he allows her."

"I hate to sound like a broken record, but we still haven't figured out why Brian and his family are at the center of all this. Why the Dark Bride latched on to them."

Father Neal looked at me. "You'd better go, Aidan. Pick me up after the meeting. Celestine and I will try to figure things out."

I nodded and went to the door. As I glanced back, I caught Celestine staring at me with a sad expression on her face.

# CHAPTER TWENTY-FOUR

I TRIED TO FIND SOME ORDER IN THE JUMBLED EVIDENCE AS I DROVE back to the church. We knew a lot—and nothing. We knew that the Grinning Man and Morgan, the Dark Bride, were behind everything on the farm. We knew about Celestine and her secret order of dark magick hunters. We knew about the history behind everything. But the thread that would bind all of them together remained hidden.

What could it be? The slavery issue obviously contained the key, but I couldn't make head or tails of it. Slavery had been abolished through a long and bloody war. I knew that slavery existed in other parts of the world, but I highly doubted it found its way back to our shores. Morgan obviously had a thing for torturing and enslaving her fellow human beings. Brian had most likely brought all this on through erotic Internet chat, but I couldn't see why she would torture him to this extent.

I sighed as I pulled into the church and saw everyone had already arrived. It seemed as if everyone had been anxious to get started as soon as possible. I wouldn't be the least surprised if the committee voted to recommend Cole to the congregation tonight.

I walked into the building. Elder John was there on the couch, as if he had been waiting for me.

"Pastor Aidan, how are you? Did your dinner renew your strength to do the Lord's work?"

I smiled. "Yeah, John, it did. I had Cajun at that new restaurant in Franklinton."

He frowned. "The wife and I tried that restaurant last week. Too many pagan symbols on the wall, especially that evil witch, Marie Laveau."

I made light of his comment. "Ah, John, by all real accounts, she was a good Catholic woman who didn't practice Voodoo later in life."

He made a face as if being a Catholic might be worse than practicing the dark arts. I let that pass as I asked, "What can I do for you, John?"

"I have something burdening my heart, Pastor Aidan, and I need to speak to you about it."

"Come in, we have a half hour before our meeting with Cole."

He came into the office and sat down. I sat at my desk and waved him on. "So, what's on your heart?"

"Well, Pastor Aidan, it's come to my attention you spend a lot of time with a Catholic priest."

I smiled. "He isn't Catholic, John. He is Anglican, high church, but Anglican."

"Yes, well, that's somewhat better. Can you tell me the nature of your relationship with him?"

I frowned. "He is my friend, John, and has become something of a mentor for me lately. Is that a problem?"

"I would prefer to see you seeking out the counsel of some of our ministers in the presbytery. I think they would be more suitable to be your mentors."

"And why is that?" I didn't bother to hide the disgust in my tone at his questioning.

He shifted in his seat, "Well, I'm sure that Father Neal loves the Lord and means well. But he just isn't Reformed."

"How do you know?"

"Well, he is Anglican. He wears robes, makes the sign of the cross, and kneels during prayers, yes?"

I nodded. "That he does. Even more shocking, he uses candles, too."

He shook his head. "I'm not the only one concerned, the whole session is, even Bill."

I leaned forward. "What exactly do you object to, John? Father Neal is one of the godliest men I have ever known. His commitment to Christ is without question."

He put up his hands. "Oh, Aidan, I didn't mean . . ."

"Yes, John, I think that's exactly what you meant. You are trying to question Father Neal's integrity because of his commitment to Anglicanism, aren't you?"

"I . . . well, no, but I think he is in error to commit to a church system that is broken beyond repair."

I stared at him. "And how do you figure that?"

He shifted in his seat again. "Well, I mean, he reports to one man, a bishop."

"We report to a group of men, John, it's called a presbytery."

"Yes, but, the power is not in one man's hands, less room for abuse that way."

"And the presbytery and elders don't abuse their power?"

I had him, but he wouldn't admit defeat. "Well, they do, of course, but checks and balances are better."

"Says who?"

"The Bible."

"Does it?" I hammered away at him. "It seems to me the Bible speaks of a pastor to pastors, one man, watching over the ministers of local churches, someone who is above petty congregational disputes. I'm positive it doesn't always work the way it's supposed to, but I sure like it better than what we have."

The words spilled out of my mouth before I realized what I had said. John stared at me with a shocked look on his face.

"Pastor Aidan, are you saying you are questioning our system of government yourself?"

"I am, John."

He shook his head. "It seems as if we didn't go deep enough when we counseled you about your crisis of faith. It has warped you into this."

"John, you are right, my crisis of faith led me to this point, of that you can be sure."

He looked at me with eyes full of sadness. His heart was full of genuine concern for me. I still wanted to hit him.

"John, I can assure you, my faith in Christ is stronger than it has been in my whole life. That is not what is at issue here."

"Then what is, Pastor Aidan? Tell me how I can help you."

I came out from behind my desk and sat down near him. "I don't feel the need to be helped. My crisis is not of faith, but of practice, of trying to figure out the nature of the church."

He was stunned. I knew what whirred through his brain right now. How could Aidan Schaeffer, son of a famous reformed Presbyterian theologian and a pastor himself, be saying such things? Despite myself, I felt sorry for John. I'd rocked his world. What if I told him about the Five Sorrows? I think he would need adult diapers.

"Pastor Aidan, I don't think you can be the minister here much longer."

"I know, John. Father Neal has offered me an intern position at Saint Patrick's. After the call to Cole, I will announce to the congregation my desire to be Anglican and study for the priesthood. But I'll make you this promise: I will not utter a word about my convictions to anyone here until that announcement. I'm not going out in a blaze of glory."

He shook his head. "It makes me sad, Pastor Aidan."

"I know it does, John, but there is no need. We're still on the same team, after all."

"Yes, I suppose you are right."

I knew that had cost him everything to say. "John, let me tell you, I have always been wrong about you. I know your heart is always on Christ and what he wants. I didn't appreciate that very much for a long time, but now I do."

He nodded, tears in his eyes. "I just don't understand why, Pastor Aidan."

I sighed. "John, I just see the Presbyterian and the larger evangelical world as broken. We keep running after one trend or another. We need something larger, more historic, and more grounded."

I spoke in language he would get, even though my reasons for becoming Anglican ran much deeper. When it came down to it, the supernatural element in my life of the past year had utterly convinced me of Christ's power in a bishop-run church. The proof, as Father Neal loved to say, had been in the pudding.

John sighed. "So be it, Pastor Aidan. I think I always knew you would leave, but for entirely different reasons. I figured you would try to get your own pastorate somewhere."

I smiled. "And I still might, John. I still might."

He nodded. "Do you want to tell the other elders yourself?"

"Yes, I would prefer that, if it is acceptable to you. I want this transition to be smooth for Knox. The Lord knows this body of believers has been beaten to a bloody pulp. They don't need me to mess with the waters just as things are looking smooth."

He gave me a weak smile. "That means another search committee. Can I tell you, in complete confidence in the Lord, that I dislike these meetings immensely?"

Shocked, I said, "Wow, John, I never thought . . ."

He chuckled. "I am human, Aidan. There are times I would rather be at home watching *American Pickers* than sorting through pastoral résumés."

I laughed. "Sorry about that. Maybe you can get Bill to replace you."

"Possibly, although thanks to the blessed invention known as DVR, I haven't missed a show."

We stared at each other for a moment, and then John said, "Well, we should probably get in there and finish the job."

I nodded. "Go for it. I'm going to grab some coffee."

He left and I stared after him. I hadn't planned to blurt out my Anglican plans like that, but I didn't regret it one bit. God does work in mysterious ways, and maybe he figured the time had come. Whatever it had been, I felt good, as if a huge weight had been lifted from my shoulders. I had finally said aloud what I had been feeling and thinking. My life had begun to change with Amanda's murder, and I felt the process coming to an end.

I smiled at the thought. Everything was starting to fall into place. I knew I wanted Jen for the rest of my life. I knew I wanted to be a priest. The direction I had missed for so long finally had come into sharp focus. The path stretched before me, and I would walk it.

I walked into the kitchen humming "Mysterious Ways" by U2 and poured some coffee. I thanked God that our congregation contained coffee snobs who always bought good coffee for the church. I needed the shot of concentrated energy to get through this meeting.

My phone rang right before I stepped into the conference room. I looked down and saw it was Brian.

"Hey, bud, are you okay?"

I heard a shuffling and a man sobbing.

"Brian, are you there? What's wrong? Did something happen?"

"Aidan. I—"

"Brian, slow down, I can't understand you."

"Lily, Aidan, Lily—"

Chills ran up my spine as I gripped my coffee cup. "What about Lily, Brian? Is something wrong? Where is Ashley? Did you see more lights?"

"Gone, Aidan. Lily is gone."

# CHAPTER TWENTY-FIVE

**"WHAT DO YOU MEAN? IS SHE HIDING?"**

"No, Aidan. I have looked everywhere, even outside. I can't find her."

I clutched the phone. "Then call the police."

"I can't, Aidan, Ashley is having some sort of . . . attack."

I looked into the conference room, and everyone had arrived. Well, if anything qualified as a pastoral emergency, this did. I caught John's attention and motioned to him.

"Okay, Brian, sit tight. Keep Ashley safe from hurting herself. I'll call Jen and have her send out a squad. I'll be out as soon as I get Father Neal."

"Hurry, Aidan. Please hurry."

I hung up the phone as John stepped into the hallway.

"John, there is an emergency out at Brian and Ashley's farm. Lily has gone missing."

He looked like someone had struck him.

"Missing? I don't understand."

I shook my head. "Neither do I. Hopefully, she is just hiding in a closet somewhere. But, I have to go."

"Of course, we will pray for her and for you. I'll take things from here."

I gripped his arm. "Thanks, John, for trying to understand everything."

"Pastor Aidan, there are many things I don't understand, so I rely on the Lord to lead and vouchsafe our future."

I grinned. "Amen, Brother."

I ran out to the car, dialing Jen as I jumped in. The phone rang and I got her voice mail. Damn. She must be in a meeting. I texted her.

"Need police help. Emergency."

As I drove to the restaurant, Jen called. "Where is the fire?"

"Lily is missing."

She paused for a moment. "You are fucking kidding me."

"I wish I were. And Ashley is having some kind of an attack, so Brian is trying to keep her restrained. Can you have a squad go out to the farm?"

"Yes, of course. I'll go out there myself."

"Good. I'm picking up Father Neal. I think the shit has finally hit the fan."

"I think you're right there. I really think my case and Brian's stuff is related."

"Oh? Can you share?"

"Soon. Weaver is talking to the FBI people about letting you in on the investigation. But I can tell you, I'm scared to death."

"That makes two of us."

"I love you, Aidan. I'll see you at the farm."

"I love you, too." I hung up the phone and drove like a mad man through the streets of Columbus. I figured that Jen would get my ticket fixed if a cop pulled me over. I got to the restaurant in record time and ran inside.

Father Neal sat at a table surrounded by some of the most beautiful women I'd ever seen. Besides Celestine, two redheads with flowing ringlets down to their shoulders, a beautiful dark-skinned woman who looked Middle Eastern, and a short, blonde-haired woman with glowing blue eyes encircled the good father as they all stared at him with adoring eyes.

Despite everything, I couldn't help but laugh. They all turned to me, and Father Neal smiled. "Ah, Aidan my lad, you are early. Meet the Daughters of Madame Marie Laveau, the twins, Brigit and Aislinn."

The redheads gave me a cute curtsy.

"And Aisha, from Lebanon."

She regally inclined her head.

"And, of course, Emily, who I must say, is a bit of a firecracker."

Emily smiled and said, "Oh, Father."

"Everyone, this is my son in the Lord, Aidan Schaeffer."

I found my voice. "Hey, I wish I had more time to talk."

Father Neal stood as he looked at me. "What's wrong?"

"Lily has gone missing, Father, and Ashley is being attacked again."

The air went out of the room as the girls all frowned.

"Then we must go," he said.

He turned to the girls. "It has begun; you know this."

They all nodded.

"Please find out what you can, and then meet us at the farm. Something tells me we will be there for a while."

As we started to walk out of the restaurant, he paused and turned back to Celestine. He reached into his bag and pulled out the knife.

"Keep this safe for me, my dear. And use it if you need to, do you understand?"

Celestine smiled like a Cheshire cat. "With pleasure, Père."

He raised his hands over them and they bowed their heads. "May Michael Militant uphold you and the power of the Three in One protect you."

Father Neal limped out with me. I turned to him. Despite the fear I felt about Lily, I had to ask, "So, having a good time in there?"

He smiled, stretching the lines in his face. "They are lovely and delightful girls." Then he frowned. "And dangerous, most dangerous."

"Why?"

"They have dedicated their lives to the killing of one person, the Dark Bride. In doing so, they have explored magick more than they should have. All of them are older than you would think."

"How old?"

He frowned. "I can't be sure. At least as old as I am, even if they don't look it."

I made my way onto the highway and gunned the engine. "That's what I don't get, Father. The Grinning Man, Morgan the Witch, and the girls, how do they keep being young?"

He frowned as he stared out of the window, his favorite pastime when riding in my car.

"There are many ways, all of them unnatural at the very least, downright horrible at worst."

I felt my skin crawl. "You don't think the girls have done . . ."

Father Neal shook his head. "No, my dear boy. They have other means, Voodoo means, that aren't nearly as horrible. Unnatural, but there are levels."

"So Morgan . . ."

"Given what we know of her history, she most likely either kills or uses dark magick to extend her life."

"Do you think that is why she took Lily?"

His knuckles went white as they gripped his cane. "Let us hope not, my lad, let us hope not."

I pulled into the farm. Jen stood outside a patrol car, talking to two uniformed officers. As we got out of the car, Jen ran up to me. "Brian wouldn't let us in until you got here."

I nodded as I gave her a quick kiss and ran up to the porch.

"Brian, it's Aidan, I have Father Neal and the police. You have to let us in, bud. Come on."

Brian opened the door and I gasped. Blood oozed out of five long scratches on his face, and his lip had swollen like a bloated worm.

"Brian, what the—"

He whispered, "Ashley. Upstairs."

Jen took Brian to the couch, and Father Neal and I made our way upstairs. We could hear whispered screams and words: "No. Why? No . . . you said. You said."

Ashley moaned and laughed with a voice not her own. *What I said and what I do are often two different things. And now, you will pay.*

The sounds of cracking bones, Ashley's high-pitched screams, and breaking furniture assaulted our ears. I busted down the door. Father Neal, face full of fury, raised his cane and commanded, "Come out of her, in the name of Christ!"

Ashley flew back into the wall, writhed against it and crumpled to the floor. She looked up at me, face pale and full of horror. "Aidan . . ."

I ran to her and gently picked her off the floor. She moaned softly. "My girl, my precious girl is gone."

I laid her on the bed and smoothed out her dress. I found a blanket and covered her.

"Aidan, Lily is gone. They took her."

Father Neal kneeled down at the bedside. "Who took her, my dear?"

She struggled and stuttered. "I c-c-can't. They won't let—"

He nodded and put his hand on her brow. "It will be all right, my dear. Rest." Behind his back, he motioned me to the door. I went out into the hall and he followed. "We are missing something."

"What the hell are you talking about? "

He shook his head. "I don't understand why Ashley is so affected. Her torment should be over."

"I'm not sure I follow. I mean, Brian did something bad on the Internet and now they are attacking his family. Seems pretty simple."

"Yes, so it would seem."

I looked back at the door. "You aren't convinced?"

"No, not at all. Brian's actions played a part in this, I have no doubt. But there is something else." He sighed. "I need you to call Darrin, tell him to go by the church, get my 'house kit,' and bring Kate with him. This is going to be a long night."

I heard Jen and the cops talking to Brian downstairs.

I dialed Darrin and he answered, "Yo, Preacha, you interrupted my Halo tournament this evening. This better be good."

I told him about Lily and what Father Neal said. "Damn. I'll be right out, Aidan. I just have to get Kate. I'll see you in thirty minutes."

"Thanks, bud." I hung up. "He is on his way. Are we going back in there?"

Father Nealshook his head. "I never go into the room with a woman alone, especially one in Ashley's condition. It is why I took Jen with me the other night."

"Good thinking. Is there anything I should do?"

"Let's find out together."

We went downstairs and saw the officers taking Brian's statement. Jen motioned for us to meet her on the porch.

"Well, what did he say?"

She frowned. "If it wasn't Brian, I don't know that I would believe a word he is saying."

"Why?"

She shook her head. "It might just be the trauma, but his story doesn't line up in some places."

"What do you mean?"

"He said that he put Lily to bed at seven and went down to work on some things. He went up to check on her at eight and she wasn't in her bed."

"That sounds pretty straightforward to me."

She nodded and then frowned, her scar stretching down to her chin. "Yeah, but it's the next half hour that I can't account for."

"What do you mean?"

"He called you at about eight thirty, right?"

I looked at my phone and said, "Yeah, eight thirty-two, actually."

"Then what was he doing for half an hour?"

"Looking for Lily?"

"But how long would that take?"

"It depends. Maybe he looked over the whole farm."

Jen looked skeptical. "Maybe."

"You obviously think something else."

"I think he went in and accused Ashley of something. They got into a fight, but he is leaving that part out. He just said she went crazy and he had to restrain her."

All three of us looked in the house as I voiced our fears. "This isn't a JonBenét Ramsey situation, is it?"

She shook her head. "I have no idea, Aidan. But we have more squad cars on the way. This is no longer a private matter. It could get messy, you know."

As I digested that, a light flared in the field beside the house. I ran to the edge of the porch. "What the hell?"

We watched as the light danced in the field, making some sort of pattern.

"What is it doing?" I asked.

Father Neal replied, "Delivering a message, I would guess."

Jen shook her head. "You know, the day you two came into my life . . ." She grabbed both our hands.

More squad cars began to pour into the farm.

"I need to go and brief everyone before we start a thorough search," Jen said. "Aidan, when we are ready, can you help?"

"Is that allowed?"

She nodded. "I'm allowing it as the ranking officer on scene."

"Darrin is coming. Do you want him as well?"

"The more the merrier," Jen called over her shoulder.

I looked out at the field.The light had disappeared.

"So, now what?"

Father Neal sighed. "I have no idea. I don't know if this is the Grinning Man or the Dark Bride."

"Do you think they are split on this?"

"Yes, I think so. I think he gave us her most prized possession."

"Can she still do magick without it?"

"Yes, but it's more uncontrolled and less focused, remember? Plus, I think that knife had, ah, sentimental value to her."

"Why do you think he is doing that to her?"

He gave me a grim smile. "I think that is the way he operates, don't you?"

"I guess. I just don't see why."

He nodded. "That is what we need to figure out. Brian and Ashley's involvement in this is no accident."

"What do you mean?"

"I can only guess, but I'm thinking this is about you, Aidan."

I gripped the rail. "I guess. Just seems like an elaborate plan. If he wants me, he could have killed me in the woods."

He frowned. "Well, I'm sure it's not all about you. It seems the Grinning Man has interweaving plans. Besides, he doesn't want you dead. I told you that."

"What is happening to Brian and Ashley is my fault?"

"No, my lad. When Brian opened himself up, it gave the Grinning Man an opportunity."

"You think he monitors my friends that closely?"

"I have no doubt."

Chills ran over my body in spite of the soupy heat.

"As I have told you, Aidan, there is much for you to learn."

Jen shouted from the driveway. "Aidan, come here."

I walked to join her.

"This is Pastor Aidan Schaeffer. Yes, we are dating, but that's not relevant to this investigation. He is best friends with the victims and knows this farm like the back of his hand. I want you to listen up as he tells you where to conduct your search."

I nodded and stepped up. "Ladies and gentlemen, this farm has been here for a long time. There are a lot of hidden places on the grounds, some wells, and places in the woods where a little girl might go. To begin, the house has an extensive cellar that you must investigate. Again, lots of hidden nooks and crannies."

Jen pointed to two women officers. "Strong and Donne, take

the house. Bottom to top sweep. Keep your eyes out for *anything*. Do not go into the master bedroom, where the mother is. I'll take care of that myself."

She gave me a look and I took over. "The grounds contain a barn, an old chicken shed, and a few wells. You'll see the well coverings. Lily shouldn't have been able to get in those, but it doesn't hurt to check."

"Simko, Ro, Hoover, and Hermann, search the grounds. Note everything unusual, out of place, no matter what it is. Got it?"

They nodded and went toward the barn.

I pointed to the field and the woods. "We are going to need a whole team out there. In the woods, there is a foundation for an old cabin. There used to be another farm here, so I don't know if there is a hidden well somewhere. I hope to God not, but just be aware."

Jen looked at the six uniformed cops remaining. "The rest of you, hit the field first and then the woods. Stick together. No wandering off on your own."

The cops went out to the field and started to climb the fence.

"I hope the Grinning Man doesn't decide to show up," Jen said as she stared out to the field.

"So do I, although, Father Neal is here."

Jen chewed on her lip.

"What's wrong, love?"

"I'm pretty sure someone took her, Aidan."

"I know."

She frowned. "I think we are going to have to pull Brian's chats."

"I wondered about that."

She grimaced. "It won't be pretty, you know. You might find out things about him you would rather not know."

"I already know some of it, love."

Jen fiddled with my shirt. "I don't want to have to do that, but I may have no choice."

"The important thing is finding Lily; that's all that matters."

She nodded as a tear rolled down her cheek.

"Is there something else?"

"This is how it started with my ex, Aidan. He got busted in an Internet sting operation, by thinking he was going to have sex with a fourteen-year-old girl."

I hugged her. "I'm not sure I follow, love."

"Brian."

"Well, he didn't have cybersex with a teenage girl. They were all of age, I think."

"So we would hope."

My skin crawled at the thought. "Come on, Brian wouldn't sell his daughter."

She shook her head. "You can't know that for sure, Aidan. Something else is going on here, other than Brian getting fired for participating in erotic chat at work."

My shoulders slumped. "I know."

"Until I know more, Aidan, Brian is a suspect. I just wanted you to know that. I know this is hard, and you are hurt badly." She touched my ribs.

"I'll be fine. Just never would have suspected in a million years he would get himself into this sort of trouble."

She caught my arm. "No one does. Everyone has secrets; some are just worse than others."

I stared into the living room, where Father Neal prayed with Brian. "I just hope Brian's secrets aren't in the worst category."

"So do I. I hope he is not connected to"—Jen hesitated—"to what I'm investigating on the task force."

"It's related?"

"Well, the crime certainly might be, although I hope to God it's not."

I felt sick. I started to get an idea of what Jen might be investigating. Something that had to do with sex on the Internet and its illegal boundaries, boundaries I never wanted to explore even in my worst nightmares, much less in the life of my best friend.

# CHAPTER TWENTY-SIX

**IN THE LIVING ROOM, BRIAN HELD A FROZEN BAG OF PEAS TO HIS LIPS.** I sat down next to him. "Jen's people are searching the grounds. Hopefully, we are going to have something soon, Brian."

He nodded, staring off into space. Father Neal and I looked at each other.

"Brian, is there anything else you want to tell us?"

He looked at me. "What do you mean?"

"Look, there is no one else here but me and Father Neal. You know what I'm talking about."

He grimaced. "Aidan, that stuff stopped two months ago when we moved here. I don't even go on the Internet to check sports scores anymore."

"Jen is going to have to check your computer, if we can't find Lily."

He nodded.

"She is going to have to talk to your chat site and pull records."

He nodded again.

"And you have nothing else to tell us?"

He took the frozen peas and threw them at my head. "Aidan,

my daughter is missing, and you are kicking my ass over something I stopped doing months ago."

I threw back the peas. "Well, asshole, your actions 'months ago' have probably caused your daughter to go missing."

He got up out of his chair, and I did the same. Brian balled his fist, and I braced myself for the punch. Father Neal leaped up faster than I thought possible and stood between us.

"Boys, that's enough." The authority in his voice stopped us both as we glared at each other.

"We will not find Lily by both of you trying to prove what men you are."

Ashamed, I dropped my head. "I'm sorry, Brian."

He nodded and sat back down.

Darrin came through the door, bringing Father Neal's bag.

"Hey, Father, I came as soon I could. Kate is talking to Jen."

He looked at Brian. "I'm sorry about Lily, man."

Brian mumbled, "Thanks."

Kate came in the door and Father Neal said, "Come, Kate, we have no time to lose. Upstairs, please."

When Father Neal put his foot on the stairs, we heard screaming from Brian and Ashley's room. The voice echoed throughout the house.

*Stay away, Priest, if you know what's good for you. She's mine. They're both mine.*

Father Neal crossed himself and turned to Kate. He reached into his bag for holy oil and dabbed some on his fingers. Kate bowed her head as Father Neal made the sign of the cross on her forehead, hands, and breastbone, saying, "May Christ guard your mind, your hands, and your heart."

The screaming grew louder as they climbed the stairs.

*Damn you to hell, Priest, take your little whore and go! You're not welcome here.*

I watched them disappear into the darkness and said a silent prayer.

I turned to Brian. "I'm sorry, bud, I was just trying to tell you what's going to happen."

He nodded. "I understand."

Jen poked her head in the door. "Aidan, I need you, please."

I looked at Brian who continued to stare out the window. His reaction bothered me. I couldn't tell if shock or guilt had short-circuited his brain.

I leaned toward Darrin. "Watch him, will you?"

He nodded. "Not a problem."

At that moment, another scream came from the room. *Get your damn Jesus away from me. Bastard son of Mary, filthy son of a bitch whore. I know you, Priest, I know you. I know what you did.*

Darrin and I both crossed ourselves without thinking. I went out onto the porch. The moonless night prevented me from seeing very far. Jen ran up to me and grabbed my arm.

"They found something in the woods I want you to see."

"By the cabin?"

She nodded and walked me off the porch. The light from her flashlight played along the ground as it guided us to the fence. I stared at the woods and paused.

Jen looked at me. "What's wrong?"

I gave her a weak smile. "The last thing I want to do is go back in those woods."

"I'm sure."

I took a deep breath and climbed over the fence. I held up my hand and helped Jen down. She held on to my hand as we walked to the woods.

"Do you know what we are going to see?"

She shook her head. "No, I don't. Officer Strong found it, and she sounded near tears. I changed her orders to search the woods. Glad I did."

I nodded, feeling a lump in my throat. My ribs ached as the painkillers wore off.

I found the path easily enough, and we wound our way back to the cabin. A patrolwoman stood silhouetted in the dark.

"Detective, is that you?"

"Yeah, Julie, it is. I have Pastor Schaeffer with me."

"It's over there, right in the middle of the hearthstone you all found."

I went numb as I knew what would be there: another message from the Grinning Man.

Jen shined the light to the middle of the cabin, and I saw a glimpse of something pink. Horror gripped me as I ran to the object.

Please, God . . . please, God . . . please, don't let it be Lily, please.

I took a deep shuddering breath of relief when I didn't see a little body lying on the ground. Instead, I saw a pink bear—Smokey, Lily had named her—and a blue blanket.

"Damn it, it's hers."

"Are you sure?"

I snapped back, "Of course I'm sure. I'm the godfather to that little girl, and she's like my own daughter."

Jen rested her hand on me. "Easy, Aidan."

I nodded, taking deep breaths. "I'm sorry. I just . . ." I couldn't hold back the tears running down my face. I went down to get the bear and Jen grabbed my arm.

"No, Aidan. There might be fingerprints. We can't disturb anything."

She turned to the patrolwoman. "Julie, go get some tape, cordon off this area. Grab one of the others and stay here until I relieve you."

"Anything else, Dectective?"

"Yeah, call Lieutenant Weaver. Tell him to send out the Major Case Squad. I'll run point for the investigation."

Julie Strong nodded.

"If he objects, just tell him I think this is related to our case. He'll understand."

Officer Strong ran off into the dark, and Jen turned to me.

"Do you think he has her?"

"There is no doubt about it, is there?"

She shrugged. "I can't say for sure. Maybe she wandered out here and left these things."

I frowned. "It's possible, but I doubt it. Way too much of a coincidence for me, don't you think?"

Jen put her hands on her face. "Yes, it is."

She rested her hand on her gun. "I don't know how to investigate this, Aidan. I can't tell my people to look for a magickal man running around the woods."

"No, you can't. There is another possibility."

"Oh?"

I told her about Celestine and our conversation about Morgan.

"You think she was one of the women Brian had cybersex with? Still presents problems with what I can tell my team."

"Yeah, it makes the most sense. Can't exactly say, 'Look for a six-hundred-year-old woman who looks like she is in the prime of her life.' "

"We're going to have to get Brian's computer records. Do you think he'll give them up willingly?"

I knelt on the ground, looking at the blanket and the bear. "God, I hope so, Jen. Otherwise, it means he's more involved in this than I want him to be." I looked around in the dark. "Hard to see if there is anything else here, isn't it?"

She nodded. "We are going to get the floodlights out here. Forensics is part of the squad."

"Does the squad always get called out for missing kids?"

She shook her head. "No, but I have good evidential reasons for doing so. Weaver won't question me, especially since I told him this is part of our task force investigation."

I sighed. "Are you going to be able to tell me about this task force now?"

She nodded. "You do realize one of the reasons I didn't tell you was to protect you, right?"

"No, I don't understand."

She stared off into the woods. "You have so much on your mind, with your job, all the darkness you see there, that I didn't want to add this weight to your shoulders."

"Ah, the old discussion of you making decisions on what is best for me without talking to me first."

She smiled. "Yes, that's exactly what I did. Plus, I couldn't tell you anyway without Weaver's permission."

"Now you have it?"

She nodded and took a deep breath. "I was talking to him when you called. What I'm investigating is—"

Her radio crackled. "Detective Brown, something really weird happened here."

She replied, "What is it, Officer Ro?"

"Ma'am, you just need to see it to believe it."

I said, "Let's go, you can tell me later."

We ran along the path as fast as my bruised ribs would allow. Panting, Jen asked, "Ro, what's your position?"

"Top of the barn, ma'am."

"What the—" Jen muttered as we raced alongside the field, climbed over the fence, and ran toward the barn. We hit the barn door and climbed up the rickety ladder to the loft.

I gasped for breath as my ribs radiated pain with each breath.

"Where are you?" Jen shouted.

A muffled response came from above us, "Up here, ma'am. Go through the hole in the roof at the left side of the attic."

We found the hole and wiggled our way through. Ro stood on the roof staring over the field. Jen and I concentrated on making our way to him so we didn't slide off the edge.

"What is it, Ro?"

He pointed out to the field. "Look."

We glanced out to the field, and Jen gasped. She nearly lost her balance, and I had to steady her. I gazed at the field. A huge smiley face, carved into the half-grown corn, glowed in the night with a faint greenish light.

"The lights," I whispered.

"What?"

"Earlier, the lights came back to the field. I could tell they were drawing something, but I lost interest once I got in the house."

She grabbed her radio. "Strong, did you get hold of Lieutenant Weaver?"

The radio crackled. "Yes, Detective. He is on the way to the farm."

Jen responded, "Tell him he needs to bring the FBI agent, too."

Ro and I looked at her.

"I need you to go down and help direct traffic. Things are about to get really busy here."

"Yes, ma'am."

Jen waited until Officer Ro climbed through the roof and we heard him making his way down the ladder.

"The FBI, Jen?"

She nodded, taking a deep breath. "Are you ready to hear? I'm warning you, you might wish you hadn't."

"I think I have to now."

Jen sighed. "Yes, I think you do. That thing is why," she said, pointing out to the field.

As we stood on the roof, we stared out at the dark fields as flashlights bobbed in the dark. The night air was thick with humidity and I took a few deep, calming breaths. She grabbed my hand and our fingers intertwined.

"How much do you know about modern-day slavery?"

I shrugged. "I know about the work of International Justice Mission."

"What do you know?"

"I know they free people from slavery situations around the world and raid brothels where women are held against their will. I listened to a talk by their founder a few months ago on a podcast. I sent them some money."

She nodded. "Yes, they do most of their work overseas. Do you know what area has one of the highest sex-trafficking rates in the world?"

"No."

"Here, in Ohio, or rather, the wider Midwest."

"What? You can't be serious."

"I would never joke about this, Aidan."

I looked down. "Sorry, I know."

"A few years ago, the FBI conducted a raid in Toledo as part of a nationwide operation known as Operation Cross Country. Hundreds of people were arrested and numerous children were freed from prostitution."

The words *children* and *prostitution* in the same sentence made my stomach tighten.

"As a part of that sting, the FBI became aware of a larger network, but I have not been able to break them."

"Let me guess, they use a smiley face as their symbol."

Jen's face hardened. "Yes, that's exactly what they do. They use it to mark their territory all over the Midwest, rubbing it in our faces."

"Why the Midwest?"

"The economy, Aidan. Girls are easy prey here, especially single moms who have to fight to keep roofs over their heads and food in their kids' mouths. Or high school girls who are fleeing poor and abusive homes. The pimps offer them love and then trap them. There is no way out for them, and they are sold as sex slaves."

I had to sit down, otherwise I would have fallen off the roof. That grin in the middle of the field had now taken on the sinister aura of the Dark Mark, the Death Eater's brand of a skull and snake, in Harry Potter.

"Dear God, Lily . . ."

"That's what I'm afraid of, Aidan. So afraid, I feel like I'm going to throw up. I have to go down there and lead, but dear God, I don't want to."

Jen sank down next to me on the barn roof and leaned into me. Her warm body pressed into mine as I held her tight. She began to shake with sobs.

"It's just like . . . just like Joe, my ex-husband. I had to do this, Aidan. I had to."

I nodded and kissed her head. "I know, love, I know."

We sat there for a moment as Jen let it out. I felt like crying for Jen, for Brian and Ashley, for Lily, for all the girls trapped in this shit. Deep down, I knew the Grinning Man stood behind all of this. The slavery stuff, Morgan's sadism, it all lined up. Were there reasons for anything he and the Dark Bride did? Or did they do it for pure thrill of pain in others?

I paused. No, the Grinning Man wasn't the only one responsible for the slavery part. Jen said it was a bigger network, something more moneyed and protected.

Jen sat up and wiped her eyes. "I'm sorry, Aidan. I have wanted to tell you for so long."

"Honey, you don't have to apologize."

She stared at me. "Are you okay?"

"Why do you ask?"

"You have a scary expression on your face."

"I'm pissed off. For a long time, I have been afraid of the Grinning Man. Now, I just want his head on a platter." I winced. "And my ribs are on fire."

She nodded, never taking her eyes off my face as she gently touched my chest. "Shall we get to work?"

"By all means. Let's kick this thing's ass and save Lily."

# CHAPTER TWENTY-SEVEN

WE WENT BACK DOWN TO THE FARMYARD. ALL THE OFFICERS HAD ASsembled near the porch. The crying and vulnerable Jen became an ass-kicking cop as she issued orders.

"All right, people, listen up. We have the Major Case Squad on the way, as well as the FBI. As you can guess, this is more serious than a child wandering from her house."

They all nodded.

"I need reports. What did we find, other than the belongings in the woods?"

"Nothing in the basement or the rest of the house."

"Did you find anything unusual in the child's bedroom?"

"Yeah, we found an open window in the middle of suffocating June weather, in an air-conditioned house."

Jen wrote that down. "Good. I want you to rope off that room and guard it until Forensics gets here, got it?"

They agreed and left.

"We already know about the woods and field. What about in your search of the grounds? Find any footprints?"

Officer Simko spoke up. "No, ma'am. The ground is too hard, probably."

Jen looked skeptical. "There had to be something."

"No, ma'am. I looked under the little girl's window for a long time. Nothing. No broken bushes, no broken grass, nothing."

Jen looked mystified. "That makes no sense at all. Even if Lily climbed out herself, there had to be some sort of mark."

Simko shrugged. "Yes, ma'am, I don't understand it."

"Okay, thanks."

She wrote it down, and only I could see her hands shake.

"Now, people, I need you to set up a perimeter around the farm. No one gets in or out of here without my permission, got it? Let in Lieutenant Weaver and the FBI when they get here. No press."

"What if they start clamoring for information, Detective?" Simko asked.

"Tell them someone will talk to them at eight in the morning, no sooner, got it? Tell them we have a missing girl and that time is important. Hopefully, they'll understand."

"Command post, ma'am?"

"The front porch, until the Major Case Squad gets here with their command unit. I'll be in the house running point. Officer Simko will be the guard on the porch, got it?"

Everyone nodded, and Jen continued. "If any of you talk to the press about anything you see here, your asses are mine, do you understand? There are a lot of lives at stake, not just Lily's. One screwup will destroy thousands of hours of hard work. You'll feel my wrath if that screwup comes from any of you, got it?"

They tried hard to hide their smiles. I could tell they all loved Jen and were used to her threats. But she wouldn't hesitate to carry them out.

"Good." Jen nodded. "Now get to work. Report anything unusual."

They all scattered to their posts, and she turned to me. "Why are you smiling?"

"You are kinda hot when you're all authoritative and stuff."

She smiled. "As long as you think so."

A scream came from inside the house, and we both quickly turned. "Guess we should get back in there," I said.

We found Brian curled up on the couch, staring into space.

"How long has he been like that, Darrin?" Jen asked.

"Since you left. I tried to talk to him, but I'm getting no response."

I heard more screaming from Brian and Ashley's room. "Jen, I think I need to go up there."

She nodded. "I'll stay here with Darrin."

I made my way up the stairs and saw Officer Hoover standing guard at Lily's bedroom door. Ashley was still screaming, and his face had gone white. I put my hand on his shoulder. "Brandon, right?"

He whispered, "Yes."

"It's okay. Father Neal and Kate are experts. They can help."

He nodded as I walked down the hall. I could feel something push against my chest, a force I hadn't felt since Serpent Mound.

*No, damn it. No, I don't want the prick in this room. No more ministers. No more Nazarene-lovers. No!*

I said a prayer and the force lessened. I pushed against a blind wall and made my way to the door. With a grunt, I opened it.

Ashley lay on the bed, bound by restraints so she couldn't hurt herself as she thrashed. Candles lit the room, illuminating Father Neal and Kate praying at the foot of the bed. I shut the door and they both looked up.

Ashley let out a loud, cackling laugh. *Hellllo, Aaaidan, why don't you—*

Father Neal held up his hand. "Silence, in the name of Christ."

Ashley acted as if she had been slapped, but she didn't utter another word.

"I take it things aren't going well," I said.

Father Neal got off his knees and hobbled to me. He took me into the corner. "No, not at all, my son."

"Is she possessed?"

He shook his head. "No, sadly. If she was, it would be easier to take care of."

"Then what is it?"

"Magickal influence, and that is what troubles me."

"Why?"

"She would have had to open herself up to it at some point."

I gripped his shoulder. "What?"

"Such influence can't happen against a person's will. It has to be allowed somehow."

"Okay, but how?"

Father Neal looked at Ashley. "I have no idea. I do know it's not Ashley speaking to us."

"The Dark Bride?"

He nodded. "She has spoken in French several times."

"What did she say?"

He sighed. "She wants the knife back, of course. She said, *Give me the knife and I'll return the girl.*"

"Then we give it to her."

Father Neal shook his head. "No, Aidan. She wouldn't give Lily back, and the situation would be much worse."

I looked at Ashley as she leered at me and rolled her tongue along her lips. Sweat ran in small rivulets down her face and her hair stuck to her skull in blood-red ringlets.

"Ashley gave the Dark Bride influence in her life?"

"So it would appear."

"You sound skeptical."

Father Neal frowned. "I don't know what to say, Aidan. I can only give you guesses from the evidence I see."

"Okay."

We stared at the bed as Ashley let out a long, hair-raising, maniacal laugh. *You, you fucking priests. All the same. Child molesters. Hypocrites. At least I'm open about exploiting children. Lily will fetch a good price.*

A *whoosh* filled my ears, and I began to see red. I went for the bed, and Father Neal grabbed my arm. "No, Aidan!"

I shook off his arm and stared into Ashley's eyes. They turned black as she smiled. The spirit in Ashley said, *Hello, sexy. You are a strong one; no wonder my lover wants you.*

"Tell your lover he might as well give up. I'm going to hunt him down and destroy him, got it?"

She laughed, *This from the boy-wannabe-priest who didn't know his own faith a few months ago? I'm sure my lover will be trembling in fear.*

She spat in my face and I wiped it off.

I raised my hands with palms facing her.

"Let Ashley go, in the name of Christ."

Anger rose in her black eyes. *No, she is mine; she is ours; she said so.*

"I don't think you heard me; I said in the name of Christ, let her go. I want to speak to Ashley. Now." My voice echoed in the room as a rushing wind whipped around me.

Ashley screamed and the voice said, *I'll be back, boy . . . I'll be back.*

I couldn't figure how I'd cast out the spirit, and Father Neal didn't.

The candles flickered and then went still. Ashley moaned and said, "Aidan, Aidan, where am I?" She pulled at her restraints. "Why are my hands tied?"

"For your safety," Kate said from the bottom of the bed.

"My safety? What happened?"

Father Neal limped to the bed. "Do you remember anything?"

"No, not really. Just bad dreams, bad dreams of Lily being missing."

We looked at each other, and Ashley's eyes widened.

"What? What is going on?"

"Ash, Lily is missing. Someone took her."

Her face crumbled as if someone had punched her. "No, God, no, please no."

She cried in racking heaves as Kate unbound her straps. When Ashley had her arms free, she clung to me. I forced down the revulsion I felt at her touch. I reminded myself that the leering maniac had departed. . . . For now.

"Did Brian call the police?"

"Yeah, Jen is here with a squad. More reinforcements are on the way. Don't worry. We'll find her."

She sobbed and curled up in the bed. "Please, Aidan, find her. Save her."

"I will, Ashley, I promise."

I motioned to Father Neal, and we went out into the hall. I whispered, "Are you going to find out what she knows?"

"I'm going to try. But it will be difficult."

"Why?"

"Because if we say anything wrong or ask the wrong question, we could invite Morgan to reestablish the connection."

"It's that strong?"

"Yes. I figured it would break now that we have the knife and doll. I guess not."

"What would that mean?"

Father Neal fingered the wooden cross around his neck. "There are many possible explanations, Aidan. The connection is stronger than I realized. We must find out how she extended the invitation."

"Any ideas on how?"

"Not yet." He frowned. "The FBI is on the way? Why?"

I looked down the hall at the patrolman, who looked the other way. I whispered, "I'll explain more later, but there is more going on here than simple family terrorism. We have stumbled on a major work of the Grinning Man."

"Yes, I think so. I wonder what the Daughters of Laveau will be able to tell us."

"That is a good question. When are they supposed to report?"

"Tomorrow night."

"I hope that's not too late."

Father Neal gripped his cane. "Me too, my lad, me too."

# CHAPTER TWENTY-EIGHT

I WENT BACK DOWNSTAIRS TO SEE BRIAN BEING QUESTIONED BY JEN. HE answered in a monotone.

"No, I didn't notice anything wrong when I put her to bed. The windows are always locked."

Jen leaned forward. "From the inside?"

Brian nodded. "And I always check them. Lily has a bit of an adventurous side, so I'm always afraid she will try to crawl out."

"Could she have unlocked the window herself?"

Brian thought for a moment. "No, I don't think so."

"Thanks, Brian. We're doing everything we can, okay?" Jen said.

She motioned for me to go with her on the porch.

"What's up?" I asked.

"I don't think he did it."

"Why?"

She chewed on her lip. "Well, for one, the way he is answering the questions. He keeps talking about Lily in the present tense."

"I don't get it."

She looked out at the driveway as a huge mobile command center made its way to the house. "Sometimes, suspects will be tripped up in their use of simple grammar. I have had murder cases cracked wide open because the perp used past tense verbs to refer to the victim."

"Makes sense."

"But . . ." She paused.

"What?"

"How am I going to explain this to Weaver? A woman who should be dead, going around taking children? He isn't going to buy it."

I folded my arms. "No, probably not."

"I wish I could spare Brian the investigation, but I can't. The wheels are in motion."

"When do you think they will summon the computer records?"

Jen played with the scar near her lip. "Probably right away, once I tell him the situation. My first order of business is to take him up on the roof. That's the biggest piece of evidence at this point, that and what the bear and the blanket show us."

"Couldn't you have a look at both of their computers?"

Jen nodded. "We have Brian's, and he gave us access to all of his email accounts. I'm about to ask Ashley for hers."

I furrowed my brow. "I don't know if that's possible. When I left the room, she had passed out from exhaustion. Do you really need them now?"

"Yeah, we can at least pick up her computer. I can always get the passwords when she wakes up. We have other fish to fry," Jen said, glancing back inside.

I nodded as we watched the command center park. The door opened and a muscular marathon runner, Lieutenant Scott Weaver, dressed in jeans and a golf shirt, made his way toward us.

"Aidan. Jen. This better be more than a missing child case. I was on a very hot date with a Brazilian model."

Jen walked down and said, "Come with me."

They walked to the barn and Darrin came outside.

"I feel kinda useless right now, Preacha."

"Yeah, me too."

I gripped the wooden porch rail and stared out into the night.

"Are you doing okay?" he asked.

"As well as I can be."

Darrin leaned on the rail beside me. "Is Kate okay up there?"

I gave him an encouraging smile. "Kate is doing just fine. She is stronger than either of us, you know."

He laughed. "Oh, believe me, I know."

We stood in silence as we watched the police bustle around us. Jen and Weaver came out of the barn at a slow run.

"Schaeffer, get your ass in the command center. I need you," Weaver shouted.

I patted Darrin on the shoulder and ran down to the command center. I opened the door and stepped into a hive of activity. Every person in the center wore street clothes, called in while off-duty, as they set up for the investigation. A blonde female detective hooked up her computer to a projector in the middle of the center. With a few furious clicks on the keyboard, she brought up the Google satellite images of the farm. I caught snatches of conversations as I followed Weaver to the front of the RV.

". . . is this just a missing child case?"

"Not really sure why we are here . . ."

They all looked at me with questioning glances. I realized that I didn't know many of Jen's fellow detectives. It made me wonder if she talked about me at all.

Weaver raised his voice. "All right, people, settle in right now. We are going to have a briefing, and then we are going to get to work."

He motioned to me. "Ladies and gentlemen, this is Pastor Aidan Schaeffer. He has consulted with the department on a few cases, and this farm belongs to some friends of his. Plus, he is godfather to the little girl. I want him to point out the important features of the farm in a few moments, so you all can go over it with a fine-tooth comb." He paused. "Now, I'm going to tell you the main reason you're out here late at night."

Weaver nodded toward the blonde detective, and with a few clicks she brought up a PowerPoint presentation.

"What I'm about to tell you people is classified. If any of you leak this, you'll be fired. Is that clear?"

His brutal, straightforward honesty shocked me. I was used to passive-aggressive church discussions, where everyone hid his or her real meaning.

I looked around and could tell the warning hadn't been necessary.

Weaver continued, "Now, quick chain of command. I'm in charge of the command unit, but Detective Brown is in charge of the investigation, got it? We're going to be running a liaison with the FBI as soon as they get here."

I noticed a few eyebrows raised. Weaver nodded to the blonde detective again, and she clicked on the next slide. The words *Operation Underground Railroad* appeared on the screen.

"Now, as you know, Detective Brown and I have been part of a secret joint task force that I'm sure has been the subject of station gossip everywhere."

Everyone chuckled.

"Well, what was hidden, I'm about to reveal to you."

He pointed up to the screen. "Operation Underground Railroad started four months ago to fight a large sex-trafficking ring. We've every reason to believe their headquarters is right here in Ohio."

A dark-haired detective raised his hand and Weaver said, "Johnson?"

"Sir, is this related to the rings in Operation Cross Country?"

"We found out about it during that sting, but investigative efforts have been slow in coming. At first, we thought this group might just be an urban legend. However, the more the Cross Country task force interviewed pimps and victims, the more we realized the bust of two years ago had only scratched the surface. From everything we learned, a secret group using a smiley face as their calling card is running things." He nodded to the detective who brought up a painted smiley-face image.

"Sir?" asked a female detective. "How do we know this isn't just kids being stupid? I mean, a smiley face isn't exactly very scary, is it?"

Jen and I looked at each other. I'm pretty sure we had the same thought: if they only knew.

Weaver gave a thin smile. "Detective, trust me, there is nothing scarier than a smile. It can conceal so many things." He paused. "Besides, there are numerous examples of child sexual abuse-rings using signs of innocence to mask the horror. This sign is how we learned about the group in the first place. Take it from me; they are real. Consider it a gang sign, a way to mark their territory."

Everyone nodded.

"You are probably wondering how this applies to this case. I'm going to let Detective Brown take over."

Jen shot me a sideways glance and stepped up to the podium. She gave them a rundown of that evening's events and paused before saying, "This is what we're going to need."

Everyone took out notebooks and iPads, ready to take notes.

"First, we need Forensics to investigate the smiley face in the field. I want to figure out who made this face, how, and why. Second, I'll take a few of you to the site in the woods where we found the bear and the blanket. I want a thorough search of the area in a two-hundred-yard radius around the site. Take note of anything unusual or out of place. Third, I want a complete set of Internet usage records for Brian and Ashley, especially records of any chats they might have had."

Everyone looked up at that and a redheaded detective raised her hand. "Are the parents suspects?"

Jen said, "They are until we prove otherwise, as usual. However, there might be other possibilities that come from the chat records. I want that as a private report to me and Lieutenant Weaver, is that understood?"

They all nodded.

"And fourth, I need a full forensics sweep of the house, especially Lily's bedroom. We need to issue an Amber Alert as soon as possible."

She looked at all of them and said, "Listen, I don't think I need to give a dramatic speech here. You all know a little girl's life is at stake. Time is not on our side with these people. They're like ghosts. We have been investigating them for months, and this is the first time we have been able to catch them at the tail end of a kidnapping. Not only can we save Lily, but we could also save the lives of hundreds of other girls. So, let's get to it. Aidan, can you give us the layout of the farm?"

I stood up and used the map to point out the features of the farm. They all took notes without asking any questions. I sat down and Lieutenant Weaver said, "Thank you, Aidan. Now, people, let's get to work. Move."

Everyone launched into activity, pulling out cell phones, sending emails, and then going out into the night. Weaver, Jen, and I sat down at a table to wait for the information that would pour into the command center.

"So, you two, tell me, how are the parents reacting?"

Jen said, "They're out of their minds, to put it bluntly. Ashley has lost it and is under the care of Father Neal right now."

Weaver grunted. "To be expected, and Brian?"

"Nearly catatonic," I said.

Weaver played with his pencil. "Do you think either of them had something to do with this?"

Jen didn't look at me. "I think it's possible, Lieutenant. I think the chat transcripts will help us on that score."

Weaver turned to me.

"Do you think either of them is capable of giving Lily to these people?"

I wiped my face with my hands. "I wouldn't have thought so, Scott. These people have been my friends forever, almost my family, really."

To my surprise, Weaver gave me a sympathetic look. "I know,

Aidan, it has to be hard. Can you handle helping us on this investigation?"

I looked up. "Do you mean, can I put away my personal feelings completely? No. But I'll do anything to save Lily. If her parents have compromised her safety, I'll fulfill my vows as her godfather. Is that enough?"

"It is. Do you have any other information that would be useful?"

My mind pored over all the supernatural events, and I tried to figure out a way to explain it to him. I had no idea whether Weaver believed in God or the supernatural. I decided that once I started, I wouldn't be able to stop. I decided to wait.

"No, there's nothing right now. Jen knows everything I know on the personal side. She might be able to give you a more objective view of things."

"Thanks."

I looked at them both and said, "What do you want me to do?"

"Stay with Brian and Ashley. Monitor them. Let us know of anything unusual. We need to keep track of them, know what they are doing, and how they react to any news. When Ashley wakes up, get her passwords. That'll save time getting a court order," he said.

"Should I tell them about the bear and the blanket?"

Weaver shook his head. "No, not yet. I want Forensics to go over those in depth, okay?"

I nodded and stood up. "I'll get right on it."

Weaver looked at me and said, "Oh, and prayers on our behalf wouldn't hurt, Pastor."

I smiled. "That can be done."

# CHAPTER TWENTY-NINE

**I WALKED BACK TO THE HOUSE AND MET FATHER NEAL ON THE PORCH.** "How is Ashley?"

Father Neal sighed. "She is asleep, for now."

"Any more ideas on how the connection happened?"

"Many, but none of them has become the frontrunner." He paused. "You said we may have stumbled on a major work of the Grinning Man. What did you mean?"

I filled him in on Operation Underground Railroad. As I talked, I saw Father Neal's expression change into a look of undisguised hatred and revulsion. I'd rarely seen that expression on his face, and it made me step back. He noticed and said, "What's wrong, dear boy?"

"You. The look I just saw on your face."

"You mean my righteous anger?"

"Yeah."

"Don't you feel it, lad?"

"Yeah, yeah I do. It makes me sick to my stomach and angry."

"Good. It is good to be angry at the right things, you know that?"

I said, "I was raised in evangelical circles to suppress my anger and outrage. It wasn't very polite."

"Understood. Hear me, Aidan. Anger is a good thing when used for the right reasons. Anger at the destructive power of sin and injustice is a beautiful thing. Use it."

We looked out at the flashlights running around the field, and Father Neal said, "I doubt they'll find out anything there."

I nodded. "It's like a crop circle."

"Yes, exactly. They'll find the smashed corn and have no ability to explain it. No footprints, no DNA. You know that, right?"

"Yeah. How do we break up this ring, Father? Can we destroy him?"

He shook his head. "No, we aren't going to be destroying him. Not yet. The means to do so are out of my hands at this moment."

I raised my eyebrow. "I'm not sure I understand."

He smiled. "You will, lad, once I understand. You know me; I don't like to give evidence until I have most of the threads in my hands. I'm afraid I'm very much like Sherlock in that way."

"Fair enough. But can we at least destroy this smiley-face ring?" I asked.

He lowered his brow and raised his cane. "By the power of the Trinity, and the angels in heaven, I swear to break this abomination in half."

"I think we let the detectives do their thing and we do ours. What do you think?" I asked.

He smiled. "My thoughts exactly."

Father Neal limped inside and called up the stairs. "Kate, Darrin, can you please come down here?"

Kate and Darrin came down to the porch.

"Any change in Ash's condition?" I asked.

Kate shook her head. "No, not yet. She's still asleep, thanks to the very large sleeping pill she took. I don't think she'll wake up for quite a while, and when she does, it's probably not going to be pretty."

I nodded. "I figured. And Brian?"

We all looked through the window. Brian sat with his head in his hands, mumbling to himself.

"I don't think he is going anywhere right now," Darrin said.

"Good, because we can't let them." I explained the investigation. As I talked, Kate put her arm around Darrin, who held her close.

"Now that we know what we are dealing with, we need to get the team together."

Darrin nodded. "Do you think that'll help? I mean, we don't have any more evidence beyond what we recorded that night."

"We will have more very soon. We have some, ah, unusual friends."

Darrin looked puzzled. "What sort of friends?"

Father Neal smiled. "Let's just say it's a group of ladies who have been tracking the Dark Bride longer than we have. They are gathering information as we speak."

"And when will we hear this information?" Darrin asked.

"Later today, I should think. We'll all get together and share information. We need to move as quickly as possible."

"So what do we do until then?"

Father Neal said, "We wait and we pray. Keep watch over Brian and Ashley."

No sooner did he finish those words than we heard a loud screaming from the bedroom.

"Stay with Brian, Darrin. Don't let him go upstairs."

Kate, Father Neal, and I went up the stairs, past the cops who had begun to make their way to the bedroom. Father Neal stopped them. "There is no need; we'll take care of her."

We found Ashley balled into a fetal position.

"My dear, are you there?"

"Yes . . . yes, Father, she is trying to come back. She wants . . . she wants—" Ashley threw her body back on the bed and her eyes went black. *Hellloooo, Faaather. . . . Reconsider my offer yet?*

Father Neal's face twisted in revulsion. "No, Morgan."

Ashley, or at least Ashley's voice, cackled in hair-raising laughter. *I have her, Father. I have her. The little girl is with me, safe and sound . . . for nowww.*

Father Neal raised his cane. "Tell us, where is she?"

She laughed. *Oh, I will, once you bring me the knife and tell me how you got it.*

"How we got it is easy to tell. Your master gave it to us," I said.

The black eyes burned with hate. *You lie, you piece of filth.*

"I never lie, my dear Morgan. We found it at the cabin."

*Show me; prove to me that you have it.*

"Nah. It is in other hands."

*Whose? Tell me or the little girl suffers.*

"Some old friends of yours, Morgan. And now that I've given you a hint, how about one to where we can find the little girl?"

Ashley laughed as she moved her body around the bed. *Oh, dear Father, such a clever man. I really wish I could have you.* She paused while we waited anxiously. At last, she continued. *Very well,* mon amour, *your hint is: by the strange lake, she will be.*

Ashley slumped to the bed, breathing hard and moaning. "My girl, my little girl."

Father Neal put his hands on her forehead, murmured something and said, "She is safe for now. Take her downstairs, get her out of this room."

I helped Ashley down to the living room and into a chair. She joined Brian in staring out of the window. I couldn't stand being in the same room with them now, so I went out on to the porch.

Jen gave directions to people as they reported in and went about their assignments. I leaned against the door and watched her. I memorized her every movement as she frowned, smiled, and tucked her long black hair behind her ears. She could be mine forever, but fear gripped me. I didn't want to turn out to be like Brian and Ashley.

No, we won't be like them. We won't start as Mr. and Mrs. Perfect. We're too flawed for that, I thought.

Jen must have felt me staring at her, because she turned to smile at me. Everyone cleared off the porch for a moment and she walked over.

"What are you thinking about, love?"

I smiled. "You. Us."

She put her hand on her hip. "Is that so, mister? Are you going to share?"

"Yes, eventually. But this isn't exactly the time or place to do it."

She looked around and didn't see any of her people around. Reaching up, she kissed me on the cheek. "Whenever you are ready."

I kissed her back, breathing her in. "I promise, it's a good thing."

I marveled that we could stand on the porch, the world seemingly ending around us, and express how much we loved each other. The story of my life, God giving me grace among the crap piling up around me. I realized that probably could be said about most people, including the beautiful woman standing in front of me.

"There you go, smiling again. What's going on in that head of yours?"

"I told you, later, dear. Tell me about what's going on."

She sighed. "It's hard to see in the dark. I think if the bear and the blanket hadn't been at the cabin, we might not have found them yet. We are just going to have to wait for the morning. The lights don't seem to be helping in the woods."

"What, really?"

She nodded. "It's like something is sucking them of their energy."

"Of course there is."

She shrugged. "Can't prove it. Everyone is chalking it up to a bad power source."

I scoffed. "Then they don't know Olan. That man kept this farm up-to-date. He installed a full-on modern power grid when I first moved here."

"I know, but they aren't going to believe the alternative."

She folded her arms and watched the detectives search the property.

"Anything new from Ashley?"

I told her about what had happened upstairs. She wrinkled her nose. "By the strange lake, what does that mean?"

"I have no idea. It's not the lake on the farm, obviously."

"Some kind of riddle," Jen said.

"Yeah, I'm not very good with riddles."

She snorted. "What is it with the spirit world and the vague mysterious statements? Why can't they just spell it out?"

"That's a very good question."

"What does Father Neal think?"

"I don't know, my dear; I have just been puzzling that one out." Father Neal limped onto the porch. He looked tired and worn.

"Have you found anything?" he asked.

Jen shook her head. "No, Father. Not yet. We just have to wait. It's going to take some time to get Brian's computer records and really search the farm. Once the Amber Alert goes out, things are going to get really hairy. The press will be camped outside the fence."

I rubbed my face. "Oh man, I forgot about the press."

"Yeah, but don't worry too much. I have a total lockdown on information right now. We got here before they found out, so we can establish a larger-than-normal perimeter around the farm."

She peeked into the living room. "Is Ashley stable, Father?"

"For now. I do not know when the Dark Bride will reappear. I'm assuming you want to question her, yes?"

Jen nodded. "Yes. I need to do it now, if that's possible."

Father Neal opened the door and limped inside. We followed him into the living room. He touched Ashley's arm. "Ashley, Jennifer would like to ask you some questions, would that be acceptable?"

Ashley nodded but didn't look at him. I stood in the doorway as Father Neal and Jen sat on the couch.

"Ashley, I'm going to try and make this as painless as possible. Okay? But I need information. It could help us find Lily."

Ashley mumbled, "Okay, Jen."

"Can you tell me what happened before Lily disappeared?"

Ashley didn't say anything.

"Ashley, please."

"I'm trying to remember, Detective." She touched the dark circles around her eyes in a slow rubbing motion. "I was . . . I was in my room. Watching TV, I think."

Brian spoke up. "And on the computer, I heard you typing."

She stared like a robot. "Yes. Yes, I was, it's true."

"What were you doing on the computer?"

No response.

"Ashley, please, what were you doing on the computer?"

Ashley rubbed her face faster. "I think I was talking to a friend online."

"Did you hear Brian put Lily to bed?"

"It's hard not to hear them. Brian roughhouses with her too much before bed. She needs to be calm so she can sleep."

"She likes it and it's not ever a problem."

Jen raised her hand to shut them both up. "Brian, what is the bedtime routine for Lily?"

He turned to her and said, "We wrestle around a bit, brush her teeth, and change into her jammies. I read her a story, then the Bible, and we pray."

"And what time was that?"

"Around seven. I can't be sure of the exact time."

Jen wrote it down. "Then what did you do, Brian?"

"I went down in the basement to work on a little wine cellar I have been building. It's a perfect place, cold, damp, and dark."

"So you were using power tools and everything?"

"Yes."

"Could you hear upstairs at all?"

He shook his head. "No, not at all. The table saw is pretty loud, and I had music on as well."

Jen turned to Ashley. "Ash, did you hear anything from Lily's room? You were the closest?"

"No, I was . . . concentrating on my conversation and the TV was on fairly loud."

Jen frowned. "And you didn't hear any bump, scream, or anything?"

Ashley slowly shook her head. "No, no, I didn't."

Jen leaned forward and touched her arm. "Ashley, if there is anything, anything you can remember, please tell me. I need all the information I can get."

Tears started to run down Ashley's face. "There is nothing, Jennifer. Nothing. Don't you think I would tell you?"

"Frankly, Ashley, I don't know, I'm not exactly buying your story."

Ashley launched herself at Jen and started pounding on her. "How dare you! How dare you! She's my daughter, you bitch! I'm telling you the truth!"

I ran and pulled Ashley off Jen. She kicked and screamed as I launched her back into her chair. She looked at me with a hatred I'd never seen from her, facial muscles contorted and eyes bulging. Any trace of the genteel Southern belle destroyed.

"Don't, Ashley. Don't move." She seemed to wilt under my gaze and curled up into the fetal position in her chair. I turned to Jen, seeing a large red mark begin to appear on her cheek.

"Babe, are you okay?"

Jen nodded as she stared at Ashley.

"Let me get you some ice." I went into the kitchen. I looked around and could feel the sadness take hold of me. This place had once been a place of peace and refuge, warmed by Olan and Edna's love.

Not any longer.

I grabbed a plastic bag and filled it with ice. Grabbing the paper towels, I went back into the living room and gave the ice to Jen.

"Thanks, Aidan." She held the bag to her cheek.

"Jen, I'm sorry, I don't know what prompted that," Brian said, shocked out of his catatonic state.

"Don't worry about it. Shock can do weird things to people."

Jen gave me a sideways look that told me otherwise. I'm pretty sure if Ashley hadn't been our friend, she probably would have gotten her ass beaten and been handcuffed.

"It seems like Lily disappeared somewhere between seven and eight, would that be right, Brian?"

He nodded. "That's when I went to check on her."

"I hate to make you relive this, but tell me what you found."

Brian shut his eyes as he had to relive the nightmare. I knew at that moment that Brian had nothing to do, directly anyway, with Lily's disappearance. The tension went out of my chest as I listened to the pain in his voice.

"I came upstairs to check on her. I heard . . ." He paused and then said, "Ashley typing on her computer. Knowing she probably hadn't been paying attention, I opened the door to check on Lily. She wasn't in her bed. I thought she might be hiding under the bed or playing in the closet. She does that sometimes."

He rubbed his face and said, "But I couldn't find her anywhere, and then I noticed the window had been opened. In a panic, I ran to the window and looked down to the ground. Nothing, so I ran into our bedroom to ask Ashley. That's when we both started looking around the house."

Brian didn't quite meet Jen's eyes as he gave this statement. Jen noticed and said, "Why did you wait so long to call someone?"

"Because, Jen, I wanted to make sure Lily wasn't playing hide-and-seek somewhere."

Jen nodded. "And you looked everywhere?"

"Not everywhere. I knew she wasn't in the basement, but yeah, everywhere else."

"When did Ashley start to lose it?"

Brian paused. Those hesitations really started to get to me. Brian always answered questions right off the bat.

"About right before I called Aidan. I had to get her to the room and lock her in there. I couldn't call the police with her like that, so I asked Aidan to help."

"Thanks, Brian."

He leaned forward. "Jen, tell me you can find her. Please. I can't . . . I can't . . ."

Brian came apart and wept, his body wracked with sobs. He fell on the floor as he moaned, "My baby . . . my baby girl. God help us. Help us."

Father Neal leaned down and put his hand on Brian. Jen motioned with her hand toward the kitchen.

Jen said, "Ashley, I need one more thing. I need all your passwords to your computer, email, Facebook, and anything else social media–wise."

Ashley glared at her. She reached for a notebook lying on the table, wrote down her passwords, and gave the notebook to Jen.

Jen motioned for me to go in the kitchen. Gripping my arm, she whispered, "They are both lying about something."

"I know, I know."

"The thing is, I'm not even sure if they are lying about Lily. I don't know what is true in their statements and what isn't," Jen hissed in frustration.

"I don't get the sense they are lying about the basic facts, but I feel like I'm missing something," I said, rubbing my head.

Jen slapped the counter. "Until we have more evidence, we can't be sure. Forensics needs to have free rein of the woods until the morning. When they are done, I want that bear and blanket analyzed."

"You think that's going to tell us something?"

"Yes. I think whoever took Lily left those to taunt us. If it's this Dark Bride bitch, it would seem to be her MO, yes?"

"No doubt about it."

Jen checked her watch. "My team won't have a report until eight a.m. We won't know anything more until then unless Ashley decides to go crazy again."

I moved her hand and the ice pack. I winced.

"That bad?" Jen said.

"Well, let's just say one side of you will look like a raccoon for a bit."

She nodded as she put the ice back on it.

"What are you going to tell the squad?"

"You mean, about my eye?"

"Yeah."

She shrugged. "The truth. It happens more than you realize. Most of the time we don't press charges. It's like I said, grief does weird things to people."

"But you don't think it's grief, do you?"

She shook her head. "No, it's something else." She paused and looked at the passwords. "I need to get these to my team."

Father Neal had gotten Brian up to the guest bed, and Kate had taken Ashley back to the master bedroom. They both came down the stairs as Jen and I came in from the kitchen. Everyone looked exhausted from the past eight hours.

Jen said, "Kate, you and Darrin might as well go home."

Father Neal spoke up, "No, we must stay here."

Surprised, I turned to him. "Are you sure?"

"Yes. Things are coming to a head. I will not leave, and neither will these two. Reg and Zoe can't make it out tonight."

Darrin and Kate nodded. Kate curled up on a chair, and Darrin lay at her feet like a protective dog.

I motioned to the couch. "Take the couch, Father. I'll grab one of Brian's camping mats."

"Thank you, my dear boy."

He lay on the couch and closed his eyes.

Jen laid her hand on my shoulder. "Why don't you curl up on the bench outside and get some sleep. I'm going back to the command center for any updates and see if the lady from the FBI has arrived yet."

I felt fatigue hit me like a truck. "Not a bad idea, dear. I could use some sleep. When are you going to get some?"

She smiled. "You know I'm part vampire."

"Are you going to suck my blood?"

"If you are lucky," she said as she walked out the door.

I made my way to the porch and stretched out on the huge bench. I tried to relax and let sleep come, but my brain whirled through the images and conversations of the past few hours. Prayers came to my mind faster than I expected.

*Lord, be with Lily. Please keep her safe.*

I heard her giggles in my head and pictured her showing off her new dress the last time I'd seen her.

*Lord, be with Brian and Ashley. I don't know how to pray for them.*

I pictured them as a smiling couple on their Tennessee farm, walking arm in arm in the twilight.

*Lord, be with Father Neal and me. Help us figure this out and save Lily.*

Not exactly the most earth-shattering prayers in the world, but that's all that came out. I knew God would hear them anyway, but I couldn't shake off the old Presbyterian mindset of making our prayers as long as possible. It's as if we had this idea that God had a scorecard and judged who had the greatest verbal prayer gymnastics.

I must have dozed off, because the next thing I knew, Jen was shaking me awake. The early morning sun shone through the window, and I blinked. "Jen, what's wrong? Everything okay?"

"Okay is a relative term, dear, but nothing is pressing. We are about to have another briefing on what we found so far."

I sat up and rubbed my face. "Ugh, I could use some coffee."

She smiled and held up a cup. "I think you have become an addict."

"Yes, I think you are right." I sipped my coffee as we walked out to the command center. At the end of the driveway, I could see the TV trucks lining the main road.

"When did they get here?"

"About an hour ago. We are going to have to give them something at some point."

"Who gets to do that?"

She grinned. "Probably Weaver. They are all afraid of him, so they usually don't ask too many questions."

I chuckled. "I bet."

We walked into the trailer, and I took a position in the back of the small gathering. Jen walked up to the front and said, "Okay, people, you can sit.

"First, let me introduce our FBI liaison in Columbus who is going to be with us, Special Agent Emily Jordan."

I about dropped my coffee cup when the small, cute blonde-haired woman from Celestine's stood up and waved to everyone. She gave me a secret wink as she took her seat.

So, the Daughters of Laveau had eyes and ears everywhere. Clever.

"Now, I'm going to give you the parents' version of events. There are going to be questions about their story, but I want you to hold off for a bit until we get everyone's report, okay?"

They all nodded.

As Jen wrote times and events on the board, I couldn't help but stare at Emily. Questions began to flood my mind. Who were these Daughters of Laveau? How far did their influence stretch? Something told me I would be finding out all about it very soon. Maybe more than I wanted to know.

Jen's voice broke into my thought train. "So, that's the history of events, as far as we can tell at this moment. We can poke holes later. Let's hear the reports. The woods first, please."

A male detective stood up. "Forensics just finished sweeping the woods. No footprints. No fingerprints. Nothing."

Another detective raised his hand. "How is that possible, David? Someone had to put that teddy bear and blanket there."

David shrugged his broad shoulders. "I have no idea. If anyone has any suggestions, I'm open."

"Is it too dry out?" I asked.

"Yeah, that's a possible explanation. However, with as many sticks as there are in those woods, you would think we would have found some broken twigs, bent branches, torn cloth, something. A little girl couldn't just wander around in the woods and not leave a trace."

"You're right, David. Any theories, people?" Jen asked.

Special Agent Jordan spoke up. "Could the girl have been carried there somehow?"

David said, "Assuming the girl was out there at all, yeah. But again, same problem. An adult tromping around the woods would have left a sign."

Jen broke in. "Okay, people, there doesn't seem to be anything to learn from the woods right now. Let's put that aside for a moment. What about the bear and the blanket?"

A woman detective stood up. "The preliminary analysis showed a ton of fine red hair strands, probably from the girl." She paused. "But we found a little slit in the bear, most likely done with a knife."

I leaned forward as Jen said, "Go on, Leigh Ann."

"Inside the tear, we found a roll of parchment, possibly sheepskin; we aren't sure."

"What? Seriously?" Jen asked.

Leigh Ann nodded. "Yeah, we didn't quite understand it, either. When Forensics pulled it out, they found writing." She moved over to the projector, switched from computer mode, and laid the parchment on the glowing light. A crinkled piece of parchment appeared on the screen. Leigh Ann used a laser pointer to focus on the wrinkles in the paper. "Now, see how the parchment has been rolled into a little scroll." She enlarged until she focused on a letter.

"Wait, what does it say?" David asked.

"I'm getting to that. But I want you to notice something first. Note the scratches on the paper and the smeared ink. The writing wasn't done with an ordinary pen."

"What do you mean?" Jen said.

Leigh Ann hesitated. "If it had been done with a pen, there would be no scratches or smears on the parchment. This is just a wild, uneducated guess, but I think it was done with a quill."

"What?" I asked.

"A quill, you know, like George Washington used."

"Why would someone take the trouble of writing a message on parchment with a quill? Wouldn't a pen and notebook paper be easier?" Weaver spoke for the first time.

"That is a good question. We have no educated guesses," Leigh Ann responded.

Weaver nodded. "Why don't you show us the message."

Leigh Ann took a deep breath. "Okay." She shrank the screen and the writing came into focus. What I read chilled my blood.

> *I give myself to him. I renounce all claims to myself. I give myself to his lordship. I give myself for his pleasure. I give him my body for his pleasure. I give him my mind for his pleasure. I give him my soul for his pleasure. I pray that he accept this offering so that I may be his bride. May he come to take me as his own. So be it.*

The whole RV got quiet as we stared at the words.

"I don't understand," David said.

Leigh Ann shook her head. "Nor do I. Neither did anyone in Forensics."

Jen looked at me and glanced at the writing. I nodded. Father Neal had been educating me on how to recognize magick ritual. This formula had been his first lesson, because, as he had told me, "It's one of the most heinous."

Weaver looked at me. "Anything for us, Pastor Schaeffer?"

"It's a magick ritual of some sort, a selling of the soul, if you will."

Everyone glanced around. I could tell they thought I had a screw loose. Jen noticed and stepped in. "Aidan is an expert in the occult and occult signs."

"The nature of the language is ritualistic. It's an offering up of a person's whole being."

I took the laser pointer from Leigh Ann. "Notice the beginning. You can see the intent of the ritual and the renouncing of all other claims by the person who is doing the ritual."

"Why is that important?" Weaver asked.

"Because, if you are giving your soul to another, you want to break all claims, or so the logic goes."

"Go on."

"This particular ritual is designed to be said from a female perspective." I hesitated, and Jen smiled to encourage me. "Because, well, it's designed to be a female surrendering to a male master. You might say it is an infernal wedding vow. The ritual is sealed with a gift."

Leigh Ann asked the question I dreaded. "So, did the bear and the blanket seal the deal?"

I shook my head, and a lump in my throat prevented me from speaking for a moment. "No, Lily was the offering. She must have dropped the bear and the blanket when—"

The whole room went silent, and I knew I didn't have to finish. They all understood. Someone had taken Lily and given her to another person, or rather, someone who had once been a person.

"So, it has to be one of the parents, right?" David asked.

Jen looked over at Emily. "Special Agent Jordan , do we have any information from the Internet search?"

Emily shook her head. "We need the records. They are processing a high volume of requests. We were bumped to the beginning of the line due to this being a missing child case. If you get the passwords, we can get started right away on Ashley's computer and fill in the blanks later. The preliminary search of Brian's computer showed nothing."

Jen spoke up, "We've got the passwords. Come see me after we are done. All right, people, until we get into Ashley's, we may not know more. I want you all to comb the farm again. Anything out of the ordinary, report it. So, that's the story, people. Let's get back out there, do the work, and find Lily."

# CHAPTER THIRTY

**AS I WENT OUTSIDE, EMILY CALLED OUT TO ME, "PASTOR SCHAEFFER,** can I have a word?"

She followed me to the driveway. "You're probably surprised to see me."

"That's a bit of an understatement."

"I thought about contacting you after we met at Celestine's, but we still had to keep things under wraps. I hope you understand."

"Not really. How is it you are in both the FBI and the Daughters of Laveau?"

She laughed. "You act like they are mutually exclusive."

"Shouldn't they be?"

Emily cocked her head. "We are both trying to put an end to evil, Aidan."

I looked around and said, "But you have an agenda, right? Stop the works of the Dark Bride at all costs, right?"

She frowned. "Not at all costs, Aidan. That would make us no better than the Dark Bride."

"Fine. But you do realize there is more going on here than just Morgan, right?"

"We're starting to see that."

I pointed out to the field. "You know where the smiley-face sign came from, right?"

"Actually, no, we don't."

I couldn't believe it. I had figured they knew everything about magick, secrets, and certainly the Grinning Man.

"You're serious?"

She nodded. "Yes. That's why we needed to meet with you and Father Neal. There are large pieces of the puzzle we're missing. He had started to tell us when you walked in last night."

"I would apologize, but . . ."

She waved her hand. "No need. This little girl is your best friend's daughter, yes?"

I nodded. "She's like my own. I'm her godfather."

"We are going to find her. In the hundred and twenty-five years of the Daughters, we have never been this close to Morgan. We'll have her."

"How old are you, Emily?"

She smiled. "How old do I look, Pastor Aidan?"

"About twenty-three, if I'm guessing."

"You are off by about seventy years."

I shook my head. "How is that possible?"

She sighed. "It's not natural, if that's what you mean. We keep ourselves this way for a purpose."

"Is it that much of a sacrifice?"

Her face went white, and I thought she would faint. "Very much so, Pastor Aidan."

"I guess you aren't going to tell me."

She shook her head. "It's forbidden. Too much temptation."

"Doesn't sound like it."

"Stopping aging? Not dying? Believe me, it's more temptation than most can handle."

"Why do you do it?"

She clenched her fist. "Because, Pastor Aidan, the fight against evil is a real fight, with real casualties and real sacrifices."

"Yeah, but it would seem the ultimate sacrifice is death."

She grasped my arm. "That shows you are very young, Pastor Aidan."

At that moment, Jen walked up and looked at the both of us. "Are you two okay?"

Special Agent Jordan recovered her cheery, cheerleader disposition. "Oh yes, Jen. We were just talking about the farm."

"Emily knows, Jen. At least she knows about the *other* stuff."

"What other stuff?" Jen gave me a sideways glance.

"The Grinning Man."

Jen's eyes widened. "Aidan, you can't say that."

"It's okay, Jen. Emily probably knows more about all this than you and I combined."

"What do you mean?"

I sighed. "It's kind of a long explanation."

Jen crossed her arms. "We've got time."

"Go ahead," Emily said.

I explained about Celestine and the Daughters of Laveau. Jen stared at Emily the whole time.

"Special Agent, you know that is a conflict of interest."

"Is it?" Emily frowned. "I thought we are on the same team here, Detective."

They glared at each other, and their bodies tensed.

"You mean this whole time we have been searching for child predators, you had another purpose?" Jen said, spitting out every word.

Emily stepped closer to Jen. "How dare you. The person my sisters and I are chasing *is* the predator."

"What the hell are you talking about?"

Jen looked at me, and I realized I hadn't told her anything about Morgan. "Jen, it's my fault. Things have been moving so fast, I didn't have a chance to talk to you."

They both turned on me and I braced myself for the onslaught.

"Start talking, Preacher Boy."

I explained about Morgan and her status as the Dark Bride.

"How in the world am I supposed to convict a woman who should have been dead a hundred and twenty-five years ago?"

Emily softened and put her hand on Jen. "Conviction in a court of law may not be the way to go."

Jen shrugged Emily's hand off her shoulder. "It has to be. Otherwise, what are we doing here?"

"Destroying an evil that should have been stamped out long ago," Emily said. "Putting her in jail will not do that."

Jen looked at Emily as if she'd sprouted tentacles. "You can't be serious. You are talking about killing this woman, yes?"

Emily answered in a low voice, "Yes. That's exactly what I'm talking about."

"And you call yourself a law-enforcement officer. You can't just kill someone because you feel like it."

"What are you going to do, turn me in?"

I couldn't help but be curious about Jen's response. The anger and hurt over her own past had driven her to this task force in the first place. By her own judgment, not exactly going by the books. I didn't bother pointing that out, but I said, "Jen, even Father Neal thinks this is a battle we can't fight through the law."

Jen's muscles relaxed. "I just don't understand any of this."

Emily nodded. "I think we need a meeting of the minds. As soon as possible."

"We can't do it here," I said, looking around the farm.

"My sisters can meet anywhere; don't worry about getting them into the scene."

"And how are they going to do that?"

Emily smiled. "Just watch. Where do we meet?"

I gazed toward the woods. "At the cabin."

"Okay. Let me make a call."

She walked a few paces away, and Jen said, "This is crazy."

"I know, but I don't think we have much of a choice."

Jen rubbed her face and swayed. I steadied her and said, "Seriously, you need to lie down for a bit."

"I will, when we hear from these Daughters of Laveau."

"Can you clear the woods so we can meet there?" I asked.

Jen nodded. "I'll tell everyone to pull out of the center of the woods so that we can have another look around."

"Won't that arouse suspicion?"

Jen smiled. "They aren't going to question me and an FBI agent."

Emily walked up. "They'll be here in half an hour. We will be able to put the puzzle together, or at least arrange the pieces into a workable order."

"Let's get Father Neal," I said.

We walked over to the house. Lights from the windows penetrated the darkness. I looked at my phone and saw the time, 3:00 a.m. Darrin's snores rattled the windows and I smiled for the first time all evening. I touched his leg with my foot and he woke up with a start. "Aidan, Jen, I'm sorry."

I smiled. "Some guard dog you turned out to be. Where is Father Neal?"

"Inside."

I went in and found Father Neal still asleep on the couch with his mouth hanging open. I hesitated before I woke him up. His pale face looked gaunt, and dark rings circled both of his eyes. I didn't want to wake him, but I knew he would beat me with his cane if I didn't.

I touched his arm. "Father?"

He mumbled in his sleep. "No, you are not allowed."

"Father, it's Aidan."

"Please, please, they are innocent. Leave them alone."

"Father, wake up!"

He jolted awake and his eyes blazed. I took a step back and raised my hands. "Father, it's Aidan."

The blaze went out of his eyes. "Aidan, what time is it?"

"It's around three in the morning, I think."

"What day?"

I checked my iPhone. "It's Wednesday, June twenty-second."

He relaxed. "Good, very good. There is still time."

"I didn't understand anything you just said. Are you sure you're awake?"

He nodded as the lines in his face went taut. "Quite awake, dear boy. Why did you disturb me?"

"The Daughters of Laveau are coming to the farm to meet with us."

He gripped his cane. "Are they now? Why?"

I looked over my shoulder at the porch where Jen and Emily waited. "Turns out one of the Daughters, Emily, is an FBI agent, Father, and has been working on this case with Jen since the beginning."

He smiled. "Is that so? Excellent, excellent. So, we are going to have a meeting of the minds?"

I nodded and he gave me his hand. "Help me up, dear boy. This is exactly what needs to happen."

I helped him up, and we walked outside. Emily smiled and said, "Father Neal! I'm so sorry we had to wake you up. Are you okay?"

He smiled and turned on the English charm. "Yes, my dear. Now, take my arm, and we shall walk to the woods together."

Jen watched them go down the stairs together. "He is a real charmer."

"Unlike me," I said as we followed them to the field.

"You have your moments, Preacher Boy."

We followed along the path behind Father Neal and Emily. When we arrived, the Daughters of Laveau stood in a semi-ciricle around Celestine. They all wore white dresses that glowed in the moonlight and they arms rested at their sides. Each of them wore an expression of serenity combined with an inner fierceness that made me stop walking. They looked beautiful and terrible at the same time. A man could have fallen in love or been destroyed on the spot.

Celestine bowed her head. "Père Neal, and Aidan, welcome. The time has come to end the Dark Bride. All the signs point to it."

Father Neal nodded. "It is the twenty-second, the day before Saint John's Eve."

"Most certainly," Celestine said.

Celestine turned to Jen, and to my surprise embraced her. She kissed both cheeks. "It is wonderful to meet you, Sister."

Jen looked stunned as she said, "I, uh, I'm not . . ."

"You are, even if you haven't joined us. Emily has told us about you. We even considered asking you to join us, but"—she looked at me—"it seems someone has already claimed you."

Jen grinned. "Or I claimed him, whichever."

All the girls giggled and I said, "Can we get to the point, please?"

"Of course, Aidan," Celestine said. "Let us sit in the boundaries of the cabin. The spell of the Grinning Man has already been broken."

We all sat on the ground and Father Neal asked, "Who should start first?"

Emily said, "I have a better idea, why don't Jen and I tell the story? Then you and Aidan can fill in the blanks."

Jen and Emily took turns bringing everyone up to speed on the official investigation of the smiley-face group. Father Neal, with interjections by me, filled in the gaps on the Grinning Man.

After he had finished, everyone sat in silence. The enormity of everything hit us hard. We stared at the hearthstone that the Grinning Man had used to mock us and lead us along by the nose.

Celestine broke the silence. "Thank you all for sharing what you know. Now, it is our turn." She traced her lips with her finger and then grimaced. "We lost track of Morgan around 1968."

Father Neal leaned forward. "Why, my dear?"

All the Daughters of Laveau hung their heads as Aisha said, "It is one of our greatest shames, Père. We had her cornered in Memphis, before . . ."

"Before what?" I asked, as Jen elbowed me for my insensitivity.

"Before Martin was shot. We had everything in place to

destroy Morgan, and then we lost her in the chaos after the shooting."

"Wait, are you saying she shot Martin Luther King?"

They all shook their heads, and Emily said, "No, of course not. She just played a role in the events."

Eager, I probed further. "Like how?"

Jen interrupted, "I don't think that is really relevant at this point, do you? We're running out of time."

"Sorry, continue, Celestine," I said.

"We have been searching for over forty years for any trace of her. It's almost as if she vanished from the earth. We decided to see if we could pick up a trace of her in Ohio."

"Is this because of the Underground Railroad?"

Brigit nodded. "We knew, of course, that Morgan had prowled this state just before the War Between the States. What we didn't know, until you shared your vision with us, Aidan, is what she did during those years. She fed her bloodlust for slaves by capturing them along the Underground Railroad."

I looked around. "They used this farm as a trap, a fake station on the Railroad."

Celestine said, "That is correct, *mon amour.*"

Jen tensed beside me and I grabbed her hand. "So, I guess I did see a residual haunting."

Father Neal said, "Yes, I believe so, lad. It's like a recording on a tape. Someone recorded the events on the landscape."

Jen broke in. "How did you figure out she had come back to Ohio?"

Brigit said, "Something happened when we went to the Underground Railroad Museum in Cincinnati. First, we saw a picture of Morgan in one of the displays about slave bounty hunters."

"How do you know it was her?" Jen asked.

"The Dark Bride is a strikingly beautiful woman. Her eyes are as black as coal and stare right through you. She is not easy to forget, Detective," Celestine said.

"We all felt it as we stared at her. We knew she was near," Aiselinn added, tucking her hair behind her ear.

Jen shook her head. "Why did it take the picture to feel that? Why couldn't you do it before?"

All of the Daughters of Laveau looked down. "Because Morgan knows the magick of Marie Laveau. She can sense us," Brigit said with a shiver.

"I had to go to Toledo that same day for the final raid that broke up the sex-trafficking ring there," Emily put in. "When I was there, I sensed Morgan's presence so strongly, I thought she would jump out at me any moment."

"Did you know that she was behind a sex-trafficking ring?"

Emily shook her head. "Sadly, no, I looked at them as unrelated. It wasn't until Celestine's conversation with Madame Laveau that everything started to click into place."

"So, how do we use all this to rescue Lily?"

Father Neal broke his silence. "She gave us a hint through Ashley."

Celestine raised her eyebrow. "What did she say?"

"She told us that Lily would be found on the shores of the strange lake. Does that ring a bell?" I asked.

They all looked confused. Emily replied, "No, not at all. It doesn't make sense."

Father Neal asked, "Does anyone know anything about a lake in Ohio with any unusual associations?"

"No, none that I know about," I said, frowning. "Zoe and I had a long conversation about weird places in Ohio. I don't recall her saying anything about a lake."

Jen had bowed her head and was staring at the ground.

"It's a riddle," I said. "I don't think we are looking for a lake with strange associations. I'm guessing the name of the actual lake is there somewhere, maybe an anagram."

We stared at the hearthstone as if it would give us the answer. Something told me the Grinning Man would stop giving us more hints. Jen looked up and said, "I got it."

I felt a surge of hope. "What, what is it?"

She gave me a smile. "It's so stupid and simple, as most riddles are when you know the answer." Jen looked at everyone else. "What's another word for strange?"

"Weird," Emily said.

"Uncanny," Brigit chipped in.

"Bizarre," Aisha offered.

Father Neal smiled at Jen. "I think eerie is the world you are looking for, my dear."

"Exactly."

"So, the eerie lake . . ." I stopped short. "That's it! You're right, Jen. Lake Erie. Good Lord, how did we not see that?"

"Because we were being too smart for our own good, that's why."

Emily stood up. "Maybe it's Toledo again. I can get the Bureau there on alert."

Celestine held up her hand. "We can't forget Saint John's Eve."

"What's that?" I asked.

"Saint John's Eve, June twenty-third, and Saint John's Day are prime Voodoo days. It is the day Marie the Second did her rituals on Bayou Saint John in New Orleans."

"Why is that significant here?" Jen asked.

"I'm not entirely sure, to be honest. But it seems as if everything here—the events on the farm, Lily's disappearance, and Morgan's knife—all point to something significant happening tomorrow night and the morning of June twenty fourth. Father Neal?"

He studied Celestine for a moment. "Madame Laveau appeared and told me. She was about to tell more when Aidan woke me up."

Jen's radio crackled. "Detective Brown, are you there?"

Jen responded, "This is Brown, go on."

"Ma'am, we need you back here ASAP."

Jen looked irritated as she responded, "Can't it wait, Ro? I'm in the middle of something."

"I'm afraid not, ma'am. The wife has disappeared."

Everyone looked as stunned as I felt.

"I'm sorry, Ro, can you say that again?"

"The wife, Ashley, the redhead, isn't in her bedroom. That girl Kate checked on her, and she wasn't in her bed."

"What about the rest of the house, Ro?"

"We are checking that, ma'am, but so far nothing."

# CHAPTER THIRTY-ONE

JEN, EMILY, AND I RAN BACK TO THE HOUSE. AS WE CLIMBED THE FENCE, Leigh Ann, one of the squad detectives, met us with news. "We couldn't find her."

Jen walked fast, and Leigh Ann struggled to keep up.

"You checked everywhere?"

"Yes, ma'am. We looked through the basement, the attic, the barn, and every possible nook and cranny."

"Check again, Detective."

Leigh Ann nodded and spoke into the radio as she ran back to the command center.

"Are you two thinking what I'm thinking?" Emily said as we got to the house.

"That Brian is completely innocent in all of this?" Jen asked.

"I don't know about that," I said.

"What do you mean?"

"I'm not sure yet, but I don't think the answer is that simple."

They both looked back at me.

Emily said, "Do you think he knows more than he's telling?"

I shook my head. "No. But I can't shake the feeling the computer records are going to tell the tale."

Jen and Emily looked at each other, and Emily said, "I think he's right."

Jen spoke into her radio. "Leigh Ann, have the computer records come in?"

The radio crackled back. "Just the email records for Ashley's Gmail account. By the way, Ashley gave us false passwords. Brian's stuff won't come in until later."

"Bitch," Jen muttered. "Where are the records?"

"They were still being printed out when Darrin told us about Ashley. We had to run out and try to find her."

"Thanks, Leigh Ann. Let everyone know I want them at the command center in fifteen minutes."

"Yes, ma'am."

Jen closed her eyes as she returned the radio to her belt. "Any thoughts?"

"Many, and none of them are good. I want to see the emails before I share them," Emily said. "But we should probably start by looking at her emails from the past week."

"Then let's go look at them," Jen said.

They started to go inside the command center and I said, "I'm going to go talk to Darrin, Kate, and Brian. I want to see if there's anything they can tell us."

Father Neal met me on the porch, and we walked into the house. Darrin and Kate sat on the couch holding hands. Brian sat in a chair opposite them with his head in his hands.

"Are you okay, Darrin?" Father Neal asked.

"It's all my fault, Father. I have no idea how she got out."

Father Neal settled himself in the chair near the couch. "Why are you apologizing?"

"It was my responsibility."

"Why don't you tell us what happened and then we can assign blame," Father Neal said.

Darrin took a deep breath. "I had just made some coffee, pretty strong stuff I might add, and all three of us were starting to drink it when the air changed."

"The air changed?" I asked.

"Lame, I know. I don't know if I can describe it."

Father Neal leaned forward. "You have to try, Darrin, it's important."

Kate spoke up. "It's like the air shimmered and distorted, as if someone had bent it."

Darrin nodded. "Everything distorted, and all the angles went all wrong."

"Go on," Father Neal said.

"The next thing I knew, I woke up on the floor. Kate was passed out, too. I woke her up and she went to check on Ashley. She was gone."

Father Neal put his hand on Brian's shoulder. "Don't blame yourself, Darrin. You are the victim here."

Darrin looked mystified. "I don't understand."

"Magick, Darrin. Someone put you all to sleep."

"Who would that have been? The place is crawling with cops. We had one stationed right outside her door. How could anyone have gotten in the house?"

"Surely they didn't put everyone to sleep," I said.

Brian, who had been staring at the wall this whole time, said, "Maybe the person didn't come from the outside."

All of us got quiet. The answer hung in the air, and none of us wanted to say it.

Kate broke the silence. "Ashley. She did it."

"As crazy as that seems, I don't see any other explanation. But I still don't understand." I paused and looked at Father Neal. "The link. It's become so strong, the Dark Bride can use Ashley as a concentration point to do magick."

"I do believe you're right, Aidan."

My phone buzzed, and I checked the message. COMMAND CENTER, ASAP. BRING FATHER NEAL AND DARRIN.

I looked up. "Jen needs us. Kate, can you stay here with Brian?"

"Of course."

We went outside and walked to the command center. Darrin asked, "What's going on?"

"My guess is that Jen and Emily found something in the emails."

"Emails?"

"They pulled Ashley's emails for information."

Darrin nodded as we reached the command center. When we got inside, everyone had already gathered and Jen started with the briefing.

"As you can see from these few emails, Ashley had contact with a person unknown. Leigh Ann, if you would."

A few clicks and the first email popped up on the screen.

*From: chillindrid@gmail.com*
*To: redhairmomma23@gmail.com*

*My lover,*

*I'm coming to you soon, are you ready for our marriage and to bind yourself to me? I shall consume you and absorb you into me. You shall be my own, my possession. Look for my sign.*

*—I*

"Do we know who owns this account?" David, one of the male detectives, asked.

Jen shook her head. "Google had no idea. It was registered under a false name, and the account was always accessed from a different IP address, usually a local library. The address is a dead end."

"What was the false name?" Father Neal asked.

Leigh Ann wrinkled her nose. "It's really dumb and senseless. Indrid Cold."

"What was Ashley's response?" I asked, dreading the answer.

Jen nodded to Leigh Ann, who pulled up the next email.

*From: redhairmomma23@gmail.com*
*To: chillindrid@gmail.com*

*My master,*

*I'm ready to give you everything, my whole life, body, and soul. I want to be yours, consumed and folded into you. I will do what you say. I'll obey what you say. Come to me, my love, and I will join myself to you. I await your signs.*

*—A*

"So basically, Ms. Ashley gave herself to someone on the Internet she had never seen. The question is, how did they meet?" David asked.

"Brian got fired three months ago for getting on an erotic chat site on his work computer. It's my guess that's not the only place he accessed it," I said, saving Jen the trouble.

The lightbulbs went on around the command center. "So Ashley decided to jump on to see what her husband was into and got lured in herself," Leigh Ann said.

"That would be my guess."

"Does Brian know?" Emily asked.

"No, otherwise he would have told me. He knew he did damage to his family with all of this, but I doubt he knew this."

"We are going to have to question him, Aidan," Jen said.

"I figured as much."

"We have more; pay attention to this one, people," Jen ordered.

The next email came on the screen.

*From: Chillindrid@gmail.com*
*To: redhairmomma23@gmail.com*

*My slave,*

*As you see from my signs, I have arrived with my Dark Bride. You will learn to serve her as much as you serve me. In doing so, you will one day replace her. It is now time for you to show your absolute dedication by giving up your daughter to me. She will be sold to one of my associates as final proof of your allegiance. He lives in the South, so dear little Lily will be right at home!*

*Tonight, you will take her to the cabin in the woods, my old home. Cut her arm and say these words:*

*"I give myself to him. I renounce all claims to myself. I give myself to his lordship. I give myself for his pleasure. I give him my body for his pleasure. I give him my mind for his pleasure. I give him my soul for his pleasure. I pray that he accept this offering so that I may be his bride. May he come to take me as his own. So be it."*

*My bride will come to you and receive the offering. Await my instructions.*

*—I*

The image of Ashley taking a knife to Lily made my stomach churn and my vision blur. I put my head in my hands and felt Father Neal's hand on my back. I heard him whisper, "The strength of Christ be with you, my son."

I felt a surge of warmth and regained control. The room had grown quiet and David broke in. "What the hell is going on?"

Jen responded, "My guess is that whoever runs this trafficking ring sought to get Ashley and her daughter."

"Sick assholes," Leigh Ann said.

Emily frowned. "That doesn't even begin to cover it, Detective."

"But why the pseudo-magick formula shit?" David asked.

"I haven't shared this yet with Detective Brown, but I just received some new information as we sorted through these emails."

Jen gave her a sideways glance. I wondered if this was Emily telling the detectives what she had learned from her Sisters.

Emily held up her phone. "I got an email from the FBI office here in Columbus. A woman has come into the office, claiming she was a victim of a smiley-face gang. She has told the agents there she had been sold to a group of people who forced her to perform a lot of magick sex rituals."

Father Neal's hand shook as he steadied himself with the cane. I touched his arm. "Are you okay?"

He shook his head. "Sex magick is a powerful dark ritual, Aidan. Very powerful. Much more powerful than anything Mike or Daniel, servants of the Grinning Man, ever did."

I remembered my near-death experience on Serpent Mound as we battled those two assholes. The fear, the pain, and the terror struck me hard as I breathed deep. I thought I couldn't imagine anything worse.

"I think I need a bath," Leigh Ann said.

Jen nodded. "Before this is all over, we are probably going to have to put ourselves in decontamination because of the crap we will have waded through."

"Is that all of the emails?" Darrin asked.

"No, we actually got one more before you three got here. Apparently, it had been sent early this morning to Ashley's account."

"What does it say?" I asked.

"It's not what it says, but what it shows."

Jen stared at me with tears brimming in her eyes. I knew it

couldn't be good if Jen would be on the verge of crying in front of her team. She nodded to Leigh Ann, who put it up on screen.

I saw Lily with tears staining her cheeks as she stood near a wall of white stone brick. Someone had typed over the picture, COME HERE AND YOU WILL BE REUNITED WITH HER.

Hot tears streamed down my face, and I hated the Grinning Man with all my heart and mind. I couldn't bear to see Lily in the control of that sick bastard. The blood rushed to my head, and I had to fight the urge to tear up the command center. I wanted to go in the house and punch Brian in the face. Lily had become an offering on the altar of a failed marriage.

"Where is she standing?" Father Neal asked.

"I have no idea. We are trying to find out. It could be anywhere."

I looked at Jen and mouthed, *Lake Erie*. She nodded and then said, "However, we have some indication it might be Lake Erie."

"Why?" Leigh Ann asked.

Emily lied. "We have every reason to believe this ring of sex traffickers is using the Great Lakes as a pipeline."

"Pipeline?" Father Neal asked, keeping up the charade.

"Yes, since the Great Lakes are a major international waterway, they can use boats to ship girls to other US cities and around the world."

I stared at the white stone and couldn't shake the feeling I had seen this place. The name of the location seemed just out of my reach.

Jen followed Emily's lead. "There are also indications something will happen to Lily and Ashley tomorrow night. Most likely, it means they will be shipped out, as you can see from the emails."

"That doesn't give us a lot of time to figure out where they are," David pointed out.

Jen said, "No, and this is why no one is leaving until we can figure out this picture."

Everyone nodded and Jen continued. "So what do we see?"

I tried to calm myself and focus on the picture. I needed to find some sort of objective and forget about the face of my goddaughter. Her eyes kept drawing me back and shattering me. I had to put my head down and listen to the sounds of everyone whispering to himself or herself. The dull thump of people typing on their iPads or phones as they searched the Internet for hints. I heard Darrin mutter, "No, that's stupid; they would never go for it."

"I have an idea on how we can figure out this picture," Darrin said to me.

"How?" I prodded.

"Well, it's crazy as hell," he said as he looked around the room.

I gripped his shoulder and pointed to the screen. "Look at her eyes, Darrin. See the fear? Think about it."

He looked at Lily's picture and raised his hand. Jen noticed and said, "Darrin, did you figure it out?"

"No, but I have an idea on how we can find out."

"How?"

"Well, there is a site on the Internet . . ."

"Wikipedia? Ohio tourism?" Emily fired off.

Darrin shook his head. "Not exactly. It's a site I used to visit before I, well, met Father Neal."

"Okay," Jen said, leaning on the table. I held my breath, as I had no idea what site Darrin would recommend.

"It's not what you are thinking," Darrin said, looking around the room. "It's an utterly free, anonymous posting site called 4chan."

"Sounds a bit dodgy," Father Neal said.

"Parts of it, sure, but it's not all bad. It's an online bulletin board where you can post anonymously, and there is no registration. I wouldn't recommend spending time there, but the posters have done some pretty funny stuff, such as pranking Oprah. They also do some really good stuff, such as busting people who posted pictures of animal cruelty."

"How did they do that?"

Darrin gave us a crooked smile. "They went over the details

of the picture one by one until they figured out this person's location, found their IP address, and turned them in to the authorities."

"Sounds like some pretty scary people."

He shrugged. "They have their own sense of justice and what's right. I don't think I have ever seen them break someone who didn't deserve it. They are the true Pirates of the Internet."

Emily looked at Jen. "Are you suggesting we put evidence of a crime investigation on the Internet?"

"Yeah, I am. It's not like you don't use the media to do the same thing, am I wrong?" Darrin took out a cigarette and began to fiddle with it.

All the detectives tried to hide a smile as Jen said, "What if we do?"

"Exactly. This way, no one needs to know about it except those of us in this room. No one will be able to track who posted the picture just by your username. You can delete the post after you get your information."

Jen looked at Darrin. She might as well have been a sphinx; I couldn't read what she might be thinking.

"Darrin, I just don't think we can do that. We have to figure out something else," Jen said.

I started to get up and object. Father Neal gripped my arm and whispered, "Wait, son." I looked at him as he stared at Jen.

"All right, people, I need you to go out to the surrounding houses within a five-mile radius. Start asking questions and see if anyone says anything."

As everyone filed out, Jen said, "Aidan, Darrin, Father Neal, and Emily, I need to talk to you for a few moments."

She waited for everyone to file out. "What we are about do is probably illegal and could get me fired. Everyone might get thrown in jail. Do you understand that?"

We all nodded. Jen walked back to Ashley's computer. We watched on the projector as she copied the picture.

"All right, Darrin, now what?"

"I still have my login. I'll post it."

"Will it be easier to trace that way?"

Darrin shrugged. "Maybe, but if they ever investigate me, I'll just say I stole it from the crime scene in an act of vigilante justice. Besides, all of them know me, or rather knew me. I got to be pretty popular. That's important, because they'll know I'm not full of shit."

Jen moved so Darrin could log on. With a few quick keystrokes, he got into his account. He pasted in the picture of Lily and wrote, "Important. Hey, Anonymous, I need your help. A friend of mine had his daughter kidnapped last night. I need to know where this picture might have been taken. I think it's a place by Lake Erie. This isn't a prank. You all know me. Godofkenyon."

He posted it and checked to see if it posted to the feed. Darrin smiled as he said, "There it is."

"Godofkenyon, eh? Interesting name," I said.

Darrin shrugged. "I used to be an atheist."

Emily laid a hand on his shoulder. "What's next, Darrin?"

He sighed. "We wait, and I'm hoping not long."

Sure enough, the first time he refreshed we got a response.

*Godofkenyon! We miss you. The stone in the picture is granite without a doubt.*

Darrin refreshed again, and more comments joined the thread.

*It is granite, cut into blocks. Whatever this damn thing is, it's pretty big and tall.*

Refresh.

*Yeah, like a monument or something.*

Refresh.

*I would agree, it looks like the Washington Monument, but it can't be. Do you see how there are curved grooves?*

I watched as replies poured in and added new information with each post.

"This is unreal," Emily said. "It's like they are doing the work of a whole team of detectives."

Darrin gave us a grim smile. "You have no idea. You don't want to piss these people off. They could ruin your life."

He hit refresh again.

*Damn, you are all right. A monument with curved grooves. My guess it's a column of some sort. And it's by . . .*

*Idiots, it's a Doric column. That's why you have grooves there. Open your F'n eyes.*

The next ten responses came fast in colorful language that played variations of curse words I had never heard before.

Jen looked closely at the picture. "I can't believe they figured out all this information in, what, five minutes?"

I nodded. "I don't think they are done."

Darrin refreshed.

*Put it all together, everybody. Just did a Google search for a large Doric column that looks like a monument on Lake Erie. . . . Could it be, drum roll . . . the Perry Monument on South Bass Island near Put-in-Bay, Ohio?*

Darrin pulled up a picture of the monument and whispered, "That's it."

"Right on the shores of the strange lake," Emily said.

"Well, more *in* the lake, it's on an island, but same thing," Jen said as she smiled. She reached for her phone and dialed. "Lieutenant? It's Brown. We got a location on where we think the picture was taken, but we have every reason to think she won't be there until . . ." She looked at Emily and Father Neal, who both mouthed "midnight."

"Midnight, the start of the feast of St. John, June twenty-fourth. We belive this has some kind of occult group association."

She paused and shrugged her shoulders. "Father Neal says the twenty-fourth, the feast of Saint John, has some kind of draw for these occultic groups."

Jen listened and said, "Yes, sir, it's concrete, I promise you. I'm going to leave a few detectives here and have the rest of the team come back to the station. We need the Canadians, the Coast Guard, the State, and I'm sure the FBI will want to join us.

"That's right. Command center and everything. I have a feeling we are going to be able to break the ring right here. However"—she looked at Emily—"Special Agent Jordan and I need to be in charge of the operation. How soon can we get it going?"

"Yessir. Hauling ass right now." Jen hung up the phone and said, "Are you all sure about this? Really sure?"

We all nodded and Darrin said, "If the picture is real, the 4chan people nailed it."

Jen said to Emily, "Do you think you can keep your sisters at bay while we arrest this Morgan?"

Emily shook her head. "Our vows are not to you, Detective. The Daughters of Laveau will go where we must. We haven't been this close in a very long time."

"Very well. I might shoot this woman myself, if it comes down to it."

"I wish you could, but she can only be killed with a special weapon. Morgan can't be killed by guns."

"Then by what?"

"Celestine would know. She is the one who will do the killing."

Jen looked at the rest of us. "Are you all okay with that?"

Father Neal said, "My dear, it is the only way. It is a horrible thing, but it must be done."

"I sure as hell am not going to lose sleep over it," Darrin said.

Jen looked at me and I said, "Think of what she has done. Not just to Lily, but to all the girls you have been trying to save."

She chewed on her lip, and I could guess the battle going on in her head. Jen had a strong sense of justice that often conflicted with her job. She had to obey the law, but sometimes the law stood in the way of justice in her way of thinking.

"Okay, if I can get the cavalry to hold back for a bit, do you think that will be enough time?" Jen said.

Emily cocked her head. "Do you think we can do that?"

Jen nodded. "I can tell them we have hostages. That'll be enough. As for what happens when you get there, that's up to you."

"We will make our way north. Call me when you get there."

To my surprise, Jen and Emily hugged. "May the Lord of Life go with you, dear sister," Emily said. When they broke apart, Jen wiped her eyes as Emily headed for the door, reaching for her cell phone.

"So, what do we do?" I asked.

"Nothing. You wait here with Brian until this is all done."

I shook my head. "That's not an option. I'm going up there."

Jen sighed. "I can't take the whole Scooby gang. It's just not possible."

"I didn't say you should. Take me and Father Neal."

"My dear, like it or not, you are going to need us both. You would put the lives of every law enforcement officer at risk. This isn't an ordinary criminal."

She steadied her hand on the desk. "Damn it. If I hadn't been with you two at Serpent Mound, I would say you are both certifiable."

Father Neal and I looked at each other. I grinned and said, "Well, we still might be certifiable."

Jen touched her scar. "Fine. But you two have to go separately. As in, right now. Get to the island and hide out in a hotel."

"We must be cautious. Morgan may be able to sense us. Actually, there is an Episcopal church up there. I'm on very good terms with the rector. She will hide us. It's not far from the monument, as a matter of fact."

He gave me a sidewise glance. I was pretty sure this meant the Five Sorrows would guard our presence.

"Fine. You should catch Emily and tell the Daughters of Laveau to go there. That will be the best place for them as well, don't you think?"

"Yes, I will go get her." Father Neal hobbled out the door.

Jen came around the table and collapsed in my arms. She sniffled, and I could feel my shirt getting wet from her tears. Darrin walked off to give us some privacy.

"Are you okay, love?"

She nodded. "I just need a little sleep."

"When will you be able to get some?"

"When we get up to Sandusky. We are going to have to get a command center going and brief everyone involved. It's going to be a huge undertaking. As I said, the Canadians will probably be in on this."

"Why?"

She smiled. "You keep forgetting your geography. The Canadian border isn't too far from the island. If they cross the line, we are going to need them. Plus, I'm guessing there is some sort of ship in the lake ready to take Lily and Ashley aboard."

I nodded, and she lifted her head up. Her eyes were glazed from her tears. "I really love you, Aidan."

"And I love you. I want to be with you the rest of my life, you know."

The words came out in a rush. I hadn't planned to say them because of everything going on. Seemed like horrible timing, but then again, I have never won awards for tact.

She clasped me to her. "Do you really mean it, Aidan?"

"Without a doubt. But I won't propose right now. Would like a better spot and circumstances, you know?" I said with a self-deprecating shrug.

Tears started to flow down her cheeks as she leaned in to whisper in my ear, "And I will say yes, just so you know."

We hugged for a moment, and I didn't want to let her go. I had no idea what the next twenty-four hours would bring.

"We have to go," she said, her voice muffled in my shirt.

"Don't want to."

"Lily, Aidan, we must get Lily."

I let her go. "Well, shall we saddle up?"

She looked up at me and her eyes had returned to hard-ass cop. "Hell yeah."

We went outside, and Jen started giving orders to pack up. Father Neal said, "The Daughters will meet us at Saint Michael's later this evening."

I stared at the house. "We have to tell Brian."

"Yes, my lad, we do. Do you want me—"

I cut him off. "No, Father, I'll do it. Tell Darrin and Kate to get everyone together to pray at the church. Have them call Olan and Edna as well."

Every step I took toward the house felt like walking through water. I didn't want to tell Brian what was going on. Then again, he probably suspected Ashley's involvement.

Brian was sitting on the couch, staring out the window. "Why are they leaving, Aidan?"

I sat down next to him. "We think we know where Lily and—"

"Ashley gave her over to him, didn't she?"

I nodded and my reply came out in a throaty rasp. "I'm afraid so."

"To whom? How?"

I would rather stab myself with a knife than tell him the truth.

"Aidan, tell me. Now."

"Ashley . . . She found your erotic site. She must have wanted to check it out for herself. The Grinning Man must have gotten to her there."

I figured he would break apart on me, but he didn't.

"I figured as much. It is my fault."

"Partially, yes. I won't lie to you, Brian."

"You don't need to."

He kept staring out of the window. "Where are they?"

"I can't tell you that."

"Are you going?"

"I can't tell you that, either."

He grabbed me by the shirt. "Bullshit. I need to know. Something tells me you shouldn't be going, either."

He had me. "No, we shouldn't be."

"We?"

"Father Neal is going with me."

Father Neal walked into the house and said, "Are you ready, Aidan?"

"Yeah, just—"

"Father, let me come," Brian said, tears falling from his eyes.

Furious, I said, "Brian, you can't!"

He cut me off with a wave of his hand. "I'm not talking to you, asshole. I'm talking to Father."

Father Neal examined Brian with his blue eyes. "Very well, my son. You have a right. I won't deny you."

"But, Father . . ."

"No arguments, Aidan. Brian must go, do you understand?"

"Not in the least."

"Then you'll have to trust me. We will wait until Jen leaves, so she won't be held responsible."

I fumed as we watched the departure of the command center and the uniformed officers. Jen loitered around the house, talked to a few officers, and then left.

"Do you think they'll leave a guard to keep the press out?"

"Yeah, it's still a crime scene. Jen is very thorough, Brian."

He nodded and said, "Can we go?"

I sighed. "Yeah, let's get on the road. I want to be there before dark."

# CHAPTER THIRTY-TWO

AS THE FERRY PULLED INTO THE DOCK ON SOUTH BASS ISLAND, THE PERRY monument loomed in the distance. The grooved stone column rose over the island like a lighthouse, complete with a cupola capping the top.

We arrived at Saint Michael's around five thirty in the evening. As we stepped off the dock, a tall, skinny, salt-and-pepper-haired woman greeted Father Neal with a hug.

"John, it's great to see you. How are things at the parish?"

"Very well, Mother Rebecca. Thank you for putting us up on such short notice."

She smiled. "You came at just the right time. We just had a parish vestry retreat leave this morning. You'll have the place all to yourself."

"Is it okay for us to have access to the sanctuary?"

"Of course. And you'll have some ladies joining you as well, yes?"

"Yes, they'll be joining us later tonight." He looked at us and said, "Forgive my rudeness, this is Aidan Schaeffer. He is going to start training as a priest in a few weeks."

Mother Rebecca enclosed my hand with hers. "So nice to

meet you, Aidan. You couldn't be training under a more beautiful and godly man."

When her skin touched mine, light flashed all around me. The pulsating sensation I felt in Father Neal's office, and in the forest, engulfed me. Mother Rebecca's face transformed from that of a mid-fifties woman to a goddess in an instant. Her flowing black hair reached to her shoulders and her skin shone from some unseen light. As I looked into her face, I gasped. Red rivulets began to run down her face, as if tiny thorns pierced her skull.

A member of the Order, I thought. Her wound was the crown of thorns.

I shook my head to clear the vision. Her words came into focus as the world returned to normal. "You are more than welcome here any time, Aidan."

As I tried to gain composure, I reverted to my inner smart-ass. "Thanks, Mother Rebecca, I appreciate the offer. As for Father Neal, I'm not sure about the beautiful part."

Father Neal, who watched me with a look of concern, rapped me on the ankles. "He also has no respect for his elders."

Neither of them seemed to realize what I'd seen or they pretended not to notice. I tried to catch my breath from my vision.

Rebecca laughed as she turned to Brian. "Welcome, my son."

Brian tried to force a smile. "Very nice to meet you, Mother Rebecca."

She waited for Brian to say more, and when he didn't, she motioned up the dock. "I have golf carts waiting for us. Seamus insisted on driving you himself, Father."

"And how is he?"

Rebecca rolled her eyes. "Still the cantankerous Irish sexton you know and love."

Large oak trees protected us from the heat of the late afternoon. I breathed in their sharp, woodsy smell as we walked. As we rounded the bend to the golf carts, a short, old man slid out of one and greeted us.

"Good to see ya, Father," Seamus McGammon said in a thick, Northern Irish accent as he extended a gnarled hand.

"And you, Seamus, how are you?"

"Ah, well, the joints ache and the doctor won't let me eat red meat anymore. Plus the damn kids keep tearing up the fellowship hall, if you'll pardon me."

"Seamus, our guests had a long drive," Mother Rebecca said.

"Ah, too right, Mother Rebecca. Let's get you back to the church and get food in your bellies. I'm guessing you're thirsty, too. You won't turn down something a bit more spirited, eh?"

I laughed. "As long as it burns my throat when it goes down."

"It'll put hair on your chest, lad. I think you and I will get along."

We loaded our overnight bags on to the carts. I sat with Mother Rebecca while Father Neal and Brian rode with Seamus.

Our cart followed Seamus's as he drove along the roads. I could see Brian lie back in his seat and stare at the scenery. His face had taken on a gray cast, as if he had just had a bout of food poisoning.

"So, you are a novice now, Aidan," Mother Rebecca said.

"You knew I saw you?"

She smiled. "Of course. First I knew from the look on your face. John was right, you can't hide your facial expressions. Plus, I felt the transformation."

"The transformation?"

"Surely, you know that when the veil is ripped away between this world and the unseen, you can feel it."

I nodded. "Yeah, true. Behold, right?"

Mother Rebecca chuckled. "Behold indeed. I assume you've seen the Guardians?"

"Yeah, I have. Powerful. I guess they are angels?"

She smiled. "I suppose you could call them that, although they may not quite fit the description."

"I don't understand."

"Well, they aren't very old. They came into being during the Lord's death. Or at least, some could perceive them."

Father Neal cleared his throat from the cart in front of us. Mother Rebecca blushed.

"Ah, he is right, I'm telling too much. I'm sorry, Aidan."

Bah, I'm going to get that old man, I thought.

"How long have you known him?"

She smiled. "That is an interesting question. Long enough."

I groaned. "You're as bad as he is."

"I'll take that as a compliment. You have already looked into the unseen world quite a bit. Now that you have made the decision to join us, there is going to be a whole lot more."

I didn't know how to handle Mother Rebecca's mysterious hints, so I tried to make a joke about it. "Gee, and here I thought I knew everything already."

She smiled as she stared ahead. "You'll see."

Our carts pulled into Saint Michael's as the sun began to set. The fossils of the limestone blocks glowed in the light, giving the church a heavenly glow.

"Mother Rebecca, the restorationists did an amazing job," Father Neal said.

"Restorationists?" I asked.

Mother Rebecca nodded. "Yes, we had a problem with vandals a few months ago. We had to have the limestone scraped, polished, and cleaned."

"What sort of graffiti?"

"Oh, you know, stupid kid stuff. It's been happening all over the state. Kids are losing respect for just about everything."

We got out of the carts and I grabbed my overnight bag. Seamus limped up to me. "So, you're Pastor Aidan, eh? Pastor, would you like a wee nip in the lodge?"

Mother Rebecca sighed. "Seamus, you really shouldn't bring alcohol into the retreat center."

He waved his hand. "Ah, come on, Mother, no one will know. We aren't going to get drunk or nothing."

"Very well. Father, is there anything else you need? I must call my sister this evening."

"Not at all, Mother Rebecca. Thank you very much. I'll join you for the morning service, if you don't mind."

She smiled. "Not at all. In fact, if you want to assist, I would love it. My deacon is on vacation."

"Would love to."

Mother Rebecca walked back toward the rectory as Seamus showed us to the lodge. We walked into a cozy, stone structure built around the time of the Great Depression. The setting sun poured through the windows and illumined the lounge area. A few comfortable-looking leather couches were placed about, and a large moose head dominated the fireplace.

"All of ye sit. I'll fetch the whiskey."

Brian, Father Neal, and I sat down on the couches. Brian looked about ready to break and I asked, "Bri, are you okay?"

Brian burst out, "No, I'm not okay. My wife and daughter are in the hands of a madwoman while we are going to sit here drinking whiskey."

"I know it's hard, Brian, but we have to wait. We need the Dark Bride to show herself and bring the girls out in the open. Jen is setting up all the agencies. We are putting our trap into place, don't you see?"

"No, I don't see. Each minute means something could happen to them!" Brian shouted.

He buried his face in his hands. The strong man I once knew, crumbled by the wreck of his life. I swallowed hard and fought my tears. Brian needed my strength. I came over to him and put my arm around his shoulder.

"Brian, there is nothing to be done until tonight. We have no idea where they might be hiding. This is our best and only option. I know it is terrible, but we are doing everything we can."

Brian gripped his hair in his hands. "It's all my fault. If Ashley hadn't seen those chat sites, we wouldn't be here."

"Listen to me, Bri. Yeah, you shouldn't have gone on those sites, but Ashley made her choice. She's the one who sold your daughter to these people. You didn't. What you did was bad. What she did was a million times worse."

"But I'm the guy, I'm supposed to protect my family, be the guardian."

"It's not your fault," Father Neal said as he leaned in. "We are all responsible for the choices we make. That is the way God has made it. The idea of the male being the only one responsible is a bit dated and a misunderstanding of the Bible."

Brian looked up with tears streaming down his cheeks. "Why? Why? I have always wanted to have the perfect family. I wanted everything to be like Christian families should be."

Father Neal shook his head. "Such a thing doesn't exist. There is no perfection in Christian families. That is a lie sold to us by the devil. Families are a mixture of people with all of our complex personalities, beauty, and sin. We have turned the beautiful idea of family into a bloody idol, sacrificing anything for it. Like all idols, it must be smashed to pieces, like the idol of Dagon before the Ark of the Old Covenant in the Old Testament. Remember, worshipping the pieces is even more pathetic."

"Yeah, think about it, Brian. If God's family is dysfunctional, why wouldn't everyone else's be?"

Father Neal rapped his cane on the floor. "Well said, Aidan."

Brian gave me a thin smile. "That's true, I guess." He looked at us and asked, "Will we get them back?"

"We are doing everything we can. That's all I can promise."

He nodded and slumped back into the couch. "I'll fight for them, if I get them back. I'll make sure we are never in this position again."

Seamus limped back into the lounge area. "Here we go, gents. Good ol' Irish whiskey, shipped to me from me brother back home."

He poured us generous amounts and we sipped under the watchful eye of the moose. About halfway through my glass, I heard the door open behind me. Seamus's eyes went wide as he said, "Mary and Joseph."

I looked behind my shoulder. The Daughters of Laveau stood in the doorway with Celestine in the lead. They wore identical white summer dresses, and their beauty radiated through the room. Dark skin, white skin, it didn't matter, because all of them glowed with an inner holy light. Their faces were fixed in an expression of grim determination that would cause even the strongest man to take a step back.

Father Neal stood. "Welcome, my daughters."

Celestine smiled. "Good evening, Father. We have a long night ahead of us."

"Yes. The sanctuary is open for your use. Mother Rebecca gave me the key."

"Um, am I missing something?" I asked. "What are you doing this evening?"

They all looked at me, and I had to fight the urge to run away.

"We are going to prepare ourselves for death, Aidan."

# CHAPTER THIRTY-THREE

**I TOSSED AND TURNED MOST OF THE NIGHT. JUST AS I WOULD DRIFT** off to sleep, a barrage of images would fill my mind. Lily's tearstained face. Brian's haggard sickness. Ashley's look of hollowed-out shame. A woman in a white dress with long black hair and pale skin. A grinning death's mask.

I must have drifted off to sleep at some point, because a knocking on my door jarred me awake.

"Aidan, are you okay?"

"Jen, hey, yeah, I'm fine. Hold on."

I threw on a shirt and opened the door. She wore faded jeans and a Ramones T-shirt.

"Hey, beautiful, come in."

She walked in and sat on the bed. I looked at the clock. Noon.

"Father Neal sent me to check on you."

"What time did you get here?"

"Just now."

I sat on the bed and put my arm around her. Dark circles under her eyes told me she hadn't slept at all.

"Is everything in place?"

"All set. We have had to blend in with the tourists." She smiled. "Which is why I borrowed your Ramones T-shirt."

"As I have always told you, there's nothing sexier than you in my T-shirts."

She lay her head on my lap and I held her. "The Coast Guard is standing by in Sandusky. The state police have already set up a command center, and Emily has agents walking through the city."

"I'm guessing they haven't found anything."

"Not a trace. You would think they would have left some sort of mark you could pick up on."

"Like what?"

"Oh, I dunno, you would think someone would notice a crazy woman leading around a woman and her daughter."

"What did Weaver say about the whole thing?"

"Not much. He is in Sandusky trying to quarterback with the Canadians. He is letting me run the show on the island. He thinks our 'tactics' are sound."

I scoffed. "Yeah, I doubt he would feel that way if he knew you were letting Emily and the Daughters of Laveau have the first shot."

She closed her eyes. "Yeah, let's not think about that, shall we?"

"When do you have to be back?"

"Weaver made me take a few hours to get some rest. He wants me back at the state police command center at four."

"Then sleep here in my bed. I'll go hang out in the lounge."

"No you won't. You'll stay right here with me."

I lay down and she snuggled up to me. We fell back asleep and woke to Jen's phone ringing. She answered, "This is Brown."

She listened for a moment and said, "I'll be right there."

"I have to get to the command center. The Ohio State Patrol wants to be in charge of the operation. I need Emily. Do you know where she is?"

"Check the church."

She kissed me and stared into my eyes. "Please be careful.

I'm worried about this whole thing. It doesn't feel right to me at all."

I nodded. "I know, me neither."

Jen touched my cheek and said, "I'll be watching over you, I promise."

I smiled. "I think that's supposed to be my line."

She hit me. "Get over it, you Neanderthal. This is the twenty-first century."

"Just because it's the twenty-first century doesn't mean I can fight my male instinct to protect you."

She smiled. "Fair enough."

She kissed me again, got out of bed, put on her gun holster, and said, "I'll see you tonight."

I took a shower and made my way to the lounge. I grabbed some coffee and saw Brian sitting on the deck, staring out the window.

I went out and sat down next to him.

"I'm coming with you."

"And why would you do that?"

Brian frowned. "Isn't that obvious?"

"I don't think that is such a good idea. Besides, I doubt Emily or the other Daughters would allow it."

"I'm not asking for permission, Aidan. I have a right and you know it."

I sighed. "Do you really want that, Brian? You might see things you wish you hadn't."

He nodded. "I'll live with it."

I gripped his arm. "Will you? Because let me warn you, bud, you'll never be rid of those images." I pointed to the monument. "Your daughter and your wife will be there tonight. Who knows what condition they are going to be in? Do you really want to remember that for the rest of your life?"

"You think they'll be dead?"

I shook my head. "No. But, there are some things worse than death."

"What are you not telling me?"

The image of Lily next to the monument flashed in my head. I wouldn't tell him. I would take that to my grave. No father should ever see his daughter with that look of abject fear.

"Nothing, Brian. I'm just saying, I don't know what these people may have done to them."

Brian gripped the arms of his chair. "You think that is going to help me not think about it? My imagination is already doing a fine job of filling my mind with horrific images. I wonder if reality is any worse than that."

I didn't feel like arguing anymore. "Okay, Brian."

Father Neal joined us on the porch. "Is everything okay?"

Brian walked past him. "Just fine, Father."

Father Neal looked at me and I shook my head.

"Tell me, what's going on with the law enforcement side of things?"

"Jen was here a few minutes ago. The law enforcement pieces are in place. She is talking to Emily about the Daughters of Laveau's plans. Do you know anything?"

Father Neal nodded. "We will meet in the church for the Eucharist at nine tonight. When it's finished, we are going to walk to the monument from here."

"Why are we walking?"

"The same reason as at Serpent Mound, Aidan."

I nodded, remembering the wall of resistance we had met. "Will it be worse?"

"I think we can count on that. But, the Five Sorrows will be with us."

"Will the rest of the Order join us?"

Father Neal shook his head. "No, just me. Mother Rebecca will be praying for us. Your powers are growing. Faster than I've ever seen, truth be told. You're able to call on the Sorrows without much of a problem. That is rare early on, my son."

"And here I just wanted to be a humble priest." I smiled.

"That means putting a target on your back for the dark forces of Tellus, who stand behind the Grinning Man and the Hellfire Club. The Watchers, the Nephilim. Mike and Daniel at the Serpent's Mound were child's play, Aidan. Two-bit magicians who dabbled in darkness."

"Yeah, because the murder of Amanda was only mostly evil." I frowned.

Father Neal rapped my shins. "Don't be sarcastic, boy. This is serious."

"I'm being totally serious, old man."

"Let me ask you a question, Aidan. The evil we are about to face, up at that monument, don't you think it's worse than what Mike and Daniel did?"

I looked at the gleaming white of the monument. "Yeah, you are right."

"What you have stumbled on, or rather what Brian and Ashley stumbled on, is a window into what evil is doing in the world: destroying people. The group has fought this sort of thing for ages."

"This evil, is it led by the Grinning Man?"

Father Neal shook his head. "No, but they are using him for something. What that is, I'm not sure of just yet."

I looked toward the monument. "Do you think he'll be out there tonight?"

He shrugged. "I don't know. That remains to be seen."

"Are you ready for that?"

He smiled forbiddingly. "That, too, remains to be seen."

I rubbed my head. "People are going to die tonight, I can feel it."

Father Neal looked grim. "Yes, I think you are right. That is why we are having communion tonight."

"Prepare our souls and all that?"

"Yes, exactly. Will you assist me?"

"Of course. I figured you would have Mother Rebecca do that, though."

"She will help as well. I want you to watch my movements and get an understanding of the service."

"Who all will be there?"

"I want the Daughters of Laveau, Brian, you, and Jen, if she can make it."

"I don't know if Jen will. She is trying to run interference at the command center for us. Apparently, the State boys are trying to throw their weight around."

Father Neal shook his head. "I hope Jen wins, because there will be even more deaths if they get involved."

"Come on, wouldn't a fully armed SWAT team do the job, Father?"

"No."

He looked up at the sky. Dark, towering clouds started to build and roll toward each other. "We are going to have some serious storms tonight. That sort of energy in the air will make things worse."

"I don't understand."

"Morgan will have much more energy to play with in her magick. A SWAT team would be burned to death in seconds."

"From what?"

"Lightning strikes."

"She has the power to direct lightning?"

Father Neal nodded. "We must assume it. Although her not having the knife will be an advantage for us. She'll be wild and undirected. That has its own dangers, but also opportunities. In any case, it is important that Jen keeps the law enforcement people at bay."

"She took Emily with her to throw her weight around. The task force is supposed to be commanding this operation. So whatever trouble the State people are causing should be cleared up rather quickly."

He got up and groaned. "I think this old body is not meant to sleep on metal-spring beds anymore. Don't worry. I will tell you everything. It's time to pass on the leadership."

I furrowed my brow. "Father, I don't know anything. Why would I be the leader?"

He smiled. "All in good time, Aidan. I'll see you in the chapel at nine."

Father Neal limped inside. I decided to take a walk along the water to collect my thoughts. I reflected on the changes in my life in the past year and half. My parents dying. Amanda being murdered. My crisis of faith. Jen. Father Neal. Each felt ordained and ordered, as if this filled holes in my life. I had always felt it, a nagging sensation of something just beyond the horizon. During my crisis of faith, I had tried to dismiss that feeling into a naturalistic oblivion. God had brought it back with a roaring intensity as He reminded me of the limits of my own logic. Oddly, I hadn't jettisoned science and rationality. In fact, Father Neal had taught me that my beliefs ought to be the logical end of those sorts of discussions. What could be seen is only a part of the larger puzzle, a greater mystery. I felt as though I had just begun to scratch the surface.

I looked up at the clouds beginning to build in spiraling towers above my head. The storms tonight would be epic, both in the seen and unseen worlds.

I muttered, "I just hope we all survive."

# CHAPTER THIRTY-FOUR

I WALKED INTO THE CHAPEL AT 8:00 P.M. THE LIGHTS WERE OUT, AND candles lit the darkening chapel. The Daughters of Laveau knelt in a pew and didn't move. Brian sat a few pews behind them with his head bowed. The church radiated peaceful stillness, and I could smell the tang of incense, the scent of holiness. I missed Jen, but I knew she needed to get the cops in order.

Father Neal and Mother Rebecca knelt in front of the altar, dressed in white robes. I wasn't sure how Father Neal wanted me to help, so I stood behind them in silence. He looked up and nodded his head toward the sacristy. I opened the door and Father Neal followed me.

He grabbed a white robe and held it up. "This is an alb, in case you didn't know."

I nodded as he continued, "Not a robe, as I'm sure you will be tempted to call it more than once."

I slipped it on over my head. "Well, I'm still Presbyterian, after all."

"Yes, but you have to start changing your mindset now, Aidan. Your new life has begun."

"Yes, Father." I pulled the alb over my head, adjusted the cincture, and stood at attention.

He appraised me with a look and then said, "You'll do. Now listen, stay at my right hand when I do the words of institution of the sacrament, okay?"

I nodded.

"Watch my every move. Don't worry about the exact words. That is what the prayer book is for. Everything else will flow naturally, okay?"

"Yes, let's do it."

Mother Rebecca came in. "Are you two ready?"

Father Neal said, "Let us proceed."

Mother Rebecca led us out to the altar. She stopped, bowed her head, and took her place behind the altar. I followed and stared up at the cross.

Father Neal bowed and took his place behind the altar. He lifted up his arms and said, "May the Lord be with you!"

Everyone responded, "And also with you."

"And now, brothers and sisters, let us confess our sins and ask for God's protection using the Litany."

Father Neal raised his hands. "Lord have mercy."

We responded, "Lord have mercy."

"Christ have mercy."

"Christ have mercy."

Father Neal said, "Let us pray.

"From all evil and mischief; from sin; from the crafts and assaults of the devil; from thy wrath; and from everlasting damnation."

"Good Lord, deliver us."

"From all inordinate and sinful affections; and from all the deceits of the world, the flesh, and the devil."

"Good Lord, deliver us."

The litany washed over me as I repeated the responses with everyone. I started to grasp why I had wanted to become an Anglican. Everything about the worship grabbed the senses, engaged the mind, and made me feel intertwined with the nexus point of heaven and earth. Heaven and earth truly joined as God's people celebrated the true joining of flesh and spirit.

When I shook myself out of my thoughts, Father Neal started in on the communion service. "We break this bread to share the body of Christ."

We responded, "Though we are many, we are all one body because we share in one bread."

Those words nailed me. No matter how badly Christians fought, no matter how much we displayed contempt for each other, the Lord's Supper told us something else. That God wanted his people to eat his body and blood in unity.

Father Neal said to us, "Come to the altar and receive the grace of Christ. Anyone who freely confesses their sin and their utter need for Christ may come."

Father Neal gave communion to Mother Rebecca, who came over to me and said, "The body of Christ, the bread of heaven."

I took a thin wafer and said, "Amen."

She handed me a chalice full of wine and said, "The blood of Christ, shed for you."

"Amen." I drank deep and crossed myself. When I did, the air vibrated and Mother Rebecca touched my ribs. Heat flowed into me. I felt my ribs, my eardrum, my bruises, and my whole body mend. All the aches in my body disappeared. She gave me a small smile and turned to walk to the railing where everyone knelt.

Father Neal motioned to me and I came up to the altar. He whispered, "I want you to distribute communion."

He gave me the cup full of wafers and the chalice full of wine. The Daughters of Laveau and Brian knelt at the altar. Celestine took the wafer and dipped into the wine. I went down the line, giving Aisha, the twins, and Emily the Lord's body and blood.

After the Eucharist, Father Neal said, "Now that we have partaken of the body and blood of Christ, I will anoint you with oil for the night ahead."

He motioned for me to join everyone, and I knelt beside Emily. "Aidan, may this oil represent Christ's holy protection as you fight against evil this night. May it guard your heart and mind through the power of the Holy Spirit. May it make you strong in heart, mind, and spirit. May it help your hands work for holiness and not darkness."

Father Neal anointed my head, my heart, and my hands with the sign of the cross. The oil glistened in the candlelight, and the holiness of Christ covered my head. I felt strong, ready, and I had no fear of death. I hoped it would last.

When Father Neal finished with everyone, he said, "May the love of God the Father, the salvation of God the Son, and the unity of the Holy Spirit guide and protect you. May he send his holy angels to watch over you, led by Saint Michael, the sworn enemy of Satan. May they guard you in all things through the finished work of Our Lord. In the name of the Father, the Son, and the Holy Spirit. Go in peace to love and serve the Master."

We responded, "Amen."

Celestine stood up and said, "Daughters, it is time."

# CHAPTER THIRTY-FIVE

THE SKY TURNED RED AS THE SUN REFLECTED OFF THE STORMCLOUDS that had gathered over the island. If anyone had decided to go for a late-evening stroll, they would have gotten a shock as Rebecca led us through a path in the woods toward the monument. I walked behind her, followed by Father Neal and Brian. The Daughters of Laveau brought up the rear, still dressed in their white dresses.

The Perry Monument lay hidden by the trees as we made our way along the path through the small forest. The Daughters began to sing in quiet whispers, and I could just make out a few French words. They called for protection, strength, and the defeat of the enemy.

A low roll of thunder broke the stillness and a flash of light filled the woods. Father Neal held up his hand. "She knows we are here."

Out of nowhere, wind began to rush through the trees at hurricane force. Limbs blew off trees and flew around our heads. Splinters filled the air and pricked our skin. We hit the ground with arms covering our heads. Dust kicked up and swirled around us. My mouth filled with dirt and leaves.

Father Neal shouted in a language that sounded both guttural and lilting. He raised his cane as the winds whipped his body. The winds broke and the air became still. Limbs and debris dropped from the sky. A tree limb fell on me, and I cried out in pain.

Celestine crawled over to me. "Are you okay, *mon amour*?"

I grimaced. "Yeah, other than this tree limb on my shoulder."

She, Emily, and Brian moved the limb, and I stood up. Pain shot up my arm as I got to my feet. Breathing hard, I said, "Why is it every time I make contact with the magickal world, I receive some sort of horrible injury."

Everyone chuckled, and I heard the relief in their voices.

"Because, lad, dark magick is jealous of your good looks," Father Neal said.

"Yeah, well, it can have them."

Celestine asked, "What was all that, Père?"

Father Neal gave us a grim smile. "The outer line, as it were. Merely a sentry."

"A sentry?" Brian said.

"Yes, lad. The Dark Bride has made contact with some local spirits, it seems."

He pointed with his cane. "Onward, fellow soldiers. We have broken through the first line. The next ones will not be so easy. She will have plenty of time to plan more nasty surprises."

As if to prove his point, lightning flashed and thunder rolled overhead.

"Care to elaborate, Old Wizard?" I asked.

He shook his head. "I can't. I don't know what she will come up with. It could be anything, so watch your step."

We reached the end of the forest trail, and the monument stood in front of us.

Father Neal motioned for us to come to him. He huddled us together and whispered, "How far do you think the monument is from here?"

"I'd say about two football fields, give or take a few yards."

Brian nodded. "And all on open ground."

Brigit pointed to a strip of white that lay just under the monument. "What is that white line over there?"

We all looked. I couldn't make out anything, other than that the line of white seemed broken up by spaces.

Father Neal slumped against me. "Dear Lord, no."

I held onto him. "What is it?"

"People, Aidan. There are people lying on the ground."

"Women," Celestine said, and her face paled at the realization.

"Potential slaves," Aisha broke in.

The truth of her words hit me like a blow to the chest. Ashley and Lily weren't the only ones who would be sacrificed to the "colleagues" of the Grinning Man. I tried to count out the bodies lying on the ground.

"I can make out about twenty."

Father Neal nodded. "That seems right from what I can see. Celestine?"

"I agree," she said as she pulled out a knife. I looked at it and I gasped.

I looked at Celestine. "Why the hell did you bring that thing along?"

Celestine glanced at Father Neal, who eyed the blade with obvious distaste. "It's the only way to kill her: with her own knife. We have to get close enough to plunge it into her heart."

"You can't be serious," I said.

"It's the only way, Aidan."

"That thing is evil, at least you said so. How can we even think to use it?" I couldn't help it. I spat on the ground.

"Aidan, we're not using the magick. It will be used as a weapon only. Never fear."

"Fine, but how are we going to get that close? We have to cross two hundred yards of open ground and"—something caught my attention—"deal with those guys who are guarding the women."

Lightning flashed to reveal dark outlines walking around the bodies as they stood guard. I couldn't make out any guns, but that didn't mean anything, I knew. They probably still had them.

Father Neal smiled. "Well, this just got interesting, didn't it?"

My stomach churned and my pulse raced. Still, I tried to downplay my fear. "Understatement of the year."

Brian leaned in and said, "What's the plan?"

Father Neal looked over the ground. "You are wrong. The ground isn't totally flat. There are some hills and ridges off to the left. Daughters, you need to take that path. We will be the diversion."

"And how are we going to do that?" I asked, dreading the answer.

"We are going to walk straight across the field and right up to the guards."

"Damn fool, I knew you were going to say that."

"Who's the fool, the fool who goes in or the fool that follows him?" Father Neal said, whipping out a *Star Wars* line.

"All right, Obi-Wan, lead us. I didn't want to live long anyway."

Emily held up her hand. "We have to get hold of Jen. I promised to let her know our plans."

I checked my phone, but the display kept going in and out.

"My phone is going out. I can't call her."

Emily smiled as she looked over my shoulder. "Why don't we just tell her?"

Arms encircled me from behind, and I heard a familiar voice say, "My, you have a fine ass, come here often?"

I turned and gave my black-clad girlfriend a hug. Her face was smeared with black camouflage paint, but her eyes reflected the familiar twinkle.

She pointed out to the guards. "You've seen them?"

I nodded. "Bastards."

"Don't worry. There are only two places they are going tonight: prison or hell."

She pointed out to the lake. "The Coast Guard has cleared the waters. They have two patrol boats out there. They just radioed that a large yacht had just crossed the border and is headed our way."

I checked my watch: 11:50 p.m. "Just in time."

"I can keep everyone at bay for a while. They know that Em is on the ground with some other agents. They'll all wait for my signal. What's the plan?"

Emily told her and Jen said, "I don't like it."

Father Neal put his hand on Jen's arm. "Don't worry, my dear. I'll bring Aidan back in one piece."

"This is stupid," Jen argued.

I shook my head. "We have to give the Daughters of Laveau a way in. Besides, even if the guards do have guns, something tells me the Dark Bride doesn't want us shot dead."

"You don't even know where she is."

"True, but she has to be somewhere near the women, wouldn't you say?" I pointed across the dark field.

"Yes, but she could be anywhere, like hidden behind one of those trees," Jen said, folding her arms and frowning.

"I realize that. But do you have any better plans?"

I could tell I had struck home as Jen said, "This is bullshit. I can't stand to watch you walk across that field."

I touched her cheek. "Then don't watch."

Jen hit me in the arm. "Damn it, Aidan." She turned to Emily. "If anything happens to him, I'm going to hold you and your sisters responsible, got it?"

Emily nodded.

Jen checked her phone. "Fine. Go. I'll move in when I get your signal."

She turned to me. "You better come back to me, boy."

Jen disappeared into the woods. My stomach clenched at the thought I might not see her again.

*Dear God, please bring me through this. Please let us be happy. I love her.*

"All right, are we ready?" Father Neal asked.

I nodded. "Brian?"

He started walking. "Let's do it."

The old priest grabbed his arm. "I think I should go first, lad."

"Hold on," I said as I grabbed a long stick. "Time to put the shillelagh lessons to good use."

We walked in a single file line out onto the field with Father Neal in the lead. I couldn't help but think of Pickett's charge as we started crossing the open ground toward the monument. I imagined the Confederates felt just as hopeless as they marched across the field, knowing a hail of bullets would mow them down.

Mist began to form in the air around us, swirling in a steady wind. Very soon, we could see only about two feet in front of us. The fog muted any sounds, and everything went silent. However, the fog glowed with a dim green light as it shifted and swirled.

"I guess fog is the next weapon," Brian said.

"No, my dear boy, the fog is merely the beginning." Father Neal pointed, and the fog formed into humanlike shapes. My skin chilled as I watched slaves by the hundreds lurch toward us. The crabbed, broken-limbed slave who had haunted my dreams scuttled toward us on the ground. A two-headed monstrosity moaned its pain as it begged for death.

"The ghosts of Morgan's victims?" I asked.

Father Neal shook his head. "No, it's . . ."

The figures pressed in closer to us and I could feel the cold on my skin as they touched us with their wispy gray fingers. Moans filled my ears as I knelt on the ground.

*. . . knives, they cuts us . . .*

*. . . broke my limbs . . .*

*Starved us. She starved us.*

The moans rose to a fevered pitch, and I heard Brian cry out. I tried to crawl to him, but the icy hands forced me down. The fingers began to tear at my hair and rip my clothes.

"Christ . . . Christ have mercy," I gasped.

I heard Father Neal say the same, and the green light began to flicker. The figures began to squirm and scream as the light swallowed them up.

Brian stood and almost fell over again. He steadied himself with his fighting stick. Father Neal leaned on his cane, looking at the turbulent sky about us. I felt the hair on my arms raise and the air began to crackle.

Father Neal shouted, "Run!"

We ran as fast as we could across the field. Thunder rolled, and the air began to heat up with energy. Lightning flashed and bolts began to strike the ground all around us. Dirt kicked up in the air and sprayed us with debris. I made it to the concrete surrounding the monument, Father Neal hobbling behind me. I stopped and he yelled, "Keep going, lad. She can't hurt me."

I ran as fast as I could, bolts hitting all around me. I could hear the voice of a woman whispering in French, *Elements, voici mon ordre. Détruisez-le. À la poussière, il reviendra.*

"Elements, here is my command. Destroy him. Unto dust, shall he return."

My breath came in ragged gasps as I reached Brian and collapsed on the concrete steps in front of the monument.

"Where is Father Neal?"

I motioned back toward the field and wheezed. "Should be . . . coming . . . soon."

We watched the field, straining to see Father Neal's familiar form.

"I don't even see his body lying on the ground," Brian said.

"Me, either."

We looked again. Nothing.

"You don't think . . ."

"He was vaporized? No, I don't think so. Lightning doesn't do that to people. It's too quick."

He grimaced. "That wasn't ordinary lightning."

I nodded. "He'll turn up, don't worry." I tried to force myself to believe my own words as I caught my breath.

"Now what?"

"We go after the guards." I twirled my stick.

He grinned. "What are we waiting for?"

We raised our sticks in the charge position and crept around the base of the stairs. Four guards with dark masks covering their faces stood with their backs to us.

I put my finger to my lips, and Brian nodded.

"Well, these girls are smoking hot. I imagine the Archon in Cleveland wants them? He'll have a good time, eh?" said the guard in the middle, turning to his companions.

"Asshole. These aren't for his pleasure. I don't know if he even has sex anymore, to be honest," said the guard on the right.

"Why do we serve him anyway? Don't we obey the Grinning Man? Isn't he our master?" The guard on the left stretched his long arms over his head.

The middle guard shrugged. "They're working together, that's all I know. Something is going on in Cleveland, though; that's for sure. You can practically feel the darkness gathering. Loved every minute of it. The power is growing here, that's for sure."

So, all the girls seemed bound for Cleveland. Why didn't they just take them by car and save the hassle? I couldn't figure out what I was missing. Or maybe only some of them? Who the hell was the Archon?

I pointed to the guards and put up four fingers. Brian nodded and motioned to the two guards on the left. He crept slowly over to the left, and I readied myself. I raised the stick and pointed forward. Without a word, we attacked.

I hit guard number one with the full force of the stick. With a few quick strikes, I knocked him flat on his back. A final whirl with the stick and a crack to the head put him down for the count. Guard number two swirled out two knives.

"Ready, my friend?" I smiled.

The guard moved, slashing at me with both knives. I twirled my stick and whacked him in the head. He grunted with the force of the blow but didn't go down. His eyes glinted with hatred as he stared at me through the mask. With a flurry of twirling, he swung his knives, and I barely parried each swipe. He overreached himself and left his stomach wide open. With a quick thrust, I put the stick into his stomach. He doubled over, and then I brought my stick around in a swift arc. The stick made a loud cracking noise as it whacked him on the side of the head with full force. He crumbled to the ground without a sound.

I turned to watch Brian. He finished off the last of his two guards when I saw another one creeping up behind him. With horror, I yelled out, "Brian, look—"

The guard plunged a knife into his back. Brian cried out and sank to his knees. Blood pounded in my ears as I rushed forward. I hit the guard in the face with my stick and drove him to the ground. Remembering my golfing technique, I took a full swing into the side of his head. Blood spurted out, and I sank the butt of my stick in his mouth. The guard passed out from the pain. I kicked the guard over in my fury and I nearly stuck him again when something grabbed my stick.

"Peace, my son, it's over."

Father Neal's voice soothed my anger, and I let him take the stick from me. We knelt down over Brian. Father Neal tore Brian's shirt to look for an outer knife wound. Seeing none, he said, "Brian, I need you to turn over, can you?"

Brian nodded and turned over. Blood soaked the back of his shirt. Father Neal tore off the rest of the material. The knife had entered between the spine and the shoulder blade. Father Neal looked concerned as he said, "Can you breathe?"

Brian gasped. "Yeah, but every breath hurts."

"I think the knife may have gotten to the lung, but I can't be sure. You need a hospital, and you need it now."

Brian motioned to the line of girls in white. "Are they over there?"

Father Neal and I ran over to the girls. My heart did flips as I gazed at the faces of the women who'd been marked for slavery. Every one of them wore a white robe, and their arms were crossed over their chests. Their eyes were closed, as if they'd lain down for a good night's sleep, and their faces radiated a serene peace. All of them seemed between sixteen and twenty-two or so. Most of them were probably farm girls who had been looking for work and were stolen by the assholes we had just taken out.

"What's wrong with them?" I asked.

Father Neal knelt down and pressed his hand on the forehead of a beautiful blonde girl about seventeen years old. The innocence in her face almost made me weep.

"They have been put into a deep sleep. How, I'm not sure," Father Neal answered.

"Magick?"

He shook his head. "No, most likely some sort of drug."

"I don't see Ashley or Lily."

Thunder rolled and lightning flashed. We looked up to the top of the monument as it rose above our heads. The Daughters of Laveau came out of the trees to the right of the monument. Celestine looked at the girls and Brian with an expression of suppressed rage.

"Where is she, Father?"

He pointed up with his cane. "There, my dear. My guess is that is where she is waiting for us, at the top."

"Then to the top we will go," I said, already aching at the thought.

# CHAPTER THIRTY-SIX

FATHER NEAL STARED AT THE TOP AS THE DAUGHTERS OF LAVEAU BEGAN to enter the monument.

"Are you going with us?"

He shook his head. "No. I need to take care of Brian and the women. They shouldn't be left alone."

"I'll stay with them. The Daughters are going to need you."

He put his hand on my shoulder. "They have you."

"Yeah, but I don't know any magick, Father."

Father Neal smiled. "That is why they need you. Magick will not win this situation, and I'll be too tempted to use it."

I looked at him and understood. Using magick his whole life had taken so much out of him that any more might kill him. I didn't think death scared him, but I also didn't think he wanted to meet Christ in that way.

"You just don't want to climb those stairs, old man."

He chuckled. "Indeed. Now go, my son. I'll watch over the injured."

I entered the monument and paused. The circular marble room was flanked by curving stairs on each side. A star dominated the floor and friezes of British and American soldiers lined the walls. A sign told visitors that three British soldiers and three American soldiers lay buried below the monument. A voice spoke to me from the right stairway. "Pastor Aidan, we are over here."

With a deep breath, I joined the Daughters of Laveau at the bottom of the stairs. Emily smiled. "Are you ready to climb?"

I shook my head. "We won't have to. There's an elevator."

They all looked at me as if I had lost my mind and Aisha said, "Uh, Pastor Aidan, she can conduct electricity, so an elevator isn't the best idea."

"That's where you are wrong. She'll be expecting us to come up the stairs. You don't think she'll have more nasty little surprises for us along the way? I'm not too excited to meet any more."

They all looked at one another. Celestine smiled. "Well, you aren't just a pretty face, are you?"

I frowned. "Funny. Let's just get going."

We climbed the stairs to the elevator, and I punched the UP button. The elevator dinged and the doors opened. I motioned with my hand, "Ladies, after you."

They all piled into the elevator, and the door shut. We rode in silence as we stared at the ground. Despite confidence in my plan, I couldn't help but wonder when we would be hit with lightning and go plunging to a crushing death. As the elevator rose, my stomach did flips with each metallic noise and click.

The elevator shuddered, and we heard a ding, announcing our arrival at the top. The Daughters of Laveau all drew out knives, and Celestine cradled Morgan's knife to her breast. I gripped my stick, hoping it would be enough. I felt like the kid who was about to watch two gunfighters shoot it out in the streets.

The doors opened, and we stepped out onto the observation deck. The Daughters' white dresses shone in the darkness, but I couldn't make out any other light.

"See anything?" Brigit asked.

I turned to answer her, and her head snapped back as if pulled by some unseen force. Her eyes went wide with shock as she fell to the floor.

"Brigit! No!" Aislinn screamed as she hit the floor. We all knelt down. Blood trickled out of her mouth. Emily felt her neck.

"Emily?" Celestine asked hesitantly.

"She's dead. From the sound and feel of it, it's a broken neck."

No. I'd just talked to her. She couldn't be—

A high, fierce female laugh rattled in the darkness around us. *Hello, my sisters. Glad you could join me.*

I felt a hot prick in my skin, then another, and another. My whole body felt as if it were being bitten by fire ants and I cried out, "What the—"

*And you brought Aidan with you. How lovely. Do we get to have our way with him, Sisters?*

We looked around, but dark shadows started to envelop the entire observation deck. Everything shifted in perspective and I couldn't make out any tangible forms or shapes.

"Don't respond, that's what she wants," Celestine said as she stared at Brigit. Aislinn tried to hold back her grief. She clutched at Emily, who held her tight.

A voice filled the air, but I couldn't locate its source.

*So, you finally caught up with me, after all these years. Was Marie finally able to break through and tell you were I was?* Her tone dripped with scorn.

"No, your master betrayed you," I said.

A scream tore through the darkness. My right eardrum burst with a stabbing pain. I cried out as I put my hand to my ear. Warm blood oozed over my fingers, and I fell to the ground.

*He did not betray me, you lie!* the voice shrieked.

Celestine stood and held up the knife. "Then why do I have this, Morgan?"

Wind tore through the room and whipped through our clothes with hurricane strength. The Daughters of Laveau's dresses began to tear, and my Green Lantern T-shirt began to rip in half.

*You stole it. Someone stole it. He would never give it you, not a knife of the Nephilim.* A voice screamed in the wind as it lessened in fury so we could hear.

Nephilim. Dear God, that knife belonged to the Nephilim, not just the Grinning Man.

My legs wobbled as I stood by Celestine. "We told you: your master gave it to us. Apparently, he no longer requires your services."

The monument shook as if a giant had struck it with his fists. Celestine fell into me and I steadied her. Aislinn, Emily, and Aisha stood by us, their dresses torn, hair disheveled, but with death in their eyes.

"Show yourself, Morgan, whore of the Dark Masters. The Daughters of Marie Laveau have come to end you."

*Fools, fools! If you end me, you'll end yourselves,* the voice screeched.

Emily smiled. "We'll gladly do that."

Everything went silent, and then the voice whispered, *Why don't you come to the top, my dears? We can talk. I have beautiful ladies you might be interested in, maybe we can bargain.*

Celestine nodded toward the door, and we made our way outside. Lake Erie lay about three hundred feet below us on the left side and the town of Put-in-Bay on the right. Emily took out a metal cylinder. "I think it's time for the cavalry."

She tore a metal lanyard and launched a bright red flare into the night toward the town. A few moments later, a flare came up in response. We could see cars begin to move toward the monument. I looked out toward the lake and saw two Coast Guard ships flip on their lights as they made their way to the black yacht.

A whisper broke in. *I'm up here.*

We looked up and saw a metal platform that rose above the stone circle that held the elevator. Girders crisscrossed to support a metal dome that looked like a spaceship.

In the middle of the cupola room, Ashley and Lily hung suspended in the air, illumined by a greenish glow. I suppressed the urge to cry out when I saw Lily's face. Someone had cut thin lines into her forehead that looked like Hebrew writing. My stomach churned as memories of Amanda flooded my mind. Mike and

Daniel had cut words into her head before they killed her. I didn't pay any attention to Ashley because her face just filled me with anger I didn't need now.

Below Brian's girls, a dark figure stood with arms outstretched. When I looked at the head, a shimmering visage came into view. Morgan's beautiful, pale face, ruby lips, and dark eyes probably seduced more men than I cared to think about.

A voice whispered into my ear, *Hello, beautiful boy. You want me. I can feel it. Your energy . . . pulsing.*

I swallowed hard and said, "*Kyrie Eleison. Christe Eleison. Kyrie Eleison.*"

The face of the figure turned into a skull with empty sockets. Black and red flames flickered over the facial bones. My prayers showed her true being to me—death, the destroyer.

"Aidan, are you okay?"

Celestine touched me on the shoulder and I looked up. The figure disappeared.

"Yeah, yeah, I'm fine. Morgan was just here. She appeared to me first."

"That is because you're a man, *mon cher*. Easily seduced by her."

I frowned. "Not that easily."

She smiled and put her finger to her lips. Emily motioned for us to take up separate positions around Ashley and Lily. No one spoke as we waited for Morgan to make her next move.

The stillness stretched on until I wondered if I should say something to the Daughters. As I opened my mouth, a warm, inviting laugh echoed through my head.

*My, my, what a gathering: a delicious young pastor and his consorts with Madame Laveau's handpicked bitch at the head.*

I gripped my wooden branch. "Come out, Morgan, and fight us. Your plan is falling apart. It's over."

She laughed, the sound piercing me.

*Oh, Aidan, you've come to play. I'll try not to bite . . . hard.*

A gust of wind hit me full force and knocked me to the ground.

Air sucked from my lungs, and I took deep gasping breaths as I struggled not to pass out.

When I sat back up, I heard Celestine scream, and I turned as she launched herself at the Dark Bride. She hit the witch with full force and knocked her to the ground. Celestine raised the knife, but Morgan stuck out her hand and said something in a language I couldn't understand.

My stomach clenched as a strong gust of wind hit Aislinn and she flew in an arc off the monument.

"NO!" Aisha screamed as Aislinn fell into the darkness. She made to run toward the edge, but I grabbed her.

"No, Aisha, no. Don't. She's gone."

She screamed and beat my chest. I wouldn't let her go, and Emily ran over to help me.

Celestine fought Morgan with body blows and punches to the face, looking for another opportunity to use the knife. Her rage took over as the fighting pair rolled over the metal platform. Emily and Aisha rushed in to help. The Dark Bride uttered a few more words, and the two girls flew through the air toward me. I caught both of them as they flew by me and we collapsed to the ground in a heap.

"Are you two okay?" I gasped.

No response.

As I stood, I saw both of them lying motionless on the ground.

"Please God, no, not them, too."

I felt their pulses and breathed a sigh of relief.

I turned around to see Morgan throw Celestine to the ground, and the knife clattered toward the middle of the platform. Blood oozed from both their mouths as the Dark Bride raised her hand. I ran at her with my stick, whirled and cracked her on the head. She shrieked in pain and planted a hand into my chest. The force of the blow threw me back to the metal floor.

Morgan laughed. *Foolish man. The good priest has not taught you enough tricks to take me on, lover. I think I shall enjoy having you for a slave.*

She turned to Celestine, raised her hand, and lifted her into the air. *As for you, my sister, the Daughters of Laveau come to an end tonight. There'll be no more hunting. Only pain.*

Morgan stood at the edge of the platform, silhouetted against the lake. Her hands raised in triumph as she began to utter her spell of destruction. Celestine cried out and writhed in agony on the metal floor.

*All of you are mine. I'll take the good priest, too. He is almost dead anyway. But I'll keep you alive for my . . .* She paused and leered at me.

She motioned and pinned Celestine against a metal beam. Unseen cords bound her to it. Morgan walked up to Lily, pulled her down, and laid her beside me. *Such beauty in a young girl. I think I'll adopt her. What do you think, Aidan? Her parents certainly don't deserve her.*

"Go to hell, you bitch," I spat out.

She laughed. *No, I don't think so, Aidan. I shall never die, don't you know?*

With that, she faced the waters. *Now, it's time to take care of your friends below.* Her long, thin arms began to move in a circle and the clouds began to respond. I tried to get up, but her left hand flew out to pin me down.

Morgan began to chant in English, *Death. Death. Death.*

I prayed for guidance, and warmth started to envelop me. As I stood, words began to pour from my mouth unbidden, and I felt a surge of power course throughout my body as I screamed, "*Ecce sanguis Christi virtutem.* Behold!"

A bright light exploded into the darkness, and I closed my eyes in pain. Morgan let out a high-pitched shriek and a string of curses. I braced for their effects, but nothing.

When I opened my eyes, I saw the Five Guardians, holding their objects and pointing them at Morgan. She writhed in pain as she fell to the floor.

*How? The Order? How?* Morgan gasped.

I said in a low, commanding voice, "They stand here, with the five objects that absorbed the blood of the Slain Lamb. Look at them."

Morgan screamed, her eyes squeezed shut. *The Master, the Club, the Archon, they never told me you were part of the Order of the Five Sorrows. Why?* She moaned, light starting to eat at her flesh.

"Because they serve the ultimate liar, Morgan. Of course they would never tell you. They used you, as they've used others."

The Dark Bride screamed as light began to burn away her flesh.

"You may turn, even now, Morgan, turn and repent. You will be forgiven by the Slain Lamb."

A soft bleat echoed in the chamber as the Five Guardians raised the Sorrows above their heads in exultation.

*No, I will not bow to that mongrel thing; that mixed bastard son of Mary.*

"Think carefully. Behold the Sorrows, Morgan. They contain the blood of Christ. Will you not turn?"

*No! Fuck your Christ! Fuck your God!*

I held up my hands, not understanding anything I did, and said, "Then go, with the power of Christ—"

She screamed as flesh fell from her in long, thin strips. With a final grunt, she pushed her hands forward and caught me square in the chest. The light went out for a moment as I banged my head on the metal flooring.

*I have you. You're not strong enough. You're mine.*

Forgive me, Jen. I wasn't strong enough, I thought.

Footsteps ran along the metal of the platform, and I heard Morgan grunt. Her hold released and I looked up. A figure battled with her on the edge of the platform.

*Fool, no . . .*

She tried to raise her arms to conjure more wind, but the stranger blocked her with a sharp rap of a stick. The Dark Bride screeched in rage, and then gasped as she appeared to recognize the person before her.

*You. My Internet lover come for—*

The unknown assailant put a hand over her mouth, and she bit down hard. The attacker roared in pain and pushed Morgan back to the edge. Teetering on the brink, the person raised a knife. The metal gleamed in the lightning, and the shadowy figure plunged it into her heart. Morgan's scream tore at the air as she teetered toward the edge. Darkness poured from the knife with dark guttural chanting. The figure grappled with her over to the edge. They launched themselves into the night as lightning crashed around them. Morgan's screams echoed as she fell to the ground far below with her killer.

# CHAPTER THIRTY-SEVEN

I CLIMBED TO MY FEET AND THE WORLD SPUN. MY RUPTURED EARDRUM threw off my balance. As I steadied myself, I made my way to Celestine. I bent down, and she opened her eyes.

"Where is she?"

I pointed to the edge. "She went over the edge with someone. I couldn't see. Whoever it was stabbed her in the heart."

She gave me a thin smile and coughed. "She is dead. I can feel it."

Celestine sat up and pointed to Emily and Aisha. "Are they okay?"

"As far as I know. They're breathing, anyway."

A faint voice said, "We're okay." Aisha and Emily helped each other to their feet. I gave a hand to Celestine and pulled her up.

"You saved my life, *mon cher*," Celestine said.

I shrugged. "Thank the shillelagh lessons."

She gave me two quick pecks on each cheek and reached out for her sisters. "She is dead. We have succeeded."

Emily and Aisha nodded as they stared at Brigit. We walked over to join them, and I said, "At least they went together."

All three of them broke into tears and began to chant in a language I couldn't understand. When they finished, Celestine said, "We prayed that God would receive their souls."

"I have no doubt he will."

Sirens broke the still of the night and bright spotlights shined on the tower. "We should probably go down," Celestine said.

"Who is going to carry them?" Emily asked me as she pointed to Lily and Ashley.

"I'll—"

"Aidan? Is that you?"

I went over and bent down over Ashley. "Yeah, it's me. Are you okay?"

She looked puzzled and then she caught sight of Lily.

"Oh God, Lily. Aidan, is she . . ."

I shook my head. "No, she is fine. Just drugged, I think. Like you."

She began to tremble. "It's my fault, all my fault. I gave her to them. I couldn't . . ."

The full force of what she had done hit her. Her face crumpled in horror and she clung to me.

"Oh God, forgive me . . . forgive me. What have I done?" She began to scream, over and over, "What have I done?"

Ashley clung to me, and I winced as she dug her nails into my back. I looked to Emily for help and she knelt down to whisper to Ashley. "It's okay, she is fine, but we need to leave here, do you understand?"

Ashley shook uncontrollably as she stood. "Aidan, where is Brian? Aidan, is he okay?

I lied. "He's fine. He is helping Father Neal. He is waiting for you."

"Do you think he'll forgive me, Aidan?"

I didn't know what to say. There was no doubt Brian would have forgiven her online shit. He'd done the same thing, after all. But she'd sold their daughter to be abused. I didn't know if he had that much forgiveness. I'm pretty sure I wouldn't have.

"That is something we are going to have to work through, Ashley. You have both done your damnedest to destroy each other"—I nodded to Lily—"and her. It's only by the grace of God she isn't on that yacht out on the lake."

My words broke her in half, and I didn't care. I tried to demonstrate God's grace to her, but I didn't feel it. I knew it would be there for her when she asked him for it. I hoped he would heal her, but I knew I couldn't be the agent of that healing.

"Emily, take Ashley. I'll carry Lily. Celestine, you and Aisha are going to have to leave Brigit where she is for the moment."

They looked at Emily, who said, "Yes, and then we must disappear. Meet us back at the church. If anyone questions you, tell them that you work for the monument and you let me in, got it?"

Celestine and Aisha nodded. I picked up Lily and said, "Time to go."

We made our way to the elevator and rode down to the stairs. As I started down the stairs, the jostling woke up Lily. Her blue eyes looked into mine and she smiled. "Hi, Uncle Aidan. Is the bad lady gone?"

I smiled. "She is, dear. Your daddy and I saved you. Now go back to sleep."

Her eyes fluttered closed as I kissed her on the forehead. As we walked out of the door, Father Neal met us with a grave look on his face.

"I need you. It's Brian."

My stomach churned as I handed Lily to Emily. I walked with Father Neal to a group of paramedics who surrounded two bodies. I ran over to them, and I saw Brian lying in the middle next to Morgan with the Nephilim knife sticking out of her heart. Her vacant eyes stared off in the glaze of death.

I pushed my way through the paramedics and knelt at Brian's side. His face was smashed from the fall, and his arm stretched above his head in a weird angle. The bone jutted out of his skin, and his face was the color of ash. I looked up at the paramedic who shook his head. I fought back my tears as I touched Brian's arm. "I'm here, Brian."

His eyes fluttered and opened. "Aidan . . . my brother . . . are they?" He coughed, and blood came out of his mouth.

God help me, I didn't know if could handle this. I fought for words. "Yeah, they are fine, Brian. You saved them. How did you get up those stairs?"

"Father Neal . . . touched . . . healed . . . Is the bitch Morgan . . ." He struggled as he choked on blood.

"Yeah, you got her, right in the heart. She is dead. You did it, buddy."

His bloody hand clung tightly to mine. "Take care . . . of them. It's not going . . . to be easy . . . on them."

Tears rolled down my cheeks. I couldn't hold back anymore. "I promise, Brian. I promise I'll take care of them both."

He groaned, coughed, and blinked his eyes. He raised his eyes and he smiled.

"Time to go . . . Amanda and I'll trade stories. Tell my daughter I love her . . . and I'm always . . . with her."

His grip went slack as his last breath escaped his lungs. My body wracked with sobs, and I heard a scream. Ashley pushed me aside. "Brian? Brian!"

"Ashley, he is . . ."

She hit me hard. "No. No. No!"

I nodded to the paramedics, who pulled her off. They took out a sedative and stuck her arm. She went limp as I heard her whisper, "My fault . . . mine."

I felt a light touch on my arm and turned around to see the most beautiful sight in the world: Jen. I grabbed her in a tight hug and let my grief out. She held me tight, and I cried as I clung to her. She touched my ear and said, "You're bleeding."

She turned around and yelled, "Hey, I need some medical help over here, right now. Move it."

"Jen, it's—"

"Shut up, Aidan."

The paramedic looked into my ear and pronounced a burst

eardrum. He cleaned off the blood and turned me back over to Jen.

"What now?" I asked.

She looked around. "We have to figure a way to explain Brian. And you, too, for that matter, without getting me and Emily fired."

I looked around. "Looks like Celestine and Aisha are gone."

"So, any ideas?"

"Yeah, easy, we came to the church to pray and await news of the raid. Brian slipped out and we followed him. We got into a struggle with Morgan, and Brian killed her as we got to the top of the monument."

"That's pretty thin, Aidan."

"Prove it wrong, Detective."

She frowned. "Sadly, it's probably the best thing we have. Truth be told, no one is going to be sorry this one is dead." She kicked Morgan lightly. "Those assholes on the boat are some serious bad guys."

I raised an eyebrow. "Oh?"

"Yeah, major international sex traffickers. This is a massive bust and probably just the beginning."

I looked at Brian as the paramedics covered him with a white sheet. "So, he didn't die for nothing."

"No," Jen said, clasping my hand. "What are we going to do about Ashley?"

I frowned. "She can't have Lily back, not now."

"That's for damned sure."

"Temporary insanity, commit her to a mental hospital?"

"That's possible. I have to take her into custody, regardless. Can you take Lily?"

A lump rose in my throat. "Can I?"

"Yes, I'll authorize it. You are ordained clergy. I'll release her to you on the understanding you'll get her to her next of kin. But you have to do it within a week or she has to go into foster care."

"I understand."

She whispered, "Get her out of here. Go back to the church. Emily and I'll clean up, okay?"

I nodded and looked at Brian's covered body one more time. I whispered, "I'll take care of them, my friend."

Jen and I walked over to the uniformed officer who held Lily.

"Officer, you can release this girl to Pastor Aidan Schaeffer. He is going to be responsible to hand her over to her next of kin. I'll take full responsibility, understand?"

The patrolwoman handed Lily to me, and Father Neal walked up.

I turned to him and said, "We have to go back to the church. Emily and Jen are going to take care of everything else."

Father Neal nodded, and we headed toward the woods. As we walked, Lily opened her eyes and said, "I had a dream about Daddy, Uncle Aidan."

Tears welled up and my breath caught. "Did you, love? What was it about?"

"He told me that he is with Jesus and not to be sad. He said you would take care of me. Will you?"

I kissed her forehead. "I will, dear. I promised him."

She fell back asleep on my shoulder. Tears flowed again and the pain hit me full force. I held Lily tightly. Father Neal placed his hand on my shoulder.

"Talk to me, my son."

"I . . . I can't, Father. Lily . . ."

He nodded. "Who will get her?"

"I have no idea. The last time I checked, Brian's sister is supposed to. He told me about their will."

I turned to him as we walked. "Why, Father, why? This little girl has no parents anymore."

Father Neal didn't answer as he limped along with me.

"Aren't you going to say anything?"

"I don't have an answer for you, at least, not the answer you want. Or one that will comfort you."

I nodded. "I know, I know."

We walked in silence toward the stone church. Mother Rebecca met us as we came out of the woods. "Celestine and Aisha are inside. I took care of their physical injuries as best I could. I don't think anything is broken."

She looked down. "Is this the girl?"

I nodded, not trusting myself to speak.

Mother Rebecca sighed. "Always the innocent suffer." She reached for Lily and I pulled back. "Aidan, you need to rest. I'll take the girl and put her in bed. Trust me."

I held on to Lily and then said, "Okay . . . but put her close to my room, please?"

Mother Rebecca nodded and carried Lily into the lodge.

Father Neal gripped my shoulder. "Now it is time for you to rest."

"I don't think I can."

"I insist. You are tired and worn out."

As much as I wanted to protest, his touch and voice made my limbs feel heavy. "Stop it, you wizard, I don't want to sleep."

He didn't pay any attention to me as he led me to my room.

"Sleep, my son, and forget your grief for a little while."

I slumped onto my bed. My eyes closed and I plunged into blessed forgetfulness.

# CHAPTER THIRTY-EIGHT

**A WEEK LATER, I PREPARED TO PRESIDE OVER MY BEST FRIEND'S FUNERAL.**

"Pastor Aidan?"

Elder John's voice broke into my thoughts as I zipped up my robe. I turned around and all the elders had filtered into my office.

"Hey, guys, is everything ready?"

They all nodded, and Elder Bill said, "All the family has been seated. We are still waiting for the cello player. She had a flat tire."

"Always something."

They all looked at one another as if they had something else to say. "Come on, guys, what's up? Spill it."

John said, "We hesitate, Aidan, because we don't want to wound your soul on this day."

I tried not to roll my eyes. I really wished he would learn to speak normal English. "John, I'm fine. I don't know how I'll be in the middle of the service, but I'm okay for now."

John looked at Bill, who said, "We are going to call a congregational meeting to call Cole as our pastor."

I smiled. "That's great, you all. Congrats. Cole is a good man, and if you nurture him right, he'll be a fantastic pastor."

They all looked relieved, and I added, "Did you think I would be offended by that?"

John looked down and didn't respond. He knew the truth, but the others didn't. Kudos to him for keeping his mouth shut.

Bill said, "We didn't want you to take it the wrong way, Aidan. We love you and want you to stay."

I smiled. "And I love you guys. We have been through a lot, haven't we?"

They all nodded.

"But I'm not going to stay. Knox deserves a brand-new start. Plus, I'm no longer a Presbyterian by conviction. Even if I wanted to stay, it wouldn't be right."

Everyone but John looked stunned. I picked up a white envelope and handed it to Bill.

"This is my letter of resignation. I'll stay for the next two weeks to get everything cleaned up and ready for Cole. I'll also inform the presbytery."

John nodded. "They are probably going to have something to say about you leaving the church."

I smiled. "I'm not leaving the church, John. I'm stepping over into another room."

Bill rubbed his chin. "Which one?"

"Anglican, of course. Father Neal has offered me a job over at Saint Patrick's. I'm going to start training for the priesthood."

Silence descended in the room as they all stared at me. Bill shuffled his feet and looked up. "I think we're all a little stunned. Maybe you should take some time to think it over. You have had a rough few months."

I put my hand on his shoulders, "Bud, there is only one other decision I have been more sure of in my life. And that's not something I have acted on just yet."

John gave me a smile. "This wouldn't have anything to do with a certain lady police officer, would it?"

"You are a smart man."

Bill grabbed my arm. "But still, Aidan . . ."

"Bill, sometimes—well, all the time, it seems—God uses turmoil in our lives to get us to change things around, wouldn't you say?"

They nodded.

"I'll tell you this, if you all mess Cole up, I'm going to crack all of your heads."

They smiled and started to come up for hugs. I gave them each a good, backslapping Christian-male hug.

"Now, let's pray that God will be lifted up in Brian's funeral and that Brian's soul will rest in Jesus."

We all stood in a circle in my office, arms around one another's shoulders. As I listened to each of them pray, I thought about how much these guys used to annoy me. My cheeks colored at some of the thoughts I used to have about them and their lives. No matter what they had done, they stood faithful to the church and to me. Leaving them was turning out to be harder than I thought.

I finished the prayer with, *Jesus, give me strength. Give me strength to bury the man whom I loved more than life, a man who served you with all his brokenness and gave his life for his family. Give me the words that will bring comfort and peace to his family. Let me speak Christ and no one else. Be with Lily and Ashley who aren't with us today. Bring peace to Lily. Fix and change Ashley's mind with Your grace. Help her to repent and get well so she can be the mother of her daughter again.*

I paused as my throat tightened. This funeral would be brutal. I had almost let Father Neal or Cole do it, but I couldn't let Brian be buried by anyone else. I knew it had to be me. I just didn't want to cry and choke my way through it.

I said a quick "Amen." The elders gave me a pat on the back as they headed out of the office. I took a few deep breaths as I tried to collect myself.

"You look pretty handsome in that robe, mister."

I looked up to see Jen in the doorway. Her dark hair curled as it hung down to her shoulders. She wore an elegant black dress that clung to her at the right places. Amazing how she could make me forget everything else in the world.

"You look beautiful."

She smiled. "Odd thing to say about a funeral dress."

I went over to hug her, and she encircled me with her arms. I held her tightly and breathed in the scent of her light coconut perfume.

I whispered, "I don't know if I can do this, love."

Her arms rubbed my back as she whispered into my neck, "I know, baby. But you can do it. God is with you, and I'm here."

I held her for a few moments, drawing from her strength. With a few deep breaths, I let her go. She looked into my eyes and touched my cheek. "Are you ready?"

I nodded. "Go on in, I have to finish some things here."

She gave me a kiss and then walked back to the sanctuary. The cello player had made it and she began to play. The strains of "Be Thou My Vision" began and tears rolled down my cheeks. With a deep breath, I opened the door to the sanctuary and walked down the aisle.

From the sounds of the congregation, there didn't seem to be a dry eye in the place. Muffled sobs and cries made me fight not to add my own to the chorus. I prayed for strength as I walked up the aisle. Celestine, Emily, and Aisha sat toward the back. No one knew how deep their grief was as they mourned their own sisters. Father Neal, Darrin, Kate, Zoe, and Reg sat closer to the front with Jen. They all turned to me and gave me small smiles of encouragement.

Brian's and some of Ashley's family occupied the front two rows. All of them wore looks of shock. It would be some time before they would come to grips with what had happened. Brian's sister, Jill, gave me a small smile as I passed the front row.

I paused before Brian's coffin. I put my hand on the lid and whispered, "May it go well with you on your journey, my friend."

I walked up to the pulpit and raised my hands as I said, "The Lord Jesus Christ has conquered death. It has no more sting for those who believe. But, we still mourn when we have to say goodbye. Those tears aren't evil or sinful."

I paused as I looked around at the congregation. "We come to say good-bye to a man we all loved, me no less than all of you. This man, Brian, was my best friend, my brother, and the guy who helped me through many dark times. His death personified his life. He gave himself up for others. He was the best man I've ever known, even if he rooted for Tennessee."

Everyone gave me a relieved chuckle.

"He gave himself up for others because he loved Christ, who gave Himself up for sinners, people who didn't love Him. In Christ's death, He not only accomplished the forgiveness of sins, but He brought us into a family, the church."

I paused and looked out at the congregation. "We are a pretty messed-up bunch, aren't we? But we are family. God loved us enough to put us together as a family, because that is what a church is, a family. And it's at times like this that a family pulls together."

As I continued the service, I felt the absence of the two people closest to Brian: Ashley and Lily. Jill and I had agreed Lily shouldn't attend the funeral. She'd dealt with the death of her father better than the rest of us. She kept talking about how her father never left her. Jill, a psychiatrist, had been worried it demonstrated a denial on her part. I just smiled and told her not to worry. I didn't think of explaining to her that Lily spoke the truth.

Ashley hadn't been allowed out of the hospital to attend. I hadn't wanted her there anyway. I still fought to forgive her. I knew I would have to visit her and give her absolution eventually, but the grief and anger still clung to me.

After the ceremony, we went to the cemetery, and I made the burial service as brief as possible. The heat radiated in the air, and everyone had begun to sweat in their black funeral clothes. As the service broke up, Jill gave me a hug and said, "Lily has been asking about you. She wants to see you before we go back to Tennessee."

I nodded. "Jen and I would like to take her to the zoo tomorrow, will that work?"

Jill said "We are trying to get Brian's personal stuff situated at the farm, so that would be perfect."

I lowered my voice. "How are things with Ashley's family?"

Jill looked around. "Tense. They don't like that I have Lily, but they can't dispute it. The will is clear. I'm going to work out a visitation schedule with them. I think that helped diffuse the tension a bit."

I nodded as Jen walked up. "Jill, this is my girlfriend, Jen."

They shook hands as Jill said, "I have heard a lot about you from Brian. We're all glad Aidan found someone like you, Jen. Aidan's like my little brother, but he can be a pain in the ass, just to warn you."

Jen chuckled. "I knew that from the beginning, Jill. That's part of his charm."

She walked off to join the family, and I filled Jen in on what we'd discussed. Then Celestine, Aisha, and Emily walked over to us. Celestine said, "Beautiful service, Aidan. It helped us mourn our sisters."

"When will the funeral for them be?"

Celestine said, "We are going to take them back home in a few days. They would want to be buried in New Orleans."

I nodded as Emily said, "We were going to ask you to join us for lunch tomorrow before we go. Can you make it?"

Jen smiled. "Of course. Aidan and I are going to pick up Lily for a morning excursion. Besides, Celestine, I haven't tasted your cooking yet."

Emily brightened. "Good, it's a date then. See you tomorrow."

Jen turned to me. "I have to get back to work. It's brutal, but there are mounds of paperwork on this thing."

"I figured as much. Don't worry; I have some things to take care of around here. Late dinner tonight?"

She kissed me. "Count on it, preacher boy."

# CHAPTER THIRTY-NINE

**A FEW DAYS AFTER THE FUNERAL, I FELT READY TO ASK JEN TO MARRY ME.**

"Lily's shoe is untied. Go on ahead, we will be right there."

Jen made her way up Shrum Mound and I bent down, pretending to tie Lily's shoe. I reached into my pocket and pulled out a ring box.

I whispered, "Do you know what this is, Lily?"

She shook her head. I opened the box, and the diamond shone in the sunlight.

"Ooh, Aidan, that's pretty. Is that for me?"

I laughed. "No, dear. Someday, a guy will love you as much as your daddy and I do. He'll give you one of your own. This is for Jen."

I motioned up the hill. "I'm going to ask her to marry me. Do you think she'll say yes?"

Lily giggled. "Yes!"

"Now, I need your help. I need you to put it in your pocket it and pull it out when I tell you to, okay?"

She nodded, squirming with excitement. Her face beamed as she looked off to the right.

"What's up?" I asked.

"Daddy wants me to tell you he is excited for you, Aidan."

I felt tears well up again. With a deep breath I said, "Well, let's all go up and do this, shall we?"

She grabbed my hand. "Don't be nervous, Aidan. She'll say yes."

I chuckled and made a mock nervous face. "You think so?"

She nodded in a solemn five-year-old way. I gripped her hand and said, "Thanks, Lil' Red. I don't think I could do it without you."

We walked up the steps, and Jen stood gazing at the quarry. "Seems like forever since we found the dead chickens."

"I was just thinking about that."

Lily giggled and smiled at Jen.

"And what are you laughing at, silly girl?"

"Oh, nothing." Lily covered her mouth and looked at me. I could tell I would have to do this soon, or Lily would spill my secret.

"Lily has something she wants to give you, Jen."

Jen turned to Lily and I knelt down. Lily fumbled with the box, and she finally got it out. Jen took it, opened it up, and gasped. She turned and saw me on my knee. Tears began to flow down her cheeks as I said, "Jennifer Brown, we met under strange and bizarre circumstances—still better than a singles bar, though—but I can tell you without a doubt, I want you in my life forever. I love you and you are my soul. I need you. I love you. And I want to marry you. So, will you marry me?"

She knelt by me and kissed me with fire. Her tears flowed onto my cheeks as she whispered, "Yes, Aidan, yes . . . with all my heart, yes."

We hugged each other tight and Lily joined us. "Can I be the flower girl?"

Jen laughed. "I think we can arrange that. Would you like to be?"

"Oh yes! Mommy always said I look beautiful in weddings."

Jen and I looked at each other. Then Lily asked, "Can Mommy come to the wedding with me?"

"Maybe, dear, we'll have to see if she can get out of the hospital."

We had all told Lily that her mom was very sick and needed care. It was the best explanation I could think of at the moment. I hoped to God that no one ever told her that her mom had almost sold her into slavery.

We held each other on top of the mound for a few moments until I said, "You know, I think it's time for lunch. We should probably go to the restaurant, don't you think?"

Jen smiled. "Yeah, I have to show off my ring, after all."

Lily ran ahead of us and started down the steps. Jen grabbed me and kissed me deeply. When we broke apart, she said, "I love you, Aidan Schaeffer. I'll be good to you."

I smiled and said, "You better."

She hit me. "Don't push your luck, bub. Don't forget I have a gun."

"I'll keep that in mind."

We got in the car and drove to the restaurant. Father Neal, everyone from the Scooby gang, and the Daughters of Laveau had already arrived. Celestine busied herself bringing out food that smelled of Cajun/Creole goodness: muffalettas stacked in a neat triangle near bowls of jambalaya and gumbo.

"Father, will you pray for us?" Emily asked.

"Of course, my dear. Let us pray."

We all bowed our heads as he said, "Dear Father, we are here to eat and remember those who are with You now. Let us eat in celebration of their reward and remember with joy everything they brought to our lives. Let them be with us as we rejoice together. In the name of the Father and of the Son and of the Holy Spirit. Amen."

Jen said, "Before we all eat, I do have an announcement." She grabbed my hand. "Aidan and I are going to get married."

A general shout of excitement greeted her announcement as everyone rushed up to congratulate us. They all hugged us, oohed over the ring, and toasted our happiness. We sat down to eat and told stories about Brian and the twins. Lily didn't seem sad at all. She shared stories about her dad along with the rest of us.

Celestine sat beside me and said, "Congrats, Aidan. Jen is a wonderful woman."

I smiled. "Yeah, God often gives us better than we deserve."

She chuckled. "Too true."

"What's next for the Daughters?"

She looked at Father Neal as she chewed on her lip. "It seems as if our task may not be done."

"What, the Dark Bride can come back from the dead?"

Celestine shook her head. "No, Aidan. Of course not. Father Neal told us some things last night after the funeral. It seems we might have new goals."

"And those would be?"

She smiled. "He made us promise not to tell you yet. I think he wants to do that himself. Let's just say, we are coming back here after New Orleans. The Grinning Man is still out there, you know, as well as . . . others. . . ."

"I'm trying not to think about that."

Celestine's eyes flashed. "You better, Aidan. Things aren't going to get better. What happened to Brian and the twins is child's play. Father Neal is a part of something larger. You know that, right?"

"Yeah, but I don't know what that is, do you?"

"Some. Father Neal promised to give us more information when we return."

"Well, I hope he is going to tell me, because I'm in the dark."

"Enjoy the food and your ignorance, Aidan. Both aren't going to last very long, but they are nice for now."

Celestine got up to talk to Jen. I pondered her words as I ate. When I finished, Father Neal touched my shoulder.

"Aidan, a word."

We walked outside and the heat felt good after the air-conditioned cold.

"Congrats, dear boy. I'm very excited for both of you."

I smiled. "Do you know any old, annoying priests who would be willing to do the ceremony?"

Father Neal chuckled. "I think I can dig one up."

"I turned in my resignation to the elders."

"How did they take it?"

"As well as can be expected. They were shocked, of course, but I feel the more they think on it, they'll see it's the right thing."

"So, are you ready to start with us?"

"More than ready, Father. But something tells me starting with *us* means more than just the priesthood, am I right?"

Father Neal paused and then said, "Yes, my son. The Elder and the Order are waiting for you. In a few weeks, you'll go see him. I've arranged it. Don't worry; you'll get more answers than you can possibly handle."

I smiled. "Good, I was starting to worry."

As we stood there for a moment, Father Neal touched my shoulder. "What's on your mind?"

"The Archon in Cleveland, to be honest. Where were those girls going? What is going on there?"

"I'm checking into that. I'm hoping to have some answers in a week or so. I do know something up there is not right, but it's always hard for me to tell."

"Yeah, why is that?"

"Because, you should know this: In Ohio, we dwell in darkness. The sleeping Nephilim that lay under our feet still have a dark presence here. As to how powerful it is, I'm still trying to figure that out without using magick. Why do you think I was so deceived by Mike and Daniel?"

"I often wondered."

"While the light is stronger than the dark, it is often hard to penetrate evil's secrets. That is why Christ alone must reveal them to us through the Five Sorrows."

"And that's what you told the Daughters of Laveau last night, I'm sure. They'll be joining us?"

He nodded. "Along with Darrin and Kate."

I sighed. "Well, I know better than to pump you for information, old man. I'll wait."

Father Neal rapped me on the ankles. "Now you are getting it, my son."

"There is still one thing I don't understand."

"And what is that?"

"The Grinning Man . . . Why did he betray the Dark Bride?"

Father Neal gave me a grim smile. "I thought that would be obvious."

I shook my head. "Not to me."

"The Grinning Man, and those like him, don't have personal attachments. You are still thinking in terms of love, loyalty, and compassion. Even the worst people in the world have some twisted version of these things. The Grinning Man has none of these things. He is the utter negation and twisting of the soul. He gave up Morgan because he was done with her. Plus, I think she became a convenient way to test you and see what you were made of."

Not knowing what do with that, I changed to another uncomfortable subject. "Well, as for me, I discovered I might have one thing I can't forgive."

Father Neal nodded. "Ashley."

"Yeah, I can't find it in my heart to forgive what she did."

He stared at the empty street. "Remember, son, the agents of darkness are master manipulators. We are most vulnerable to them in our grief and in our anger. Ashley and Brian are perfect examples of that. What Ashley did was terrible. What Brian did was awful. Their combined sin led to this destruction. You understand that, right?"

His words struck home, and I hung my head. "I know you're right, but I don't feel it."

"Yes, feeling it will take a very long time."

We stood in silence for a moment. Then I said, "Tell me again this wasn't a situation where interest in me got people killed."

He shook his head. "Most certainly not. He isn't God, not even close. The opportunity presented itself, and he took it. If it worked, he would have had more slaves and destroyed more lives. As it didn't, for the most part, he still found out much about you."

"I don't understand his interest in me."

"Not just his, the others as well."

"Do these others have a mysterious island in the Pacific somewhere?" I said in a facetious reference to the old television program *Lost*.

He grimaced. "Not funny, Aidan. There are things you are going to learn in the next few months that will alter you."

I laughed. "You mean, more than I've already been?"

"I'm afraid so, son."

"Well, if God wills it, so be it."

A burst of laughter interrupted us as he said, "Now, let's get back in and stuff ourselves. This is your engagement day. We should be celebrating."

I nodded as I moved away. "I'll be there in a sec," I said before stopping to look back at him. "When will I see the Five Sorrows again?"

Father Neal paused, as if listening. "Soon. The Elder comes first."

He limped back inside, and I stared at the streets of Franklinton. I didn't know how to take Father Neal's words. They hit me like they always did, mysterious, strange, and unsettling. I had no idea what my future would be or what dark things lay on the horizon. What would happen to me? What would happen to the people I loved? Could I just run away with Jen? Find a nice beach town somewhere and start some kind of business for tourists?

The faces of Brian, the twins, and the women all popped into my mind. What happened to them is what happened when people didn't fight evil. If I turned and ran, more victims of the Grinning Man and his crew would pile up. They'd been doing this shit for a long time, and it was time to stop them. I couldn't run away. I wouldn't back down. I would do whatever it took.

Another burst of laughter came from the restaurant. Jen saw me and came outside.

"Everyone agrees you didn't go cheap on the ring."

I laughed. "Is that so?"

"Yes."

She hugged me tight. "Are you okay?"

I looked down. "I am. And even if I'm not in the future, I know you are going to be there with me. That's all I need, really."

"Come back inside, Aidan. Father Neal is telling some stories about his college days."

I rolled my eyes. "I bet those are entertaining."

"They are; come on."

I took her hand and held her tight. We walked in to join our new family. It made me realize that family, especially God's family, can never just rely on blood, it must come from the soul. Celestine shoved another plate of food in my hand, and Lily jumped onto my lap. I looked around at the faces that greeted us, and their happiness surprised me. I realized that no matter how dark and evil things got, light, love, happiness, and good food were always more powerful. All of these things acted like sacraments in the community so that the darkness could never win.

No wonder God gave us each other.

www.ingramcontent.com/pod-product-compliance
Lightning Source LLC
LaVergne TN
LVHW050927080826
845145LV00001B/237